"Julie Moffett writes spirited, well-crafted historical romances that truly satisfy the reader."
—*Romantic Times*

PASSION'S PRICE

"I told you the conditions for walking about my estate," Stefan said sharply. "You agreed to them. Do you always break your word so easily?"

"I did not break my word," Hanna said, her mouth set in a stubborn line. "I told you I would escape."

"You will not escape from me, Hanna. Ever."

The look on Stefan's face was so fierce and possessive, Hanna retreated. "May I return to my room now?" she whispered.

"You may not. You must first pay the price for your disobedience. Come here, Hanna."

Hanna shook her head warily. In a flash, his fingers shot out and caught her wrist, drawing her close.

"You will not disobey me again."

Hanna raised her eyes to meet his and gasped as she saw his silvery eyes had turned dark and turbulent.

"One kiss, Hanna," he whispered thickly. "That is all I ask."

"Kiss?" she asked, her voice sounding curiously breathless.

Stefan let his gaze roam boldly over her. Lord help him, he knew he was playing with fire, but he could not stop himself. "Aye, Hanna, one kiss is the price you will have to pay. Do you still dare to disobey me?"

Other *Leisure Books* by Julie Moffett:
FLEETING SPLENDOR

A Touch of Fire

Julie Moffett

This book is dedicated to the two best sisters a girl could have:
Sandra Moffett Parks
Elizabeth Craig Moffett

Book Margins, Inc.

A BMI Edition

Published by special arrangement with Dorchester Publishing Co., Inc.

If you purchased this book without a cover you should be aware that this book is stolen property. It was reported as "unsold and destroyed" to the publisher and neither the author nor the publisher has received any payment for this "stripped book."

Copyright© 1994 by Julie Moffett

All rights reserved. No part of this book may be reproduced or transmitted in any form or by any electronic or mechanical means, including photocopying, recording or by any information storage and retrieval system, without the written permission of the Publisher, except where permitted by law.

Printed in the United States of America.

Kingdom of Poland 1655

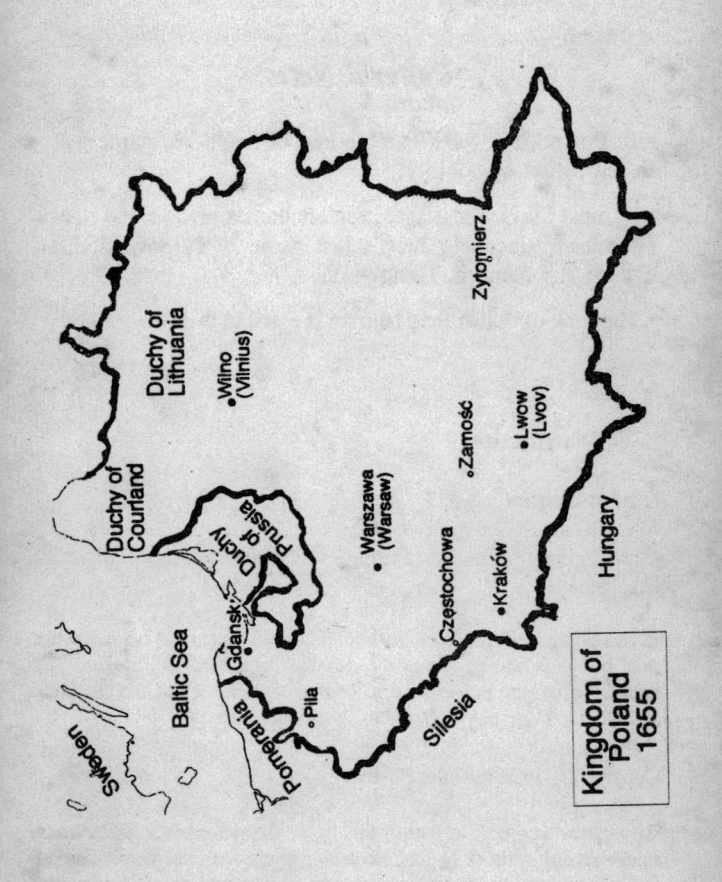

Cultural Notes:

- In Poland, the "ski" on the end of one's last name was an indication of nobility.

- In most Slavic languages, female names always end in a. Therefore, since our hero's last name is Tarnowski, his sister's last name is Tarnowska.

- The rank of Polish field hetman is equal to that of a general.

A Touch of Fire

Prologue

London, England 1642

There was no fog in London on this crisp and frigid spring night so his view was unobstructed as he stood in the shadows of a rowhouse, ignoring the brilliant sapphire stars that glittered in the evening sky. His dark eyes darted up and down the street until he was satisfied that it was empty of passersby.

As he strode down the street, his richly cut cloak was unfastened despite the cool wind. His steps were sure and determined, his face twisted with a seething anger that boiled his blood, making him oblivious to the coldness around him.

Damn her, he thought for the hundredth time. She had dared to defy him and had almost succeeded. *Almost,* he reminded himself. It had taken him nearly five years, but he had finally found her.

He came upon the house he sought and paused, letting his jeweled fingers rest lightly on the wrought-iron gate. *She was here in this house, within his reach.* He felt himself tremble with anticipation and took a deep breath to calm himself. Slowly, he opened the gate and walked up to the house.

Calmly, he raised the brass knocker and brought it down three times. Within moments, an elegantly dressed manservant opened the door. Upon formally stating his wish to see the lady of the house, the manservant immediately ushered him into the parlor. A slow smile curved across his face. No questions had been asked. Clearly, the manservant was impressed with the cut of his cloak and the sparkling jewels on his fingers.

Curiously, he looked around the room as he waited, his fingers trailing over the back of a heavy, ornate chair. She had done well for herself, even without him. The parlor was richly furnished and decorated with the utmost care and taste. Elaborately carved furniture was comfortably placed about the chamber and large, beautiful paintings hung on the walls. A delicate spinet stood in one corner of the room and he wandered over to it, lightly running his fingers across the ivory keys. Then, slowly, he moved to the hearth, holding his hands out to the warmth of the fire.

He knew the exact moment she entered the room. Her scent was distinct, like a roomful of fragrant roses. After she had left he had not been able to stand the smell of them.

"'Tis a cold night to be out and about," she said, her voice carrying a trace of a foreign accent. "How may I help you, sir?"

He remained standing at the hearth, his back to her, savoring the sound of her voice. God, how he had missed the melodic notes of her voice and her precious laugh. Slowly, he turned to face her.

She was exactly as he had remembered. She would be twenty now, just two years younger than he. She was dressed in a magnificent gown of blue velvet, cut low on the shoulders and finished with a delicate lace collar and matching cuffs. Her fiery red hair was loosely tied with a matching ribbon and her blue-green eyes widened as she looked at him, first in surprise and then in shocked recognition.

"*Dobry wieczor, moja różyczko,*" he said in fluent Polish. "Good evening, my little rose."

All color drained from her face as she took a trembling step backwards. "My God, Jozef. It is you. Wh-what are you doing here?"

Jozef leaned casually against the back of a chair, turning his dark eyes upon her. "I suppose I could make up some story to explain my presence, but we both know why I am here, don't we, Alexandra?"

She shook her head, tears filling her eyes. "You were wrong to follow me. I had to leave you. You frightened me with your jealousy, your possessiveness and cruelty. I could not breathe. I could not live."

His expression remained emotionless. Casually, he picked up a vase from a nearby table and examined it with the utmost interest. Then, abruptly, he threw it against the hearth, where it shattered into a hundred pieces, scattering across the floor. The manservant who had escorted Jozef to the parlor came rushing into the room, but Alexandra waved him back.

"It's all right, Sebastian. I know the gentleman," she told him reassuringly, and then she closed the door behind him.

Taking a deep breath to calm herself, she turned to face Jozef. "Stop this childish display. Your anger changes nothing."

Jozef's fists clenched at his side. "You still belong to me, Alexandra. Running away to England did not change any of that."

Alexandra took a deep breath, running her fingers across her high cheekbones to calm herself. "You are wrong, Jozef. It changed everything. I am married and have become an English subject. I'll not go back to you. Not now . . . not ever."

His face contorted into a furious scowl as he strode across the room and grabbed her by the arm. "What you want is no concern of mine. You will come back with me if I have to take you kicking and screaming." He threw his cape back around his shoulders and she gasped as she saw the glitter of jewels sewn into his tunic.

"Aye," he whispered as he followed her eyes to his chest. "I am rich. Richer than you could have ever imagined. My wealth can be your wealth, Alexandra. Come back with me and live the life you were meant to live."

She shuddered and closed her eyes. "Your riches do not interest me. I have a comfortable life here and I am happy. Buy yourself another woman, Jozef."

"You are the only woman for me, Alexandra." He spoke with such conviction that she felt a chill creep up her spine.

"I will not be intimidated by you," she said with a firmness she did not feel. "I am no longer the naive girl who fell under your dark charms. You do not own me and you never did. I will not go back."

He reached out for her arm, his fingers painfully pressing into her flesh until tears sprang to her eyes. "No one leaves me, Alexandra. No one. Especially not you."

He dragged her close and brought his lips down on hers, harshly tasting her sweetness. He had taken plenty of women to his bed, but there was no one like her. She set his heart and soul afire until it threatened to burn him, dragging him down into her fiery depths. Cupping her face with a fierce grip, he looked deeply into her blue-green eyes, the same eyes that had haunted his dreams for as long as he could remember.

She was crying, almost hysterically now. Smiling, he released her. "You will come with me tonight," he commanded quietly.

Before she could answer the door opened, and a little girl about three years old came running into the room, holding a doll.

"Mama," she said shyly, running over and hiding her face in her mother's skirts.

"Hannka," Alexandra gasped, using the diminutive of the child's name. "*Mama jest zajęta. Idź się bawić,*" she said, sweeping the child into her arms.

A Touch of Fire

"Mummy is busy. Go and play." She rushed to the door with the child, but Jozef's firm hand on her shoulder stopped her movements.

"The child is yours?" Jozef asked curiously. Alexandra hugged the little girl to her breast protectively but said nothing.

Jozef stared at the little girl. She looked exactly like Alexandra, with a cloud of red curls and a sprinkle of freckles across her face. Abruptly, he reached out and took the child's chin in his hand.

"Nay," Alexandra gasped, trying to pull the child away from him.

Jozef's voice was harsh. "If you move again, I will force her from your arms. I warn you, I will not be gentle."

Alexandra froze, and Jozef nudged up the chin of the child, until he could look directly into her face. Wide blue-green eyes stared back at him, oddly unafraid.

Shocked, he dropped his hand and took a step backwards. "*Jezus Maria,*" he said hoarsely. "She has your eyes."

Tears streamed down Alexandra's face. "God help me, Jozef, if you dare to harm this child . . ." She let her sentence trail off, unable to finish.

The little girl promptly dropped her doll and began to wail, sensing her mother's distress. Alexandra stroked the child's curls, whispering soothing words of comfort. Hanna immediately stopped crying and began to suck her thumb, resting her head on her mother's shoulder.

Jozef smiled slowly. "We leave tonight. All of us, including the child."

Alexandra set the child down in a chair and walked over to face Jozef. Her fear for her child's safety suddenly gave her new courage.

"Nay, Jozef. I will not go. We are no longer in Poland and I will not answer to you. I belong to another man, and he will kill you if you dare to abduct us."

Jozef took a deep, impatient breath, forcing himself to control his anger. "I know your husband is not in London,

Alexandra. He left two days ago for a trip to Wales. I also know that there are only a few servants on the premises tonight. I will kill them if it becomes necessary."

Her gasp of horror gave him a thrill of delight. "My dear, dear Alexandra," he continued with a sigh, drumming his fingers on the back of the chair, "do you really think I would be so stupid as to come here tonight without a plan? I have been in London for months, following you, watching you, waiting for just the right moment to approach you. That moment has come. Now, either you come with me peacefully or I will force you. The choice is yours." He casually reached over and picked up the fire iron, holding it loosely in his hand, as if to make a point.

She drew in her breath sharply, tightly clasping her hands together. "All right, Jozef. Your point is well made. I will go, but Hanna stays behind."

He laughed hoarsely. "You are in no position to bargain with me. I will take both of you, if I so desire."

Alexandra put her hands on her hips defiantly, her fiery hair sliding loose from its ribbon. "Nay. You will not touch my child. You are a sick man, Jozef Czarnowski, and I will not allow you to ruin my daughter's life as you have tried to ruin mine. Leaving you was the best thing I ever did. I never for a moment regretted my decision and I never will."

A fury so powerful that he could barely breathe swept over him. She still dared to defy him, after he had traveled all this way to find her and bring her home. *The ungrateful wench!* Without thinking, he reached out and grabbed her slender neck between his hands, shaking her with all his might.

"Nay, Alexandra," he growled through his fogged anger, "you belong to me and you know it. How dare you haunt my dreams with your eyes and then spit on me when I declare my love for you. You are mine, and you'll stay mine forever. Do you hear me?" He could hear the child crying but could not concentrate on anything except his consuming, blinding fury.

"Say you love me, damn it," he ordered furiously. "Say it." After several moments had passed and she did not answer, he released her, still shaking with anger. She slid to the floor, her red hair covering her face.

Jozef looked down at the still form in horror. As if in a dream, he knelt by her side, brushing the hair back from her face. He lifted her head and shoulders, but she remained limp and motionless.

His heart stopped beating as he looked at her face. Her eyes were open and still. The blue-green orbs stared at him emptily, without feeling.

"My God," he whispered, pressing the back of his hand to his brow. "What have I done?" Carefully, he placed her head back down on the floor.

"Nay, nay," he shouted, pounding the floor with his fists. *It was all wrong. She was supposed to return to Poland with him, become his wife and love him forever ... until their destinies were fulfilled. She belonged to him, damn it. But now she had slipped through his fingers. Again.*

Mad with grief, Jozef came to his feet and looked around the room. The doll still lay on the floor where it had been dropped, but the child was gone, the door slightly ajar. Grabbing the doll, he stuffed it in his pocket and stumbled wildly out of the parlor, tears running down his face. Heading for the door, he wrenched it open and fled into the cool London night. He flung open the gate and paused for a moment to look back at the house.

"I know you live on in that child, Alexandra," he whispered hoarsely. "You cannot so easily escape me."

Slowly, he pulled the doll from his pocket, turning it over in his hand before tightly clenching it shut.

"Next time, my little rose," he promised softly. "Next time, I come for you."

Chapter One

London, England 1655

Sixteen-year-old Hanna Quinn stood completely motionless beneath the warm summer sun, her breath checked, her delicate brows knit in fierce concentration. A small bead of sweat slid down her nose, and she wiped it absently on the sleeve of her left arm. Her right hand hovered over the lightweight sword attached to the belt on her side, but she did not draw it. *Not yet.*

Taking a deep breath, she forced herself to move forward, careful to keep her footsteps light and quiet. As she inched toward her destination, she reminded herself of what she had been taught. *Look for the unexpected. Be ready for anything. But above all, be patient. Don't let your eagerness outweigh your judgment.*

A hissing sound split the air behind her and surprised, she flung her slim form around, swiftly drawing the sword from the sheath. Instinctively she crouched, ready to strike, when a large alley cat leaped from the bushes and rushed past her, disappearing into the street.

After a moment of shock Hanna dissolved into laughter, falling to the grass. Her sword clattered harmlessly to the ground beside her. Reaching up with one hand, she wiped away the tears spilling from her sparkling blue-green eyes. God help her, she had cornered a feline!

Still laughing, she removed the belt from her waist, tossing it to the ground. Had it really come to this? Would her greatest challenge in life be fighting cats? Carelessly, she flipped several long strands of hair over her shoulder, ruefully shaking her head. At least it was better than wielding a sword, day after day, against a series of mock enemies, she thought. Lord, if only Jim could see her now, after all the time he had spent training her so meticulously. She thought of his deep blue eyes crinkled with mirth and his rough, callused hands showing her again and again the proper way to hold a sword.

Learn your enemy's strengths and weaknesses, he had told her. *Don't let your emotions show.* But eventually, even Jim had given up on that point. Fondly, he had told her that it was God's will she had been born with fiery red hair and a fitting temper to match.

Hanna felt an unbidden flash of sadness rip through her at the thought of her old friend. She missed him so much. He had been the one bright spot of light in her life; a life filled with so much loneliness and pain. And now she had no one. No one at all . . .

"Where are ye, ye little twit?"

Hanna scrambled to her feet at the sound of her uncle's shout, and she raced into the house, where he waited for her impatiently. Fleetingly, she wondered if he was drunk again.

"You called, Uncle Mason?" she asked breathlessly, absently tucking a stray tendril of her unruly hair behind her ear.

"Aye, I called ye, imp. What took ye so long?" He eyed her up and down before a sudden frown crossed his face. "What the hell did ye do to yer dress?"

He raised his hand as if to hit her, and Hanna cringed instinctively in a defensive move, bracing herself for the blows that would fall, as they always did when he was displeased with her.

But this time the blows did not come, and Hanna wondered why. Curiously, she looked past her uncle's large form into the parlor, where an elegantly dressed stranger sat. She hardly had time for a quick glance before her uncle placed his heavy hand on her shoulder, pushing her into the room.

"If ye ruin this deal, I'll see ye pay for it for the rest of yer life," he whispered angrily. "Now look sharp and speak only when ye are spoken to."

Hanna nodded silently, wondering what her uncle was up to this time. He had insisted that she bathe and dress in her finest gown, showing an unusual interest in her appearance and well-being. Usually he didn't care whether she slept or ate, for as much attention as he paid to her. Except when he was angry. Then she received his attention, all right, but it was mostly painful and left her black and blue for days.

As she approached the stranger, her uncle's hand gripped her shoulder until she was forced into a curtsy in front of him.

"Pleased to meet you, sir," she murmured.

The stranger came to his feet slowly, his mouth opening in astonishment at what he saw. The girl was absolutely exquisite; her hair the color of a burnished sun, her eyes a blue-green sea of promise. Reaching out, he gripped her chin in his hand, turning her face from one side to the other. Hanna grimaced at his touch, her brows furrowing together in a frown.

"Exceptional," the stranger said softly, his voice carrying the trace of an accent. "She is sixteen, yes?"

"Aye, sixteen tomorrow," her uncle answered proudly. "And as smart as a whip. She speaks two languages, English and Polish. Her mother was Polish and her father English. A real lady she is."

Hanna looked at her uncle in amazement. Never once had she heard him say a kind word about her.

The stranger let his gaze rake over Hanna, his eyes

gleaming. "There is no other living relative who could interfere with our little arrangement?"

Mason shook his head. "Nay, it's just the girl and me. It has been that way since me brother passed on, God rest his soul. Died of a broken heart, they say, some years after the girl's mother was murdered. I've been raising her all by meself."

Hanna felt a fierce flash of anger sweep through her. Uncle Mason had had little to do with raising her. Except for ensuring that she receive a daily dose of his wrath, he had spent most of his time drinking, gambling, and whoring about the city. Hanna bit back the retort that hovered on her tongue, knowing that it would only bring her a beating later.

The stranger cocked an eyebrow at Mason. "The girl's mother was murdered? How frightful. Did they catch the scoundrel?"

Mason shrugged. "Nay, they never did. To this day, I can't figure out who would have wanted to hurt such a pretty little thing." He leaned over closer to the man, speaking in a hushed whisper. "They say she knew the man who did it, though. Methinks it was some kind of sordid affair."

Hanna glared at her uncle, her temper flaring. He had no right to speak such dreadful lies about her mother. Not only was it immoral, it was unfair. A determined look suddenly flashed in Hanna's angry eyes. This time she would not let the insult pass, even if it meant a painful beating later.

Taking a deep breath, Hanna moved to stand squarely in front of her uncle, her flaming hair curling defiantly around her face. "That's enough, Uncle Mason," she warned quietly. "I won't stand here and allow you to speak such falsehoods about my mother."

Mason looked at her with a mixture of shock and surprise on his round face. Then he snorted with laughter, bawdily slapping his open palm against his thigh. "Aye, a saucy wench, ain't she?" he chortled at the stranger.

Hanna frowned, her cheeks flushing an angry red. "I

bloody well mean what I say, Uncle Mason," she warned. "Don't ever speak of my mother like that again."

The smile immediately faded from Mason's face. He took a meancing step toward her, his eyes narrowing into tiny slits. "Ye watch yer mouth, luv," he threatened in a low voice. "We have a gentleman in our presence, not the scum from the docks ye are used to chumming about with."

Hanna stiffened, her hands clenching at her side. "Don't you dare speak ill of Jim," she hissed. "He was more of a gentleman than you will ever be."

Mason growled deep in his throat, his face turning beet red. "Ye are wrong about that, twit. The old sailor was nothing but a pockmarked, ignorant lout."

Hanna nearly choked on her anger. Old Jim might have been unschooled, but he was far from ignorant. Gray-haired, with a kind and gentle heart, it had been Jim who had taught her the value of self-worth and confidence, taking an interest in her when no one else would. Seeing the bruises on her arms and face, he had also shown her how to protect herself by using her hands, as well as a sword and knife. He had been like a father to her, and Hanna had cherished every minute they spent together. When he died she had been inconsolable. Even now a lump swelled in her throat at the thought of him, and she blinked furiously to keep back the tears.

Curiously, the stranger watched the exchange between the feisty young woman and her uncle. A slow smile of satisfaction curved across his face as his eyes took in Hanna's hotly flushed cheeks, bright eyes, and fiercely clenched hands.

"Magnificent," he breathed in admiration. "Simply magnificent."

Mason glanced at the stranger out of the corner of his eyes and saw a gleam of approval in the man's eyes. Realizing that the girl was making him for a fool, Mason's fury grew.

"Enough of this," he growled angrily. "Ye keep yer mouth shut and open it only when I tell ye. And ye're not to speak again of that sailor scum."

A Touch of Fire

Hanna bravely stepped closer to her uncle. Despite his beatings she had always refused to cower in front of him.

"He was not scum," she said, her voice quiet but steady, "and I'll speak of him whenever I want."

A heavy silence followed her words before the stranger burst out in uncontainable laughter. Mason's mouth dropped open, his neck and face turning crimson with rage. He growled in anger, his hands curling into fists as he loomed over Hanna. She immediately tensed, readying herself for his blows. At that moment the stranger put his hand on Mason's arm, his eyes sending a clear warning of restraint to him.

"Now, now, there has been quite a bit of tragedy in this family, especially for one so young and beautiful. There is no need to dwell on such matters, nor to be overly upset." He rubbed his chin with a gloved hand, staring thoughtfully at Hanna.

"Mowisz po polsku?" he asked her, smoothly changing the topic. "Do you speak Polish?"

"Tak, mowię biegle po polsku," Hanna snapped, and then exhaled deeply, letting a bit of the tension flow from her. "Aye, I speak fluent Polish."

A Polish nanny had cared for her until the old woman had passed on two days before Hanna's eighth birthday. Hanna had continued studying Polish diligently under a tutor, mostly because the sound of her mother's native tongue somehow brought back warm memories of a distant time when she had been cherished and loved.

The stranger nodded with satisfaction and looked at her again strangely. Hanna felt uneasy from his gaze. He was an elegantly handsome man, probably near his fortieth year of age, Hanna thought. Yet there was something queer in the way he looked at her, and it made her stomach knot in apprehension.

She instinctively took a step backwards. "Why are you asking all of these questions?"

His mouth curved into a dark smile. "Does it frighten you?"

"I don't know," she said hesitantly. "But I don't like it."

Her uncle came from behind and shoved her back toward the stranger. "What ye like is of no importance. Ye'll do as I tell ye, girl."

The dark-haired man laughed and caught her around the waist, pulling her into his lap. "Ah, a beauty with spirit," he said, smiling, showing a gleam of white. "God, she tempts me already. How much did I promise you?"

"How much?" Hanna screeched and struggled to remove herself from his lap. The stranger held her tightly, refusing to let her move.

"Ye paid me half of the money four years ago," her uncle said, picking his teeth with his fingernail. "As I see it, ye owe me the other half plus interest for keeping her safe and sound, just for ye." His face squinted as he attempted to make the calculations.

The stranger frowned and then stood, dumping Hanna ungraciously from his lap. Hanna landed hard on the floor, yelping both in pain and anger.

"You English swine," the man said threateningly. "Don't you dare try to cheat me."

"Cheat you?" her uncle said, having the grace to look appalled. "I'm an honest man, making an honest deal. After all, she is my niece. . . ."

The dark-haired man laughed cruelly. "And she'll be my wife."

"W-wife?" Hanna gasped in horror, but both men ignored her.

"Now I'm willing to offer you a fair price," the stranger said coolly. "Probably more than you will ever see in your lifetime." From under his cloak he pulled out a heavy velvet bag and threw it at Mason's feet. Mason reached down and opened the bag, his eyes gleaming, gasping with amazement at what he saw.

"W-why it is even more than ye offered," he stuttered, letting the coins fall slowly through his fingers.

"I am well pleased," the stranger said arrogantly.

For a fleeting moment Mason had a flash of doubt as he looked into the dark eyes of the stranger. Then he felt the weight of the gold in his hands and his doubts vanished.

"Then the deal is settled. The girl is all yers," Mason said accommodatingly.

Hanna still sat on the floor where she had fallen, looking in shock at the two men. She thought she might be ill, both from her uncle's behavior and from the hungry gleam in the stranger's eyes when he looked at her.

"Good," the tall man said slowly. "I will return tomorrow to take her. I must first prepare a suitable traveling companion for the girl and secure our passage on the next available ship."

The stranger walked over to Hanna and pulled her off the floor. He dragged her close roughly, bending down to press his lips against hers. It was such a cold and repulsive gesture, Hanna gagged and took a step backwards.

The man laughed. "Get used to it, girl. You will learn to please me, *moja rozyczka*." With those words he turned and walked out of the room.

Something painful tugged at Hanna's memory with the sound of his voice, but the recollection eluded her. She watched him go with her hands clenched at her sides before turning to face her uncle. He was still looking at the coins in wonder, his eyes filled with greed and lust.

"Uncle Mason," she said softly. "How could you? I am your brother's daughter."

He didn't bother to look up from his gold. "'Tis my duty to see ye married. Ye should thank me, girl. After all, ye are already sixteen and no one even made me an offer, except him. He didn't even care that ye don't have a dowry."

Hanna winced inwardly at his words. It was true that no one had asked for her hand in marriage, but it was primarily because Uncle Mason had squandered her father's fortune and had drunk away every scrap of respectability the Quinn family had ever had.

"Not that I would have accepted, even if someone had offered," her uncle continued, oblivious to the hurt look in her eyes. "Nay, I promised him four years ago that on yer sixteenth birthday ye would wed him. So be happy, twit; ye fetched a fair price. Ye certainly did yer uncle proud."

Hanna was stunned. "Y-you promised my hand in marriage four years ago?"

"Aye, I did. He gave me a sack full of money even then. I wasn't sure that he'd come back. Ye see, four years is a long time for a man to wait, especially a man as rich as he. I was sure he'd be able to find something better than ye. But much to me astonishment he arrived today, right on schedule. Have to say, it did surprise the hell out of me."

A mixture of anger and unhappiness filled Hanna. She bit her lower lip so hard, she could taste the blood. A small tear slipped from the corner of her eye and she quickly brushed it aside. She would not give her uncle the satisfaction of seeing her cry.

"Who is he, Uncle Mason?" she asked as calmly as she could manage.

Her uncle put the gold back into the bag and tied the string tight. "Well, ye see, it is a bit of a strange tale. When he came to me four years ago he didn't want to give me his name. Said he wanted to keep the request a discreet matter, him being a nobleman back in his country. He said he'd seen ye on the street and liked yer red hair. Said he was drawn to ye like a moth to a flame, those being his exact words. Me being a man and all, I understood exactly what he was talking about, although I like dark-haired ladies meself." He chortled into his hands.

Hanna fought down the bile that rose to her throat. "How utterly fascinating, Uncle. Pray continue."

Mason narrowed his eyes at her tone. "He offered me money for ye on the spot. I told him that he couldn't have ye until ye turned sixteen, because of yer father's will. Ye see, if ye left me before that, I would have been left without a coin to my name. The money was in yer name, and me being yer guardian and all . . . well, I could draw on the money whenever I wanted. If ye had married, yer husband would have taken control of the fortune." His eyes studied her shrewdly. "Once ye turned sixteen, it

A Touch of Fire

didn't matter. Ye became the sole owner of the fortune and could have cut me off, if ye so desired."

Hanna stood in stunned silence and then suddenly threw herself at her uncle, pummeling him with her fists. "You bastard," she shouted, tears coursing down her face. "You've already spent it all."

Mason grabbed her fists easily, twisting his face into a sneer. "Ye watch yer tongue and yer temper, luv. Ye'll be married to a fine gentleman who'll not be as easy on ye as I was. Besides, I don't see why ye object to yer uncle having a little retirement money. After all, I took care of ye, didn't I?"

Hanna wrenched herself from his grasp and ran toward the door. "I'll never agree to this marriage," she cried, stopping at the doorway, her chest heaving with emotion.

Mason took a threatening step toward her, his face turning purple with anger. "Ye'll do as I say, girl. And if ye do anything to ruin this deal, I'll throttle ye good with me own two hands. Ye'd better know that I'd not stop until ye'd wish ye were dead." He waited a moment to let his words sink in. Then, slowly, he cracked his knuckles one by one.

"I see it this way, Hanna. Ye can either marry him or stay here with me. What will it be, girl?"

With a choked sob, Hanna turned on her heel and fled from the room.

Chapter Two

Warsaw, Poland 1655

The funeral procession wound slowly through the streets of Warsaw as the sky opened, pouring torrents of rain upon the mourners. A deep roll of thunder sounded, followed by a jagged fork of lightning that lit the gloomy sky. Still the mourners continued their slow plodding toward the church and the cemetery that stood on the hill.

Curious onlookers crowded the streets in spite of the rain, whispering and crossing themselves as the coffin passed. Some of the bystanders were bolder, shouting curses and hurling spiteful comments at those carrying the coffin.

A tall man with dark hair and a long black cloak led the procession, balancing the front corner of the coffin on his right shoulder. He looked neither to the left nor to the right, nor did he appear to hear the insults as he guided the procession toward its final destination. Only the brightness of his eyes and the tension with which his hand clenched the casket gave any indication of his anger.

Slowly the group reached the cemetery, but instead of entering the gates, the mourners walked to a small rise overlooking the church, where a shallow grave had been dug. Gingerly, the pallbearers lowered the coffin into the hole. As the rain continued its steady downpour, the mourners gathered around the grave.

There was no priest among the mourners, so the tall man stepped forward. He lifted the hood from his cloak, uncovering his head. A long mane of dark hair fell to his shoulders, wet with rain. His straight, blunt face was as emotionless as stone, and though the rain relentlessly pelted his face, he did not blink. The wind whipped his light cloak around him as he stood in front of the group, his legs set wide apart, his hands on his hips. Another loud clap of thunder sounded as he raised his voice to be heard.

"We lay to rest our beloved sister, Danuta Tarnowska," he spoke, his voice rising above the storm. "May God bless and forgive her kind and gentle soul."

Pausing for a long moment, he listened to the fierce rumbling of the storm and the sound of the rain as it fell against the ground. Then, slowly, he pulled out a single white rose from the folds of his cloak and dropped it gently on top of the coffin. "Good night, dear sister," he whispered softly.

One by one, the mourners approached the coffin, dropping flowers on it and paying their last respects. Eventually, the tall man was left alone on the hill, save for a young man with sad eyes. As the two men stood side by side in silence, the resemblance between them was remarkable. Both had strong, hard faces and the exact same color of dark brown hair. Their only difference was in height and size, the older one being considerably larger.

"Stefan," the young man whispered, "it can't end like this. He has shamed her and our family. It is not right."

Stefan put a gentle hand on the young man's shoulder, wondering if the anguish he could see in his brother's eyes was as evident in his own. "It does not end here, Mikhail," he said quietly. "We shall see that justice is served."

The two brothers' eyes met, and a silent promise passed between them. The rain tore at them, but they held the gaze steady. Suddenly, Mikhail turned away and fell to his knees at the edge of the grave, sobbing into his hands.

Stefan watched his brother in silence for several minutes before reaching down and pulling him to his feet. "Grieve now, Mikhail," Stefan said softly, pulling him inside his cloak. "For soon there will be no time for tears. Have no doubt that Jozef Czarnowski will suffer greatly for what he has done to Danuta. I swear this on her grave."

A crack of thunder sounded as lightning ripped the sky. The rain continued its slashing, blinding fury, but the two men did not notice. On the hill, at the grave of their sister, the young man put his head on his brother's chest and cried bitter tears of grief.

Chapter Three

Stefan Tarnowski strode into the library, shrugging out of his cloak and shaking the rain from it. Shutting the door behind him, he carelessly tossed the cloak over the back of a chair and walked toward a wooden cabinet. He pulled out a bottle of vodka and filled a goblet, draining it in one movement. Quickly, he poured himself another and put the bottle back on the shelf.

Walking to the hearth, he stoked the flames with a fire iron, watching as the sparks leaped and hissed. He was deep in thought when a soft knock sounded on the door. Irritated that he had been disturbed, he walked to the door and flung it open.

An old priest with silver hair stood in the doorway, his robe damp from the rain. He said nothing, but looked for a long, silent moment at Stefan.

Stefan raised one eyebrow in surprise and then, bowing slightly, gestured for the priest to enter the room. The priest obliged him and walked slowly across the threshold.

"Father Witold," Stefan said, closing the door behind him. "How utterly Christian of you to come to us in our hour of grief." He lifted his glass in a mocking salute and then drained the last of his drink.

The priest showed no offense at the tone of Stefan's voice. "You know I would have been there if I could," he said softly.

"Of course you would have, Father," Stefan agreed, his voice coldly sarcastic.

The priest sighed. "You judge me harshly, Stefan. I loved Danuta as if she were my own and you know it. Have you no idea how it tore my heart to know that precious child could not be buried in holy ground?"

Stefan stiffened and turned his back to the priest. "You expect my pity?"

"Nay, only your understanding."

Stefan set his glass down on the table with a loud crash. "I understand nothing of you and your kind. She loved you and everything the Church stood for, yet you turned your back on her."

A tear formed at the corner of the priest's eye and slid down his cheek. "I am deeply sorry, Stefan, but the Church has very strict rules. Because she—" The priest stopped, choking on the words. "Because she took her own life, there was nothing I could do."

Stefan whirled to face him. "She did not take her own life, Father," he said angrily. "Her life, as she knew it, ended the night she was forcibly taken by Jozef Czarnowski. He killed her as surely as if he had run a sword through her heart."

Father Witold sank into a chair, raising his troubled brown eyes to meet Stefan's. "Do you think I do not know this? If it is any comfort to you, I have said a prayer for her soul."

Stefan clenched his hands at his side. "Nothing you can say would give me comfort now. Damn you and damn the Church for its rigidity."

Father Witold paled visibly, and Stefan could see how deeply his words had wounded the priest. Angrily, he picked up a log and threw it into the hearth, watching the sparks fly about madly.

The priest clasped his hands together and bowed his head. "I fully deserve those words, Stefan. Danuta was the light of my life. Her soul was as pure as gold. Had I the courage, I would have been there today to wish her a final farewell." He whispered the last words, his voice thick with emotion.

Stefan heard the priest's sorrow in his voice and sighed deeply. "I am not my sister, Father. I do not forgive so easily." He paused for a long moment, staring deeply into the flames. "But somehow I know that she, of all people, would have understood your absence."

Father Witold took a deep and painful breath. "That doesn't make it any easier. I will have to live with myself and my actions."

"And Jozef Czarnowski will pay for his actions. Danuta's death will be avenged." Stefan's face was as cold as stone.

The priest carefully lowered his eyes. "Aye, my son, God will justly punish him for his sins."

Stefan's eyes hardened. "That is not what I mean."

Father Witold sighed and clasped his hands in his lap. "I know what you mean, Stefan."

"Justice will be served, but on my terms, not God's."

"I will not condone violence," the priest said softly.

Stefan's jaw tightened. "I am not asking for your permission."

The priest stood slowly, rubbing his hand across his brow. "I am well aware of that. I want only to remind you that revenge does not always turn out the way it is planned. Often the innocent are harmed."

Stefan laughed hoarsely. "And were there none more innocent than Danuta?"

"Violence begets violence, Stefan," Father Witold reminded him gently.

"And isn't it also said, 'An eye for an eye, a tooth for a tooth'?"

The priest shook his head sadly. "I only ask that you think about what it means to take revenge. It will not bring Danuta back."

Stefan laughed hoarsely, but there was no humor in his voice. "Nay, unfortunately, it will not. But it will give me the satisfaction of sending that foul man to his death."

"You must do what you think is right."

"Then you know I will kill Jozef Czarnowski."

Father Witold exhaled heavily and returned to his seat. "Aye, you will do what you must. It is part of the reason I am here today."

Stefan arched an eyebrow in surprise. Silence hung heavy between them before the priest spoke again.

"If your heart is set on revenge, my son, then see that your actions are swift. A dark shadow will soon fall across Poland."

Stefan frowned. "You wish to speak to me in riddles?"

Father Witold shook his head. "This is no riddle. There are rumors, dark rumors, from the city of Gdansk."

Stefan lifted his head sharply. Gdansk was at the northern tip of Poland and a major trading port for merchants from all over the world. There, people exchanged not only goods but valuable information as to world events.

"A German merchant returning from a trip to Sweden told me the Baltic Sea is full of Swedish warships and that shipbuilding in Gdansk is at a frenzy," Father Witold continued. "He sold out his entire shipload of iron works in only one day."

Stefan could not hide the look of surprise in his eyes. "It sounds as if Sweden is preparing for war."

"So it does," the priest answered quietly.

A deep frown furrowed its way across Stefan's face. "Sweden already controls most of the Baltic land north of the Duchy of Lithuania and several northern German territories. Perhaps they are only planning to reinforce their claims on those territories."

"Perhaps," Father Witold said mildly.

Stefan leaned forward in his chair. "You don't think Sweden prepares to attack us? The truce of Sztumska Wies is to last twenty-six years. There are still six years left to this treaty."

Yet even as he spoke the words, his mind quickly calculated the possibility of a Swedish offensive. As the youngest colonel in the service of His Majesty Yan Casimir, King of Poland, Stefan had a reputation as a brilliant strategist and an excellent swordsman. He and his men had returned from the Russian front just four months ago. Poland was still warring on two borders, with the Cossacks and with the Russians. In fact, he and his men were currently waiting reassignment by the king. Stefan had assumed they would soon be sent back to the Russian front, but given this new information, perhaps he had been too hasty in his assumptions.

He looked at the priest thoughtfully. "Forgive me, Father, but I sense that you don't believe the treaty will hold."

The priest sighed sadly. "I don't. Two days ago a high-ranking envoy arrived from the Vatican to speak with King Casimir."

Stefan whistled softly. The Pope was by far the Polish king's staunchest ally. As Poland was a fiercely Catholic country surrounded by mostly Protestant neighbors, the Vatican kept a close eye on events in the country, often informing the king of potentially dangerous situations.

Stefan's heart began to beat uncomfortably in his chest. The Swedes had an enormous army of well-trained and battle-seasoned men. If they were set loose on Polish soil, the results would be catastrophic.

"You think the Vatican envoy is here to warn the king?" Stefan asked, his mouth dry.

Father Witold nodded. "I believe King Gustav of Sweden longs to seize the rest of the Baltic coast and silence his cousin's dreams of one day ascending to the Swedish throne."

Stefan muttered a curse under his breath. King Yan Casimir was, indeed, cousin to the Swedish king. Polish noblemen, fearful of making any one of themselves too powerful, had three times in succession elected a member of the Swedish royal family to be their king.

Although Yan Casimir had publicly renounced his Protestant upbringing and been baptized as a Polish Catholic, as had the two Swedish kings before him, there were still persistent whispers in the kingdom that Yan Casimir secretly dreamed of becoming the next King of Sweden.

Stefan brought his fist crashing down on the mantel. "Damn," he shouted. "Not now."

The priest stood, his brown eyes calm. "There is not much time, my son. Whatever you must do to avenge that young girl's soul, it must be done soon. Before you are called away again to serve your country."

Stefan raised his head sharply, appraising the priest's words. "I thought you did not approve of violence, Father," he said slowly.

Father Witold absently smoothed his robe with his hands, avoiding Stefan's eyes. "As a servant of God, I do not. As a weak and humble man . . ." He let his words trail off as he slowly walked to the door and opened it.

Stefan eyed the priest with new appreciation. "Thank you, Father," he finally said quietly. "The information that you have given me is most valuable."

Father Witold acknowledged the words with a tip of his head. He turned to go and then stopped, as if remembering something.

"By the way, there is something else you should know, my son," he said slowly, without turning around.

Stefan rested his hands against the back of the chair. "Aye?"

"Jozef Czarnowski is to be wed in one week."

A look of surprise flashed in Stefan's eyes, and then a slow smile spread across his face.

"God bless you, Father," he said quietly as the priest closed the door firmly behind him.

Chapter Four

It was stiflingly hot in the small chapel. Hanna Quinn paced back and forth in front of the altar, nervously fingering the gold and ivory threads of her wedding dress. She was alone, a bride in seclusion before the marriage ceremony.

Stopping suddenly, she sank to her knees on the padded step, resting her elbows on the small wooden gate surrounding the altar. She clasped her hands together and closed her eyes in prayer.

"Lord God, I know I have not been a true and faithful servant. But please, no matter what transgressions I may have committed in my lifetime, I beg you to deliver me from this evil man."

She waited a moment and then opened her eyes, looking up at the heavy golden cross on the altar. The sight of Jesus's suffering face as he hung limply from the cross brought back the words of Father Leszek as he had spoken them that morning at her confession.

"My child, you must accept your burden and carry your cross without complaint, as Jesus did."

Sighing, she got to her feet. It had been her first time at confession and oddly, she had felt better after pouring out her soul to the gentle-eyed priest. It had been a while since anyone had really taken the time to listen to her. Speaking haltingly at first, she had told Father Leszek everything, releasing the pent-up emotion of the years of pain and abuse she had suffered under the heavy hand of her drunken uncle. She had barely been able to finish her confession, she was crying so hard. The priest had soothed her by murmuring soft words of comfort.

Hanna sighed at the memory and pressed her hand to her brow. In many ways she did not regret being in Poland. The sound of her mother's native tongue brought her comfort and kindled memories of being warm, safe, and loved. In fact, if it weren't for Jozef Czarnowski, she might not regret it at all.

God help her, Jozef Czarnowski frightened her more than her uncle ever had. She twisted her hands together tightly. The trip across the English Channel had been a nightmare. Although properly accompanied by a chaperone, Jozef had done everything in his power to trap her alone. Her careful avoidance of him seemed only to excite and encourage him.

He had caught her once, in a corridor below the deck. Forcing his fingers into her hair, he had released the pins and let it fall about her in a red cloud.

"Jezus Maria," he had whispered softly. "Hair the color of fire . . . the same fire that burns in my soul for you."

Frightened by the look in his eyes, she had struggled to get away, but he had held her tight, twisting her arm painfully when she tried to move from him.

"You are a witch, my sweet. I always knew that you would be mine, that you would come back to me. You cast a spell on me with those eyes of yours . . . the color of an endless sea. At night, when I slept, they beckoned . . . called out to me. That is when I knew that you had never really left me."

Hanna was completely bewildered by his strange words

and his odd obsession with her eyes and hair. The flushed, hot look in his eyes frightened her senseless, though she could not explain why.

Thankfully, her chaperone had appeared, and Jozef had released her, but not before he had promised her there was more to come.

Hanna shivered at the memory, nervously fingering the beads on her gown. *How is it that my life has gone from rotten to wretched in just a few days?* A tear slid down her cheek and she brushed it away angrily. There was no one to look out for Hanna Quinn except Hanna Quinn herself. She would have to rely on her wits to get her through this ordeal.

"What will become of me?" she whispered, running her hand across her brow, feeling the dampness along her hairline.

Sighing, she began pacing again until she heard the door open behind her. Whirling, she gasped in horror when she saw Jozef standing there, a smug smile on his dark handsome face.

"Jozef," she breathed, her heart hammering in fear. "What are you doing? Don't you know it is bad luck to see the bride before the wedding?" As soon as the words were out of her mouth, she felt like laughing hysterically at the irony of her statement.

Jozef didn't answer, but took a step toward her, his eyes drinking in her beauty. God help him, she smelled of roses. Hungrily, he let his gaze linger at her breasts. The shadowed dip of her cleavage and the soft swell of her bosom aroused him painfully.

"You are beautiful," he whispered in awe. "And today you will finally be mine."

Hanna felt a cold finger of fear wrap around her heart. She opened her mouth to say something, but the words froze in her throat. Jozef took a step closer and reached out to trace a line across her cheekbone to her lips. She shuddered, a cold chill creeping up her spine.

"Do you not think I am handsome too?" he asked her in a husky whisper.

She fought down the urge to run and slowly looked into his eyes. For the first time she really looked at him. He was a handsome man; almost pretty. Although he was much older than she, the dark, mature beauty of his face and his well-sculpted figure would set most women's hearts aflame. But she felt nothing but coldness, emptiness, and fear when she looked at him.

"I . . ." she croaked, and then she cleared her throat. "I suppose so," she whispered hoarsely.

A frown flitted across his face, and his arm shot out, grabbing her by the waist and pulling her toward him. She put out her hands to stop him but found them crushed against his chest. "Nay," she said in a choked voice, struggling to free herself from his grasp.

His breath was hot on her cheek as she turned her head away from him. "I have been cursed," he said, gripping her tighter. "Ever since the day I saw you, your eyes have followed me, taunting and teasing until I burned with desire. Flames as hot as the fires of hell have tormented me, crushing my will and making me want you more than I have ever wanted anything in my life. I have waited for years to claim you, to put an end to the agonizing burning in my soul. I will not let you escape again, my little rose. Today you will be mine—for now and for all the days of eternity."

Hanna trembled, horrified by his rambling confession. He saw her fear and smiled. "Good, good, my sweet. I want you to fear me. Fear and desire go hand in hand. Soon you will open your soul to me and I will teach you the joys of my body and yours. I will make you want me as much as I want you."

He brought his lips down upon hers, crushing her body against his. Forcing his tongue into her mouth, he sucked at her until it seemed he was drawing the very breath from her lungs.

"Nay," Hanna gasped, tearing away from him. As his hands painfully gripped the flesh of her arms, she raised her knee, hitting him squarely in the groin. Howling in pain, Jozef dropped to his knees while Hanna scrambled away, trying to catch her breath.

After several moments Jozef stood, his face contorted with anger. "You will be punished for that, Hanna. I will take you again and again until your soul crumbles before me, until you beg for mercy. This I promise you, Hanna Quinn."

With those words he turned and left the chapel, slamming the door behind him. Hanna closed her eyes in momentary relief, and then dropped to her knees in front of the altar. "Lord God Jesus," she prayed, tears falling from her eyes, "please have pity on my soul and deliver me from the evil that awaits me."

So earnest was her plea that one might believe that God would indeed take pity on her soul.

Chapter Five

Mikhail Tarnowski gripped the hilt of his sword tightly in his hand, trying to contain the fierce excitement that coursed through his veins. He always had this strange sensation in the pit of his stomach when he knew he would match skills and wits with an enemy. His nerves were stretched taut with tension and anticipation, his hands and brow sweaty. Christ's blood, how he liked a good fight. He often wondered whether it was fear that drove him or reckless courage.

How different he was from his older brother. With a mixture of pride and envy, Mikhail looked over at Stefan, who sat calmly astride a dark brown steed, scanning the thick walls of the Czarnowski estate from the edge of the forest. A man of great physical stature and bronzed skin from constant exposure to the weather, Stefan cut an impressive figure to the men gathered about him. One hand loosely held a shield; the other rested against his brow, protecting his eyes from the bright sun. His large profile was firm and steady, his very presence emanating strength and security. Mikhail both revered and respected his brother, as did most of the men who followed him.

Digging his heels into the side of his mount, Mikhail reined in next to Stefan. "What is it, brother?" he asked quietly.

A slow smile of satisfaction crossed Stefan's face. From what he could see, the wedding festivities had made Jozef Czarnowski careless. Not a single soldier could be seen standing guard at the open gate, nor was the sentry at his assigned position. It was just as he had hoped.

"Czarnowski will meet his death today," he said, looking at his brother steadily. "There will be no mercy."

Mikhail nodded and quickly wheeled his horse around, giving instructions to the men behind him.

After several moments Stefan raised his hand high in the air and then brought it down quickly. Spurring his horse into a gallop, he led half of his men toward the gate, while the others circled around to the back of the estate and began scaling the walls from the other side.

Stefan charged through the gate and into the courtyard. A Czarnowski sentry heading for his post shouted a warning but was quickly silenced by one of Stefan's men. Screams of terror filled the courtyard as elegantly dressed wedding guests scattered and fled about the grounds in a crazed panic. A lone Czarnowski soldier bellowing with anger charged Stefan and tried to pull him off his horse, but Stefan coldly cut him down with a swift stroke of his sword.

Alerted by the screams, Czarnowski's soldiers began to spill out onto the courtyard. The sound of clashing steel filled the air. The deafening noise mingled with angry shouts and agonizing cries of pain. Stefan wielded his sword easily, methodically removing anyone who got in his way.

The fighting ended quickly, with Stefan's well-trained men easily overpowering Jozef Czarnowski's ill-prepared soldiers. With a flick of his hand, Stefan motioned for his men to round up the wedding guests. Reining in his horse in the center of the courtyard, he searched the group for Jozef Czarnowski. There was no sign of him.

"Where is Czarnowski?" Stefan shouted at the guests as his steed pranced restlessly about the courtyard.

The wedding guests looked at him in horror, no one daring to answer the fierce, angry soldier.

Stefan's mouth curled in contempt. Jozef Czarnowski was a coward, the last man to be found in the thick of a fight, the first one to run at the sight of trouble. As always, he let his men fight his battles for him, protecting the one thing he held valuable above all else, his own skin. Wheeling around his steed, Stefan let out a shrill whistle. Mikhail was instantly by his side.

"What is it?" he asked his brother breathlessly, his eyes ablaze from the fight.

"We will search every inch of this estate until Czarnowski is found. I don't want a single stone left unturned."

Before Mikhail could answer, a young soldier rode up to Stefan, an anxious look on his face. "Jozef Czarnowski has escaped, sir," the soldier said, panting for breath. "He rode out of the stables with several soldiers, riding as if the devil was after him. Piotr took a bad cut from one of them, sir." He wiped his hand across his brow. "We chased them, but they got away."

"Czarnowski ran from his own home?" Mikhail asked incredulously as Stefan's face darkened with anger. "*Psia krew*," Mikhail shouted, then spewed a series of other curses. "The damn coward. Has he no honor? He leaves his home, his guests, and even his new bride unprotected, and for what—to save his own hide?"

Stefan thought for a moment. "Aye, it was careless of him." He urged his horse a few steps forward. "Bring me the bride of Czarnowski," he commanded his men, his voice ringing clearly through the courtyard.

A few of the wedding guests gasped, and two women fainted as his men ran off to do his bidding.

Coldly, Stefan turned to his brother. "You and Feliks search the church," he ordered. "She may be hiding there."

Mikhail nodded as he and Feliks slipped off their mounts and entered the church. The massive stone building was empty, but Mikhail thought he heard a noise from an adjoining chapel. With a flick of his head, he motioned for Feliks to approach it. Feliks drew his deadly shortsword, ideal for fighting in small places. Cautiously, he headed for the door.

At that exact moment, the door was flung open and a young woman with stunning red hair, dressed in an ivory and gold wedding gown, stood in the doorway. As she met their eyes, her mouth dropped open in astonishment.

"Nay," she screamed in terror when the two men began to advance on her. Quickly, she slammed the door shut behind her, drawing the latch.

Immediately, the men began throwing themselves at the door. Hanna saw at once that the latch would not hold for long. She had no idea why these two men were approaching her with drawn swords, but Jozef's threat still rang in her ears. *"You will be punished for that, Hanna."*

"God help me," she whispered quietly. "Jozef has gone truly mad and I am without a weapon to protect myself."

Suddenly, her eyes fastened on the heavy gold cross on the altar. Saying a quick prayer of thanks under her breath, she lifted the cross off the altar and hurried to place herself behind the door. Holding the cross above her head, she held her breath and waited.

The men hit the door a few more times and the latch gave way, hurling one of them into the room. Murmuring a prayer asking for forgiveness, Hanna brought the cross down on his head and then reached over to take his sword into her hand. Whirling around, she stood ready to face the next man.

Mikhail crashed through the door and stopped in amazement when he saw Feliks lying facedown on the ground.

"What the hell?" he said, looking around for someone else before realizing that the girl held a sword in her hand.

Hanna tried to stop her hand from shaking. "I d-didn't mean to hurt him. He is alive. I felt his pulse when I took his sword."

"You did this?" he asked incredulously.

She bit her lower lip. "I won't let you hurt me. I don't know for what evil purpose he has sent you here, but I won't remain passive in the face of such cruelty. Either you leave me alone or you kill me. In fact, I would prefer the latter, if I may have a say in the matter."

Mikhail thought the girl had gone utterly mad. "Put down the sword. You'll only hurt yourself."

The young man looked as if he had honest eyes, so she hesitated for a moment. "Can you honestly say, sir, that you mean me no malice?" She paused, looking at him squarely. "You had best tell the truth. Remember, you are in a house of God."

Mikhail looked over his shoulder at the empty altar and frowned. "Put the sword down, woman," he said irritably. "I'll promise you nothing."

Hanna nodded. She had expected no less from one of Jozef's men. Slowly, she took a step backwards, mentally sizing up her opponent. He was young but strong and could easily knock the sword out of her hand if he caught her unaware.

Better to let him think I am inexperienced and have no idea how to hold this sword. She said a silent prayer of thanks to Jim for all the times they had practiced together. *My one and only friend,* she thought sadly.

Hanna took a cautious step backward, nearly tripping on her dress. Silently, she cursed the heavy material for restricting her movements. At the first chance possible she would have to free herself from the heavy gown or she would never be able to move as quickly as she needed.

Feliks began to moan and Mikhail knelt down by his side, keeping a wary eye on the girl.

"What happened?" Feliks asked groggily.

"The girl hit you over the head with a cross." Mikhail couldn't help but grin as he said the words. God help him, but this would make a good story back home.

"A what?" Feliks said, sitting straight up and then groaning with pain.

Mikhail didn't have a chance to answer; the girl suddenly tore the material of her gown with the sword. Before the men could close their gaping mouths she shrugged out of the gown and stood facing them calmly, clad only in a thin chemise.

Mikhail forced himself to close his mouth and stood slowly. Feliks, too, rose to his feet, still holding his head.

"The girl has gone completely mad," Mikhail said in a low voice to Feliks. Feliks nodded, his eyes still reflecting astonishment at her actions.

Turning to her, Mikhail held out his hand. "Give me the sword," he said gruffly.

Hanna shook her head, shifting her weight to her back foot. "Nay. I'll not let you torture me. You'll have to kill me first."

Mikhail and Feliks exchanged a puzzled look of disgust and then Mikhail moved forward. He thrust his sword at hers lightly, hoping to knock it from her hand, and howled in surprise when she easily slapped his to the floor.

"What the hell?" he said looking first at his hand then at his sword, as if he could not believe his eyes.

"Stay away from me," Hanna warned again.

Mikhail ignored her words and lunged at her, attempting to grab her hand with the sword. She easily sidestepped him, slicing a long strip of material from his sleeve. At the same time, Feliks made a scramble for Mikhail's sword and snatched it from the ground. The two men stood facing her, panting and angry.

"I tire of this game, Mikhail," Feliks drawled slowly, circling to her left. "Let's end it as soon as possible. I say we show her no mercy." He hoped his words would frighten the girl into surrender.

Much to their amazement, she smiled. "Now, this is a true challenge: two against one. Let's see how you do, gentlemen."

Feliks and Mikhail exchanged a look of disbelief before their eyes hardened. Being mocked by a woman was something neither of them would tolerate.

"We shall take you, madam, even if it takes two of us," Mikhail said, his voice cold.

"Then we shall see, won't we?" Hanna said sweetly, raising her sword.

Stefan Tarnowski was halfway down the aisle of the church when he heard the sudden clang of blade hitting blade. Quickly, he strode toward the noise, pushing open a splintered door that stood slightly ajar. His mouth dropped open in astonishment at what he saw.

A young woman, half clad, was defending herself against two of his men. Furious that his men had dared to raise a sword against a woman, he started forward before he abruptly stopped in his tracks.

The young woman clearly knew how to use the sword. Despite the fact that she was half the size of either of the men, she handled her sword with such ease and dexterity that her two opponents were making little progress against her.

Stefan slowly relaxed as he realized she was in no danger. She was small but skilled, and it was a joy to watch her. He even smiled as the girl moved forward, actually forcing both of the men back a step. Mikhail had begun to sweat profusely as he attempted to push her off balance, and Feliks had become careless, slashing recklessly at her.

Stefan leaned against the doorway, crossing his arms against his chest. He'd be damned, but the girl was actually winning. He watched as Mikhail took a step back to wipe his brow and get a second breath. Left alone with only Feliks to tend to, the girl immediately pressed her advantage, focusing all her attention on him. She easily deflected one of his blows, then slipped her sword through to snap clean through his belt. As his pants fell around his ankles, Feliks uttered a foul oath.

"Shame on you, sir," Hanna scolded him. "Please remember that we are in a house of God."

Stefan could contain himself no longer and roared with laughter. Mikhail and Feliks turned quickly, flushing bright red when they realized their commander had been watching them for some time.

A Touch of Fire

Hanna gasped as she looked at the man who stood in the doorway. He was the largest man she had ever seen. His powerful arms were crossed against a broad chest and his thighs were as thick as tree trunks. His eyes, although amused now, looked as if they could chill a summer's day if he was displeased. Her breath caught in her throat. Lord help her, but she would never be able to fight this man. He was enormous.

The two men stepped aside deferentially, and Hanna guessed the big man was their leader. Biting her lower lip, she raised her sword at him.

Stefan laughed. "You mean to fight me, too, woman?"

She nodded firmly. "I'll run this sword through you if you come another step closer."

He heard the slight accent in her voice and frowned. "You are a foreigner?"

"You don't know?" she asked, surprised that Jozef had not told his own men that she was English.

He raised an eyebrow. "Should I?"

She thought for a moment, her delicate brows furrowed. "I d-don't know. My mother was Polish," she finally conceded.

"And your father?"

"English."

"I see," Stefan said thoughtfully. His frown deepened as he let his gaze sweep slowly down her body to the floor, where the shredded wedding gown lay in a heap. Lord, he couldn't help but notice what a fiery beauty she was. The ringlets of her flaming red hair fell like silk around her bare shoulders and her skin was fresh and rosy. Her flashing blue-green eyes met his, though he could see from her heaving breasts that she was frightened. Still, he respected her for having the courage to stand up to him. Jozef had chosen well, he thought to himself.

He forced his mind back to the matter at hand and casually took a step forward. "Well?" he asked calmly. "Do you mean to run me through?"

"I w-won't give you another chance," Hanna warned again, wishing her voice would stop wavering. "Don't come any closer."

Ignoring her threat, Stefan moved forward again until the steel tip of her blade pressed against his chest. "Well, madam, I suggest you make good your threat . . . or surrender your sword."

Hanna drew in her breath and looked into his eyes. They were the most unusual color she had ever seen: a deep shade of gray, the color of a stormy sky, with long black lashes covering them. He had a small scar near his left eye, and she wondered how he had received it. She felt her heart skip a beat. Lord, he was a handsome one, and his presence emanated strength.

"I am waiting, madam," Stefan repeated patiently.

Closing her eyes, Hanna let the sword slowly drop to her side. She knew she didn't have it in her to kill a man, even if it meant her life.

"I will not spill blood in a house of God," she said quietly.

Feliks rushed over to take the sword from her hand, but froze abruptly at Stefan's harsh command. "Don't touch her, Feliks."

Feliks nodded slowly, exchanging a puzzled glance with Mikhail. Mikhail shrugged slightly and looked away.

Stefan reached out and took the sword from her hand. The young woman moved back a step in fear, but he made no attempt to touch her, simply staring until a rose blush crept across her cheeks. As her color deepened, Stefan found himself physically reacting to her. She was thin, a bit too underfleshed for his taste, but she had spirit. In spite of her rather precarious position her flashing eyes never ceased to challenge him. At that moment, he thought he had never met a woman so lovely and vibrant.

"May I ask where you learned to handle a sword like that?" he asked her. Damn, but he couldn't keep a trace of admiration out of his voice.

"I learned in order to protect myself," she said, lifting her proud eyes to meet his.

"Protect yourself?" he asked, his eyebrows arching. "Had you no man to protect you?"

Hanna flushed but straightened her shoulders. "I need no man for that. I can take care of myself," she said haughtily.

"So I see," Stefan answered noncommittally, but he had seen a brief flash of pain in her eyes.

What troubling secrets did she hide behind that mane of dazzling red hair? he wondered, surprised that the thought should cross his mind. He shook his head and grunted. Whatever her secrets, one thing was certain: She intrigued him greatly.

Hanna watched his eyes move across her body and had the distinct feeling he was undressing her with them. She suddenly became self-conscious, aware of how scantily she was clad. What had earlier been to her advantage was now appearing to be quite a disadvantage.

Purposely, she crossed her arms over her breasts. "I demand that you stop looking at me like that. If you wish to kill or hurt me, I ask you to do the deed now and get it over with."

Stefan looked at her as if she had gone daft. "Kill you?" His laughter was deep and husky. "I have no plans to kill you, madam. You are much too valuable to me."

"Forgive me if I say I don't believe you," she answered, pressing her lips together and raising her head to meet his eyes.

Stefan laughed and then held her stare. They stood coolly appraising each other for several long moments, neither willing to be the first to look away.

Finally, Stefan loomed over her in his most intimidating stance. It had sent many a man running, and he had no doubt that she would soon dissolve into tears, begging for his mercy. Confidently, he put his hands on his hips and waited.

She raised her chin in defiance and glared furiously at him.

Stefan's dark eyebrows arched in surprise. So, she was not one to be easily intimidated. She seemed determined to defy him; he could see it in the way she pursed her lips.

His gaze raked across her face and lingered on her lips. He felt his pulse quicken. God help him, he should never have brought his attention to her full, round and thoroughly sensual lips. They were far too enticing for a man's peace of mind. He suddenly imagined pulling her into his arms and exploring the tender recesses of her mouth. . . .

Disgusted with his train of thought, he abruptly grabbed her around the waist and tossed her over his shoulder, as if she were a sack of potatoes.

Gasping in outrage, Hanna balled her fists and hit his back as hard as she could. "How dare you touch me! I insist that you put me down immediately."

He ignored her, motioning for his men to leave the chapel. Hanna decided the man was completely deranged. Taking a deep breath, she let out a scream loud enough to send vibrations echoing through the church. She waited for some kind of reaction from him, but he seemed totally disinterested in her noisemaking.

He carried her to the courtyard before setting her down. Hanna stood ready to tell him what she thought of his unpardonable behavior when she suddenly noticed the bodies of Jozef's soldiers strewn across the ground. Covering her mouth in horror, she looked around quickly and saw the group of terrified wedding guests surrounded by her captor's soldiers. She did not see Jozef anywhere.

Dazed, she looked up at the man towering over her. "My God, sir, have you lost your senses? You k-killed these men. M'lord Czarnowski will be furious."

His eyes narrowed darkly. His face looked so cold and forbidding that Hanna's breath caught in her throat. She took a shaky step back, wishing she had never opened her mouth. As she watched in growing terror, he slowly pulled off his shirt and took a step toward her.

Hanna nearly fainted from fright. He stood directly in front of her, his tall form looming over her. Closing her eyes, she said a small prayer for courage in the face of the beating she was about to receive. When several moments had passed and nothing had happened she cautiously opened one eye. The huge man stood in front of her, one hand on his hip, the other holding out his shirt to her. Astonished, she opened the other eye.

"Wh-what are you doing?" she stammered.

"If you have no wish to cover yourself, madam—" Stefan shrugged and began to put his shirt back on.

Hanna suddenly realized her state of undress, her cheeks flushing crimson. The soldiers in the courtyard were staring at her openly, and the wedding guests gaped at her bare legs in horror.

Quickly, she snatched the shirt from his hands and thrust her arms through the sleeves. The shirt fell to her knees.

Slowly, Stefan turned to face the cowering wedding guests. "Tell Czarnowski that if he ever wants to see his bride alive, he'll have to face me first." His voice, coldly formal, rang through the courtyard. Nodding to his men, Stefan swiftly mounted his horse. Silently, he stretched out his hand to the young woman.

Hanna took a trembling step backwards. "Who are you, if you are not Jozef's men?"

He ignored her question, still extending his hand. She took another step backwards.

"You can mount with dignity or you can be forced," Stefan said, shrugging. "The choice is yours, madam."

Hanna shook her head stubbornly. "I will not go anywhere until I know who you are and why you are doing this."

Stefan sighed in exasperation and spurred his horse forward, leaning down to grab her by the waist, dragging her onto his horse.

"Nay," she screamed as he pulled her in front of him and forced her to sit snugly between his legs. Mortified, Hanna realized her bottom was firmly plastered against his hard thighs. Before she could open her mouth to protest he urged his steed forward in a gallop.

"Stop," she cried, trying to wiggle out of his iron grasp.

"Be still, woman," her captor said coldly, his arm tightening around her waist.

Realizing that she would break her neck if she fell from the horse, Hanna ceased her struggle. He rewarded her by slightly lessening his grip. They galloped at breakneck speed from the estate as he led the way. When they were off the Czarnowski grounds they slowed to an easier gait.

Fighting back her fear, Hanna sat stiffly until her shoulders ached. Knowing that her captor was shirtless, she dared not lean back lest she touch his bare chest. Had he no shame for putting her in such an indecent position?

Hanna kept her body rigid as he guided the steed forward, his thighs pressing tightly against hers. She squeezed her eyes shut, trying to block the image of this fierce warrior from her mind. But even with her eyes closed, she could feel every inch of hard muscle in the arm that was wrapped tightly around her waist. Moreover, his scent penetrated her nostrils, a masculine mixture of sweat and smoke. Oddly, Hanna discovered that it was not an unpleasant scent. Instead, she found it unusually intriguing and compelling.

Dismayed by her thoughts, Hanna tried to shift her weight to ease the pain in her shoulders. It was useless; her abductor's left arm was like an unyielding band of steel. Unable to move, the pain began to spread from her shoulders to her back until her eyes filled with tears.

With a groan of annoyance, he suddenly pulled her firmly against his chest. Hanna gasped in indignation even though it brought relief to her aching back.

"You'll be more comfortable riding like this," he said quietly, his voice a husky whisper. "We've still a way to go."

Hanna felt her cheeks flush at the intimate position in which she found herself. She tried to pull away, but he held her firmly. To some extent she was grateful; it was a more comfortable position, and she didn't relish the idea of sitting rigidly for the entire journey, however long that might be. Still, it was clearly improper, captive or not, and she tried once more to wiggle from his grasp. The man held her tightly against his chest, a fierce growl coming from his lips. With a sigh of resignation, Hanna finally relaxed, letting the tension drain from her shoulders.

They rode for some time without speaking until Hanna could no longer stand the silence or her curiosity.

"Milord?" she asked suddenly, turning slightly to look up at him. "Won't you at least tell me who you are?"

He stared straight ahead, not answering her. Hanna frowned when she realized he was deliberately ignoring her. Her delicate brows furrowed in frustration, but her eyes took on a glint of stubborn determination. She would have her answer if it took the entire journey to get it.

"You know, it is quite rude of you to ignore me," she persisted. "It would greatly ease my fears if you would extend me the courtesy of telling me your name."

Stefan groaned inwardly. It appeared that his captive intended to drive him daft with her insistent questions, despite his determination to ignore her and the soft body so intimately pressed against him.

He had been more than aware of her presence during the journey thus far. Her hair had escaped from its pins and gently caressed the skin of his bare neck and shoulders as they rode along. Worse than that, she smelled fresh and wonderful . . . like a field full of flowers. He exhaled loudly. Hell and damnation, he could see it was going to be a long ride to his estate.

"I am Stefan Tarnowski," he said curtly, hoping it would end her questioning.

"Stefan Tarnowski," Hanna whispered, letting the name roll over her tongue. "May I call you Stefan?" she asked hastily, struggling to look up at him.

He was surprised at her question. "Why would you want to do that?" he asked curiously.

She blushed. "I think it sounds better than 'milord.'"

He thought for a moment and then shrugged. "You may call me Stefan."

Encouraged by his response, Hanna smiled back. "Then, Stefan, may I ask for what purpose you have abducted me?"

A long silence hung between them. "You may not," he finally answered gruffly.

Hanna gave a small gasp of outrage. He was proving to be a most difficult man. "Bloody rotten and rude swine," she muttered in English under her breath.

His hand tightened around her waist. "Quite a colorful vocabulary for a lady," Stefan said in perfect English.

Hanna twisted around in the saddle, her eyes wide with astonishment. "Y-you speak English?"

A smile touched his lips. "I do."

The heat rose to her cheeks as she remembered what she had called him. "B-but how is that possible?"

He smiled wryly. "For a Pole to learn English? Or for me in particular to know the language?"

She heard a hint of amusement in his voice and smiled in spite of herself. "How did you learn to speak English?" she clarified.

He wondered if he should answer and decided no harm could come from it. "I spent three years in London, training under General Robert Lyle."

"Training in London? Why?"

"I'm a colonel in the service of His Majesty, King Yan Casimir. He has a particular fondness for English strategy."

Hanna considered his words for a moment. "Three years in London," she mused. "Why didn't you tell me earlier that you spoke English?"

He shrugged. "Why should I?"

She frowned at his indifference. "Well, I don't know. It simply wasn't very polite of you." She blushed as she said the words, realizing how silly it was to accuse a man of impoliteness when he was in the process of abducting her.

Stefan nearly laughed, but he managed to catch himself. Sweet Mary, the last thing he wanted was to like his captive, but she was making it damn hard. Her perfume and their conversation was beginning to have the oddest effect on him.

Sighing, he clamped his lips together. It was time to end this senseless chatter. Getting to know his captive would only lead to complications. Scowling, he turned his concentration to the ride at hand.

"Please, won't you tell me where we are going?" Hanna asked after a few moments.

Stefan shook his head, determined to end their conversation. With a low whistle and firm pressure from his thighs, he urged his horse on faster. Hanna felt the heat rise to her cheeks, acutely aware of how each movement of his powerful legs pressed him tighter against her.

Angrily, she forced her mind back to her perilous situation. Apparently, her captor wasn't interested in anything she had to say, nor was he concerned about her welfare. Well, she would not be intimidated, his size notwithstanding.

"I'm not afraid of you," she suddenly announced to him in Polish.

Stefan rolled his eyes, wondering how she dared not to be frightened.

"In fact," she continued firmly, "I would like to thank you for saving me from Jozef Czarnowski. When you are finished with your little game I hope you will allow me to leave and go on my own way."

He pulled on the reins with such fierceness that she would have gone flying off the steed had he not been holding her tightly.

Sliding off the horse, he pulled her none too gently out of the saddle. His men came riding up behind him, alarm written all over their faces.

"What's wrong?" Mikhail asked, dismounting and coming to stand beside his brother.

Stefan didn't answer, simply looking at the young woman, scowling. "I think it is about time for some answers. What is your name?" he asked, his jaw set in a hard line.

She flinched at the cold tone of his voice. "H-hanna," she answered. "Hanna Quinn."

"Why did Jozef Czarnowski go to London to find a bride?"

She was puzzled by his question. "I don't know. My uncle said he saw me on the street and liked my hair." Her cheeks flushed scarlet as she heard a snicker from one of the soldiers.

Stefan narrowed his eyes at the men, and a deathly silence filled the air. He turned his attention back to the girl. "Are you trying to tell me, Hanna, that Jozef Czarnowski went all the way to England to find himself a bride with red hair?"

Hanna nodded nervously. "Aye, that is what I am saying."

Stefan took a deep breath. "My patience is wearing thin, woman. I suggest you tell me the truth."

Moving toward her, he stopped in his tracks when he saw her cringe, instinctively turning to protect her vital organs. He had seen the movement many times; he taught it to his own men when instructing them on how to protect themselves from an enemy blow.

His mouth opened in astonishment. Good God, did she think he was going to hit her?

"Hanna," he said softly, reaching out to gently take her by the shoulders. She opened her eyes slowly.

"What do you want from me?" she asked, lifting her chin defiantly.

He could see she was very much afraid, despite the challenge of her eyes. "Why are you glad that I have taken you from the home of Jozef Czarnowski?" he asked softly.

Although it was a warm day, she wrapped her arms around herself to keep from shivering. "Why should you care?"

Stefan frowned, summoning patience. "Just answer me, Hanna."

She looked at him fiercely but backed down when she saw the determined expression on his face. "There is something odd about him," she said slowly. "He frightens me."

"What do you mean 'odd'?" he asked, noticing that her shoulders had begun to tremble. When she didn't answer he raised his voice a notch. "Hanna?"

"I truly don't know," she finally answered him. "He is touched in the head over me. It is an obsession, I think. He wants to h-hurt me." She spoke so softly that he could barely hear her.

Stefan clenched his jaw and abruptly dropped his hands from Hanna's shoulders. "God help me," he growled, "but I have just been given another reason to kill that bastard."

They stood in silence until Stefan finally ordered his men to remount. Then, with surprising gentleness, he swept Hanna into his arms and placed her on his steed. In one fluid motion, he joined her and urged his mount forward.

Suddenly, Hanna could not stop trembling. The events of the past hours had rendered her drained and defenseless.

Stefan felt her slender shoulders shake and frowned. Damnation, he hadn't meant to frighten her, but he needed her to bring him Jozef Czarnowski. It was important that he know whether Jozef valued the girl enough to risk coming after her. Still, he felt like a cad for scaring her. Sighing, he drew her close, hoping his warmth would reassure her.

Momentarily surprised by his actions, Hanna did not struggle. Worn out from the overwhelming emotions she had experienced in the past few hours, she wanted nothing more than to close her eyes and pretend that someone in this world cared for her. Oddly, sitting there in his arms, she did feel protected and safe.

Stefan felt her snuggle closer. He was startled by the surge of protectiveness that swept over him as he rested his chin lightly on top of her head.

They rode on for a long time without a word until she spoke, startling him from his thoughts. "Stefan," she whispered.

He looked down at her head and marveled at the burnished red color of her hair. "Aye, Hanna?" he whispered back, his voice gentle.

The way he said her name sounded like a caress, and her heart suddenly fluttered in her breast. "I know why you abducted me. You will use me to draw Jozef to you."

He was silent for a long moment. Suddenly, for some unknown reason, it was important that he not lie to her. "Aye, Hanna, that is why."

His answer brought tears to her eyes. She blinked rapidly to keep the tears from falling. The warmth she had felt in his arms suddenly vanished.

Stefan felt her stiffen and leaned over, his cheek brushing the hair back from the side of her face. "And will he come for you?" he whispered softly, putting his mouth close to her ear.

Hanna shivered as she pictured Jozef's dark, cruel face. *"You will be mine, Hanna Quinn, this I promise you."* His words echoed malevolently in her ears.

"Aye," she finally managed to whisper back. "Aye, Stefan Tarnowski, you can be certain that he will come for me."

Chapter Six

It seemed as if they had ridden for days, although Hanna knew it had only been for a few hours. Stefan had not spoken a word to her for the rest of the ride, nor had he further explained his reasons for abducting her.

She was unbearably sore when they finally arrived at the Tarnowski estate. Her bare legs were chafed from rubbing mercilessly against the saddle. Stefan dismounted and then lifted her off the horse, his large hands easily spanning her waist. Her legs almost collapsed as they touched the ground, and she grabbed his arm to steady herself. Looking up at him, she saw he had an amused look on his face.

"Excellent with a sword, but not much for horses," he observed dryly.

She stood stiffly, removing her hand from his arm. "I happen to enjoy horses very much . . . when I ride them alone," she said coolly.

Stefan shrugged; then he strode toward the stable. One of the men who had attacked her in the chapel motioned for her to follow.

Sighing, she began to walk after him and then stopped in amazement to look about the courtyard. The Tarnowski castle was magnificent. Made of the finest stone, the walls of the enormous structure loomed over her. Two tall towers, one to the east and one to the west, flanked the castle, and Hanna could only imagine what a breathtaking view they would present of the surrounding countryside.

Her eyes slowly traveled to an immense church by the side of the house. A tall spire on top of the massive stone structure seemed to reach up to the very heavens. It was such a stunning sight that it took her breath away.

"This is his estate?" she whispered in awe, her eyes fastening on Stefan, who stood in the entryway.

"It is the Tarnowski estate," Mikhail said, grabbing her roughly by the elbow. "And I am a Tarnowski too; Stefan's brother. You are fortunate to step foot on our land."

Hanna stopped in her tracks and tried to yank her arm from his grip. "Why are you so angry with me? Are you still thinking about what happened back at the chapel? I was only trying to protect myself."

"You dare to put such a question to me?" he shouted.

She was taken aback by the vehemence of his words, but she drew herself up straight. "I don't think it is too much to ask why you frown at me as though I have offended you in some way."

Mikhail snorted. "Am I supposed to believe you have no idea of what happened?"

She gave him a perplexed frown. "You speak in riddles to me."

Mikhail leaned close to her face. "Jozef Czarnowski and those whom he loves will pay dearly for what he has done," he sneered. "Despite your touching words back in the forest, that means you, too, milady."

He looked at her with such anger and loathing that she took a step backward. "I am to pay for the sins of Jozef Czarnowski?" she whispered, the words suddenly stuck in her throat. "My God, what did he do?"

Mikhail gripped her arm tighter. "Don't play the innocent with me. Everyone in Warsaw knows what Jozef Czarnowski did to Danuta."

Hanna shook her head slowly. "But I am not from Warsaw. Who is Danuta?"

Mikhail looked at her incredulously; then he grabbed her by the shoulders, shaking her painfully. "Don't you dare speak her name aloud," he shouted.

Hanna was stunned at the look of raw pain and anger in his eyes. He shook her so hard, her teeth began to rattle.

"Mikhail," she heard Stefan shout angrily as he strode across the courtyard. "Damn it, take your hands off her . . . *now!*"

Mikhail abruptly released her and stepped back, his face blotched red with fury. He faced his brother, a defiant look in his eyes.

"She claims to be ignorant of all knowledge of Danuta. Yet I know she lies. She is the bride of Czarnowski." His voice was loud and threatening.

Stefan towered over his brother, his eyes dark. "You will not touch her again. She is our captive, not our enemy. You would do well to remember that."

Trembling, Hanna instinctively moved closer to Stefan, her hand creeping into his. Stefan blinked and looked down at her, astonished both by her touch and the fierce wave of possessiveness that swept over him as she clung to his hand.

"But, Stefan . . ." Mikhail began to protest hotly.

"I said that is enough, Mikhail." Stefan raised his eyes to meet his brother's, his voice dangerously soft.

Mikhail met Stefan's unflinching stare and finally backed off. "She deserves no less than what happened to Danuta," he muttered under his breath before turning and walking away.

Stefan looked down at Hanna and saw that her shoulders were shaking. Sighing at the odd array of feelings she had suddenly stirred in him, he began to lead her toward the house in silence.

"I d-don't understand," she suddenly said quietly.

"You must not speak again of Danuta."

"Please," she said, stopping in her tracks. "Who is she?"

Stefan searched her face slowly. "You really don't know, do you?"

Hanna shook her head, and Stefan turned from her, running his hand wearily through his dark, thick hair. "Danuta Tarnowska was our sister . . . a very gentle and trusting soul. She planned to dedicate her life to the church. But that was before . . ."

He stopped, his voice suddenly full of emotion. Hanna looked at him in astonishment, unable to believe that this physically imposing man could display such feeling. Oddly, she felt a bit better, as if his showing such vulnerability somehow made him more human, more approachable.

That feeling faded quickly as he turned back to look at her, his square face grim, his eyes black with anger.

"Jozef Czarnowski raped her one night as she was leaving the theater at Warsaw Castle. He killed two of my men who were with her before he committed this foul act."

Hanna gasped in horror, covering her mouth with her hand. *"Jezus Maria,"* she whispered, "I'm so sorry."

Stefan's voice was harsh. "She never told us who did it; her mind simply snapped. Three months later we discovered she was with child. She became feverish, deranged. I stayed with her, tried to help. She was restless and began to have nightmares. One night, when I was at her bedside, I heard her call out a name in fear. It was the name of Jozef Czarnowski. The next morning she threw herself off the tower." His voice was a cold, droning sound.

"I made discreet inquiries and discovered that Jozef had bragged about his deed to others. I challenged him openly, but he publicly refused all knowledge of the deed. That is when I realized I would have to force him into a fight."

Hanna hid her head in her hands, unable to absorb the full horror of what she had just heard. Tears streamed down her face.

"She could not have a Christian burial because she took her own life," he said flatly. "He took everything from her . . . even in death. And now he will pay."

Stefan was quiet for a long moment, watching Hanna sob into her hands. Slowly, he reached out a hand and pulled her toward the house, forcing himself to ignore her despair.

"I don't care if you knew or not," he said, more to convince himself than her. "You are our captive, Hanna. I need you to bring me Jozef Czarnowski. Until that time you will do as I say, act as I say. You will not open your mouth with one single word of protest. There are many in this house who would gladly kill or hurt you for the pain it might cause Czarnowski. Remember this well." His voice was soft but firm.

Slowly, Hanna drew herself up and wiped the tears from her cheeks. "I may be your captive, Stefan Tarnowski, but I will not be punished for the sins of Jozef Czarnowski, nor will I allow myself to become a pawn in your quest for revenge. I will escape from you."

Stefan looked at her in astonishment. "Escape?"

"Aye, escape," Hanna said defiantly, hoping he didn't notice how badly her lower lip trembled.

He almost smiled at her brave words. "You will not escape," he said gently.

"Aye, but I will," she promised fervently under her breath, although he was no longer listening and had already begun to lead her toward the castle.

Chapter Seven

The days passed slowly for Hanna. She was confined to a small room near the top of one of the towers that held a small bed and a wide hearth. There was one window with wooden shutters, but it was far too high to consider as a means of escape. *Still, I will escape,* Hanna thought with stubborn determination. *I must.*

A plan had already formed in her mind. As soon as she got away from the Tarnowski castle, she would try to secure a position as an English governess to a wealthy Polish family. Her language abilities in English, as well as Polish, would serve her well; she was certain of it. She had only to plot a way out of the castle.

Despair began to creep over her as she thought about the possibilities. How would she, a lone woman without money or mount, manage to find such a position? Hanna pulled her plaited hair, sighing in frustration. It didn't matter that she was without money; she would have to escape somehow. Anything was better than waiting to be recaptured by Jozef Czarnowski. Firmly, she decided her first task would be to get out of the confining tower room so she could have a look around the grounds.

She had seen neither Stefan nor Mikhail for the three days that she had been held in the tower. A manservant brought her a handful of gowns she suspected had been Danuta's. They were a bit tight in the bust, but as she had no other clothing, she wore them.

As she touched the material thoughtfully, she felt a flash of envy. Danuta had been lucky to have had a family who obviously loved and cared for her. What was it Stefan had said? *"One night when I was at her bedside..."* Good Lord, had he cared so much for his sister that he had sat at her bedside night after night, trying to comfort her? A longing so strong swept through Hanna that she ached. Closing her eyes, she searched her memory for those precious few moments she remembered of being loved and cherished.

You can dream all you want, but there isn't anyone in the world who would care for you like that, Hanna Quinn. You have no one but yourself, so you had better get used to it.

Hanna took a deep breath and thought how unfortunate it had been for Danuta to have crossed paths with Jozef Czarnowski. "It nearly ruined my life, too, and it still could if I do not escape from here," she whispered aloud.

Hanna pressed her fingers to her temples, feeling a kinship with the young girl. "I wish I could have met you, Danuta Tarnowska," she said softly. "I'm sure we would have had a lot to talk about."

Grimly, Hanna leaped to her feet, unwilling to let herself dwell on the past. She had to figure out a way to have a look around outside. Other than the manservant, she had seen no one except the young serving girl who brought her food and water. The girl was clearly frightened of Hanna, and never looked at her directly as she went about her business. Exasperated, Hanna finally decided she would do something about it.

"By what name are you called?" she asked the young girl as she came into the room, carrying fresh bedding for Hanna.

The girl jumped as she asked the question and, after darting a hasty glance around the room, looked fearfully at Hanna. "Me name is Dorota, milady."

Hanna smiled at her. "There is no reason to be frightened of me, Dorota. I won't hurt you."

Dorota swallowed nervously. "You seem nice, milady. We was told not to talk with you . . . you being a member of the Czarnowski family and all."

Hanna gasped in outrage. "Not talk to me? Are you saying they mean to keep me in total confinement without a word from anyone?"

Dorota was clearly agitated by the anger in Hanna's voice. "Please, milady, you mustn't raise your voice. Milord Stefan . . . he will be very angry."

Hanna swallowed her urge to shout. It would not serve her at all to frighten the girl. It wasn't Dorota's fault that Stefan had issued such barbaric orders. Besides, it was essential that she find out more about her captors and what they had planned for her.

"Of course; you are right," Hanna said, hoping her voice sounded calmer. "Perhaps you could tell me, Dorota, who is the lord of this manor. Surely, it cannot be milord Stefan. His father, undoubtedly, manages the estate."

Dorota shook her head sadly. "Sir Stanislaw Tarnowski died before I was born, God rest his soul," she said, crossing herself hastily. "He was a military man, like m'lord Stefan, but he lost his life during a campaign in Muscovy. Milord Stefan was just seven years old then; my mama told me so."

Hanna felt a twinge of sympathy for Stefan. She knew well what it was like for a child to lose a parent. "What about his mother?" she asked, her curiosity rising.

"Lady Marta Tarnowska died five years ago of the fever. They leeched her for twenty days and twenty nights, but she died anyway. The witching hour it was, when she passed. A bad omen, if you ask me. You can ask anyone in the castle; they'll tell you the same. A horrible curse fell on this house that day." Dorota made the sign of the cross, as if to ward off evil spirits.

Hanna pursed her lips doubtfully, but she did not interrupt. She didn't believe in superstitions, and especially not in curses. But each piece of information she managed to obtain from Dorota could prove to be useful. Sighing inwardly, she let the serving girl continue.

"Milords Stefan and Mikhail were heartbroken, but Lady Danuta was a great comfort to them. Yet it was too late to fix the curse," she said, her voice falling to a hushed whisper. "Lady Danuta was the next to fall under its spell. Aye, nothing but evil luck has fallen upon this house since that night."

Hanna frowned, suddenly annoyed at the serving girl's tale of continuing doom for the Tarnowski family. "Nonsense," she said briskly. "Our fates were decided long before we were even born. It is God's hand that directs our destinies, not some silly curse."

The serving girl nibbled on her lower lip. "I still say it is the devil's work."

"I'm afraid I don't agree with you. But come, let's not talk anymore about such distressing matters." Hanna busied herself with a thread on her sleeve, trying to look nonchalant. "I would rather know if Lord Stefan has a . . . ah . . . wife." She was mortified to feel her cheeks grow warm.

Thankfully, Dorota did not seem to notice Hanna's embarrassment. "Nay, milady, he does not. Milord Stefan is rarely home long enough to bother with such matters. I would imagine he'll be leaving soon. He has already stayed home much longer than usual."

Hanna nodded, storing away the information for future study. "Thank you, Dorota. You have been kind to me and I appreciate it."

The serving girl beamed at her words. "Why, it was my pleasure, milady. I want you to know I don't blame you for Lady Danuta's death." Her voice dropped to a whisper. "But there are many in this house who do. Milord Stefan is wise to keep you locked up here. It is for your own safety, milady."

Hanna frowned. Kept locked up for her own safety.

That, she thought, was certainly a contradiction in terms. Aye, and it was time to do something about it.

Hanna smiled sweetly. "Dorota, I simply ache for a breath of fresh air. Would you be so kind to escort me to see Lord Stefan?"

Dorota looked horrified. "Wh-what?" she stammered.

"I wish to see Lord Stefan," Hanna repeated firmly.

The girl shook her head violently. "Oh, nay, milady. He is very busy and no one dares to interrupt. . . ."

"I dare to interrupt," Hanna said, her voice rising. "He has no right to keep me locked in this godforsaken tower without company or exercise."

Dorota looked ready to flee. "Oh, please, milady. If he hears you, he will be angry. His temper is really quite fierce and . . ."

Hanna waved her hand. "I do not fear his anger. I wish to see him at once."

The young girl looked frightened out of her wits. "Milady . . ." she whispered, her eyes wide in horror. "P-please."

"Dorota," Hanna said gently, placing a hand on the girl's trembling shoulder, "do not fear you will be punished. Milord Stefan's anger will be for me alone. But you must tell him I want to see him, or I will be forced to shout at the top of my lungs until he comes in here."

Terrified, the girl raced out of the room, nearly tripping over a wooden bucket she had left by the hearth. Hanna watched her go, regretting the sharp tone she had used with the maid. She hadn't meant to frighten Dorota with her temper, but leaving this room was her utmost goal.

Deep in thought, Hanna paced back and forth, her hands clasped behind her back, thinking of what to say when she saw Stefan. She had to devise some way to persuade him to allow her a walk about the grounds.

She stopped in front of the hearth and cleared her throat. "If a lady is to be kept against her will, then at least she deserves a short walk in the garden to have some fresh air," she practiced.

A Touch of Fire

Hanna shook her head immediately. Nay, it was too polite. It would probably be to her advantage to sound firmer. "I demand that I be allowed some fresh air," she said in her most commanding tone.

She frowned. Now it was too bold. There had to be a middle ground somewhere. She had to think of something, like a plea tinged with desperation. She thought for a moment, and then she closed her eyes in frustration.

"Oh, for God's sake, I just want out of this bloody room," she finally said in exasperation.

"Is that why you wanted to see me?"

Whirling around, Hanna saw Stefan standing in the doorway, an amused look on his face. Heat rose to her cheeks as she struggled to look calm. "How long have you been standing there?" she demanded.

"Long enough to discern that you want out of this bloody room," he answered calmly.

The heat in her face intensified. God in heaven, he was always catching her off guard. He must think she had no manners whatsoever.

Stefan's amused eyes swept over her openly, taking in the tight fit of her gown across her breasts and the wisps of red hair that escaped her braid and curled gently around her face. Lord help him, but she was beautiful and deliciously defiant.

He had tried for three days to get her out of his mind, to forget the way her body felt against his in the saddle and the pain in her eyes when she spoke of Jozef Czarnowski. For three long days he had nearly come to see her a dozen times, but each time was able to convince himself not to. Still, for a mere captive, she was in his thoughts entirely too much.

Yet as soon as the serving girl had told him of Hanna's request, he had leaped from his chair in his haste to see her. When he had set eyes on her he had felt his pulse race in anticipation of speaking with her again. A fierce scowl crossed his face. *What in God's name is wrong with me?*

Hanna immediately saw his anger and wondered what had prompted it. Afraid she might have unwittingly hurt her chances of leaving the tower, she took a breath, smoothing an imagined wrinkle in her gown. "Will you deny me this request?" she asked quietly, looking him directly in the eye.

Stefan studied her face intently. She was a spirited girl, not at all meek and trembling, as he had imagined she would be. She had the most adorable upturned nose and a few rebellious freckles sprinkled across her cheeks. He wasn't sure that she feared him at all, and he frowned at that.

Slowly, he crossed his arms against his chest and leaned in the doorway. "And just why should I allow you a walk in the garden?"

She smiled at him sweetly. "Because a true gentleman would not deny such a humble request from a lady, captive or not."

Stefan laughed. "I see. Now perhaps you'll really tell me why I should grant your request."

Hanna bit back her discouragement, seeing that her coy approach was not going to work. "Please, you must allow me this one request. I can't stand the confinement any longer. I need a breath of fresh air and the feel of the warm sun on my shoulders. I'll go mad if I am left alone here for another moment." She breathed heavily, unaware of the desperation in her voice.

"Ah, much better. I prefer it when a woman is honest with me."

"Honest?" she shouted, immediately losing her temper. "You forcefully abduct me, take me miles away to some godforsaken castle, keep me prisoner in a tower so you can dangle me as bait in order to kill a man, and then expect honesty from me? Why, I have never heard such rubbish in all my life. You, sir, obviously enjoy tormenting innocent young women."

Hanna saw an angry flush stain Stefan's face as he walked toward her. "And you, madam, are trying my patience. You are fortunate that I even responded to your summons. Do you think I am at your every beck and call?"

Hanna stamped her foot angrily. "Beck and call? You have kept me locked in a tower, forbidding anyone to speak to me. Even the serving girl was frightened to death of me. What lies did you tell everyone about me?"

Stefan reached out and gripped her arm, forcing her to face him. "No lies, Hanna. Only the truth about what your husband did to Danuta."

"He is not my husband," Hanna snapped.

Stefan froze, stunned at her words. "He is not?"

She shook her head. "Of course not. You arrived before the ceremony had taken place."

Stefan gaped. God help him, he had assumed the wedding ceremony had just ended. It had been midday, for God's sake, and everyone knew it was customary in Poland to hold the wedding in the morning hours so the celebration could begin by midday and go on for days.

"You mean to tell me you have not yet wed him?" he bellowed, wondering why his heart suddenly leaped at the thought.

"And are you daft?" she bellowed back with equal ferocity. "I just said I had not."

Stefan closed his eyes. Lord Almighty, the situation just kept getting worse. He had abducted a young girl, not yet properly wed, and carted her off to his estate. How was he going to explain to her that because she was unwed he had just ruined her chances for making a suitable marriage once he killed Jozef Czarnowski? Her reputation would be utterly ruined. A widow was one thing, but an unwed captive was something entirely different. Stefan sighed deeply.

"Oh, bloody hell," he muttered, running his hand through his dark hair.

"Ah ha," Hanna said, smiling triumphantly. "And *you* said *I* had a colorful vocabulary."

Stefan couldn't help but laugh. The laughter came from deep in his chest and rumbled throughout the chamber. She made him daft, but he genuinely liked her. Even more surprising, he was actually beginning to care what would happen to her after his revenge was complete.

"You baffle me, Hanna," he said, looking at her closely. Her cheeks were flushed from their exchange, her eyes bright. She was a fighter, that was evident. Yet he couldn't help but wonder how many battles she had lost in her lifetime.

Suddenly, he shook his head, frowning. His growing attraction to her was damned dangerous and he knew it.

"Why do you have that strange look on your face?" Hanna asked him, startling him from his thoughts.

"You'll have your walk in the garden," he said gruffly. "But on my conditions. If you violate any of those conditions, this privilege will be immediately rescinded."

Hanna nodded. "All right. And what are those conditions?"

"I will set the time and length of each walk. You will be properly escorted at all times."

She sniffed. "Guarded, you mean."

"Call it what you may," he said, shrugging.

She thought for a moment and then sighed. "Conditions accepted."

Stefan raised an eyebrow. He had not offered her a choice, and yet here she was acting like a general, deciding whether or not she'd accept. Sighing, he shook his head and, sweeping his arm, motioned to the door. "Shall we begin?"

"Now?" she said in amazement.

"I said I would set the time of each excursion. I choose now. Are you coming or not?"

She grabbed her skirts and rushed past him. "I'm coming," she said hastily as she passed through the doorway.

Stefan smiled as they descended the winding stone stairs. She was clearly anxious to get outside . . . more than likely she wanted to plot her escape. He chuckled softly. He would have to keep an eye on her. It was clear that she was an unusual woman with a mind of her own. That in itself was an unsettling development. Aye, he would have to be very careful with her, indeed.

As he motioned for her to walk down the long corridor, he noticed the way she walked and the soft, provocative sway of her hips. Hell, she had a most disturbing effect on him.

When they reached the end of the corridor Stefan opened a door and led her into a huge room with vaulted ceilings. Hanna gasped in awe at the overwhelming size of the chamber. Whirling around dizzily, she thought her entire home in London would easily fit into this single room.

Catching her breath, she walked over to the enormous wooden table that was lined with long hard benches that stretched down the center of the room. It would seat at least a hundred people, Hanna thought to herself. A gigantic fireplace stood at the end of the room; rows of firewood were stacked neatly along the hearth. Fresh rushes covered the floor and a pleasant breeze wafted through an open window.

Shaking her head in disbelief, Hanna looked again at the tall stone walls surrounding the chamber. Rows of magnificent woven tapestries hung on them, adding a splash of color to the room. One particular tapestry caught Hanna's eye, and she walked over to inspect it.

"Why, it is the most beautiful tapestry I have ever seen," Hanna declared in a hushed voice, gently fingering the coarse material. "Is it a battle scene of Polish forces triumphing over Muscovy and Emperor Maximilian?"

Stefan's mouth dropped open in astonishment, amazed that she knew Polish history so well. "Aye, it is," he finally managed to say. "How did you know that?"

She shrugged. "I like to read, and Polish history has always fascinated me."

"You can read?" Stefan asked, genuinely surprised.

Hanna looked at him as if he was daft. "Of course I can. Can't you?"

A smile stretched across his face. "Aye, I can, Hanna."

"I would wager that I had a better tutor," she replied, her eyes dancing merrily. "Would you care to accept a challenge on that?"

Stefan laughed. "Some other time, perhaps. Although I

must admit that I'm intrigued by you, Hanna. There are few women I know who have such skill."

Hanna smiled prettily, oddly pleased by his compliment. "Are the gardens out there?" she asked, wandering to the open window.

Stefan joined her, gently taking her by the elbow. "This way," he said, steering her through another room and out into the bright sunshine.

Hanna smiled in delight as she felt the warm sun on her face. The garden was a beautiful sight, and she breathed deeply of the heavenly scent of the blossoms. A light bounce in her step, she headed down the narrow path lined by two groves of tall trees.

"It is lovely here," Hanna said, smiling up at him.

Stefan felt a rush of pleasure at her compliment, and then a twinge of sadness. Danuta had loved the gardens and had spent many long hours carefully tending the flowers and trees. He had not come here since the funeral but was suddenly glad that he had now.

Hanna noticed the pain in his eyes and looked up at him curiously. "Have I said something wrong?"

He sighed. "Nay, Hanna. You haven't said anything wrong."

Side by side, they walked along the path until they reached a long bench nestled between two large trees. Stefan sat on the bench while Hanna admired a flower bed full of rosemary and lavender. Kneeling down, she gently held one of the stems between her fingers.

"I've never seen these bloom so beautifully," Hanna said softly, smiling up at him.

Stefan returned the smile and bent over to take a handful of the rich, black soil into his hands. "It's Polish earth, Hanna. There isn't soil like it anywhere else in the world."

She nodded her head in agreement. "Aye, this is true. Polish land is fruitful and rich."

Stefan let the soil fall through his fingers. "It is Poland's most impressive treasure and her greatest weakness. Everyone wishes to possess such fertile land for his own." He spoke with such sharpness and emotion that Hanna raised her head quickly. Exhaling, Stefan shook the dirt from his hands and stared at her.

"You are a very unusual woman, Hanna Quinn," he said, letting his gaze linger on her face. "Please, tell me more about yourself."

Hanna immediately busied herself with a flower, and Stefan sensed her reluctance to talk about herself.

"How is it that you speak Polish so well?" he encouraged her softly. "Did your mother teach you?"

She shook her head, and Stefan smiled as the sunshine danced on the strands of her flaming red hair. "It was my first language, but my mother died when I was just three."

"Then how did you learn it?"

She took a deep breath. "My nursemaid was Polish. She died a few days before my eighth birthday. After that my father arranged for me to have a Polish tutor. I think he also liked to hear the language spoken. It brought back memories of my mother for him too." Her hands trembled slightly, but she managed to steady them. "I managed to keep the tutor even after my father died and Uncle Mason came to take care of me. Unfortunately, the money ran out when I turned fourteen. But by then it was of no matter; I already had a good grasp of the language."

Stefan looked at her thoughtfully. She had more than a good grasp; she spoke it naturally, with only a slight trace of an accent.

"Yet it wasn't your excellent command of the Polish language that drew Jozef to you," he mused aloud. "You said he told your uncle he favored your hair?"

Hanna nodded, her head still bowed. "I know it is odd that he should notice my hair and immediately ask for my hand. I was but twelve years old then."

Stefan wasn't sure he had heard her right. "He asked for your hand when you were twelve?"

"He did, but Uncle Mason refused him. If I was to marry, Uncle Mason would have lost access to my father's fortune. As my guardian, he could draw on as much of the money as he wanted. But when I turned sixteen, I gained sole control over my father's fortune. Though by then my uncle had made sure very little was left. Simply put, Uncle Mason didn't have anything to lose by marrying me off."

Stefan could hear the bitter note in Hanna's voice. Lord, she must have had a difficult life, being brought up by an uncle who drained her father's fortune and probably beat her as well. It would explain the way she cringed every time he moved close to her. Anger swept through him, and he suddenly had a desire to meet this cursed uncle and let him taste a bit of his own medicine. He took a deep breath.

"So you mean to tell me Jozef Czarnowski visited London four years ago and asked for your hand, but your uncle told him you could not wed until you were sixteen? Then, on your birthday, Jozef reappeared ready to take you off to Poland?" His tone was incredulous.

She nodded. "Uncle Mason said he even left a sack of gold the first time he was there, to ensure that I was not married off before I turned sixteen."

Stefan rubbed the back of his neck, a frown deepening his brow. Something was wrong, damn wrong, with the whole situation. Why in the hell did Jozef Czarnowski go all the way to England, twice, to find himself a bride? *And why did he insist on Hanna Quinn?*

In spite of Hanna's beauty, she obviously wasn't wealthy, and Stefan was sure there were plenty of more attractive and financially well-endowed redheads to be had right here in Poland. Jozef was a wealthy man; he could have had his choice from hundreds of available women. *Then why in God's name had he insisted on having Hanna?*

Stefan let his gaze rest on Hanna's face as she toyed with the stem of a flower. Whatever Jozef's reason had been, Stefan knew it was not out of love or concern for Hanna's welfare. Jozef Czarnowski was incapable of loving or caring about anyone other than himself.

Stefan rubbed his temples wearily. Whatever Jozef's

reasons, Stefan had to get to the bottom of it. For Hanna's sake, if for no other reason. He refused to let Jozef Czarnowski victimize another innocent woman.

"Have you no relatives in Poland?" Stefan asked curiously.

"I don't know," Hanna said, glancing up at him. "My father said my mother refused to speak of Poland at all. She just told him of a beautiful land with wonderful legends and brave heroes."

He smiled as she brought a flower to her nose and smelled deeply of the pleasant scent. Stefan thought that beneath that defiant exterior she was as fragile as the flower she held lightly in her hand. No wonder she had learned to protect herself. She had had no one else to depend on. He remembered the pain in her eyes when he had asked if she had no man to protect her.

Hanna felt Stefan's curious gaze upon her, and her cheeks began to warm. "Why have you not married?" she suddenly blurted out, horrified the moment the words fell from her lips.

A slow smile crossed his face as he noticed the crimson color of her cheeks. He folded his hands on his chest and leaned back on the bench. "I've never had the time or the inclination. Why do you ask?"

"I don't know," Hanna said, blushing again. "It was a silly question." Abruptly, she bounded to her feet and began to walk down the path. She couldn't believe she had asked him such a thing. *Good God, what has happened to me that I continue to think such thoughts about him when he is determined to use and then discard me as soon as his revenge has been satisfied?*

The burst of anger she felt at the mere thought of such cruel behavior sharpened her mind. She had no idea how much longer Stefan would allow her to be outdoors, and she had to use this time to her advantage, to plot her escape route. Looking around innocently, she took in the height of the walls and wondered if she would be able to scale them. She stopped in front of a huge tree, measuring the distance between the highest branch and the top of the castle wall. She was very good at climbing trees and had no doubt she would be able to make the jump.

"You can cease your plotting."

Turning, she saw Stefan watching her with an amused look on his face.

"You are not going anywhere, Hanna."

She glared at him haughtily. "I was not plotting," she said with as much indignation as she could muster, but her face flushed guiltily.

Laughter broke from his chest. "You were plotting, but it won't make any difference. You belong to me now."

"I wh-what?" she sputtered indignantly.

"You belong to me, Hanna. Is it not true that the victor may claim what he so desires from the vanquished?"

"I am not some thing to be claimed," she said, her eyes snapping angrily.

"Jozef Czarnowski abandoned you at the altar. As he would not give me the satisfaction of a fight, I took whatever he left behind. There are few who would argue with my logic."

"Well, I am one who would," she said furiously, trying to walk around him. "Besides, I know you are still longing for the satisfaction of a fight. Let's not forget the real reason you brought me here."

Stefan reached out and grabbed her by the arm. "Don't try my patience, Hanna. I am a man who has his limits."

"Well, I have limits too," she said, yanking her arm from his grasp and starting down the path.

"Hanna," he said warningly and strode after her.

Hanna hastened her steps until she was almost running. She hadn't gone very far when a heavy hand fell on her shoulder from behind.

"Do you remember the conditions for your walk?" Stefan asked, pulling her around to face him.

Caught tight in his grasp, Hanna nodded, her breath suddenly coming faster. "I remember."

"And didn't I say that I would clearly set the length of each walk?" he said firmly, leaning down so his face was squarely in front of hers.

Hanna nodded her head again. He was so close, she could feel his warm breath on her cheeks. Her hands were pressed against his chest and she could feel his heart beating through his cotton shirt. His size was intimidating, and she knew he could hurt her badly with his thick, muscular arms. But oddly, she did not feel afraid, even if he was angry at her. Instinctively, she knew he would never hurt her.

"And did I say the walk was over?" Stefan said, annoyed that his voice became husky as a strand of her hair brushed across his cheek. Her long braid had unraveled during her attempt to flee and her flaming hair hung in a glorious mass about her face and shoulders.

"You did not," she said quietly as her heart began to flutter in her chest. Lord, he had the strangest effect on her. Standing there in his arms, she suddenly wondered what it would feel like to be pressed up against the full length of his strong, muscular body. Abruptly, the heat rose to her cheeks, and she looked away.

Stefan noticed the flush that spread across her cheeks and how damn good she felt. Her scent filled his senses, utterly sweet and feminine. His gaze lingered on her soft, inviting lips, and then he sighed, releasing her from his hold.

"You may be surprised, Hanna, but my orders are for your protection."

"I don't believe you," she said stubbornly, crossing her arms.

A fleeting frown transformed his face. "Well, I am sorry you feel that way. Come now; I think our walk is over," he said gently, taking her arm and placing it in the crook of his elbow. He didn't say another word until they had returned to the tower room. Once depositing her there safely, he abruptly turned to leave.

"Stefan," Hanna asked quietly as he stood in the doorway. "When may I have my next walk?"

"When I think you deserve one."

"Deserve one? You . . . you brute," she said angrily.

A slow smile crossed his lips, a definite twinkle sparking in his eyes. "If your aim is to flatter me, Hanna, you'll have to work harder."

Reaching down, she picked up the pillow from her bed and threw it at him as he left the room, closing the door behind him. The pillow hit the wood and fell to the floor harmlessly.

Furiously, she walked over to pick up the pillow, crushing it to her chest. " 'When I think you deserve one,' " she mimicked him. How dare he treat her so rudely! Silently, she called him every name on her list of bad words . . . a list created through long hours spent at the docks with Jim. Although she didn't know what half of the words meant, she actually felt better when she finished.

Her temper still simmering, Hanna dropped the pillow and furiously pounded her fists against the door.

"Open this door at once," she shouted. "I require some water. You can't keep me locked in here without water." After a few moments she stopped to listen, but she heard only silence.

Pressing her lips tightly together, she determinedly reached out and pulled on the door with all her might. To her utter amazement, the door opened easily, and she fell ungraciously to the floor, squarely on her derrière.

He had not slid the bolt when he left!

Hanna came to her feet. His arrogance must have made him careless, she thought, smiling. Breathlessly, she listened for any sounds from the stairway but heard none. Forcing herself to be patient, she waited until she was certain that Stefan was gone.

When she couldn't bear another moment she quietly tiptoed down the winding stone steps. When she was about halfway down she halted in her tracks and listened. She could hear the faint sound of people laughing, but determined that it was too far away to be any threat. Carefully, she continued her descent.

By the time she reached the bottom, her heart was hammering so loudly in her chest, she was sure everyone in the castle would be able to hear it. Flattening herself against the wall, she willed herself to be calm, and then took a deep breath. Silently, she took a step forward and then another, until she reached the turn in the hallway. Painstakingly, she edged around the corner, looking first to see if anyone was there. When she saw the hallway was empty she began to walk quickly, heading for the door at the end of the corridor.

"Going somewhere?"

Startled, she stifled a scream before whirling around. "Stefan," she gasped, clutching a hand to her breast when she saw him. Although he had nearly scared the wits out of her, her eyes flashed angrily. "How dare you frighten me so!"

He cocked an eyebrow at her. "Frighten you? May I ask where you are going?"

She tossed her hair, hoping the fuming expression on her face would distract him from seeing her trembling hands. "I w-was just looking around," she said fiercely, knowing immediately how ridiculous her words sounded.

"Looking around? Do you always creep about so quietly when you are looking around?"

"When I have no wish to disturb anyone," she retorted.

Stefan laughed, and then walked up to her slowly. "Tell me, Hanna, just where did you think you were going?"

"I j-just told you," she stammered, her legs feeling weak.

His physique was downright overwhelming, she decided, and that was why her heart was hammering in her chest. His tall form loomed above her, his strong, square jaw giving his face a look of raw power. A thick, dark mane of hair hung in an unruly mass about his shoulders. He had a look of confidence and arrogance that was both infuriating and compelling.

"You weren't trying to escape, were you?" he said softly, his face close to hers. He nudged her chin up until she looked directly at him.

Looking into his silvery gray eyes, Hanna nodded, suddenly unable to say a word. A slow smile curved his mouth.

"The door to the tower will remain unlocked, Hanna. But you will not escape. Knowing that Jozef Czarnowski is expected soon, do you really think I would leave my grounds unprotected? I have fifty men protecting the walls of my castle and the woods surrounding it. Just how far did you think you would get?"

"I d-don't know," she whispered. "Anywhere would be preferable to here."

He cocked an eyebrow. "I see. And how did you expect to get to 'anywhere' without a mount or a coin to your name?"

"I'm sure I could find a real Polish gentleman willing to help a lady in distress," she said assuredly.

"You would not have taken two steps from this castle," he answered arrogantly.

Hanna huffed in outrage. "You . . . you blackguard. You actually find pleasure in tormenting me."

Stefan moved closer, intending to challenge her words, when he caught a whiff of her sweet scent again. Lord, it had an unnerving effect on him. He inhaled deeply, trying to clear his thoughts, but instead he got another full breath of her scent.

"What the hell is that?" he asked irritably.

Her eyes widened. "What is what?"

"That scent . . . the perfume you are wearing."

She looked at him as if he had gone daft. "My what?"

"That scent," he said again with a sniff. "What is it? It is damned distracting."

She angrily freed herself from his grasp. "How dare you try to change the subject to my perfume! You were just informing me of how many men were protecting your castle."

His loud sigh echoed off the walls of the empty corridor. "Must you work so hard to goad my temper, Hanna?"

"*Me* goad *your* temper? Did I forcefully abduct you and lock you in a tower?"

It was such a ridiculous statement that he could not think of an appropriate response. A scowl crossed his face; his patience was wearing thin.

"Hanna, I told you the conditions for walking about my estate. You agreed to them. Do you always break your word so easily?"

"I did not break my word," she said, her mouth set in a stubborn line. "I told you that I would escape."

"You will not escape from me, Hanna. Ever."

The look on Stefan's face was so fierce and possessive, Hanna took an unsteady step back. "M-may I return to my room now?" she whispered haltingly.

"You may not."

Her eyes widened in surprise. "Wh-what?"

"You must first pay the price for your disobedience."

Her breath died in her throat. "Price?" Her mouth had suddenly gone dry.

"Come here, Hanna," Stefan said, his voice soft but firm.

Hanna shook her head warily. Quickly, his fingers shot out and caught her wrist, drawing her close. Before she could utter a single word of protest, Hanna found herself pressed against the full length of his tall, muscular body, her hands trapped tightly against his chest. She pushed with all her strength in an effort to free herself, but it was of no use. His arms were as hard and unyielding as thick bands of steel.

"You will not disobey me again, woman," he said softly, his voice a low rumble.

Hanna raised her eyes to meet his and gasped as she saw that his silvery eyes had turned dark and turbulent. The air suddenly sparked with anticipation and her heart began to beat so furiously in her chest, she was sure it would burst.

"One kiss, Hanna," he whispered thickly. "One kiss is all I ask."

Her eyes grew wide. "Kiss?" she asked, her voice sounding curiously breathless.

Stefan let his gaze roam boldly over her, pausing on her ripe, inviting lips. Lord help him, he knew he was playing with fire, but he could not stop himself. Besides, he argued with himself, one kiss would surely end this unsettling attraction he had for her.

"Aye, Hanna, one kiss is the price you will have to pay. Do you still dare to disobey me?" His voice was ragged with anticipation.

Hanna knew instinctively that if she backed away, he would not force her. She also knew that moving away from him was the last thing she wanted to do. Her eyes lowered to his strong, hard mouth, and without any more encouragement, she slid her arms around his neck, lifting her lips to meet his.

Stefan pulled her to him, his mouth meeting hers with an easy naturalness. Hanna gasped as she felt the heat of his mouth and his fingers entwining in her hair. Using the gasp to his advantage, Stefan quickly moved his tongue between her slightly parted lips, hotly probing the soft recesses of her mouth.

Hanna was stunned by the sensations sweeping through her body. It wasn't like anything she had ever experienced before. It was as if a fire had started in her stomach and crept outward, flooding her senses with a burning-hot fervor.

As his tongue moved languorously inside her mouth, she was filled with a longing she could not explain. She let her fingers explore the rippling muscles in his shoulders and neck and then tangled them in his long, thick hair. Ever so cautiously, she reached out timidly with her tongue to brush lightly against his. Her actions were rewarded by a groan of pleasure.

Stefan slid his hands around her waist. God help him, but she was actually kissing him, and with an innocent abandon that was setting his senses on fire. Roughly, he pulled her tight against him. She was so warm and soft that he nearly lost his composure. A low growl of pleasure came from the back of his throat. She tasted unbearably sweet, kindling a desire within him that he hadn't felt for a long time.

Hanna didn't even realize she was kissing him. His fingers were lightly stroking her back, causing her to tingle with feelings of excitement and longing. His touch made it impossible for her to hold a single coherent thought.

Stefan ran his hands down to her hips and pressed her tightly against him. The feel of her body molded to his was his undoing. His mouth sought hers again and again until he was shaking with need. Suddenly realizing he would not be satisfied until he lowered her to the ground and eased himself between her legs, he abruptly thrust her away.

Taking a step back, he inhaled a ragged breath. Lord, he was appalled at his own lack of discipline. He had only meant to teach her a lesson, to point out her precarious position. Instead, she had surprised him by giving him a thoroughly arousing response to his kiss.

Hanna stood dazed at what she had just experienced. An ache so sweet filled her that she wished for nothing more than to stay in his arms and feel the hot probing of his tongue. His kiss thrilled as well as frightened her, as she realized he had stirred feelings within her that could make her vulnerable and strip her defenseless.

Suddenly, her face blazed scarlet, and she reached out and dealt Stefan a resounding slap across the face. He looked at her in astonishment.

"How dare you order me to kiss you!" she said angrily, turning away from him.

He frowned. "It was a fitting price for your disobedience. Besides, you seemed to be enjoying yourself," he added, grumbling.

Hanna stiffened in mortification at the truth of his words. "You . . . you compelled me to, you beast," she announced, as if that settled the matter.

Stefan rolled his eyes heavenward. She was innocent, all right. He'd known that from the moment he had kissed her. But Lord almighty, he had sensed a passionate woman smoldering beneath that fiery red hair. She had responded to him with a kind of reckless abandon that had inflamed him as had no other woman before her.

He scowled fiercely. Damn it all to hell, he shouldn't have kissed her. Her kiss had been dangerous and heady. Cursing softly, he ran his fingers through his hair in frustration. What was done was done, and there was nothing more he could do about it now. Lifting his arm, he pointed toward the stairs.

"Return to your room," he said coolly.

"With pleasure," Hanna muttered, gathering her skirts and hurrying past him. Tears of shame filled her eyes. She had no idea what had come over her. God in heaven, she had thrown herself at him like a common wench, and from the frown on his face he was greatly displeased with her actions.

A flush crept down her neck. For those few moments, while they had kissed, she had felt cherished and wanted. But he had pushed her away, obviously disgusted by her behavior. Her lower lip began to quiver, and she clamped her mouth shut tightly as she climbed the stairs.

Stefan watched her go, desire still aching within him. She had looked so sweet, her lips swollen, her cheeks pink. Her response had been tender and unguarded. Lord, it made him want her all the more.

"Oh, hell," he muttered, his mood turning foul.

His plan for revenge was becoming more complicated with each passing day. He didn't want to admit it, but suddenly he knew one thing for certain; he didn't want anything to happen to the redheaded beauty he held prisoner in his tower.

Sighing, he shook his head to dispel the disturbing thoughts vying for attention in his mind. Leave it to a woman to confuse the clearest of issues, he thought wryly as he turned and strode down the hall.

Chapter Eight

Hanna tossed and turned in a troubled sleep. Suddenly, she awoke and sat straight up in her bed. A soft wind blew in through the open window of the tower, gently lifting the light covers on the bed. Startled, she looked about, wondering what time it was and what had awakened her. Pressing her hand to her brow, she willed the fog of sleep to leave her.

Through the window moonlight streamed into the chamber, filling it with a silvery light. Looking around the room, she saw that everything was exactly as it had been when she went to sleep. Nothing had changed, except for the lingering anxiety that had been with her since she had awakened.

Hanna strained her ears, listening. There were no unusual sounds, yet the stillness seemed odd. Throwing the covers aside, she climbed out of bed and thrust her arms through the sleeves of a light robe. Picking up the candle she had left on her bedside table, she lit it from the embers in the fireplace.

Slowly, she walked to the door and stopped to listen.

There was no sound. She placed her hand on the latch and pulled the door open carefully, peering out into the darkness. Suddenly, a man stepped out of the blackness and grabbed her shoulder, pushing her back into the room.

She dropped the candle and managed half of a scream before a heavy hand came down over her mouth. Struggling furiously, she kicked her legs and arms. She stopped when she realized she was getting nowhere.

"Be still, woman," a voice whispered roughly. "I have been sent by Jozef Czarnowski."

She stopped her struggling and her captor loosened his grip. Slipping out of his arms, she raced to the open window.

"Help," she screamed at the top of her lungs.

The man lunged for her, but she moved aside agilely. But the room was small, and he managed to catch her by the shoulder and throw her against the stone wall, knocking the breath from her with a loud whoosh.

"Stupid wench," he hissed, pressing her to the wall and drawing a long, jagged dagger from his belt. "You dare to betray my lord. I should kill you now."

Hanna stared in terror at her attacker. The big man was dressed head to foot in black, his face concealed by a dark mask.

He pressed the knife against her throat and Hanna closed her eyes. Suddenly, she heard a noise, and the door to her room was flung open.

Mikhail ran into the room, his sword drawn. In his haste to reach her he tripped over a bundle of logs that had been left by the hearth and fell flat on his face. His sword clattered to the floor and slid across the room.

The man in the black tunic laughed and raised his dagger at Mikhail. Hanna screamed and threw herself at his arm, struggling to keep the knife from reaching its destination. Muttering an oath, the man easily threw her off, and she fell against the fireplace with a resounding thud, and then slid to the floor.

Her efforts allowed Mikhail to scramble to his feet, where he stood warily, eyeing his sword. The man laughed

A Touch of Fire

as he realized Mikhail's weapon was too far out of his reach. With a vicious thrust, he aimed the dagger in the direction of Mikhail's neck.

Mikhail threw himself to one side, and the blade entered his shoulder. With a shout of triumph, the man pushed it in, forcing Mikhail's back to the wall. Mikhail howled in pain as the man turned the blade and then pulled it out again.

Hanna watched in dazed horror, her ears ringing from the blow to her head. Struggling to stand, she felt the bundle of logs behind her. Without fully realizing what she was doing, she grabbed a log in her hand and came to her feet.

The man had raised the dagger and was about to bring it down on Mikhail again when Hanna, mustering all her strength, swung the log at his head. The log bounced off the intruder's skull, knocking him back two steps. Hanna crashed to the floor with her effort.

At that moment, Stefan came bellowing through the door. Holding his sword, he sent the dazed man flying into the wall with the back of his fist. The man crashed heavily against the stone, still grasping his knife. With a growl of rage, he lunged forward, but Stefan swiftly drew his sword, cutting him down cleanly with a single stroke.

The man faltered, clutching at his stomach, staggered, and then collapsed at Hanna's feet. Reaching out a bloody hand, he grabbed the bottom of her robe.

"You will die for your treachery," he said in a strangled voice before making a gurgling sound and falling silent. Hanna watched in fascinated horror as his limp hand slid from her clothing.

Stefan sheathed his sword and reached down to pull the mask off the dead man's face. Hanna recognized him immediately as one of Jozef's vassals.

She clutched her hands tightly in her lap, thinking she might be sick. The dead man's hand still seemed to reach for her, threatening to drag her closer to him, and to the smell of death that slowly began to permeate the room.

An ear-shattering scream pierced the tower. Stefan abruptly jerked up his head and saw Hanna screaming, staring in terror at the dead man. Swiftly, he knelt in front of her, blocking her view of the man.

"Hush, Hanna," he said soothingly. "It is all over now. I am here and you are safe."

She stopped screaming and began sobbing the moment she was in his arms. He gently stroked her hair until her trembling eased. In one movement, he swept her into his arms and stood.

"Assemble my officers," he said briskly to Mikhail as the room began to fill with his men. "And get someone to look at your shoulder."

"I'm all right," Mikhail protested, but his face was as white as a virgin sheet of parchment.

Stefan gave him a long, hard look. "Don't disobey my orders, Mikhail."

Mikhail looked at the uncompromising expression on his brother's face and nodded reluctantly. Satisfied with his response, Stefan turned to leave with his human bundle.

"Wait, Stefan," Mikhail said softly, and his brother paused in the doorway. "Before I go, there is something I want to tell you."

Stefan shook his head brusquely. "We can talk later."

"Nay, now," Mikhail said firmly, bravely moving forward.

Stefan looked at his younger brother in surprise. Twice in one night Mikhail had challenged his orders. He couldn't remember Mikhail ever doing so before and wryly wondered if the woman he held in his arms had anything to do with his brother's sudden disobedience.

His suspicions were confirmed when Mikhail stared for a long moment at Hanna. Slowly, Stefan followed his brother's eyes and let his gaze rest lightly on Hanna's face. She had fainted, but even in unconsciousness, she still gripped his arms in fear.

"She saved my life . . . twice," Mikhail said softly. "I

thought you should know that."

Slowly, Stefan raised his head and sighed in resignation. "All right, Mikhail. Tell me what happened."

Mikhail gave him a terse explanation of the events. When he was through Stefan dragged a hand through his hair. "It was damn foolish of her to put her life at such risk. What the hell was she thinking?"

Mikhail shook his head, wincing slightly as he moved his arm. "I don't know. I hoped you could tell me."

Stefan's frown deepened. "The woman is a mystery to me. But we can talk more about this later. I want you to have that arm taken care of at once."

Mikhail started to protest but saw the dark look on his brother's face and wisely offered no more arguments. Sighing, he left the room, carefully cradling his wounded arm.

As soon as Mikhail had departed, Stefan barked an order for one of his men to follow him to his quarters. Once in his chamber, he gently deposited Hanna on the bed. There was blood on her robe, so he took it off and cast it to the floor. Tenderly, he smoothed her hair from her forehead, shaking his head.

"You brave little fool," he whispered softly. "What am I to do with you?" Slowly, he turned to the man who stood at attention outside his door.

"See that the girl is attended to as soon as Mikhail is bandaged," he ordered the man. "And have someone fix up another room for her. She'll no longer be staying in the tower."

The man nodded sharply, and Stefan strode down the corridor toward the library, where his trusted officers were assembled, waiting.

The men leaped to attention as he entered the room. "Report," Stefan said crisply, striding across the room to stand behind his desk.

Alexander Walczynski, Stefan's portly field captain, stood and stepped forward. "It appears as if Czarnowski's man came alone. He approached the castle from the west, killing two of our men on the outer perimeter."

Stefan's eyes hardened. "How did he get inside the castle?"

"Through the cellar," Alexander said, frowning as he stroked his thick, bushy mustache. "He killed the guard positioned there."

Stefan frowned and sat down, deep in thought. "It doesn't make sense. It is not impossible for a single man to penetrate the defenses of a castle prepared for a full-scale attack. But he would never have escaped with the girl. She would have been too much of a burden."

Stefan's battle strategist, Marek Kaczynski, nodded in agreement. "It was an absurd attempt. There was never any chance of success."

Stefan rubbed the back of his neck wearily. "I can't believe Czarnowski would be that foolish. There must be some element we are overlooking."

The men looked at each other, shaking their heads. Suddenly, Marek's eyes darkened. "Suppose he expected to have help getting her out of here?"

Alexander lifted his head sharply. "What kind of help?"

Marek walked over and stood directly in front of Stefan. "Help from inside the castle."

"Preposterous," Alexander guffawed loudly. "A traitor within our midst?"

Stefan stood slowly and clasped his hands behind his back. After several moments of silence he spoke. "Perhaps it was a test," he said thoughtfully.

"A test?" Staszek Buczkowski, the youngest of Stefan's officers, spoke for the first time. "Of what? Our defenses?"

Alexander interrupted. "It doesn't make sense. If he simply wanted to test our defenses, why bother with the girl at all? Why not slip in and out with the information, if that is what he came for?"

"Perhaps that is not the information he came for," Stefan said quietly.

All eyes turned in surprise to their commander. "What if Jozef wished to test the girl?" Stefan explained, spreading his hands. "To see if she would resist his rescue attempts."

Marek frowned, his long, thin face showing disbelief. "That is madness. Why would Jozef's wife want to resist his rescue attempt?"

"She had no fondness for Jozef Czarnowski," Stefan answered. "And she is not his wife . . . not yet, anyway."

Alexander let out a low whistle. "Are you saying, Stefan, that the girl welcomed the abduction?"

Stefan smiled dryly. "Not exactly. She has already tried to escape once, but not with the intention of returning to Jozef Czarnowski."

Staszek shook his dark head in bewilderment. "I still do not understand. If Czarnowski suspected that the girl might resist, then he also knew he was sending his own man on a nearly impossible mission."

Stefan's face took on a dangerous cast. "Perhaps. But he had to be sure where the girl's loyalty lay. Now he will know for certain."

At that moment, Mikhail walked into the room shirtless, a white bandage wrapped around his arm and shoulder. The men nodded to him in greeting.

Alexander thought for a moment and then leaned forward on the desk, his mustache twitching. "But your theory means that someone has to take the knowledge of her reaction back to him. Czarnowski had to be able to count on that."

Stefan nodded. "Aye, and that is why I think Marek is right. There is a traitor in our midst. How else would he have known exactly where she was being kept?"

There was a stunned silence before Staszek brought his hand crashing down on the desk. "The bastard. If I find out who he is, I'll kill him with my own two hands."

Stefan's voice was clipped and cold. "That information will not leave this room, and that's an order. I'll not have a witch-hunt within my ranks."

"But sir," Staszek started; then he stopped when he saw the cold expression on his commander's face.

"There is a reason for that order, Staszek," Stefan said softly but firmly. "Our regiment has been summoned to

Pila. We leave in three days. The orders came direct from the king."

There was a concerted gasp in the room. "Pila?" Mikhail breathed. "Then the rumors that the King of Sweden plans to invade Poland are true?"

Stefan ran his hand through his thick hair, the lines around his eyes deepening. "Aye, Mikhail, they are true."

"But the treaty of Sztumska Wies . . ." Staszek protested weakly, his face turning gray. "Why would the Swedes break it?"

"The Baltic coast is vulnerable to attack and the Swedes know it," Stefan answered quietly. "Poland is weak and fighting on two fronts. Moreover, Yan Casimir may have brought this situation on himself by openly dreaming of one day ascending the throne in Sweden and perhaps uniting the two lands."

Mikhail scoffed at the idea. "The Swedes are Protestants. We are a Catholic nation. How could such a union be possible?"

Stefan sighed deeply. "It is not possible, Mikhail. Yet it is the destiny of kings to dream and the fate of their subjects to deal with such dreams. Marek is, unfortunately, correct."

"Can we stop her armies?" The question came from Alexander, who was again stroking his mustache thoughtfully.

Marek shook his head doubtfully. "This couldn't come at a worse time for Poland. Strategically, we'll never be able to defend ourselves against three aggressors at once, let alone an army as well seasoned as the Swedes'. "

Stefan frowned deeply at Marek's words. "Poland has never capitulated without a fight. Let us not forget that."

Marek straightened immediately at Stefan's words and nodded crisply. "Of course not, sir."

Stefan sank into a chair. "However, that still does not settle the matter of the girl. I can only assume that Jozef Czarnowski has received similar orders to mobilize his men. Unless he acts in the next three days to recapture her, she'll have to remain under our protection, but without our presence."

"You will leave behind a contingency to protect her?" Mikhail asked.

"Aye, to defend her and the estate. It makes matters damned complicated, though."

"We have no idea what Czarnowski will do next," Marek said. "The only thing we know for certain is that he will not act with honor."

Mikhail swore softly and sat heavily in a nearby chair. A silence fell over the room.

"Shall I inform the men that we shall mobilize in three days' time?" Alexander finally asked.

Stefan nodded. "Aye; tell them. And choose a regiment to stay behind. We'll have to rethink our strategy for protecting the girl in our absence."

Alexander nodded sharply and left the room, followed closely by the others.

When the door closed behind them Mikhail stood and moved closer to his brother. "Do you really think there is a traitor in our midst?"

Stefan ran his fingers through his hair. "Aye, though it grieves me to think so. There are more than sixty rooms in this castle. That Jozef's man was able to penetrate our defenses so exactly and move directly to the tower where she was being held is too much of a coincidence."

Mikhail began to pace across the room. "I agree. But God help me, Stefan, I still can't believe what she did. She put herself between me and that knife twice. Why did she help me? We abducted her, for God's sake. She means nothing to us. I hate her because she belongs to Jozef Czarnowski."

Stefan sighed. "You don't hate her, Mikhail, and neither do I."

Mikhail glowered; then he stomped about the room for a minute before coming to a halt before his brother. "All right; I don't hate her. But why did she scream for help?

She could have gone with him quietly."

"I think she would rather die than wed Jozef Czarnowski."

Mikhail looked at his brother in amazement. "She really has no loyalty to him?"

Stefan shook his head. "None at all, as far as I can tell."

Mikhail whistled softly. "Then I've behaved shamefully. She is no more to blame than Danuta was."

"Aye, Mikhail, I think that is true."

"Then what shall we do, brother?"

"We must leave for Pila in three days. If we cannot force a confrontation with Jozef Czarnowski by then, we will have to leave her here, under guard. I think it is safe to assume that Jozef will also be called from Warsaw. Yet I am sure he will instruct the men he leaves behind to keep trying to take her. She is in great danger now that she has resisted his attempt to free her."

"What about the traitor?" Mikhail asked.

Stefan exhaled. "There is little we can do about it now. Her protection will remain a priority. I'm going to assign Boguslaw Dobrowolski to watch her."

Mikhail raised an eyebrow. "The giant?"

Stefan smiled at the nickname. "There is no man I trust more, outside of my officers. He'll see no harm comes to her."

Mikhail nodded, gingerly touching his bandaged shoulder. "I suppose you are right."

Stefan rubbed the back of his neck. "Unfortunately, our plans for Jozef Czarnowski will have to wait for the time being. We must set our sights on the battle to come. I'm afraid the fighting will be fierce."

"And if we come across Jozef during battle?"

"We are both Poles, fighting a foreign invader. I will not raise my sword against him unless he threatens me first."

Mikhail inhaled deeply and closed his eyes. "Still, we'll have to watch our backs."

Stefan's face hardened. "Don't worry about Jozef Czarnowski, Mikhail. We will have our revenge, I promise you that."

Mikhail nodded slowly as he walked to the window and opened the shutters. Although it was nearly dawn, there was no light. The sky was black with clouds, and a low rumble of thunder could be heard in the distance.

"It seems as if we are in for some rain," Mikhail said quietly.

Stefan nodded in agreement, although he had not even glanced out the window. "Aye, Mikhail. A fierce storm is on the way."

Chapter Nine

Hanna came back to consciousness slowly. She felt a soft pillow beneath her head and snuggled deeper against it before abruptly sitting straight up in bed. The events of the night came rushing back to her, and she looked about wildly, trying to get her bearings.

She was alone in a large room; a man's room, to be sure. It was a stark chamber with a single window, a wide bed with a quilted cover on which she now sat, and a small wooden chest pushed up against the foot of the bed. An oversize chair was placed near the hearth, and Hanna flushed when she saw a pair of breeches carelessly slung over it. There were no pictures on the walls, no rugs, and not even a mirror.

Quickly, she slipped out of bed, absently running her fingers through her tangled hair. She remembered nothing after the intruder fell dead at her feet, clutching her robe with his bloody hand. Looking down, she saw she was clad only in her sleeping gown. Where was her robe?

Heat rose to her cheeks when she saw it on the floor, pushed partially under the bed. Good God in heaven, who had undressed her? She pressed her hands to her cheeks, suddenly certain she knew the answer.

Sighing, she tiptoed to the door and opened it a crack. She gasped as a man, who had been standing against it, fell into the room.

Astonished, she and the man gaped at each other until he started laughing. "Don't look so surprised, milady; I was only guarding you."

"Guarding me?" she asked suddenly, feeling faint. "Then I am still a prisoner?"

The guard reached out a hand to steady her when he suddenly went flying across the room.

"Don't ever touch her again," Stefan roared.

Hanna was shocked at Stefan's sudden arrival and his odd behavior. Seeing the terrified look on the guard's face, she turned to face him squarely.

"For God's sake," she said in exasperation, "he was only trying to help me."

"Get out," he ordered the guard. "And close the door behind you."

Hanna gasped in stunned outrage. "How dare you order him to leave us alone in this bedchamber!" Her face flushed at just the thought of it. "Don't you move from this room," she ordered the guard with such authority that the man stopped in his tracks.

Stefan gave the guard one hard look; the man fled from the room, slamming the door behind him.

Stefan approached her, his gaze cold and unwavering. "Don't ever countermand one of my orders again," he said quietly.

She raised her chin and met his stare defiantly. "I am your prisoner, not one of your soldiers. I do not have to obey your orders."

"You are wrong about that, Hanna." He spoke softly, but she sensed danger beneath his words. She met his icy gaze, but she decided it would not be wise to press the issue.

"Whatever you say, milord," she said without much conviction, turning away from him.

Stefan reached out and took her hand, firmly pulling her toward him. Immediately, Hanna felt her heart begin to race. She held her breath, wondering what he would do next, but he led her to the chair and motioned for her to sit. She sat obediently, wondering why she felt so disappointed.

Casually, Stefan leaned against the mantel, his hand resting on his hip. Her eyes traveled to his side, where she saw the dagger thrust into his belt.

Puzzled, she looked up at him. The expression on his face indicated that he had seen her reaction to his weapon.

"Are you able to use a dagger as well as you do a sword, Hanna?" he asked slowly, withdrawing the knife from his belt.

She nodded her head slowly. "Aye, I can."

Abruptly, he flicked the blade toward himself and held the handle toward her. "Then take it," he said quietly.

She looked at him in amazement. "What?" she whispered.

"Take it."

Hesitantly, she reached out and took the dagger from his hand. "Why are you giving me this?"

He put his hands on her shoulders, and she felt a shock of feeling go through her body at the warmth of his touch. "Have you ever killed a man, Hanna?" he asked quietly.

She shook her head vigorously. "Nay, of course not."

His eyes were dark, his expression unreadable. "The first kill will always stay with you."

She felt her stomach heave and looked away. "P-please. I no longer wish to discuss this."

He reached down and took the dagger from her hand. "Then why did you train with daggers and swords? They are not toys, but tools. If you draw one, you had better be prepared to use it."

She looked down at her trembling hands and clasped them tightly in her lap. "I learned in order to protect myself."

Stefan grabbed her chin, forcing her to look at him. "And what if you must fight to the death to protect your own life? Could you do it?"

She bit her lower lip. "I d-don't know."

He released her chin. "Well, you had better think about it. After your struggle tonight your life is in even greater danger."

"I know," she whispered.

Stefan sighed and ran his fingers through his hair. "You will keep the dagger with you at all times. And if you draw it, you will use it. Do you understand me?"

She shook her head slightly. "Nay, I do not understand you at all."

"I'm allowing you to protect yourself, Hanna," he said flatly.

"But you will protect me, will you not?" Her cheeks turned crimson as soon as the words left her mouth.

He crossed his thick arms. "I'm leaving Warsaw."

She looked up in dismay. "You are?"

"Unfortunately. Poland will war with Sweden, and I have been summoned to the city of Pila."

She stood, her eyes wide with surprise. "Sweden? God in heaven, Poland will be warring on three fronts. It will be impossible."

"Nothing is impossible, Hanna."

"And Jozef?" She was almost afraid to ask.

"He'll be called up as well. But that won't stop him from trying to get you back."

She nodded. "Aye, it won't." She was silent for a long moment. "How is Mikhail?" she finally asked shyly.

Stefan exhaled deeply. "Damned confused about why you saved him. But thankful . . . as am I."

She lowered her eyes. "He would have died trying to save me. I did not want to be responsible for his death."

Stefan couldn't believe his ears. "You responsible for his death? Good God, Hanna, have you forgotten that we abducted you? If it is anyone's responsibility, it is ours."

"I told you, I can take care of myself," she challenged, but much to her horror her lower lip began to quiver and tears formed at the corners of her eyes. Hanna willed with all of her might that they not fall. *I will not let him see me weak and vulnerable. Please God, oh please, don't let him see me cry.*

Despite her plea, a tear rolled down her cheek. Stefan looked at it in surprise, and then reached up to brush away the next one with his thumb.

Hell, he had forgotten how fragile and alone she really was. She never ceased challenging him, and it made him forget she was still a young woman in a foreign land who had been dragged against her will into the middle of a dangerous and deadly feud.

He rubbed his nape in frustration. Still . . . one conversation with her and he felt as though he had single-handedly fought an entire regiment of Cossacks.

And lost.

Stefan drew her to him, pressing her head firmly against his chest. "Don't cry, Hanna," he said softly. "Everything will be all right. I promise I'll not let anything happen to you."

Stefan stroked her silky hair, amazed that the words had fallen from his lips. What had come over him that he would make such a promise to her? She was clearly the most stubborn, outspoken, and willful woman he had ever met.

And she is my captive, he reminded himself. Yet God help him, responsibility wasn't all he felt for this woman. He wanted her. Badly.

Hanna lifted her tear-streaked face from his chest. "Why do you say these things? You don't care what happens to me. I am your prisoner, a pawn in your revenge."

"I do care," he whispered fiercely. "It is the damnedest thing."

Hanna closed her eyes and put her head back on his chest. His heartbeat thudded through his cotton shirt, and somehow it comforted her. She wanted so much to believe his words; that for once in her life someone would care

A Touch of Fire 103

for and protect her . . . allowing her to lower the walls she had built around herself and her emotions.

Those are words spoken in guilt, Hanna Quinn. Don't forget for a moment that you are his captive and he needs you for only one thing: to bring him Jozef Czarnowski. She winced inwardly at the thought, wondering why the truth hurt so much.

"I'm sorry, Hanna," Stefan said softly. "It is most unfortunate that things are the way they are. Perhaps if circumstances were different . . ." He let the sentence trail off, not sure what he wanted to say. Christ's blood, he didn't even want to consider the rest of that thought.

Another tear slipped from Hanna's eye. *If things were different, you would never have met me, Stefan Tarnowski. And who knows, maybe things would have been different. But we will never know, will we?*

Hanna pulled away from him, wiping her cheeks. "I'm sorry. I don't know what came over me," she said with obvious embarrassment.

Stefan reluctantly released her. Sweet Mary, she felt so right in his arms. He traced a line from her cheek to her lips with his finger. Her lovely eyes met his and shimmered. He had never seen such remarkable eyes: shifting shades of blue and green that made him think of endless ocean fathoms. Fathoms a man could easily drown in.

"Eyes the color of the sea," he murmured softly. Lord, she was truly a beauty. Her fiery red hair fell about her in a cloud of curls. For the first time he realized that she was clad only in a thin sleeping gown. He could see the soft outline of her body through the sheer material and was immediately aroused.

Hell and damnation, he wanted to kiss her. He knew how good she would taste, and the thought that she might respond to him again with such innocent abandon nearly caused him to lose his head.

Hanna watched as his gaze fell upon her lips and lingered there. She suddenly felt breathless, remembering the warm pressure of his mouth and the tingling sensations that had swept through her body when he kissed her.

Suddenly, Stefan blinked and turned from her, clenching his hands at his side. "I will not lose control again," he muttered under his breath.

"You won't?" Hanna asked, unable to hide the disappointment in her voice.

He laughed hoarsely. "I won't, though you tempt me sorely."

She looked down at her hands as he walked over to her. Carefully, he opened them and placed the dagger there, firmly closing her fingers over it.

"Hanna, Poland is a very dangerous place right now. We are going to war with a very fierce people. I don't want you to try something foolish like trying to escape. Will you promise me that you will not try?"

Hanna kept her eyes lowered, and he knelt down beside her. "Hanna?" he asked again, nudging her chin up with his hand.

"All right. I promise," she said softly after a long silence.

"Good," he said, feeling some of his anxiety abating. "Now, I am assigning one of my most trusted men to protect you. You can trust him implicitly, and I want you to take orders from no one but him. Agreed?"

She nodded slowly. "Agreed."

He touched her cheek gently. "I won't let any harm come to you, Hanna. You'll not be going back to Jozef Czarnowski. You have my word." He saw the look of relief that crossed her face and stared at her for a long moment before standing.

"Remember what I said about this," he said, pointing at the dagger.

Hanna opened her hand and looked at the weapon. Slowly, she raised her gaze to meet his. He was still watching her, an odd mixture of desire and regret in his eyes. She didn't understand the emotion in his face, nor the sudden feeling of sadness that swept over her when she realized he was leaving. Eventually, he turned from her and walked to the door.

"S-Stefan," she said quietly as he stood in the doorway. He turned to face her, his eyes questioning.

"*Niech żyje Polska,*" she whispered. "Long live Poland."

His dark eyes burned into hers. *"Niech żyje,"* he agreed softly.

Turning from her, he left the room, shutting the door quietly behind him.

Chapter Ten

The ride west to Pila was long and hard for Stefan and his men. They finally reached the camp at nightfall on the third day. Stefan thought it could hardly be called a camp; the area was a disarray of scattered tents and unattended campfires. Some of the men who didn't have shelter simply sprawled on the grass next to glowing fires.

There appeared to be no sentries, and the only people to greet them were a group of ill-dressed men who were drinking and quarreling loudly. Stefan and his officers frowned at the lack of order or discipline.

That would change immediately, Stefan thought to himself. The king had made him the commander at Pila, and he planned to use that authority to whip this ragtag band into soldiers. He rode slowly around the camp, nodding to those men who were still awake.

Stefan knew the task wouldn't be easy. Most of the men were peasant conscripts, sent to fight by the wealthy noblemen who owned them. A few of the noblemen themselves were also present, having been called up personally by the king. They had brought along wagons of personal supplies and a small army of servants to do their bidding. The other not-so-wealthy members of the gentry arrived with a horse and a single weapon. The poor came with nothing more than the shirts on their backs.

The next day, Stefan assembled all the men together in a large clearing. It was a warm summer day, and the air smelled of sweet, fresh grass and blooms. Surrounded by his officers, Stefan announced that he had been ordered to take command at Pila. Holding up the parchment from the king, he invited the men to come forth and inspect it. Although Stefan knew a great many of the men could not read, he also knew that most would be content to see proof of the king's seal.

Murmurs rippled through the group at Stefan's proclamation, but curiosity tugged at the men. One by one they stepped forward to look at the parchment. Finally, after the last man had looked at the king's orders to his satisfaction, the men huddled about nervously, looking expectantly at their new commander.

Stefan let his gaze sweep slowly over the group, a lock of his dark hair falling across his forehead. His voice rang through the clearing. "There are a few rules that need to be set down immediately. First, the camp must be guarded at all hours by at least a dozen sentries. I have no wish to be slain while fast asleep. I'm sure none of you have this desire."

A few nervous chuckles spread through the group, but the wisdom of Stefan's words hit home. Many now realized that it had been dangerous and foolish to leave the camp defenseless and open to a surprise attack. With the Swedes only weeks away, it had been a mistake born of carelessness and laziness.

"Second," Stefan continued, "each man will be provided with shelter or a tent to sleep in. We will build them ourselves, even if we must use rags and animal hides. Those with larger accommodations will be forced to share." Stefan looked pointedly at a number of noblemen, who frowned at his suggestion but offered no words of protest.

"Third, there will be no more drinking. I want each of you sharp-witted, able to fight instantly upon my command. If anyone is caught with drink, he shall be severely punished. This order goes for every man here. I want that to be perfectly clear."

Stefan abruptly snapped his fingers and Alexander, Staszek, and Mikhail came into view, rolling several barrels in front of them.

A horrified gasp came from many of the noblemen, and one rather portly gentleman rushed forward, throwing himself on one of the barrels. "My God, commander, have you no sense?" he screeched at Stefan. "This is expensive French wine. It cost me a fortune. Please, as a fellow gentleman, I beseech you."

Stefan flicked his wrist, and Mikhail stepped forward, dragging the man from the barrel. When everyone was clear Alexander lifted a musket to his shoulder and fired a shot into each of the barrels.

A loud cry of protest erupted from the noblemen, but it was silenced abruptly as Alexander fired another shot over their heads. Stunned, many of the noblemen pressed their hands to their brows in horror.

Stefan resisted the urge to smile at their shocked sensibilities, though many of the peasants were unable to hold back snickers and snorts of laughter. Finally, Stefan waved his hand for silence. Planting his hands firmly on his hips, he faced the group calmly.

"All right, men. I have laid down the rules. Now only one issue remains to be addressed. As subjects of this kingdom, we must pledge to work together to protect our king and country. I want each of you to swear your obedience and loyalty to King Casimir . . . and to me, your commanding officer. In return, I pledge not to ask of you anything other than that which serves the cause and defense of our kingdom."

A few muted whispers and murmurs went through the crowd before a fair-headed peasant lad stepped forward, kneeling in front of Stefan. "I swear my loyalty and obedience, sir," he said shyly, reaching out to kiss the hilt of Stefan's sword.

For a long time after that the men knelt before him, swearing fealty. His own officers did so as well, and at last the noblemen came, grumbling under their breaths but still uttering allegiance to king and country.

As each man withdrew, the surrounding forest filled with life, expectation, and noise. As Stefan moved into the crowd to shake the men's hands, a loud cheer rang through the trees, filling the air with the sounds of hope and purpose.

Days passed slowly, but finally the area on the outskirts of Pila began to look like an established military encampment. Men continued to arrive as the king's call to arms swept across the country. Artisans, musicians, merchants, and farmers all reported for duty at the camp. Unfortunately for Stefan, most of them had never held a sword, and even fewer had smelled gunpowder.

The noblemen at the camp were the worst to deal with. Strenuously protesting at how hard Stefan worked them, several of them refused to leave their tents. Stefan himself went into a few tents, dragging the men out by the scruff of their necks. Stefan insisted that every man would do exactly the same amount of training at the camp. When the noblemen saw that Stefan would not back down they began to follow orders, albeit unhappily. Slowly, a grudging respect for Stefan and his officers began to form throughout the camp.

Stefan set up training areas around the camp and began to teach the men how to use swords and the bow. Some of the more experienced men were taught how to handle the few muskets and small cannons they had at their disposal.

The July days were sweltering; most of the heavy training had to be done in early morning and late afternoon, when the sun was not so hot. Tempers were often high, especially among the noblemen, who continued to quarrel and complain loudly.

After one particularly grueling session Stefan assembled the officers in his tent. Sweat dripped off Alexander's nose as he fumbled in his pocket, looking for a cloth.

"Lord God have mercy on us. It is hotter than the breath of a dying Cossack out there," he said, wiping his brow.

Stefan wiped his own forehead with the back of his hand. "The weather is the least of our problems, gentlemen. The training is going slower than I had expected."

Alexander snorted. "Slower? I have never seen such a hopeless group of men. I can hardly find one of them who is strong enough to hold a broadsword for longer than a few moments. Most of the noblemen are quarreling like a bunch of women."

Mikhail plopped down on the ground in frustration. "Most of our experienced troops are still in the Ukraine or on the Russian border. But at least the king diverted some of our troops to defend the duchy of Lithuania in case the Swedes attack on two fronts."

"My concern for the moment is the western front to which we've been assigned," Stefan said dryly. "I need some ideas of how to turn this camp into a group of well-trained soldiers."

Marek took a swig of water from a wooden canteen. "I don't believe it can be done. Besides, technically speaking, we are not going to be able to hold off the Swedish forces for long. At least not here in Pila."

Stefan gave a small shrug. "Holding them off forever is not our goal. We simply need to give Polish forces time to prepare for the defense of Warsaw. That is our most important objective."

Alexander nodded vigorously. "I agree. We may not be able to outgun the Swedes, but we can at least give them a little taste of Polish hospitality."

Marek snorted, and Mikhail nodded his head in agreement. "I suppose I could add some more drills to the training sessions," Alexander said, pulling on his mustache.

Mikhail leapt to his feet impatiently. "Well then, let's get on with it. All this talking makes me nervous. At least when I'm training my mind is not dwelling on the number of Swedish troops marching toward us."

"Sit down, Mikhail," Stefan ordered. "I have something else I want to discuss with all of you. I have decided to request a Tartar regiment from the king."

Alexander gasped. "A Tartar regiment? Good God, Stefan, they are difficult to manage and not so inclined to follow orders."

Stefan nodded in acknowledgment of Alexander's concerns. The Tartars were fierce Turkish-speaking peoples, well skilled in the art of fighting. The Poles had been lucky to have many Tartar regiments available to them, although their loyalty to the Polish king had not come easily. Polish commanders had to promise them riches and the right to booty seized from enemy forces.

"I am fully aware of how the Tartars fight," Stefan said dryly. "I think they are exactly what we need."

Marek, who had been quietly listening to the exchange, suddenly laughed. "By God, it is brilliant, Stefan. The Swedes will be so startled to see the Tartars waving their swords like madmen and howling at the top of their lungs, it will surely give us some element of surprise."

Alexander rubbed his bald head thoughtfully. "I'll be the first to admit the Tartars are damn good fighters. But they are also unsettling and quite unpredictable. Is it really worth it?"

Stefan faced his officers squarely. "Unfortunately, I don't see any other alternative. Given our present situation and the conscripts at hand, we need the surprise advantage that a Tartar regiment could give us."

Marek agreed. "It would be most beneficial, strategically at least, to have the Tartars here. Of course, we'll have to make it seem as if we have more than just one regiment. The Swedes will have to think we have hundreds of them."

"Why can't we just request several regiments?" Mikhail asked curiously.

Stefan shook his head. "There is only one regiment currently in the Warsaw area. The other divisions are already stationed at either the Russian front or in the Ukraine."

"How long would it take a Tartar regiment to get here?" Alexander said, rubbing his balding head.

"One week at the least," Marek answered. "That is, if the king agrees to Stefan's request."

"He'll agree," Stefan said firmly. "He desperately needs time, and we are the only ones who can give it to him. I'll send a messenger to the king immediately."

The men nodded in agreement and filed out of the tent. As soon as they had left, Stefan sat down on a small wooden stool. It was going to be a hard fight, probably the most difficult campaign of his life. As it stood, they were clearly outmanned, outgunned, and outskilled. But this was Polish soil, and he and his men were Poles. *By God, that had to count for something.*

Still, would any of them come out of this alive? For an instant, he let his mind stray to a rebellious red-haired beauty who had fired his blood with a kiss. For the first time in his life he felt a longing for something more than going from battle to battle. It had been his way for so long, he hadn't realized that perhaps there should have been more to his life.

He scowled. Damn it, he didn't want to think about Hanna, but she kept popping into his mind. He remembered how her lips felt and the outline of her soft curves through her sheer nightgown.

Curse it, Tarnowski, she doesn't belong to you and she never will. You had better put her out of your mind, soldier, or she will be the death of you.

"Bloody hell," he muttered loudly in English. "I should never have kissed her."

Cursing inwardly, he strode to the open flap of his tent, calling loudly for a messenger to take his request to the king.

Chapter Eleven

Hanna quickly made friends with her protector, Boguslaw Dobrowolski. He was a giant of a man with light brown hair and mild blue eyes. A jagged scar that ran from his left eye to his upper lip gave him a fierce look, but Hanna was not at all intimidated by his gruff exterior. Instead, he reminded her very much of Jim; blunt and straightforward, yet with a good and loyal heart.

Boguslaw rarely left her side, even though she ventured from the house only once or twice a day for a walk in the garden. The estate was still heavily guarded, most of the soldiers making no attempt to hide their vigil. At night, Boguslaw slept on the floor outside her chamber, while another man stood guard at the door.

As the days, and then weeks, slowly passed, Boguslaw and the girl had come to know each other quite well, and he was impressed with what he had discovered about her. Hanna was smart, with a quick wit. And damn fine to look at, too, with her mane of gorgeous red hair. She had an easygoing nature and was never patronizing, as many women of her stature and looks often were with him. His initial disappointment at being handpicked by Stefan to watch the girl had long since faded. Although he missed being in the thick of battle, he couldn't say in all honesty that he wasn't enjoying himself.

One evening, as they sat quietly in the parlor, Hanna embroidering a shift for herself and Boguslaw polishing his boots, they suddenly heard a knock on the door. Boguslaw stood quickly, drawing his sword and motioning her to stand behind him.

"Who is it?" he asked, moving toward the door.

"It's me, Tomek."

Boguslaw lifted the latch, recognizing the voice as belonging to Tomek Niebudek, one of Stefan's young vassals.

Hanna exhaled the breath she had been holding as the young man quietly walked in.

"What do you want?" Boguslaw asked, sheathing his sword.

"A messenger has just arrived at the gate," Tomek reported quickly. "He says he has a message from the Polish parliament for whomever is looking after the estate in Stefan Tarnowski's absence."

"Tell him to give the message to you," Boguslaw commanded sharply.

"I did, sir, but he refused, saying the message can only be delivered directly to the proxy of Stefan Tarnowski."

Boguslaw frowned. "He rides alone?"

Tomek nodded. "He does."

"Is he armed?"

"Nay."

Boguslaw thought for a long moment. "Then bring him to me here."

Tomek's eyes lingered on Hanna. "What about her? Shall I take her to another room?"

Boguslaw shook his head and motioned to the door. "You have your orders, Tomek. Leave the girl to me."

Tomek nodded sharply and left the room. Boguslaw rubbed his hands together, his brows deepening in a frown.

"It may be a trap of some kind, milady. Nonetheless, I don't want to let you out of my sight."

He walked over to one of the heavy velvet draperies that hung at the window and lifted it. "Would you be so kind as to wait behind one of these for me?"

Hanna smiled in spite of the nervous beat of her heart. "As you wish," she said calmly, and Boguslaw felt a rush of admiration for the girl. There were no hysterics, no questioning of his decision; she simply accepted his judgment and acted on it.

Hanna scooted behind the drape and flattened herself against the wall. Boguslaw tugged and rearranged the drape until he was satisfied that she could not be detected. Then he waited, his hand resting lightly on his sword. Tomek led the messenger into the room and left, quietly shutting the door behind him.

"Are you the proxy acting on behalf of Colonel Stefan Tarnowski?" the messenger asked crisply.

Boguslaw noted that the man was dressed in a soldier's uniform and wore a white and red Polish breastplate with a crowned eagle. "I am," he answered quietly. "What is it you require of me?"

"I have been sent on a special mission by certain members of the parliament. It is my duty to inform you of a general amnesty to be granted to the houses of those Polish noblemen who do not resist the forces of His Majesty Charles Gustav, King of Sweden. The parliament is collecting those names. Discreetly, of course."

Hanna nearly gasped in shock at the statement and clenched her hands together. She could hear the surprise in Boguslaw's voice and knew he must be as stunned as she.

"Members of our parliament are doing such a thing?" Boguslaw asked, his voice sounding strangled. "While King Casimir still sits in Warsaw Castle planning the defense of our country?"

The young soldier had the grace to flush, but he ignored Boguslaw's pointed words. "Some members of parliament feel it is time to take prudent and realistic steps toward the inevitable. His Majesty King Charles Gustav assures you that the privileges of the Polish nobility and the clergy will be preserved. For those who agree to welcome him there will be no new or increased taxes, nor will the armies of Sweden be quartered in or on their land. I have come to ask you, as the appointed proxy of Colonel Stefan Tarnowski, to speak on his behalf regarding such an issue."

" 'Steps toward the inevitable'?" Boguslaw said incredulously, and Hanna could hear the dangerous undercurrent in his voice.

"Aye, sir," the soldier answered.

A heavy silence fell on the room. It was so quiet, Hanna was sure the messenger would be able to hear her rapid breathing from behind the curtain.

"Sir?" the young man asked hesitantly, shifting his weight nervously from one foot to the other. "May I have your answer?"

Bright red spots of anger appeared on Boguslaw's cheeks. "The inevitable?" he sputtered. "You are asking me this question while Polish forces are still gathering to battle with the Swedes?"

The young man blushed again. "Technically, aye. But it is only a matter of time before . . ."

"Get out, you treasonous bastard," Boguslaw shouted, taking a threatening step toward the soldier. "You don't deserve to wear the Polish eagle on your breastplate."

The young man took a wary step back. "I believe that you should reconsider your harsh words, sir. After all, I am a messenger from the parliament . . ."

"Get out, I said," Boguslaw thundered again, and Hanna quaked at the anger in his voice.

The soldier's shoulders stiffened. "Then I am to assume that the Tarnowski estate should not be counted among the friends of His Majesty Charles Gustav?"

Boguslaw took a deep, angry breath. "I don't know what kind of dribbling noblemen we have in our parliament that would cause them to sell their country so easily, but you tell your precious King Gustav that a true Pole believes he will never be welcome on an inch of this soil. I have known Stefan Tarnowski for nearly fifteen years and I am sure I speak for him when I say that His Majesty King Gustav, and all of his so-called friends, can go to hell."

The soldier was clearly taken aback at the vehemence of Boguslaw's words, but he quickly composed himself. "Rest assured that your position will be clearly stated, sir," the young man said, turning on his heel and leaving the room.

As soon as he had gone, Hanna lifted the drape and slipped into the room. Boguslaw stood leaning against the mantel, his head in his hands. She walked up behind him quietly and put a gentle hand on his shoulder.

"God help us, our own parliament is abandoning the country," he moaned.

"The parliament is not the people," she said softly, and for a moment, Boguslaw felt some hope and comfort. Then he sighed, rubbing his big, callused hands together.

"But how can it be that our own noblemen are willing to commit treason simply to protect their own selfish interests? Does no one in this country have honor?"

"Not all Polish noblemen are so treacherous, Boguslaw," Hanna said softly. "If what you say is true, then the Tarnowski family can be counted among those Poles with honor. I'm sure there are more families like them, as well. They will fight to the last man to protect Polish land and honor."

Boguslaw inhaled deeply. "You are right, milady. The Tarnowski family is one of those with honor. But is it enough to protect Poland from the greed and corruption within her own government?"

Hanna shook her head mutely, unable to answer his question. Sighing, Boguslaw rubbed his temples wearily.

"I need to have someone ride to Pila immediately," he said, his voice heavy. "The colonel needs to know, as soon as possible, what is happening in Warsaw."

Hanna nodded, wondering with no small amount of hope, if Stefan was still alive and whether or not she would ever see him again.

Chapter Twelve

Stefan Tarnowski sat astride his dark brown charger, scanning the horizon with his field telescope. Dressed in a chain-mail shirt, cotton breeches, and heavy black boots drawn up to his knees, he was hot, a trickle of sweat slipping from his brow and sliding slowly down his neck, disappearing into his tunic. It would be a blistering day for fighting, he thought to himself.

"Colonel?"

Staszek Buczkowski anxiously skidded his horse to a halt at his commander's side. Stefan nearly smiled, wondering if he had ever had as much energy and enthusiasm as his young scout.

"The Swedes are coming, sir, with several thousand troops and many lines of artillery. They are close; we were nearly detected by their scouts. I'm sure they will have discovered our position by now."

Stefan kept his face emotionless as Staszek relayed the information. "So the battle begins," Stefan said under his breath.

"Sir?"

Stefan shook his head. "Nothing, Staszek. Get some rest; I'll need you later."

Staszek saluted sharply and rode off. Stefan returned the field scope to his eye, frowning. The Swedes had far more heavy artillery and a greater number of troops than anyone had imagined. The news was grim, far grimmer than he had expected.

Alexander rode up, nudging his horse close to Stefan's. "How much time until we meet the first Swedish division?"

Stefan's eyes hardened. "Two, maybe three hours. Get the Tartar commander here at once. I need to talk with him."

Alexander nodded and rode off to fetch the Tartar officer. Minutes later, a tall man with a swarthy complexion rode up. His dark, fierce eyes were nearly hidden by large, bushy eyebrows and a long, swirling mustache. His attire was simple: baggy pants and a brown jacket. An expensive gold saber hung from his belt; surely it had been seized from a fallen enemy, Stefan thought wryly.

"Hamid-Bey," Stefan said, dipping his head in respect to the commander. "The Swedes will soon be here. Our scouts tell us they are heavily loaded with several wagons of ammunition and supplies. I want your men to focus an attack on the supply wagons. They will surely attempt to defend them, drawing their troops to the left. Our regiments will attack from the right and try to split the lines in two."

Hamid-Bey nodded slowly, as his eyes sized up the young commander. "The supplies will be ours to take?"

Stefan nodded. "As much as you can carry with you."

Hamid-Bey smiled. Serving under the Poles had made him and his men rich. "Then it shall be as you request," he said, turning his horse and galloping away.

Two hours later, almost to the minute, the Swedish troops came into view. Stefan signaled his men to stand by, waiting until the first several lines of the opposing army had entered the valley. Stefan's mood darkened as he saw the well-organized lines march in precision to the steady thumping of the regimental drums. The sun glinted off the hundreds of gleaming breastplates and pikes.

Through his field telescope, Stefan focused on the bright blue Swedish standard with its gold lion. He knew that somewhere near the standard rode the Swedish field marshal.

It will be a match of wills between you and me, Marshal. And it won't be as easy for you as you think.

Stefan turned to his standard-bearer. "Wait for my order," he said sharply. Time seemed to crawl until Stefan raised his sword. Spurring his horse forward, he brought the flashing blade down.

"To arms," he shouted as the standard-bearer waved the flag above his head to signal the order to advance. A trumpet screamed as the white-and-red Polish flags and standards were raised across the regiments. Sabers glinted in the bright sun as the soldiers charged the Swedish troops.

The howling of the advancing Polish forces from all sides was deafening. Swedish officers tried to shout orders over the din.

"Fire!" a Swedish colonel shouted, and a booming echo filled the valley.

Stefan charged into the thick smoke, whirling and slashing his saber as quick as lightning. He felt a sword hit his thick chain-mail vest and bounce off. Swiftly, he turned in the saddle, slashing in the direction of the attack. His sword found its mark and Stefan heard a howl of pain.

Again, the loud report of muskets sounded and he saw the air thicken with heavy black smoke. Wheeling his horse around, Stefan rode to the edge of the smoke and brought a small wooden horn to his lips. He blew into it three times; then he ducked as a musket ball whizzed past his head.

Looking up, he saw that dragoons of Tartars were attacking the supply wagons. The men charged head-on, flattened in the saddles, their bloodcurdling cries striking terror into the hearts of the Swedish soldiers.

Stefan smiled with satisfaction. The Swedes were scattering in every direction, exactly as he had predicted. Gathering some of his officers around him, Stefan charged into battle again, shouting encouragement to his men. He fought with cold, determined precision, icily aware of the slashing swords and thrusting spears.

Relentlessly, he pressed his men forward, driving his regiments into the Swedish lines like a wedge. The fighting grew fierce, with silver blades gleaming in an endless river of swords, muskets, and horses.

Hamid-Bey and his comrades fought valiantly as the scorching summer sun inexhaustibly beat down on the warriors until finally it began a slow descent behind the hills. The Tartars paused during a lull in the battle to have some water and became aware that the valley was now bathed in a blood-red sunset that streaked across the sky and mirrored the carnage on the ground. Thrusting his flask into a pouch on his belt, Hamid-Bey pulled hard on the reins of his mount and headed for the young Polish colonel.

Stefan was engaged with a particularly difficult opponent when he saw Hamid-Bey working his way toward him. He slashed with renewed vigor, his sword finally piercing through a hole in his opponent's chain-mail shirt. As the man fell, Stefan guided his horse toward the Tartar.

"One of my scouts has just reported from the northern border of Pomerania," Hamid-Bey yelled over the clanging swords. "There are more Swedish reinforcements assembling there. We'll have to pull back for the night and reassess our strategy."

"Damn," Stefan cursed. His plan had been working, and they had nearly split the Swedish line. He grimaced as he looked up at the fading light in the sky. The Tartar commander was right; darkness would soon be upon them.

"I'll order the troops to fall back," Stefan shouted.

Reining his horse sharply to the left, he lifted the horn to his lips and sounded one long note. The standard-bearers heard the call and began madly waving their signal for retreat. Stefan's regiments began to withdraw, slowly heading back toward the encampment. The Swedish soldiers were also retreating and regrouping, waiting for their reinforcements.

As soon as the majority of his men were accounted for, Stefan ordered a small detail back to the battlefield to pick up as many of the wounded as possible. Then he assembled the officers in his tent for a meeting.

"Report," he said crisply to Staszek.

The young man stood stiff at attention. "One of my men just returned from Drahim, near the Pomeranian border. A huge division of Swedish troops arrived there last night and was already on the move toward Pila this morning. These are the same reinforcements that were spotted by Hamid-Bey's scouts. The army is carrying heavy artillery and huge cannons, the likes of which I have never seen before."

Stefan paced back and forth in the tent, his hands clasped tightly behind his back. No one said a word, and a heavy silence fell over them. Finally, Stefan stopped and turned to face them.

"If they are pulling heavy artillery, it means they will not be able to move quickly. We must focus our attack on destroying those cannons." He didn't have to say aloud the thought on every man's mind.

If even one of those cannons breaks through our lines, Warsaw will be vulnerable to siege and destruction. It could be the end of us . . . of Poland.

Stefan thought of Hanna, and his stomach suddenly tightened in a knot.

"Send a messenger to Warsaw, warning the king of the danger," he ordered Staszek. "Then bring me the maps. We must decide how best to defend our position, given the new Swedish reinforcements."

Staszek saluted smartly and immediately left the tent to comply with Stefan's orders. As soon as he was gone, Stefan resumed his pacing, running his fingers through his hair. Not a single one of his men moved, no one daring to break their commander's concentration.

Stefan was deep in thought when Staszek returned with the maps. Ordering his officers to sit at the table, he began to plan their strategy.

Hours later, Staszek galloped off to the nearest post to pass on the new orders to the other Polish commanders. Later, in the early hours of the morning, an unexpected messenger arrived at the camp. Exhausted, the young soldier slid off his horse and handed Stefan a sealed parchment. Stefan broke the seal, unrolling the parchment on his table while smoothing out the curled edges.

"What does it say?" Mikhail asked curiously.

Stefan straightened wearily on the stool. "Field Hetman Edmund Karwicki has obviously not yet received our latest reports on the Swedes. He asks us to hold their forces at Pila for at least three more days."

"Three days? Good God, man, we'll barely be able to hold them off until tomorrow," Alexander protested.

Stefan's face hardened. "We'll give the Hetman what he wants and more. We'll hold the Swedes where they are if it takes our last man."

Alexander straightened and gave Stefan a crisp salute. "Aye, sir," he said sharply.

Stefan smiled tiredly and patted his friend on the shoulder. "Come, Alex, we have much work to do."

Wearily, the men poured over the maps, plotting their tactics and strategy.

The following days at Pila were filled with battle cries echoing throughout the valley, the thunder of horses' hooves, and the screams and shouts of men in torment and triumph.

Colonel Stefan Tarnowski's defense of Pila lasted a miraculous seven days. But at dawn on the eighth day the Swedish army broke through the lines, scattering the courageous Polish soldiers throughout the countryside.

Soon, the Swedish troops were on the march toward Warsaw.

Chapter Thirteen

It was nearly midnight when Boguslaw roused Hanna from a troubled sleep.

"Hurry, milady," he said, urging her to get dressed. "I have been informed that a detail of Swedish soldiers is on the way here."

There had been intermittent reports for days about the fighting around Warsaw. Most of the news was grim; the huge guns and cannons of the Swedish forces were systematically destroying the outer defenses of the city. It had been said that King Yan Casimir had already fled Warsaw, presumably to Krakow, to beg for foreign help. No one had heard a word from Stefan or any of the men from his regiment since the Swedish army had broken through the lines at Pila.

Hanna scrambled anxiously from the bed, grabbing for one of her gowns. Much to her surprise, Boguslaw snatched the dress from her hands and shoved a black tunic and breeches into her arms.

"Wear these," he instructed.

Hanna looked at the clothes dumbfounded. "What?" she whispered in horror.

Boguslaw strode to the door. "Please, milady, just do as I say. It is necessary."

Impatiently, he stood outside her room, waiting for her to dress. A few minutes passed before Hanna opened the door. The tunic fell to her knees and she had rolled the legs of the breeches up around her ankles. She held the waist of her pants up with one hand.

Boguslaw nearly laughed, she looked so adorable. Then, remembering their precarious situation, he sobered, drawing a piece of rope from his sack and handing it to her.

"Tie it around your waist," he ordered.

Hanna doubled the shirt over and then tied the rope about her waist, securing the breeches and the shirt. She then looked down at her bare feet and wrinkled her nose when Boguslaw handed her some stockings and a pair of old boy's boots.

"How did I know you were going to give me these?" she said wryly, sitting on the edge of the bed and pulling them on. They were far too big for her feet and she pulled them off and looked at him questioningly.

Boguslaw took a moment to evaluate the situation. Then, pulling her to her feet, he quickly untied the rope from her waist and cut off the bottom of her shirt. Hanna clutched at the breeches to keep them from falling.

Boguslaw took the sheared cloth and stuffed it into the toes of the boots as Hanna quickly retied the rope around her waist. This time when she put her feet into the boots, the fit was bearable. Then he handed her a greasy cap and told her to push her hair up into it. Hanna wrinkled her nose at the dirty hat but pulled it on her head, stuffing her hair inside as ordered.

Boguslaw evaluated her appearance. She might be able to pass as a boy, if it was dark enough. She was still too pretty and shapely, but it would have to do for the time being. Sighing, he reached out and pulled the cap down over her forehead.

"Come on, milady, we must go," he said, leading her down the hallway.

"Wait," Hanna said, turning and running back to the

bedroom where she grabbed the dagger from her bedside table. She ripped off a piece of her bedding and wrapped the dagger in it before placing it carefully in her boot. The heavy weight of the weapon felt oddly reassuring. "At least I won't be completely defenseless," she whispered to herself as she hurried back to Boguslaw.

Hanna could hear doors slamming, muted voices and the rushing feet of the servants as the castle began to come alive. Grabbing her elbow firmly, Boguslaw led her towards the garden. They were nearly at the door when two women raced past them, one of them bumping into Hanna's right shoulder. Whirling around, Hanna looked squarely into the face of the young serving girl, Dorota. The girl did not recognize Hanna in her boy's disguise and simply mumbled a hurried apology and rushed on her way.

"Where are we going?" Hanna whispered anxiously as Boguslaw directed her out into the garden and towards the castle wall.

"Over the wall," he said, taking a scaling rope from the pack he had fastened over his shoulder. With a swift throw, he tossed it over the wall, pulling the rope slowly until the metal hooks caught and held on the rough surface. He tugged on it several times until he was satisfied it was secure.

"Haven't you ever heard of a gate?" Hanna asked, laughing weakly.

"It is not safe, milady. Come now, climb on my back," he ordered her, firmly taking the rope between his hands.

Hanna's mouth dropped open. "W-what?" she asked in astonishment.

The noise from outside the castle walls was growing louder. Hanna could hear the clash of metal and the thunder of distant hoofbeats.

"Do as I say. Please, milady," Boguslaw urged, his huge hand reaching out to grip hers tightly. "Stefan has trusted me with your life. I would never hurt you."

Hanna squeezed the giant's hand. "I believe you," she said quietly, and climbed onto his back.

With a loud grunt, Boguslaw began the tedious climb to the top of the wall. Hanna held tightly to his shoulders, wondering with each passing moment whether the rope would be strong enough to hold them.

It seemed like hours until they reached the top of the wall. Hanna breathed a sigh of relief as Boguslaw readjusted the hook. Their descent down the other side was quick and easy.

Outside the castle wall, Boguslaw hastily led Hanna into the dark forest. She stumbled several times in the darkness, but Boguslaw steadied her, walking with a sure foot. Before long, they reached a clearing, and in the dim moonlight Hanna saw two horses. As they approached the animals, one of the horses gave a nervous whinny. Reaching out, Hanna soothingly stroked the velvety soft nose.

"Mounts for us?" Hanna asked quietly.

She heard Boguslaw grunt an answer as he attempted to fasten his pack to one of the horses. He must have been planning their escape for days, she thought.

Slowly, she looked about the clearing, wondering how far from the castle they actually were. Not too far, she decided, judging from the still audible sounds of the battle.

"Up you go, milady," Boguslaw said, suddenly lifting Hanna from the ground and placing her with a plop into the saddle. Her cap slid to her nose, and impatiently, she pushed it back. Boguslaw quickly mounted the horse and then looked back at her with a worried expression.

"You can ride, can't you?"

Hanna nodded. "Aye, of course I can."

Boguslaw sighed with relief. "Good, because I'm not sure how long one mount would last with two of us riding her. Keep close behind me on the trail." With a low cluck he urged his horse forward.

Hanna dutifully followed, wondering just what trail he was talking about. All she could see from the dim light of the moon was heavy undergrowth . . . nothing resembling a path of any kind. Thankfully, her mount thought differently; it was able to carefully pick its way through the dense forest. Hanna concentrated on avoiding the sharp and clutching branches that tore at her face and clothes.

They had been riding a scant ten minutes when the forest was filled with a loud, crashing noise and the sound of distant voices. Muttering a soft curse, Boguslaw slid off his mount, quickly grabbing her reins.

"Get down," he urged, and she scrambled to obey his orders. Quickly, he led the horses behind a big tree near the edge of a clearing and fastened a cloth around their nuzzles to keep them quiet.

"You are my deaf and mute cousin," Boguslaw said, putting his mouth close to her ear. "Keep your head down and don't answer no matter what anyone says to you."

Hanna nodded, her mouth suddenly dry. She stood close to Boguslaw, her heart hammering loudly in her chest. The giant suddenly bent over, scooping some dirt into his hands. Before Hanna could open her mouth in protest, he had smeared a liberal amount of it on her face. Then he reached up and pulled the cap as far down over her face as possible.

"Shh," he suddenly urged her. "Here they come."

Hanna watched in fascination as several soldiers came into view, crashing heavily through the forest and into the clearing. Hanna held her breath, hoping the men would pass by them in the darkness.

One of the soldiers' chargers whinnied and reared, catching the scent of the other horses, and Hanna heard Boguslaw curse softly again.

"Who is there?" Hanna heard a heavily accented voice call out in Polish. A Swedish soldier, no doubt, she thought.

Neither she nor Boguslaw moved a muscle, but the man's horse reared its forelegs again, and the soldier slid off his mount with a muttered oath.

"Komma här," the man shouted in Swedish to his companions. Alerted by his cry, several soldiers rode through the brush.

"Vad?" asked one soldier, wearing the markings of an officer.

"Something or someone is here. My horse smells them."

The officer dismounted slowly. "Who is there?" he called out in Polish, motioning with his hand for his men to spread out.

Hanna felt Boguslaw stiffen, and then suddenly he moved forward. "Don't hurt us; we are simple people," she heard the giant say in a Polish country dialect. She watched in horrified amazement as Boguslaw shuffled forward, his tall form slumped, his head hanging low.

The Swedish officer's eyes narrowed in contempt. "Ah, it is just a filthy peasant. How many more of you are there?"

Boguslaw kept his eyes carefully averted. "Just my cousin, sir. A deaf and dumb lad, he is. Isn't worth much except that he fetches a fair bit when he begs."

Turning, Boguslaw walked to the tree where Hanna stood and pulled her out by the arm. She kept her head down and prayed the cap covered her face.

The Swede snickered and walked up to inspect her. "*Avskum*," he muttered under his breath. "Polish peasant scum."

Hanna felt her anger rise but kept her eyes studiously fastened on the top of his boots. Soon the other soldiers returned from their sweep of the area. "No others, sir. Just two mounts," one of them reported crisply. "He appears to be telling the truth."

The officer nodded and looked at Hanna thoughtfully. "Deaf and dumb, are you?" he muttered quietly. Suddenly, he grabbed her arm, his fingers pressing deep into her flesh. Caught by surprise, Hanna nearly yelled. Biting her lower lip, she struggled to suppress a cry of agony.

From the corner of her eyes, she saw Boguslaw tense, his hand hovering perilously near the sword he had hidden beneath his light cloak. By this time, more soldiers had arrived; there were five in all, she counted. They were clearly enjoying watching their officer torment the peasants. If she cried out now, the soldiers would be upon them without hesitation.

Closing her eyes, Hanna summoned the strength to bear the pain. When she thought she could not last another moment the officer suddenly released her and stepped back.

"Be gone, you worthless parasites," he said, his voice full of disgust. "And be aware that your new king is His Majesty Charles Gustav the Tenth."

Boguslaw bowed in what he hoped was fitting humility and turned to take Hanna by the elbow. Before they had taken two steps a horse came charging through the brush, skidding to a halt beside Boguslaw. Looking up, Hanna was unable to control a gasp of surprise as she saw it was Tomek.

"This man is no peasant," Tomek announced to the Swedish soldiers, vaulting out of the saddle. "He is one of Stefan Tarnowski's men. And that is no peasant lad. I'll bet a gold ducat that she is the betrothed of Lord Jozef Czarnowski, friend of the Swedish empire and the girl you are looking for."

Tomek reached out and yanked the cap off Hanna's head. Her fiery red mane tumbled free and fell in a tangled mass about her shoulders.

There was a startled gasp from the soldiers. Tomek rubbed his hands together, laughing gleefully at the expression on their faces. Siding with Jozef Czarnowski and the Swedes had been the best decision he had ever made. It had cost him so little to switch his loyalty, and it had gained him a fortune.

"You bastard," Boguslaw growled.

Tomek smiled, delighted by the look of sheer fury on Boguslaw's face. "Come now, my dear man, let's accept defeat gracefully."

Boguslaw spat on the ground. "You were the traitor among us, you whoreson. You knew all along I would try to escape with the girl. It was you who sent these soldiers out here looking for us."

"Aye, quite true, but I never guessed you'd dress the

girl as a lad. It was most fortunate that I came along when I did. Quite clever, Dobrowolski; aye, quite clever indeed."

"Filthy traitor," Boguslaw hissed. "You betrayed your lord for nothing but a few gold coins."

Tomek snorted. "A *few* gold coins? By God, man, have you really no idea how much Czarnowski is willing to pay for her? This lovely young woman here has made me a very, very rich man." Abruptly, Tomek reached out and grabbed a handful of Hanna's hair.

"You see, I had red gold right at my fingertips all along." He threw back his head and laughed.

It was the last sound Tomek ever made. The fact that he dared to touch Hanna sealed his fate. With a low growl of rage, Boguslaw drew his sword from beneath his cloak and slashed it across Tomek's neck. For an instant, Hanna saw a look of surprise flick over Tomek's face as he realized what had happened. Then he fell heavily to the ground and lay silent. Hanna stiffled a scream against the back of her hand and turned away to shut out the grisly sight.

Stunned at the ferocity of the act, the soldiers simply watched, mouths agape. Before they had regained their senses enough to move, Boguslaw had roughly drawn Hanna behind him, holding out his sword in a silent challenge.

At that moment, two more Swedish soldiers rode up. The taller one dismounted and demanded to know what was going on.

"He is one of Tarnowski's men, Captain," the young officer explained nervously, pointing at Buguslaw. "And that woman was abducted from another Polish nobleman, apparently a friend of His Majesty Charles Gustav."

The Swedish captain thoughtfully fingered his curled blond wig while letting his eyes sweep over the woman, who was clearly a beauty despite her ridiculous costume. The fierce way she met his eyes in rebellious defiance suddenly caused his manhood to leap into a painful erection.

"What is your name, girl?" the captain asked in perfect Polish.

She glared back at him without answering. The captain sighed. "You'll have to answer me one way or the other. I don't wish to harm you."

Hanna shook her head and pressed closer to the colossal man, who looked ready to tear the captain's head off if he moved any nearer. The Swede's eyes narrowed. The man was clearly dangerous; he looked capable of taking down several of his men single-handedly.

"And who is that?" the captain asked quietly, pointing at the dead man.

"One of our Polish informants, sir."

The captain wrinkled his nose at the bloody sight. "A pity, I suppose." He turned his gaze back to the girl. "Just who does she belong to?" he asked the young officer.

"A nobleman by the name of Jozef Czarnowski, sir."

The captain felt a stab of disappointment. He had met Jozef Czarnowski many times during his tour of duty in Warsaw. It was a damn shame the girl belonged to the Pole; he would have very much liked to have kept this delicious little morsel for himself. Perhaps there was a way he could convince Czarnowski to release this beauty into his custody. It would certainly be worth his while to try. But until then, he thought grimly, he would have to see that the girl remained untouched. Sighing inwardly, he forced his thoughts back to the matter at hand. He looked directly at Buguslaw.

"What shall we do about this one?"

The giant growled a warning deep in his throat, and the officer took a step backward, in spite of himself. A heavy silence fell over the group as the captain and Boguslaw silently appraised each other.

Their concentration was suddenly broken as another horse charged into the clearing. Slowly, the man slid off his horse, his dark cloak swirling about him. Hanna's breath died in her throat as she saw who it was.

"Mary, Mother of God," she breathed softly and felt Boguslaw tense beside her.

Jozef Czarnowski was dressed entirely in black except for a striking gold sash that had been tied around his middle and held his sword. His long dark hair had been combed back and tied at his nape. His eyes fell upon Hanna and his face twisted into a cold sneer of triumph.

"Hanna, my sweet, I'm so glad you are safe," he said, his voice dripping with concern. "Come to me at once."

Hanna felt her legs begin to tremble and wondered if she might faint from sheer terror. *Nay, I must not distract Boguslaw. God help me, but Boguslaw is all that stands between me and that madman.* Taking a deep breath, she raised her head and stared defiantly back at Jozef.

The Swedish officer let his gaze flick slowly between Jozef and the girl. After several moments he turned to the Polish nobleman. "I understand she belongs to you," he said, his voice tinged with no small amount of regret.

Jozef nodded, his eyes never leaving Hanna's face. "Aye. She is mine."

The possessive note in Jozef's voice made Hanna's heart thud painfully in her chest. She had never been so afraid in all her life.

The captain lightly cleared his throat. "And what about him?" he asked, turning his gaze on the girl's protector.

A slow smile curved across Jozef's face. "Kill him. But do not harm the girl."

"Nay," Hanna screamed.

Boguslaw's jaw clenched, and then he took a deep breath. "Come and take her from me, Czarnowski," he challenged.

"I would not waste the effort on one as worthless as you," Jozef said with a harsh laugh.

Boguslaw snorted. "Coward."

Jozef's jaw tensed in anger. Abruptly, he snapped his fingers at the soldiers still sitting on their horses. "Kill him now," he ordered sharply.

The soldiers looked to their commander, who nodded slowly, confirming the order. Hesitantly, one of the men moved forward, and Boguslaw smiled at him, his grin intensifying the grotesque scar that ran down the side of his face.

Hanna clenched her hands so tightly, the blood drained from them. Silently, she said a prayer and then crossed herself.

Suddenly, Hanna saw the Swedish captain make a slight gesture with his hand, and one of the men charged his horse forward, thrusting his sword at Boguslaw. The giant easily deflected the sharp blade and forced his attacker off his horse with a loud cry. Abruptly, two others pressed forward, slashing at him.

Hanna stayed as close to Boguslaw as possible, careful not to let herself get separated from him. She knew the soldiers would be careful not to hurt her, so she remained slightly behind him, protecting him from the rear. Gritting her teeth, she noticed that Jozef stayed clear of the fighting, never once drawing his sword.

As the fighting continued and Boguslaw was not yet disarmed, Jozef's face flushed with rage. "Damn it, kill the bastard," he shouted furiously. "What in God's name is taking so long?"

Hanna felt her disgust for Jozef deepen while her respect for Boguslaw's swordsmanship grew. He deflected thrust after thrust, fighting three men at once. His movements became a blur, and Hanna wondered how much longer he could last. She felt exhausted just trying to stay close to him without getting in his way.

The fighting continued until Hanna thought the sword fight had become part of a dream. Her limbs seemed weighted down, and she was so tired she wasn't sure if she could keep moving. Yet she forced herself to maintain her position behind Boguslaw. After what seemed like hours there was a sudden pause in the fighting, and Hanna looked over Boguslaw's shoulder and saw three men dead at his feet. Moving back, her mouth opened in a silent scream.

She was jolted back to reality as Boguslaw put his hand on her shoulder. She looked up fearfully at the giant. His breathing was heavy and erratic and a strange gleam shone in his eyes. Dazed, Hanna realized that it was the look of a man fighting for his life.

Inhaling deeply to calm herself, Hanna quickly assessed Boguslaw's condition. His clothes were slashed in several places and blood dripped from a deep wound in his sword arm. Her eyes fell upon the remaining Swedish soldiers, who were regrouping for another attack. Jozef and the captain were exchanging some hasty words. Suddenly, she realized that Boguslaw would never be able to hold off the rest of the men. He would die trying to save her . . . unless she did something to prevent it.

Hanna looked once more at the giant's arm and then made a decision. Reaching down, she carefully took the sword of one of the dead men into her hand.

"Now there are two of us armed," she said quietly, while Boguslaw looked at her in utter amazement.

"Milady . . ." he started, his voice hoarse with protest, but she cut him off with a wave of her arm.

"I warn you that I know how to use a sword," she told the soldiers. "I will not allow myself to be taken without a fight. If you try to take me by force, you will have to hurt me."

A startled silence fell over the group as they looked at each other in surprise. Suddenly, Jozef threw back his head and howled, a cry filled with rage and fury. The Swedish soldiers looked at him in confusion and fear.

"Not one hair on her head is to be harmed," Jozef shouted, his face an angry snarl.

Hanna raised her sword at him. "Then let him go," she said, motioning with her head to Boguslaw, "and I will come with you peacefully."

She heard Boguslaw's gasp of outrage. "What?" he shouted hoarsely. "You dare suggest that I cannot protect you, milady?"

Hanna sighed. "I'm suggesting nothing of the sort." She stepped closer to him, her voice low. "What I am suggesting is that we outfox these soldiers. Someone must find Stefan and tell him what has happened."

Boguslaw looked at her as if she had gone completely

and utterly daft. "You are sorely mistaken if you think I will leave you here, milady."

Hanna frowned deeply, wondering how she could convince the giant to leave her side. "It is your duty to protect me, is it not?" she finally asked, her voice no more than a whisper. Boguslaw nodded slowly. "Then you must not die here or no one will know what has become of me. Please, I beg of you, find Stefan and tell him what has happened. It will not serve either of us if you perish. If you are vanquished, I have no hope. But if you escape, I may nurture the hope that you or someone else will come for me someday. I need that hope to live. Please, Boguslaw, do as I ask."

Boguslaw's face twisted with pain as he pulled a cloth from his pocket and pressed it to his bleeding wound. "Nay. I cannot do it. God help me, milady, but I refuse to leave you here in the clutches of that disgusting traitor."

Hanna felt a surge of desperation sweep over her. "In God's name, Boguslaw, I beseech you. Please. He will not harm me."

Boguslaw's mind raged with anger, fear, and helplessness. She was right. If he died here, it could be months before Stefan ever found out what had happened to her. *That is, if Stefan is still alive,* he thought wryly. And yet if Stefan was alive, he would be on his way to Warsaw. And Boguslaw knew which path Stefan would take.

Boguslaw's face contorted as a spasm of pain wracked his body. His arm was badly hurt, and it was clear that he would not be able to fight off the rest of the men. She was probably right. He would die if he stayed. Yet he did not fear death, only failure. And if he did not get help, he would fail in his duty to protect Hanna.

Aye, your duty is to protect her in whatever way necessary. She is right. Dying will not help her. You must escape and get help.

Boguslaw swallowed hard, forcing the words from his mouth. "I shall do your bidding . . . milady." Each word sounded as if it had been wrung from him.

Hanna closed her eyes in relief and took a shaky breath.

"Thank you, Boguslaw. I know it is a difficult decision. But it is the right one."

Slowly, she turned to Jozef. "He will leave," she shouted, her sword still raised. "But I will not lower my sword until I am sure he has had ample time to escape."

Jozef narrowed his eyes until they were tiny slits. "Hanna, I urge you to put down the sword now and end this foolishness. Why do you fight me?"

She ignored his question. "Go," she hissed at Boguslaw. "And godspeed."

The giant looked at her for a long moment. "As God is my witness, I promise you, milady, I will be back with others."

His expression was so solemn that Hanna's heart went out to him. Being asked to leave in the middle of a battle was probably one of the hardest things she could ever have asked of him.

She held her breath as Boguslaw turned and disappeared into the forest on foot. A soldier abruptly began to follow when she turned the blade on herself. "I am in earnest, Jozef. If they follow him, I'll kill myself."

Jozef waved for the soldier to stop. "Hanna," he said gently, moving toward her. "There is no need to be afraid of me. I would never hurt you. You need not protect the life of a worthless man. Besides, he answers to Stefan Tarnowski, the man who ruthlessly abducted you on our wedding day."

Hanna shook her head. "You are wrong, Jozef. Stefan Tarnowski saved me from you. He told me what you did to his sister."

A dark flush spread across Jozef's face as he made another move toward her. "He has poisoned your mind against me. Now I see why you resisted my attempts to rescue you. Give me the sword, Hanna. I will explain everything to you."

She pressed the blade against her abdomen. "Don't come another step closer or I will harm myself. I swear it."

Sighing, Jozef took a handkerchief from his pocket,

delicately mopping his brow. "You are behaving foolishly, Hanna. Now put down the sword immediately and let's go home."

He held out his hand, but Hanna shook her head. Jozef muttered a curse as the handkerchief slid from his hand and fluttered to the ground. Slowly, he bent down to pick it up. Hanna watched him warily, keeping the blade pressed firmly against her stomach. Too late, she saw Jozef make a quick movement with his hand and realized that he had thrown a handful of dirt at her eyes.

Momentarily blinded, Hanna stumbled. Jozef reached out and knocked the sword from her hand. Heavily, he lunged for her, hurling both of them to the ground.

"Get the other one," Jozef shouted at the soldiers as he rolled on top of her. The men thundered off to do his bidding.

"Nay," Hanna cried, beating her hands across Jozef's chest. His body was so heavy, she could breathe only in small gasps.

Jozef was surprised by her strength and determination to fight him. He ground his weight against her, breathless from the fierce desire that suddenly coursed through his veins as she struggled beneath him. God, she was beautiful in spite of her peasant costume and the dirt smeared on her face. *And she was his. She was finally his again!* He longed to force his throbbing manhood into her at that very moment, to claim finally what was rightfully his. His fingers tightened on her arm, but with excruciating effort he forced himself to restraint.

Patience, patience, he urged himself. She was no common serving wench. Hanna Quinn would be his bride, and he would not take her like a rutting animal on the forest floor. He had to be careful, very careful, or all of his painstakingly laid plans could go awry.

Allowing himself one harsh kiss, he finally rose, dragging her up with him. She fought him like a wildcat, kicking and screaming. Jozef smiled at her effort, hoping she would act with the same ferocity in bed.

"Cease your struggles, Hanna," he warned, pulling her

toward the Swedish officer who looked on amusedly.

"I don't think she likes you much," the captain observed dryly.

Jozef laughed, but there was no humor in his voice. "Oh, she likes me, all right. She just has an odd way of showing it."

Hanna kicked him hard in the shins, and Jozef gripped her arm painfully in retaliation. Dragging her to his horse, he pulled a coil of rope from the saddle. Quickly, he trussed her hands and legs and left her near a tree. Hanna struggled fiercely with her bonds but in vain; Jozef had tied them tightly, leaving nothing to chance. Frustrated and near tears, she continued struggling until her skin was raw and bleeding.

Finally, she stopped and leaned back against the tree to catch her breath. She prayed with all her might that Boguslaw had made a safe escape. She knew that with each passing moment, he had a better chance of remaining at liberty.

Minutes passed, and Jozef's mood became foul. He quarreled loudly with the Swedish captain and then came over to sit beside Hanna. He took a strand of her hair between his fingers.

"They'll find him, Hanna," he said quietly.

She shook her head stubbornly. "They will not."

A brief frown flitted across his face though he smiled at her indulgently. "Did you miss me, sweet?"

She shuddered at the mere thought of it. "Nay."

"I missed you."

She turned her head away in disgust. "It is unlikely you had the time to do so. You were too busy welcoming the enemy to Poland."

Jozef leaned close to her until his face was inches from her own. "Why must you see the Swedes as enemies? There are many Poles like me who believe we could not resist the Swedish forces."

Hanna raised her chin. "So you welcomed them? Turned your back on the country of your birth in order to save yourself and your property?"

He traced a finger along her cheekbone. Hanna flinched and turned away. "The Swedes have a powerful and well-organized army. Much better and stronger than ours. We could not have withstood their forces."

"You sound as if you admire them."

"I do. I won't hide the fact that I value strength and power above all else. There are many like me who saw an advantage in siding with the Swedes. If they are to conquer us anyway, why not join them? Our privileges will remain intact and perhaps even be expanded."

Hanna stiffened. "Have you no honor? You speak treason."

"There are some who would call it common sense. King Gustav has promised not to tax us or house any of his soldiers on the estates of those noblemen willing to welcome him. It was to my great advantage that Stefan Tarnowski did not share my sentiments."

Hanna deliberately yanked her face from his fingers. "Thank God he does not share your sense of honor. Stefan Tarnowski acts with genuine concern, courage and a love for his country. You . . . you behave without a shred of virtue, decency or courage."

A fog of rage began to build up inside Jozef. Involuntarily, his fingers slid around her throat. "You will respect me, Hanna. You will; I swear it."

Hanna struggled for air as his fingers tightened around her neck. "S-stop," she whispered, the words coming out as a choking plea. He ignored her, his fingers pressing into her flesh.

When Hanna was near fainting she felt him release her neck. He took a deep breath before bending down to put his face close to hers. "I will not let you get away from me again, *moja różyczko*. You are mine, for now and for eternity. I own you and your soul, Hanna. Don't you ever forget it."

With a weak cry, she turned from him, gulping deep breaths of air. Deliberately, he leaned over, pushing a tendril of her hair from her forehead, and placed a cold kiss on each of her eyelids.

Hanna shuddered. "Why are you doing this?" she whispered fearfully. "Why do you torment me so?"

He cupped her face in his hands. "Because we were meant to be together. It was always meant to be for us."

The bile rose in her throat and she swallowed hard. Jozef's desire was so strange and twisted, she wondered if she possessed the strength to fight it. Nausea churned in the pit of her stomach, and she was sure that she would either retch or faint. Drawing on her inner strength, she forced herself to look him directly in the eye.

"I will never be yours," she said with a firmness she did not feel.

She saw a smile cross Jozef's face, but it did not touch the cold depths of his eyes.

"You are wrong, Hanna. You have belonged to me for a long, long time."

A finger of dread wrapped around Hanna's heart at his words. Jozef Czarnowski was mad, demented and cruel. But now, more than ever, she feared that he might be right.

Chapter Fourteen

Two hours later, Hanna shifted restlessly beneath the tree, the bonds cutting off her circulation, her throat aching with a parching thirst. Minutes earlier she had watched as several of the Swedish soldiers returned from their hunt and gathered around their captain, listening to them as he and Jozef spoke quietly. Her stomach clenched with fear. *Had they captured or killed Boguslaw?*

She wet her cracked lips with her tongue while struggling to loosen her bonds. She felt them give a little when Jozef looked over and met her eyes. Patting the captain on the back, he said something to the Swedish officer, and the officer abruptly gave a signal for his men to mount.

Jozef walked over to Hanna and pulled her to her feet. "It is time to go home now, sweet," he said softly.

She turned her face away from him as he bent down and cut the bonds from her hands and feet. Gritting her teeth against the pain, Hanna grimaced as the blood charged back into her stiff hands and fingers. Seeing her discomfort, Jozef lifted her onto his horse and then climbed on himself. Grabbing the reins with one hand, he slapped them against the rump of the horse, urging it forward. The Swedish soldiers moved in behind him. The group traveled in silence through the heavy brush until they came to a well-worn path.

They passed several Swedish patrols along the way, many of them staring openly at Hanna. Twice, she saw Polish peasants being beaten by Swedish soldiers, and the rising smoke from the countryside indicated that the soldiers were burning their villages as well.

Hanna felt a lump in her throat at the injustice. Who were these people who came from across the sea to wipe out a culture as rich and beautiful as Poland's?

Stefan's words suddenly rang in her ears. *"Poland's lands are her most impressive treasure and yet her greatest weakness. Everyone wishes to possess such fertile land for his own."*

God help her, every bone in her body told her this was wrong and the Swedes had to be stopped. Poland was her adopted home now, as it had once been her mother's. By birth she was half-Polish, and this invasion was a violation of her right to learn about Poland's rich history and culture.

Hanna breathed deeply to calm herself. "May I have some water?" she asked Jozef.

He reached down and pulled a flask from the leather pack attached to the saddle. Slowly, he pulled the cork and handed it to her.

She accepted the flask, ignoring the deliberate brush of his fingers against her hand. Drinking hungrily, she let the water soothe her parched throat. Almost reluctantly, she handed the canteen back to him.

"I like when you ask things of me, Hanna," Jozef said softly. "You should know that you may have whatever you want."

Her lips thinned to hide her revulsion. "Then I wish," she said slowly, "to know what happened to the man who fought for me back in the forest."

She felt Jozef stiffen. "He's dead," he said flatly.

Hanna's heart paused in her chest. "Dead?" she managed to whisper.

"Dead, Hanna," Jozef repeated sharply. "You may forget about ever trying to leave me."

All color drained from Hanna's face. *Boguslaw dead?* For a moment, she couldn't breathe. Then a sob escaped her lips as the tears began to roll down her cheeks.

"Hanna," Jozef said, softly stroking her hair. "Why grieve for such a meaningless man?"

"I hate you," she whispered between her tears.

He laughed. "Ah, there is so little distance between love and hate. Your words only please me, my dear."

Hanna squeezed her eyes tighter as the tears continued to roll down her face. Perhaps she should have had the courage to press the blade into her stomach and end the nightmare. Yet a small part of her mind rebelled against that thought. Life was too precious to waste. She had been placed on this earth for a purpose, and she would serve it to the best of her abilities. Deep in her heart she just couldn't believe that God would give her a destiny too painful for her to handle. Aye, she had to believe it. Her faith would have to keep her going because she had nothing else left.

"You must accept your burden and carry your cross without complaint, as Jesus did." The words of Father Leszek rang in her ears.

"Then what is my purpose?" Hanna whispered, unaware that she had spoken aloud. When no answer leapt to mind she felt a profound despair sweep over her.

Jozef heard her words, and his mouth curved into a deep smile of satisfaction. "Your purpose is with me, my sweet," he whispered back softly. "Our destinies were made to be as one."

It was midday when they arrived at the Czarnowski estate. Her heart sank as the gate of the castle shut behind them with a loud, creaking slam. Jozef dismounted and reached up to pull her off the horse. Every muscle in her body ached with fatigue and a bone-deep weariness.

She was led to the room where she had stayed upon her arrival in Poland, the wardrobe still full of her gowns and shoes. She ran her fingers across the soft material, which no longer seemed to belong to her.

"I felt more comfortable in your dresses, Danuta," she said aloud, and then stopped abruptly.

Danuta Tarnowska. The name suddenly brought back a haunting reminder of the unspeakable crime Jozef had committed against her. "My God," Hanna whispered softly. "What am I to do?"

She was distracted from her thoughts by a sharp knock on the door. Opening it, she was startled as two menservants dragged in a tub of steaming hot water.

"A bath for you, milady," one of them said before making a hasty exit.

Hanna walked over to the tub and dipped her fingers into the steaming water. She sighed with pleasure as her fingers trailed lightly across the silky wetness. It seemed like ages since she had washed.

"The devil take Jozef Czarnowski," she muttered to herself. "I am going to have a bath."

Without another thought, she stripped and sank down into the soothing warmth. She stretched her sore and aching muscles as the water lapped about her shoulders. Gladly, she submerged her head beneath the water to cleanse the dirt and grime from it. The servants had left a rough cake of soap for her, and she rubbed it across her skin as if it could erase the memory of Jozef's hands upon her.

Hanna stayed in the bath until the water began to chill. Finally, she emerged from the tub, drying herself with the cloth that had been left for her. On her way to the fireplace she tripped over her boots and was startled to hear a clunk. Swiftly reaching down into the boot, she felt the heavy weight of her dagger.

"Jezus Maria," she whispered with excitement. In the midst of all the danger, she had completely forgotten about her dagger.

Quickly, she pulled a sleeping gown over her head and thrust her hands into a heavy robe. She placed the dagger into the deepest pocket of her robe and let her fingers press the hardness against her leg.

"I shall keep it upon my person at all times," she promised herself aloud, and then sat beside the fire, running her fingers through her hair to help it dry.

Slowly, her thoughts wandered to those people whose lives had been ruined by Jozef Czarnowski. *Danuta, Boguslaw, Tomek.* How many more people would have to die because of Jozef's vile existence? She felt the tears prick her eyes at the thought of Boguslaw. All her efforts to save him had been in vain.

She brushed a tear from her cheek. And what of Stefan? Was he still alive after the battle of Pila? She pressed her fingers to her temples, her throat tightening with emotion. She was wrong to think of him now, as if she really believed that he might come for her.

You are alone, Hanna Quinn. As alone as you have ever been in your life.

Restless, she stood and walked to the window. Lifting the heavy drapery aside, she gazed out into the darkness. It was not yet winter, so there were no heavy skins protecting the window, and she could feel the soft touch of the evening breeze on her face. It was a clear night; the stars burnt brightly in the dark sky.

She had to face the truth: There was little hope of escape now, especially since Swedish patrols were sweeping the city. Yet she would have to try. Her first priority would be to plot an escape that had some chance of success. And to do that, she had to learn the layout of the castle and the habits of the Swedish patrols. Soon afterward, she would make her escape. She would not live a moment longer than necessary under the same roof as Jozef Czarnowski. Her mind made up, she leaned farther out the window and breathed deeply of the cool evening air.

You are alone ... alone ... alone. The words echoed relentlessly in her mind. An eerie cry from a night owl startled her from her thoughts. Hanna looked out at the moon, shrouded in the smoky mist of the evening sky.

Are you alive, Stefan Tarnowski? Her heart ached with longing to know the answer.

"I don't care," she whispered fiercely.

But it was not true and she knew it.

Chapter Fifteen

Boguslaw Dobrowolski was on the run. Once out of sight from the Swedish soldiers, the advantage was his. *They were in his woods.* He had spent his entire life roaming this forest, and he knew it inside and out. And he had the additional advantage of darkness. The soldiers would have to hunt to find him, and he didn't plan on making it easy. They would have to be lucky. Damn lucky.

"Psia krew," he cursed softly as his wounded arm brushed against a sharp branch. Reaching out, he braced himself against the trunk of a tree with his good arm to steady himself. He took several deep breaths until the pain passed. Curse it, if anything would give him away it would be the wretched wound. Tearing what was left of his shirt, he wrapped it tightly around his upper arm, grimacing as he tied it firmly. Beads of sweat formed on his upper lip, but he clamped his teeth together until he was satisfied that the bleeding had stopped.

"All right, let's move," he muttered to himself, slipping further into the woods. The branches scratched at him relentlessly, but he stolidly ignored them, refusing to slow his pace. He had to put as much distance between himself and the Swedish soldiers as quickly as possible.

After several minutes his arm began to throb horribly. He had paused for a scant moment when he heard a crashing in the bushes and some muffled voices. Quickly, he ducked behind a nearby tree. He stood motionless until the voices moved away from him.

The Swedish soldiers were already searching for him. It meant that Hanna had not been able to hold them off for long. *But it was long enough, God bless her soul. I will see my message delivered, if it is the last thing I ever do. And by God, it just might be.*

He allowed himself a few precious moments to peer through the branches and to check the stars to chart his course. Once sure of his direction, he moved quickly among the trees, keeping a careful watch to make sure he did not leave a trail. Only once more did the soldiers come close to his position, but he stood motionless, concealed in thick undergrowth. They passed within meters of him.

When he was sure they were gone he continued his journey with slow, dogged steps. *I have got to keep going until I reach the path known only to Stefan and his men. Someone I trust will come along that path at some time. I have no other choice. It is my only chance to save her.*

He stopped only once to ease the aching throb in his shoulder. Checking his bandage, he saw blood had completely soaked through. The wound would have to be cleaned, but he did not have sterile material for another bandage. He clamped his mouth shut to stifle the groan of pain forming in his throat, knowing the wound would have to wait. But he could permit himself a drink of water. If he remembered correctly, there was a stream not too far ahead. Steadily, he put one foot in front of the other until he heard the rushing water. Halting at the stream, he quickly knelt down and gulped the water greedily, lessening the burning of his parched throat.

He dared not rest too long and struggled to his feet. His head throbbed, his vision was blurry, and each step jarred his wound open even more. Yet he told himself he must keep going. *For Hanna. Because I promised I would tell Stefan of her plight. I will not fail.*

He plodded on, squelching his fierce longing to lie in the grass, close his eyes, and rest his tired and aching body. If but only for a moment...

Nay. I may not get up this time. No rest until I reach the path. I must keep going.

Wounded and unarmed, Boguslaw made his way carefully. His stomach cramped with nausea, and twice he doubled over in pain, but he did not stop. When the sky began to lighten Boguslaw allowed himself a short rest and a drink from a bubbling creek. Pushing himself to his feet, he moved on. He was nearly there.

He reached the steep path at midday. After climbing the painful final steps up the embankment, he thankfully dropped to his knees at the grassy edge. He said a fervent prayer and crossed himself with his good arm. Slowly, he sank to the grass, the pain fogging his mind until he could think no longer.

Too late, Boguslaw realized he was perilously close to the edge of the embankment. He tried to lift himself but could not. His body rolled heavily down the hill, stopping with a thud near the edge of the trees. A searing pain ripped through his arm and he gasped weakly.

Then there was blessed silence.

A small but successful raid against a few Swedish soldiers on the outskirts of Warsaw had yielded Stefan's regiment some weapons, horse fodder, and two barrels of excellent ale. The raid had been their first since they had set up camp not far from the capital city, and it had lightened spirits among his men considerably. Somewhat reluctantly, Stefan had permitted them to distribute and drink their fill of the ale. Although it was against his better judgment to let his men drink at all, they had traveled and worked hard for days. Stefan thought they deserved a short break, if for no other reason than to release them from the ache of the bruises on their bodies as well as their hearts.

It had been a difficult time for all of them. After the battle of Pila, Stefan had gathered all the surviving soldiers he could find and set up a camp twenty kilometers from the city, deep in the forest. He dispatched a messenger to Krakow to inform King Casimir of his intention to regroup and resist with whatever able-bodied men would join him. A royal messenger had come back with orders to move the camp somewhere in the woods surrounding Warsaw. Their first priority would be to gain strength in numbers. After that, on the order of the king, they would take back the capital.

Stefan had acted on the orders of his king and moved the men to a location deep in the woods outside Warsaw. He had chosen a particular location in the forest called *Zaklęty Bór,* or the Magic Forest, to those who lived near it. The peasants believed it was haunted and rarely traversed it. Stefan doubted the Swedes would bother with it. The undergrowth was dense and dark. It was perfect for their campsite.

The same night, following their raid on the Swedish patrol, Stefan and ten of his men set off to his estate to get whatever supplies they could carry from the castle. Although Mikhail had a wicked headache from the ale, he had insisted that he be allowed to accompany his brother. Reluctantly, Stefan had agreed. It soon became apparent that Mikhail could not stay on his horse, and Stefan sighed inwardly. His brother had no tolerance for spirits and what little he had drunk had obviously been more than he could handle. Forcing himself to keep his temper in check, Stefan had ordered him to ride with Feliks and arranged to have Mikhail's horse led by someone else. It was a damn nuisance, though it might have been humorous under different circumstances. But they were nearing the Tarnowski estate and there could be no room for mistakes. Although on familar ground, it was now also enemy territory. In the darkness, they had no ability to spot a trap if one had been set.

Stefan urged his steed forward cautiously, suddenly motioning for his men to stop. He heard his command being whispered back along the ranks. They were only a few kilometers from the estate and he wanted to reevalute their approach.

Seeing his brother call a halt, Mikhail seized the opportunity to relieve himself. Sliding off the horse, he dashed down the embankment and into the bushes. He hadn't gone but a few steps when he tripped over something and tumbled headlong into the grass. Dazed, he came to his feet.

"What in God's name . . ." he muttered. Kneeling down, he examined what he had stumbled across.

"Stefan," Mikhail immediately hissed. "Come and take a look at this."

Stefan swiftly dismounted and strode over to his brother's side. In the faint light of the moon, he saw Mikhail bent over a large, huddled form lying on the ground. Several of the other soldiers also came to take a look.

A frown crossed Stefan's face. "Strike a light," he ordered sharply.

The night was suddenly filled with the rasping sound of iron striking against flint, and a small spark jumped to life against a dry brush torch. Stefan took the torch and held it over the form.

"It's a man," someone whispered.

Stefan felt for a pulse. "He's alive," he said, slowly rolling over the body. He brought the torch closer, illuminating the face. There was a concerted gasp among the men, and Stefan drew in his breath sharply. The jagged scar on the face was unmistakable.

"Bring me water," Stefan commanded, and a young soldier ran to do his bidding. He returned within moments, pressing a wooden cup into Stefan's hands. Stefan lifted the giant's head carefully and poured some water across his lips. Boguslaw spluttered and then coughed.

"Take it easy, old friend."

A smile flitted across Boguslaw's face. "Stefan Tarnowski," he croaked. "God be praised. You're back."

Stefan took the giant's hand gently in his. "This is some greeting, Boguslaw. Your story had better be a good one."

"It is, sir. You can be certain of that."

Chapter Sixteen

It had been three long, miserable days since Hanna had been at the Czarnowski estate. Thankfully, Jozef had not been there with her. Shortly after their arrival, he had hastened off to attend to some business with the Swedish marshal in Warsaw. *Probably offering him something in exchange for my safe delivery,* she thought wryly. God only knew what else he was plotting with the Swedes.

Still, she counted those days of Jozef's absence as a blessing and did not let them go to waste. She roamed about the castle, learning its structure, passageways, and exits. She had spoken with the servants to learn all she could about the guards' and sentries' habits. Then, early one afternoon, Jozef returned to the castle, thrusting her plan of action into motion. Tonight would be the night of her escape.

An hour before, a servant had told her that she should dress for a late supper. Dismayed, Hanna had feigned illness, but the servant had returned, politely saying that Lord Jozef had insisted she accompany him.

Hanna frowned, fretted, and then relented. She would have to suffer through an evening of Jozef's company in order to present a sense of normalcy. Her stomach turned over at the mere thought of having to eat while in his presence, but she forced herself to be calm. She dressed in her simplest gown and then stood by the window, looking out into the darkness and praying for the strength to make it through the evening.

She was still at the window when she heard the latch rattle behind her. Turning, she saw Jozef standing in the doorway. He had changed into a royal-blue *kontusz*, the long, flared coat of a Polish nobleman. His vest was made of silver brocade and his rich cloth shirt was pinned at the neck with a dazzling sapphire. A short, curved saber hung on silken cords beneath a golden sash tied loosely around his middle.

Jozef's mouth dropped open when he saw Hanna. Despite her attempt to appear plain, she radiated a regal beauty. She was clad in a sea-blue gown with a square bodice. The sleeves were full and the skirt gathered at her waist, where it was held by a jeweled belt. Her luscious hair had been plaited into one thick braid that hung down to her waist. His breath caught deep in his throat.

Slowly, he raised his eyes to meet hers and frowned as he saw no warmth or gratitude in them. He felt his anger rising. By God, he was a handsome man, perhaps the most handsome in Warsaw. He had wealth beyond most Poles' imagination, and now he had the ear of the new king, as well. Jezus Maria, *what more could a woman want?*

His hands clenched at his side, he had an overwhelming desire to force words of love from her mouth. He battled the urge and forced himself to take a deep breath. *Patience, man. It won't be much longer before you can have your way with her.*

A smile curved slowly across his face. "Good evening, Hanna. You look ravishing tonight. And am I not handsome?" he asked her, his hands stretched out on either side of the doorway.

Hanna couldn't help the grimace that crossed her face. Turning to look at him, she wanted to tell him that for a man nearing forty, he had all the physical attributes that would qualify him as handsome. His body was firm and fit, his face chiseled and pretty. But years of inner evil had destroyed the man on the inside, making him but an empty, attractive shell. She had never met a person so vain and selfish. It sickened her. She turned her head away, a small shiver running through her.

Jozef saw the slight shudder go through her body and wondered what she was thinking. She looked like an angel from heaven, and his heart began to race at the thought of finally possessing her. To feel her soft, satiny skin rub against his, to unwind her hair and have it wrap around his body. Heat began to pool uncomfortably in his groin and he gasped, clenching his teeth together.

God, he had to have her. Now. Abruptly, Jozef entered the room, closing the door firmly behind him.

Hanna immediately scented danger and her eyes widened in alarm. "J-Jozef," she said, hating the fact that her voice wavered unnaturally, "we mustn't be late for supper."

Jozef smiled. "There will be no supper tonight, Hanna," he whispered.

Hanna felt her heart thud with fear. "I'm hungry," she insisted weakly.

"Hungry for me, sweet?"

Hanna shook her head. "N-nay," she whispered.

Jozef saw that her hands were trembling. The mixture of his excitement and her fear was nearly more than he could handle. Striding across the room, he took her by the shoulders. Hanna tried to move away, but he held her firmly, gazing deeply into her blue-green eyes.

"Tonight I shall plant my seed in you, and together, with our son, we will rule the largest kingdom in Europe," he whispered darkly.

"Y-you are mad."

He did not answer, but bent down to press a kiss on her lips. As his hands slid from her shoulders, Hanna threw herself back, nearly stumbling over a chair. Desperate, she searched the room for any means of escape.

"You've nowhere to go," Jozef said, desire burning hot in his eyes. "I am the lord of this manor and no one will dare to interfere with me. You may scream, shout, even try to escape, but it will do no good. I shall take you now, in this very room."

Hanna drew the back of her hand across her mouth to keep from screaming in horror. Jozef had gone utterly mad. Worse than that, she knew he would make good on his threat. No one would stop him from raping the woman he planned to make his wife.

Oh God, there would be no escape for her this time. No escape . . . no escape . . .

"Hanna?"

She caught her breath, trying to stop the frantic beating of her heart. *She had to be calm. To think.*

"You are still a virgin, aren't you, Hanna? That bastard Tarnowski . . . he didn't touch you, did he?"

Hanna felt her stomach flip. "I would not grant you the decency of an answer," she managed to say.

He looked at her with some curiosity and then laughed. "By God, he didn't touch you. Is this why you have a strange urge to defend him? Did he play the gentleman with you, Hanna?"

"You . . . you sicken me."

Jozef shrugged. "I shall kill him, in time, for abducting you. Actually, it matters little whether you are a virgin or not. Bedsheets can be arranged for proof, if necessary. You see, Hanna, my word and those bedsheets are all that is necessary to seal our destinies together. That and the blessing of our new king, Charles Gustav, of course. He will bless our marriage, Hanna. In fact, I'm sure he will be absolutely delighted."

Hanna thought he had gone completely mad. There was a sick gleam in his eyes as he rambled on about the King of Sweden and the bedsheets. Yet she knew he was deadly serious about his intention to have her *now*. Her stomach knotted with a fear so dreadful, she thought she would not be able to stand, let alone escape.

Think, Hanna, think. There must be some way out of this situation. Clenching her hands against her side, she suddenly felt the heavy weight of the dagger hidden in the folds of her gown. *Mary, Mother of God, the dagger!*

Hanna felt like weeping with relief. She had a weapon. God help her, she only had to find the courage to use it. Stefan's words suddenly rang in her ears. *"What if you must fight to the death to protect your own life? Could you do it, Hanna?"*

Her heart continued to beat furiously in her chest. She would have to do whatever it took to protect herself, even if it meant sending her immortal soul to the depths of hell. She would never give in to Jozef Czarnowski, not while she had an ounce of strength left. Taking a deep breath, she turned to face Jozef squarely.

"I'll not be your wife, Jozef. Not now, not ever."

Stefan Tarnowski moved as quietly as the night, straining his eyes and ears for any hint of enemy footsteps. An owl hooted in the distance, momentarily disturbing his concentration, but he pressed ahead cautiously, motioning his men to follow him.

He stopped near a clump of bushes and waved for them to be still. From a crouching position, he scanned the walls of the castle for any sign of movement. He counted three sentries from his position alone. Jozef Czarnowski was taking no chances this time.

Stefan's hand toyed restlessly with his dagger, trying to keep his anger in check. What if he was too late? What if Czarnowski had done irreparable harm to Hanna, as he had done to Danuta?

His fist curled around his dagger, wondering how it would feel to thrust the cold blade through Czarnowski's throat. At that moment, he could think of no greater pleasure.

Impatience began to creep through his body, but he ordered himself to keep his thoughts on the dangerous business at hand. There were Swedes to contend with, as well as Czarnowski's men. What he was doing was damned dangerous and he knew it. If he meant to rescue Hanna without her being harmed, it would have to be done very carefully.

Stefan laughed inwardly at himself. *Rescue Hanna?* For God's sake, his sole mission should be the death of Czarnowski. Yet he knew he would not leave the castle without her. He shook his head, remembering the words of one of his commanders. *As soon as a soldier begins to think with something other than his head, his days are numbered.* Stefan grimaced, wondering if there wasn't some grain of wisdom in those words. Was he taking an unnecessary risk?

Grimly, he smothered an oath. It was far too late for such sentiments now. His mind was made up; he would rescue Hanna no matter what the cost. He had given his word.

Stefan motioned sharply with his hand and instantly Mikhail was at his side. In the bright moonlight, Stefan saw the eager look on his brother's face. Mikhail was as anxious to kill Jozef Czarnowski as he was.

"We'll go in from this side," Stefan said softly. "It's where Czarnowski is most vulnerable. There are three sentries posted to this side of the wall. You know what to do, Mikhail, but for God's sake, keep it quiet."

Mikhail nodded and moved back to relay his brother's orders. Stefan saw Mikhail and several of his men disappear into the darkness. Slowly, Stefan returned to his watch on the castle wall.

Time seemed to crawl as Stefan waited for their return. Summoning his patience, Stefan stretched his limbs one by one, keeping them loose and flexible. He took several deep breaths to help his concentration and then crouched back down to wait.

Nearly an hour passed before a small movement in the bushes caused Stefan and several others to abruptly draw their swords. Swiftly, Mikhail and some other soldiers emerged from the bushes carrying a heavy load. Sighing in relief, the soldiers resheathed their swords.

"Two sentries dead. Here's the third," Mikhail reported softly as he and his men dropped the heavy body of a tightly bound and gagged man to the ground. Stefan heard a groan and then leaned down over the body.

"I will not kill you if you give me the information I need," he said quietly to the man. "But speak falsely and I promise you a painful death. Do you understand what I am saying?"

The sentry nodded, and Stefan tore the gag from his mouth. The man licked his lips nervously.

"Is Jozef Czarnowski in residence?" Stefan asked.

The man's eyes flickered quickly between Stefan and Mikhail. "H-he is."

"Where are his quarters?"

The man swallowed, his chest rising and falling rapidly. "I d-do not know."

Stefan slowly drew the dagger from his belt. "I urge you to think clearly, man."

The man looked fearfully at the knife before closing his eyes. "F-first floor, corner room facing east."

"Is Czarnowski's betrothed also in residence?"

The man nodded. "Aye, she is here. Her room is next to his."

Stefan stiffened. "If what you say is true, you shall not be harmed. If you have spoken falsely, you will die." Quickly, he stuffed the rag back into the prisoner's mouth and ordered Mikhail to conceal him beneath some bushes.

Mikhail nodded and, with the help of another soldier, dragged the man off. After several minutes he returned to stand beside his brother.

"We'll be clear until we get inside the castle walls," Mikhail said quietly. "But we must make haste, for someone will soon notice that the sentries are missing."

Stefan returned his dagger to his belt. "I will go in alone. Two men will accompany me to the castle wall. The rest of the men should scatter along the walls and be prepared for a furious chase. If all goes as planned, we'll have to make a damn hasty exit."

"But I want to go with you," Mikhail protested hotly.

Stefan shook his head. "Nay, Mikhail. I'll have a better chance if I go in alone. Besides, I need you to ensure our escape goes as planned."

Mikhail stifled the argument that rose to his lips when he saw the hard expression on his brother's face. "Godspeed, Stefan," he said softly.

Stefan nodded at his brother and then signaled the men to move. The soldiers silently melted into the forest.

Stealthily, Stefan and his men approached the castle wall. Stefan threw the scaling rope over the side, pulling until the hook held firm. The rope between his hands, he began to inch his way up the wall. When he reached the top he looked around quickly, and then urged the other two to climb up. Dropping to the other side of the wall, the three men crouched in the bushes, listening for any sign of discovery. Hearing no cry of alarm, Stefan whispered one remaining order and then vanished into the darkness.

Chapter Seventeen

"I've waited a lifetime for this moment."

Jozef took a menacing step toward Hanna, who huddled in the corner of the room, watching him warily. His voice sent a chill up her spine.

"You are truly mad," she whispered.

Jozef smiled, noticing how her shoulders shook slightly. "You misjudge me, my sweet, trembling rose. But to taste your fear . . . you cannot imagine how it excites me."

Hanna looked at him with disgust. "You enjoying taking women by force, don't you, Jozef? Is this how you felt when you raped Danuta Tarnowska?"

Jozef tensed, his hands clenching by his side. Slowly, he forced himself to smile. "Ah, yes, a tasty little morsel, yet not nearly as enticing as you, my sweet."

Hanna raised her chin in defiance. "I'll not be yours, whether you take me by force or not."

"Oh, how I am going to enjoy this." Jozef roared with laughter. "It was my most fortunate day when I decided to side with the Swedes. It was so easy, so pitifully easy."

"*Zdrajca,* traitor," she whispered fiercely, moving farther away from him.

Jozef's eyes narrowed as he circled the room slowly. "Don't be so naive, Hanna. The Swedes have come to bring order to this pathetic country. We are weak and poorly organized. Yan Casimir is a dreamer, a foolish man who had no vision for Poland. King Gustav will change all that. As part of the Swedish empire, we will be strong again."

She shook her head. "You are nothing but a coward, afraid to stand up for what is right. You keep insisting that I must love and respect you. Well, if it is respect and love you want from me, Jozef Czarnowski, you will never have it. I could never love a traitor."

Jozef looked at her in a moment of disbelief, and then, with a howl of anger, threw himself at her, grabbing her painfully by the wrist. Hanna flung herself to the side, but he caught her by the shoulder, knocking her off balance and squarely into the stone wall. Hanna gasped as she hit the wall, and a nearby chair went crashing to the floor.

Jozef pressed her mercilessly against the cold wall, his body crushing hers until she struggled to breathe. After several moments he pulled away slightly, letting his eyes drink in her fiery beauty. She was utterly magnificent, as beautiful as a queen. His breathing quickened as his gaze moved slowly across her face and then lingered on her full lips. He leaned down to kiss her, but she turned her head away. Growling in annoyance, he twisted his hands in her hair, forcing her head back.

"I have waited a long time for this. You thought you could spend your life taunting and teasing me until I was mad with desire for you. But you were wrong, Alexandra. I shall finally claim you now."

Hanna froze. *Alexandra? Why in God's name had he called her by her mother's name?* But she had no time to dwell on the thought, for Jozef brought his mouth down harshly on hers.

Hanna promptly bit his lip.

Howling with pain, Jozef took a step back, touching

his bleeding lip in astonishment. Instantly, Hanna slid sideways, reaching into the folds of her gown and withdrawing the small dagger. Jozef's eyes registered surprise, but with amazing speed he lunged at her arm. Moving back, Hanna tripped over the fallen chair, and Jozef fell on top of her. As he landed, Hanna swung the knife wildly. Her vision was momentarily blurred as the full weight of Jozef's body slammed into her.

Hanna heard his scream of rage and struggled to free herself from his crushing weight. She managed to scramble a few feet away and came to her knees, crouching. Struggling to catch her breath, she raised her eyes to meet his and gasped as she saw his handsome face bleeding from a long, ugly scratch down the left side of his cheek.

"You'll pay for this," he said hoarsely, his breath coming in short, angry gasps.

Oh, God help me, I have disfigured him!

Hanna moved backwards on the floor, her heart pounding in her chest. She looked around for the knife and saw that it was well out of her reach across the room. Biting her lower lip, she felt faint at Jozef's murderous look.

His lips snarled in a twisted smile as he approached her. "I'm going to take you, Hanna, and it can be painful or enjoyable. The choice is yours."

"I would rather die first," she hissed at him, her back touching the cold stone wall. She was trapped.

Jozef pulled her roughly to her feet, raising his hand to strike her. "Nay, my sweet, you'll not die. But you will pay for what you have done, I promise you that." As he brought his fist down on her, a dark form hurled in through the open window.

"What in God's name . . ." Jozef roared. Distracted by the intrusion, his blow glanced off the side of Hanna's face. Still, the force of his hand caused her to stumble sideways, hitting her head against the wall with a sharp crack.

Hanna fought to keep her balance, wondering if the blow had caused her to lose the last vestiges of her sanity.

In her dazed state, she actually thought she saw Stefan Tarnowski scrambling to his feet to face her, a dagger in his hand.

Hanna shook her head to try and clear it, but at that moment Jozef grabbed her, shielding his body with hers. His arm wrapped cruelly around her upper body, she felt the cold blade of his saber pressed against her neck.

"If you touch me, I'll kill her," Jozef warned, dragging her slowly toward the door.

"Why should I give a damn about your betrothed?" Stefan said coldly, his hand tightening about the dagger.

Jozef's face twisted into an evil smile. "Prove that you don't, Tarnowski. Perhaps you wish to protect her, just as you protected your sister."

Black shards of ice glittered in Stefan's eyes. "You will die for that, Czarnowski."

Jozef laughed hoarsely. "If you so much as touch me, I'll kill the girl."

"You filthy bastard. Are you such a coward that you must hide behind a woman?"

"Do you refuse to kill me as long as I hold her?"

When Stefan did not answer Jozef laughed. "Ah, then I must conclude you do care for the woman. I suppose I should commend you. Your taste is most admirable, yet your protectiveness is foolish . . . almost laughable. Hanna belongs to me and she always will."

"Never," Hanna shouted, struggling to get free.

Stefan took a step forward but froze as Jozef pricked Hanna's skin with the blade. Hanna felt a warm trickle of blood start down her neck and closed her eyes.

"You see," Jozef said calmly. "I have the power of life and death over her. You touch me and she dies. I swear it."

Stefan forced himself to contain his fury. "Let her go, Czarnowski, and fight like a man for once in your life."

Jozef snorted. "Do you really think I could be tricked into fighting you? You're nothing but an outlaw, a criminal in your own country." He pulled Hanna tighter to his chest until she gasped for air. "I'll see to it that you are hunted for as long as you dare to remain in Poland. Did you know there is a sizable price on your head, Colonel?"

Stefan's eyes darkened, but he ignored Jozef's attempts to draw him into an argument. "This conversation is not about me," he said, his voice calm but dangerous. "Release the woman."

"Drop the dagger first."

A deathly silence fell over the room. "Nay," Stefan finally said, his eyes so dark, Hanna could not read a glimmer of emotion in them. "But I might consider sparing your life if you let the girl go."

Jozef licked his lips nervously. "Then I'll make you a deal, Tarnowski. I'll let the girl go when I get to the door. If you move toward me before that, I'll kill her."

Hanna gasped at his words. "Don't listen to him, Stefan. If you let him go, he'll call for the guards. You'll never escape. There are Swedish soldiers all over the castle."

Stefan's dark eyes rested briefly on her face, and she saw the deadly anger in their depths. The tightening of his jaw and the tenseness of his body made her think of a panther ready to strike. Closing her eyes, she said a silent prayer.

"All right; you have safe passage to the door," Stefan finally said quietly. "But I warn you, try to take her from the room and you will die. Even if that means the girl must die in the process. I promise you that."

Hanna began to struggle. "Nay, Stefan, it's a trick. He'll never act with honor."

Jozef smiled and moved toward the door. Still holding Hanna in front of him, Jozef reached for the latch and flung open the door. For a fleeting moment Hanna thought Jozef would drag her outside the door with him, but he suddenly pushed her toward Stefan and slammed the door shut with a loud cry.

"Guards," she heard him shout.

Stefan quickly slid the bolt across the door and then grabbed her by the elbow, propelling her toward the open window. She reached for the rope that still hung from the window, but he took it out of her hands.

"We have no time to climb down. Jump," he ordered.

Hanna looked at him in astonishment. "J-jump?" she stammered. Although they were not far from the ground, she was certain it was possible to get hurt leaping from an open window.

"Jump," Stefan repeated patiently. "The bolt is not going to hold them back for long."

They suddenly heard a muffled noise outside the door and a loud thump, followed by a splintering crash against the door. Before she could say another word, Stefan picked her up and dropped her out the window. Expecting to hit hard ground, Hanna was surprised to land in a cushion of leaves and soft grass. Stefan must have prepared it in advance, she thought thankfully. She scrambled to get up just as Stefan came hurling out the window, landing beside her.

"This way," he hissed, rolling to his feet.

Joining hands, they fled across the garden as the cries of alarm were sounded throughout the castle. Before she could catch her breath, they were at the castle wall, and Stefan barked an order to two of his men, who were waiting there. One of them immediately scaled the wall and looked down.

Stefan took Hanna by the hand. "I'm going to put you on my shoulders. I want you to grab the rope and pull yourself up as much as possible. One of my men will help you up the rest of the way. Do you think you can do that?"

Hanna nodded resolutely. "Aye, I can. I'm quite good at climbing, actually."

Stefan gave her a brief smile, but in the light of the moon Hanna could see the worry in his eyes.

Effortlessly, he lifted her onto his shoulders. Reaching up, Hanna caught the rope firmly. Hand over hand, she pulled herself upward towards freedom. When she was near the top of the wall she felt someone grab her wrist and pull her to safety.

She barely had time to draw a breath before the man put another rope in her hands and motioned down. "Don't worry, milady," he whispered encouragingly, "there is someone waiting to catch you at the bottom."

Hanna heard the cries of alarm come increasingly close to their position and knew that she had to hurry. The men would wait for her to reach safety before coming themselves.

Taking a breath, Hanna began the descent. When she was almost at the bottom she felt a strong hand on her waist. Exhaling deeply, she let go of the rope and fell thankfully against a solid form.

"Thank you," she whispered to the man who had helped her. Moments later, Stefan and his man jumped lightly to the ground beside them.

"Let's go," Stefan urged, grabbing Hanna by the hand and leading her to his mount. Her breath caught as she saw the men were riding off in different directions. Before she could bring it to Stefan's attention, he had vaulted onto his steed and reached down to sweep her into the saddle.

"Where are the others going?" she asked in bewilderment.

"Don't worry, Hanna. You'll be safe with me," Stefan said, his lips pressed against her ear. She nodded and he gave her shoulder a gentle squeeze. Unlike the first time she had been forced to share his saddle, Hanna now welcomed the warmth and protection of his arms.

The cries from inside the castle had grown to a roar, and Hanna gasped as she heard the gates opening and the thunder of galloping hooves. The wail of a horn split the night.

"God help us," she whispered. "Here they come."

Stefan urged his horse into a full gallop, silence no longer a factor. Hanna gripped the horse's mane for dear life, wishing Stefan could wrap his arm around her waist. But it was impossible; he held the reins in one hand and a shield in another, anticipating and blocking the branches that would have hurled them both from the saddle.

Soon Hanna's pounding heart began to beat in time with the horse's thudding hooves. From the corner of her eye she thought she saw a dark shape, but it was gone in a blur, and she returned her concentration to staying in the saddle.

They did not stop once during their grueling, tortuous ride through the darkness. When Hanna was sure she could not stay another moment in the saddle, Stefan suddenly jerked hard on the stallion's reins, bringing them to an abrupt stop. Quickly, he slid out of the saddle, quietly motioning for Hanna to stay where she was.

She watched him disappear into the forest, her heart thumping madly in fear and desperation. Determinedly, she clenched her hands together to keep from shouting for him to come back. Yet minutes passed and there was no sign of him. Fear began to thud heavily in her heart. *Good God, where was he?*

The horse must have sensed her despair because it gave a soft, nervous whinny. Reaching down, she patted the steed's head soothingly.

"Don't worry," she murmured. "He'll be back."

Stefan did return, but only after several agonizing minutes. Hanna sighed audibly in relief when she saw him.

"We lost them," Stefan said with a tired smile. Hanna clasped her hands together and said a silent prayer of thanks.

"Where are the others?" she asked as he helped her from the saddle.

"Hopefully in the same position we are," Stefan said, dragging some brush aside. "We split ranks in order to confuse our pursuers. Not a single one of us took the same route. A lone man is much harder to find in the forest, especially in our forest."

Hanna nodded slowly, rubbing her aching back. "How will you find each other later?"

"The camp," Stefan said, untying a leather pack and pulling out a bedroll.

"Camp?" Hanna asked in surprise.

"Aye, the remnants of Polish forces at Pila and others

have been regrouped into a small military camp on the outskirts of Warsaw. My men are there." He spread the bedroll on the ground. "Don't worry, Hanna. Everything will be all right."

Stefan motioned with his hand for her to sit, and wearily she obeyed him. A small groan slipped from her lips. Every muscle in her body ached, and she was cold.

"Can we have a fire?" she asked, wrapping her arms around herself for warmth.

Stefan frowned. He knew her gown was little defense against the cool evening wind, yet he could not risk lighting a fire. Their situation was still too precarious.

Stefan shook his head regretfully. "I'm sorry, but we are still too close to the Czarnowski estate to have a fire." He unfastened his belt and pulled his tunic over his head. "Here, put this on," he said, draping the heavy tunic around her shoulders.

Hanna felt strangely touched by his unselfish gesture. It was the second time since they had met that he had offered her his shirt. Shyly, she looked up; she inhaled sharply as her eyes swept across the broad expanse of his chest and shoulders. She had forgotten how big he was, his body emanating strength and power. After not having seen him for months, she marveled anew at his size and good looks.

"W-won't you be cold?" she stammered, blushing when she realized he had caught her staring.

Stefan shook his head. "Nay. Now drink a little of this. I think it will help."

Hanna reached out and accepted the flask. She took a big swallow and then coughed, wiping her mouth quite indelicately with the back of her hand.

"It's strong," she gasped. But he was right; the fiery liquid soon began to warm her.

Stefan smiled. "There is nothing like a bit of vodka to warm a man . . . or a woman, for that matter."

Hanna grinned wryly as Stefan knelt down beside her. "Have you ever heard this poem before, Hanna?" he asked softly, a smile in his voice. Gently he cleared his voice.

> *Brothers, brothers, to your horses!*
> *There is already a bottle on the table,*
> *Let's capture those glass weapons,*
> *And head on out to the battlefield!*

Hanna laughed. "Glass weapons? Nay, I cannot say in all honesty that I have ever heard that poem before, but I can well imagine the spirit in which it was said."

They both laughed, enjoying the moment. She turned her head toward him, and Stefan frowned when he caught a glimpse of her face in the waning moonlight. Reaching out, he turned her face toward him for closer inspection.

"Bastard," he said softly, noticing the purple swell under her eye and the red welt across her cheekbone. His touch was gentle and warm and Hanna felt her heart skip a beat.

She reached up to touch his shoulder. "I must thank you; I am in your debt once again. Jozef Czarnowski is truly mad."

Her touch was light and cool on his bare skin. "What happened? Did he hurt you, Hanna?" Stefan asked quietly.

His eyes were filled with such concern, Hanna felt her throat tighten with emotion. "Nay. He only hit me once. But I disfigured him with a cut down the side of his face. He'll never forgive me for that."

Stefan growled, his hands clenching at his side. "As God is my witness, I'll make him pay. For everything."

Hanna shivered at the chill in his voice and pulled the tunic tighter around her shoulders. Neither of them spoke for several minutes.

"Stefan," she suddenly asked quietly, "how did you know I had been taken to the Czarnowski estate? Only B-Boguslaw knew." Her voice caught on the giant's name, and Stefan raised his head quickly to look at her.

"Why, it was Boguslaw who told me. We came across him on a path known only to me and my men. He knew that if I was alive, I'd return to Warsaw via that route."

A Touch of Fire   173

Hanna looked at him in shock, her mouth falling open in astonishment. "Boguslaw is alive?"

Stefan nodded, frowning. "You did not know? You saved his life."

Hanna closed her eyes in relief. "Praise God. Jozef told me he was dead."

Stefan snorted. "Wishful thinking, no doubt."

"Oh God, Boguslaw is alive," she whispered in wonder. "Alive!"

Stefan suddenly felt a pang of jealousy. "You care for the man?" he said casually, but the words came out sharper than he had intended.

"Of course I do. He is my friend."

"Friend?" Stefan asked, raising an eyebrow. The giant had few friends; most people were intimidated by his size and looks.

Hanna heard the note of disbelief in his voice and frowned. "Is that so hard to believe?"

Stefan felt a twinge of jealousy. He supposed it really wasn't so hard to believe that this little redheaded temptress had charmed even the impenetrable giant. Aye, he could believe it, but he didn't have to like it.

"You can be friends with whomever you choose, Hanna," he said, turning away from her. "Have some more vodka and I will brush down the horse." He strode off into the darkness, and Hanna could hear the anger in his footsteps.

What did I do now? she thought in dismay. One moment he had been tender, and in the next breath he scowled at her fiercely. His actions were confusing, to say the least. Her frown deepened as she reached for the flask to take another sip.

"What did Jozef mean when he said you were an outlaw in your own country?" she called out as she heard the steady sounds of Stefan brushing the horse.

"He means I will never give up trying to rid Poland of her invaders . . . nor her traitors."

"He said there was a price on your head."

The brushing stopped abruptly. "I suppose I made an

impression on the Swedish field marshal at Pila. The Swedes still consider me a threat . . . someone who could lead a rebellion against them." There was a trace of cold bitterness in his voice.

"Rebellion?" Hanna whispered.

Stefan resumed the brushing. "This land belongs to Poland. The flames of resistance burn all the more hotly under the heavy hand of oppression."

"But how will you force the Swedes to leave? The Polish army has been all but defeated, and Warsaw has been taken. King Casimir is in Krakow, and people now say he plans to flee to Silesia. What can possibly be done?"

Stefan walked back into view and knelt beside her. "The Swedes don't understand the Polish people at all. They think by dividing us, they can conquer us. Yet they forget that there is one thing that holds Poles together, regardless of class."

Hanna thought for a moment. "The Church," she whispered, understanding dawning on her face.

Stefan nodded. "Aye, the Church. The Swedes are Protestants, and therefore threaten that which all Poles hold most sacred. As soon as the people realize this, it will be only a matter of time before we win back our country."

He spoke with such confidence that Hanna felt a spark of hope. "I pray that you are right," she said softly.

"I am right," he said with cold, hard certainty. He stood and returned to the horse.

Hanna pressed her lips together thoughtfully and took another sip from the flask. The liquid burned a trail from her throat to her stomach, and she sighed contentedly. Although they were still not completely out of danger, she felt warmer and safer than she had in weeks. Yet there were still so many things that puzzled her, so many questions she longed to ask. *Why did Jozef Czarnowski call me by my mother's name? What does it mean?*

Hanna pressed her fingertips to her brow. If she weren't so tired, perhaps she would be able to figure it all out. But she was exhausted, and the drink had made her feel light-headed.

"Hanna?"

Hanna blinked and then rubbed her eyes. She must have dozed off without realizing it.

"Aye?" she asked, shaking her head to clear it.

"You could sleep through a Cossack raid," Stefan said, a smile in his voice. "Lie down and go to sleep." He gently pushed her down on the bedroll.

Too tired to protest, Hanna settled herself as comfortably as possible, pulling a corner of the thin bedroll over her. Soon the heavy pull of sleep drugged her, and she slowly succumbed to its gentle waves. She was nearly asleep when she felt someone stretch out beside her.

Alarmed, Hanna sat up, suddenly wide awake. She was astonished to find Stefan lying beside her, a thin blanket wrapped around his shoulders, his arms crossed over his still mostly uncovered chest.

"Wh-what are you doing?" she squeaked.

"Going to sleep."

Hanna's mouth fell agape. "Sleep? Why, you can't sleep here . . . n-next to me." She felt her cheeks flush. "It's not proper."

Stefan exhaled loudly. "It is the only place to sleep. There is only one bedroll."

Hanna clutched the tunic tighter around her chest. "Then you'll have to find somewhere else to sleep."

Stefan groaned. "Need I remind you that this is my bedroll? Now, lie down, Hanna; I'm too tired to argue."

Hanna shook her head stubbornly. "I'll not lie next to you. Wh-what if you try to take advantage of me?" The heat in her face increased, much to her mortification.

Stefan almost laughed aloud at the absurdity of her statement. He was so exhausted from his past weeks' activities, he almost hadn't had the strength to brush and water the horse. It was God's truth that he could barely hold up his head.

"I'm too tired to be a threat to you, or to any woman for that matter, Hanna."

"B-b-but . . ." she started but didn't finish as Stefan reached up with lightning speed and grabbed her wrist, pulling her down alongside him. As she sputtered in indignation, he threw one of his powerful thighs across her legs and then closed his eyes.

"Good night," he said firmly.

Hanna's mouth opened in stunned disbelief. She struggled for several minutes to get free of him, and then hit her hands against his bare chest. He didn't even bother to open his eyes.

"Release me," she demanded in a low voice.

He did not move or acknowledge her words. Realizing further struggle would be useless, she clamped her lips together and lay stiffly, not daring to move lest she brush up against him.

Eventually, the heat of his body lulled her with its warmth. It was a strange sensation, lying next to a man, but she found it oddly pleasant and comforting, not at all sinful, as she had expected it would be. The heat of his breath on her cheek and neck was warm and sensual, and it gave her goose bumps each time he exhaled.

Little by little, Hanna relaxed, relishing the warmth of Stefan's body. She had never felt so safe and protected. A flash of longing passed through her. If only this moment could last forever.

After some time had passed and Stefan had not moved, Hanna was convinced he was asleep. Carefully, she turned her head to look at him. His eyes were closed, his face peaceful. His chest rose and fell rhythmically with each breath. Watching him, Hanna suddenly had the oddest impulse to touch his face and trace a line across his stubbled cheeks to his lips. He was a handsome man, but in spite of his imposing size his face was gentle when he slept. She pulled the blanket further down over his shoulders. Her fingers hovered over his cheek, and then she pulled them back, making a fist and clenching them at her side. God help her, what was she doing? Sighing softly, she managed to wiggle to her side, praying for sleep.

Yet sleep would not come. She was restless, aching to explore every masculine inch of the man stretched out beside her. Heat rose to her cheeks. Lord, how did he make her have such reckless and sinful thoughts?

At that moment, Stefan mumbled something sleepily and threw his arm across her waist, pulling her close. Her bottom fit nicely against his thighs, and his mouth rested comfortably against her neck. Sighing, he nuzzled the skin behind her ear, and Hanna's chest tightened as a flash of heat shot through her body. Stefan came awake immediately, groping for his sword.

"What the hell?" he said irritably, when he saw Hanna sitting up, staring at him with wide eyes.

She scooted a safe distance away from him. Stefan wearily ran his fingers through his hair. "What happened?"

"Nothing." Hanna answered so quickly that Stefan looked at her in surprise.

"Just my luck," he said wryly, lying down on the bedroll. "Now may I go back to sleep?"

Hanna smiled in spite of herself. She lay down, careful to leave a decent distance between them. "Stefan, may I ask you something?" she asked after several moments had passed.

Stefan opened one eye. "Will you go to sleep if I answer you?"

She pretended she hadn't heard his question. "Why didn't you kill Jozef Czarnowski when you had the chance? Were you afraid you would miss him with your dagger?"

Stefan rolled over to his side, propping himself on his elbow. "Miss?" he repeated, astonished at the question. He studied her face, but she looked back at him openly, clearly unaware of how badly she had insulted him and his abilities.

He forced away his anger. "Nay. I would not have missed, Hanna."

She frowned at his answer. "Then why didn't you throw the dagger and kill him? What stopped you?"

He reached out and brushed a strand of her hair from her forehead. "It takes a man a few moments to die. Jozef needed but a moment to plunge the knife into your throat. If he knew that he was dying, would he have spared you, Hanna?"

She shivered. "Nay," she whispered. "He would not."

Stefan lay back down on the bedroll, crossing his arms behind his head. "Then you have your answer. Now go to sleep."

Hanna was silent for several minutes. "B-but I should have been expendable to you," she finally said, her voice no louder than a soft whisper. "You could have killed him. It is what you wanted more than anything, to avenge the death of your sister."

"I will avenge her death," he said, his voice cold and distant, with a hard edge of certainty. "But not at the expense of your life, Hanna."

Her heart leaped at his words. "Y-you really would not have let me die? You said that if he pulled me from the room, you would kill him, even if that meant killing me in the process."

Stefan sighed deeply. "I lied, Hanna. . . . It was a bluff. I gambled that Jozef Czarnowski was more concerned about escaping with his own life than he was with you. You should not have doubted me. I gave you my word that I would protect you from Jozef Czarnowski. Besides, I owe you for my brother's life. And now for one of my men, as well."

Hanna felt a stabbing disappointment. For a moment, she had believed that Stefan had saved her because she meant something to him. But in truth, he had only rescued her because of his honor and the debt he owed her. *And now the debt had been paid.*

"I see," she said in a small voice.

Stefan heard the distress in her voice and mistakenly thought the day's events had finally overtaken her. He sent her a sidelong glance as he tried to think of something to say that would make her feel better.

"You were brave today, Hanna. It pleased me." As soon as the words were out of his mouth, he frowned. It wasn't exactly what he had wanted to say, but damn it, he wasn't used to paying compliments, especially to women.

Hanna leaned closer to see if he was smiling, her hair spilling onto his chest. Stefan's heart thudded loudly.

She was so close, her round, full lips only inches from his face. Her breath was warm, sweet, and sensual on his face.

Stefan's weariness instantly vanished as his desire leaped tenfold. Lord, if she did not move away, he would certainly do something he might regret. With a slow, deliberate motion, he rolled to his side, turning his back to her.

"Go to sleep, Hanna," he commanded gently. "I promise I'll not take advantage of you."

Hanna exhaled deeply, somehow disappointed. For several minutes, she moved, trying to get comfortable. An ache of loneliness and unhappiness started in her chest and spread throughout her body. *"I owe you for my brother's life. And now for one of my men, as well."* God help her, that was all she meant to him. She had been so foolish to hope for more. Tears burned in her eyes as she rolled about.

Stefan clenched his teeth each time she brushed against him. She would drive him mad with desire if she moved just one more time. Finally, she settled into one position and was still. He exhaled softly and tried to let the tension ease from his body. Lord, she affected him like no other woman ever had. Worse than that, she was so innocent; she had no idea of how she tempted him.

Stefan rolled to his back, putting his elbow beneath his head. He was no longer sleepy. The stars were beautiful and the night was crisp and clear. It was a perfect autumn night. Except that everything was wrong. A Swedish iron fist was slowly squeezing Poland's last breath from her.

He turned his head slightly as a wisp of Hanna's hair brushed against his cheek. He had risked much to come back for her. Yet he had not been able to stop thinking about her. He well imagined that King Casimir would not be pleased to hear that one of his best commanders had risked his life to save a woman from her intended husband. But the thought of Hanna in the arms of Jozef Czarnowski angered and sickened him with such fierceness that it surprised him. *Perhaps because I couldn't save you from him, Danuta. Aye, that must be why I came back for her.*

Stefan immediately frowned at the thought. He hadn't come back for revenge, or to absolve himself of Danuta's death, and he knew it. He had come back for one reason only: because he cared about Hanna Quinn.

Turning slightly, he tried to see her face in the darkness. What would he do with her now that he had saved her from Jozef Czarnowski? He no longer wished to use her in his plans for revenge, yet he could not put her in danger by keeping her close to him. He was a soldier, and now a hunted man in his own country.

There was only one thing he could do. At the first opportunity, he would have to put her on a ship back to England. But what did she have there except an uncle who beat her?

He lightly touched the silky curve of her cheek. Whatever it was that awaited her in England, it would surely be better than what might happen to her if she stayed in Poland. She didn't belong in a country ravaged by war. Her life would be constantly in danger. He could not continue to protect her; he had to fulfill his duty to his king and country. But the thought of giving her up made his body tense.

Sleepily, Hanna snuggled closer, the soft strands of her hair rubbing against his chest. Without another thought, Stefan pulled her into the protection of his arms, his chin resting lightly against her hair.

God, she was beautiful and brave. When Boguslaw told him of her actions, Stefan was furious that she had placed herself in such danger, yet oddly proud of her at the same time. He had wondered for days whether he should throttle her or kiss her. Now he pressed a kiss on the top of her head.

Hanna cuddled closer to him, and something tugged at his heart. He tightened his arms around her. God, she felt right in his arms. He closed his eyes.

Her body was much too soft for a man's peace of mind. It would be a long time before sleep would claim him this night.

Chapter Eighteen

Hanna was having the most wonderful dream. She was dancing with a handsome man beneath the stars, in a beautiful silver gown. The night was warm and the moon glowed brightly in the sky, casting a golden light around her. The arms that held her were strong, and she felt loved, cherished, and protected. As she whirled round and round beneath the moon, she wished the dance would never end.

"Hanna?"

Her eyes flew open and she looked directly into a pair of smiling gray eyes. She blinked in surprise, and then shook her head to clear the sleep from her mind.

"I trust you slept well," Stefan said, a twinkle in his eyes.

Hanna began to sit up and then froze in place. *Mary Mother of God!* She was sprawled nearly on top of him, her gown bunched up around her knees, her leg resting between his thighs. With a small cry of dismay, she rolled to her side and sat up, struggling to push down her gown over her legs.

"I'm sorry," she said in a rush, her face warm. "I h-have no idea how that happened."

Stefan gave her an amused look. "Fortunately, I cannot say the same."

Hanna felt her embarrassment deepen. "Y-you can't?"

Stefan chuckled and then stood up. "Don't worry, Hanna. You survived the night with your virtue intact."

Turning away, Hanna looked up to see the faint pink rays of dawn in the sky. *Was it morning already?* She felt as if she had barely closed her eyes. She flushed again, remembering how intimately her body had been pressed against him. *Good God, how did I let that happen?*

Stefan watched a series of emotions cross her face. Her expressions were open, honest and easy to read. He smiled as her blush crept from her cheeks down the ivory column of her neck. He held out a hand to her and she took it, hastily coming to her feet. Quickly, she reached down and picked up his tunic from the bedroll, handing it to him shyly. His smile widened as he took it from her.

"Where is the stream?" Hanna asked, trying to maintain some semblance of dignity.

Stefan pointed beyond the trees, and she set off, rubbing the stiffness from her arms and back. Kneeling at the bank of the stream, she cupped the cool water in her hands and splashed it liberally on her face and neck. It felt wonderful and refreshing, although she was shivering by the time she was through.

Sitting on the ground, she took stock of her hair. Most of it had long ago escaped from her braid, and now it hung loosely about her shoulders. Patiently, she untied the braid, running her fingers through her hair and smoothing out the tangles.

She had nearly finished when she felt someone watching her. Alarmed, she turned and saw Stefan leaning against a tree, staring intently at her. He had not yet put on his tunic, and the first rays of the sun glinted off his broad torso. In the light of day his features looked even more masculine and powerful. His body was lean and muscled, his chest covered with thick, dark curls. For the first time

Hanna noticed his scars, the longest one running from the top of his ribs and disappearing beneath the waist of his breeches. Fascinated, she counted six scars in all. Six scars that she could see, that is. Realizing she had been staring at him for some time, she quickly looked away.

Stefan watched her, oddly pleased at the admiration he saw in her eyes. He had come only to urge her to make haste as he wanted to leave the area as quickly as possible. Yet when he had found her at the edge of the stream, her red hair spread about her like a sparkling curtain, he had stopped in stunned amazement. She was achingly beautiful. Her cheeks were freshly scrubbed, and drops of water glistened like diamonds on her neck and bosom. She looked as innocent as an angel and as tempting as a nymph. Stefan took a deep breath, shaken by the force of his sudden desire for her.

"I was just fixing my hair," Hanna said slowly, coming to her feet. Stefan did not move but kept his eyes fixed on her face.

"Wh-what is wrong, Stefan?" she asked, her voice sounding curiously breathless.

"Nothing is wrong," Stefan finally answered, his voice a low, husky rumble. "I wish only to look at you. You are utterly exquisite." His burning gaze touched every inch of her, and Hanna's heart fluttered furiously as she quickly looked away.

He desires me. Oh God, he desires me! The thought of it thrilled as well as frightened her. Slowly, she raised her head to look at him. Steel-gray eyes met blue-green ones with an unspoken question.

Hanna felt a tingly ache start in the pit of her stomach. She closed her eyes, trying to make some sense of the whirling thoughts in her head, but she could not think over the pounding of her heart. Opening her eyes, she took a shaky step toward him.

A burst of white-hot desire swept through Stefan. His discipline was deserting him. He could feel it ebbing away, but he could not find it within himself to command its return. Fiercely, he told himself to turn and walk away from her. If he stayed another moment in her presence, he would have her, willing or not.

"Stay back, Hanna," he said hoarsely, his voice a ragged whisper.

Lord, she has no idea what she is doing. She is innocent and does not understand. If she touches me, she will tempt me beyond my endurance, beyond my strength to resist her.

But Hanna paid no heed to his words. A strange sense of inevitability had come over her. She wanted to be in Stefan's arms, to feel his lips on hers. She was tired of fighting with him and with herself. At least for this moment in time, nothing else mattered but being close to him. She felt it with a certainty she had not known she possessed.

A sheen of sweat appeared on Stefan's brow. He'd seen the first awakenings of her desire and how she struggled to understand it. A rosy flush crossed her cheeks and her eyes were dark with passion. He clenched his hands at his sides. Lord, he might be able to contain his own urges with supreme effort, but if she kept looking at him like that, reason would soon desert him.

"I warn you, Hanna," Stefan said between clenched teeth, "I'll not be able to deny myself if you come a step closer."

Hanna teetered on the edge of reason and desire. She wanted nothing more than to have this moment with him. Regardless of the outcome, she knew deep in her heart that she would never regret it. Taking a deep breath, she looked Stefan directly in the eye and took another step forward.

Stefan did the rest. In one swift motion, he closed the distance between them and swept her into his arms. His fingers entwined in her hair and his mouth covered hers with a burning hunger.

Hanna gasped at the fierceness of his kiss, her lips parting willingly beneath his. Her fingers curled about the crisp hairs on his muscular chest as he crushed her to him. His lips were hot and hungry as he probed the corners of her mouth, exploring and tasting until Hanna thought she would collapse from sheer pleasure.

Stefan's mouth closed over hers again and again, his kiss growing fierce and demanding. He had never desired a woman so much. He wanted to know everything about her, to explore every inch of her body and discover every secret of her soul. She was like a drug; he could not think straight when he was with her.

"You touch my soul with your sweetness," he murmured, holding her body tightly to his. Her breasts flattened against his chest, and he could feel the hardness of her nipples through the thin material of her gown. He cupped one breast, gently rubbing his thumb against the nipple. She moaned, arching her body against him, her fingers digging into his shoulder blades.

"Stefan," she whispered, her breath hot against his neck.

Stefan exhaled in a rush. God, her passion thrilled him. With a growl, his hands captured her buttocks, pressing her against his arousal. She was exquisite and thoroughly exciting. He lifted his head from her lips and took a ragged breath.

Too late, he heard the soft footstep behind him. Before he could move he felt the cold blade of a knife pressing into his neck.

"Move away from her," a voice said coolly.

Swearing softly under his breath, Stefan released Hanna, carefully stepping back. He cursed himself for doing the one thing a soldier should never do: leave himself unarmed and out of reach of his weapon.

Hanna's eyes flew open. "It's one of Jozef's men," she gasped, her heart leaping in terror.

"Shut up, wench," the man shouted at her, revealing a mouth full of rotten black teeth.

"Careful how you speak to the lady," Stefan said, his voice low and dangerous.

The man grinned evilly. "As I see it, Colonel, you're not in any position to tell me what to do. If you anger me, I'll kill you. You are worth more alive, but I wouldn't hesitate to cut your throat if you cross me. In fact, I damn well might enjoy it." He snorted his laughter, and Hanna moved back.

"Where are you going, pretty one?" he asked Hanna, his eyes narrowing. "Why don't you come over here so I can have a closer look?"

Hanna shook her head warily, and the man smiled crookedly. "It doesn't matter. I'll have my fill of you, soon enough." Shrugging, he loosened a pack from his shoulder and pulled out a coil of rope.

"Come here, girl, and tie him up," he said, tossing the rope at Hanna.

Hanna met Stefan's eyes, and he nodded slightly. Slowly, she bent over and picked up the rope.

"Hurry up," the man ordered impatiently. Hanna walked over to him as he forced Stefan to put his hands behind his back. "Tie him tightly, girl. If you make the bonds too loose, I'll cut off his ear." He laughed again, pressing the steel behind Stefan's ear.

Near enough to get a whiff of the man, Hanna gagged at his foul stench. For a moment, she hesitated uncertainly, before her eyes fastened on the steel blade against Stefan's skin. Carefully, she began to tie the bonds around Stefan's wrists. The bones in his hands were so big, she had difficulty wrapping the rope around them.

"What is taking so long, wench?" the man asked impatiently. "Hurry up or I'll cut off his ear just for the hell of it."

"Bloody unlikely," Hanna muttered in English, lowering her head closely over the bonds.

The man grunted, looking over Stefan's shoulder at what she was doing.

It was the moment Stefan had been waiting for. Shifting all his weight to his right side, he threw his body firmly against the man. Caught unaware, the cutthroat fought to keep his balance, but the sheer force of Stefan's body was too overpowering. Shouting an oath, the man fell to the ground with a thud. Stefan landed partially on top of him, tearing his hands free of the rope.

Still clutching the knife, the cutthroat slashed at Stefan's face, missing only by inches. Stefan lunged for the man's wrist, clutching flesh and metal. The man kicked back viciously, his knee connecting squarely with Stefan's groin. Grunting in pain, Stefan squeezed down on his adversary's hand with a bone-crushing grip, trying to force him to release the knife. The man howled in rage but stubbornly held on to the blade.

Hanna watched the fierce struggle, frozen in terror. Finally she came to her senses and dashed to the horse to pick up Stefan's sword. She ran back toward the brawling men and saw Stefan wrench the dagger free and plunge it into the man's throat. Turning, Hanna dropped the sword and fell to her knees, gagging. Tears burned in her eyes, and she closed them tightly to keep the wetness from spilling down her cheeks.

Stefan angrily rose, tossing the bloody dagger into the trees. He was furious at himself for allowing them to get into such a situation. His carelessness had nearly cost them their lives.

"Damn," he cursed under his breath, running his fingers through his hair. One minute with Hanna and he had forgotten everything he had ever learned. Control, iron control, was what a soldier needed. To care for a woman even a little could make him vulnerable. And for a soldier, being vulnerable meant instant death.

Damn it all to hell and back, he had been acting like a complete and utter fool. As a result, he had failed to protect Hanna and had nearly lost his own life in the process. He had learned a hard lesson today. He had bloody well better get his attraction to Hanna under control. It was dangerous for him to care for her, and even more dangerous for her to be associated with him. He walked over and knelt down beside Hanna.

"It's all over," he said softly, touching her trembling shoulder. Slowly, Hanna opened her eyes. Steeling his heart against the flood of emotions that threatened to surface, he pulled her to her feet.

"Come, we must go," he said gently. "We are not safe here."

Hanna nodded wordlessly and let herself be led to the horse. They had been lucky. Stefan had almost been killed and she had come too close to being returned to Jozef Czarnowski. A knot tightened in her throat.

Stefan helped her into the saddle and then climbed on behind her. Jerking on the reins, he spurred the horse forward. Neither spoke for a long time, until Hanna managed to calm her racing heart.

"Stefan," she said quietly, turning to look up at him. The top of her head bumped his chin.

"Hmmm?" he said distractedly, and Hanna could see his thoughts were far away.

"I'm sorry."

He looked down at her in surprise. "Sorry? For what?"

"For wh-what happened back there at the stream."

Stefan was astonished at her apology. "You are sorry?"

Hanna nodded miserably. "If I hadn't spent so long at the water..."

Stefan cut her off with a hoarse laugh. "Damn it, Hanna, the responsibility is mine. I acted foolishly, not you. I shouldn't have let it happen." His voice was harsh and final.

Shame and embarrassment swept over her. Oh God, he regretted kissing her. Tears flooded her eyes and she tried desperately not to cry.

What were you hoping for, Hanna Quinn? That a moment in his arms could take away the emptiness in your life? That he might have felt something more for you? You were nothing more than a momentary distraction. Your hopes are foolish. She clasped her hands together in her lap, forcing the thoughts from her mind.

They traveled in silence, stopping several times during their journey while Stefan carefully checked to see if they were being followed. Hanna suspected that they were moving in circles; she was sure they had passed the same way more than once.

The last rays of the sun had long disappeared when Stefan finally drew on the reins, bringing them to a stop. Wearily, Hanna turned around in the saddle to look at him, a question forming on her lips. Stefan shook his head and then surprised her by giving a shrill whistle. Several minutes later, as if by magic, another whistle answered in reply. Stefan immediately moved the horse toward the sound. This action repeated itself several times until a man stepped out of the brush, holding a sword at Stefan's side.

"Who goes there?" he challenged.

"Colonel Stefan Tarnowski." Another man warily stepped out of the bushes behind him, holding a torch.

The man peered up at the dark shape on the horse. "*Haslo*, password?"

"*Shaitan*," Stefan answered sharply.

Immediately, both men saluted. The man holding the torch moved closer and smiled widely, showing a row of missing teeth. "Welcome back, Commander."

Stefan nodded crisply and urged the horse forward. Hanna looked up at him.

"Shaitan?" she asked, puzzled.

A smile touched Stefan's lips. "It is the Tartar word for devil."

"Tartar?" Hanna asked, incredulous. She had heard of the ferocious soldiers who were legendary in their fierceness and ruthlessness. She swallowed hard.

"There aren't any Tartars here . . . are there?"

Stefan heard the nervousness in her voice and grinned. "Not yet."

"Yet?" Hanna squeaked.

Stefan squeezed her shoulder. "The Tartars are quite interesting people, Hanna. I think you will find them fascinating."

Hanna did not have a chance to answer as they were challenged once again by a sentry. They rode through more thick brush before finally breaking into a clearing. Hanna couldn't believe what she saw. It was as if the forest had parted to reveal a small village. Hundreds of tents had been pitched and rows of torches lit up the clearing. Men were gathered around fires, talking and laughing softly. Those who recognized Stefan saluted sharply.

The word quickly passed that Stefan had returned, and many of the men came out to greet him. Most stared with open curiosity at Hanna, and heat flooded her face at their whistles of approval. Still, Hanna marveled at the apparent good spirits of the men and their obvious relief at seeing their commander.

Stefan greeted many of the men by name before stopping in front of a large tent. Hanna was sure it was at least four times as large as the other tents. A young soldier who had been crouched in front of a small fire stood stiffly at attention, saluting smartly when he saw Stefan.

Stefan smiled at the young man as he dismounted. Beaming from the attention of his commander, the young soldier rushed forward to grab the reins from Stefan's hand. The abrupt action caused the horse to whinny and shy. Hanna, who was attempting to dismount without Stefan's aid, tumbled from the horse and landed squarely on her bottom with a most unladylike thud.

The young soldier looked at her in horror. "M-my apologies, milady," he stammered, rushing over to help Hanna up. He had just put his hand on her elbow when he suddenly went flying through the air with amazing speed.

"Don't ever touch her again," Stefan thundered, giving the boy a most ferocious frown.

The boy looked at Stefan, his face red with shame. Hanna's heart immediately went out to him. Turning to face Stefan, she planted both hands firmly on her hips and glared at him for frightening the boy.

"There is no need to shout, Stefan. The young man was just holding the horse steady while I dismounted. Unfortunately, the heel of my shoe caught on my gown, causing me to fall."

The soldier looked at Hanna in astonishment before turning to face his commander. Stefan's eyes were fixed firmly on Hanna. The young man swallowed nervously, looking back and forth at the two of them.

Stefan wanted to laugh, but given the serious expression on Hanna's face, he refrained from doing so. She looked like a tigress protecting her young. Her hair flew wildly about her shoulders, the fiery color matching her temper. There was a glint of steel in her eyes and an angry flush of color flared on her cheeks. He thought it endearing that she always tried to protect those around her, as if she didn't need protecting herself.

Stefan nodded curtly at the young man, dismissing him. The soldier took a deep breath of relief, shooting Hanna a look of gratitude for intervening on his behalf. She smiled at him as soon as Stefan looked away.

At that moment, Mikhail opened the tent flap. "Stefan, what in God's name took you so long?" he asked, slapping his brother warmly on the shoulder.

Stefan smiled wryly. "We had a little encounter with one of Jozef's men."

Mikhail's eyes clouded with concern as he looked at Hanna. "What happened? I nearly sent a patrol to find you."

"I disposed of him, but I wanted to make sure I wasn't followed. I took the long route, approaching from the east." Stefan was about to add more when he saw Hanna's face suddenly light up. Turning, he followed her gaze to the front of his tent, where Boguslaw Dobrowolski stood.

Hanna suddenly hurled herself into the giant's arms. "Boguslaw," she cried, "thank God you're alive!"

Stefan looked on in amazement as Boguslaw picked her up and hugged her, a half-wit smile on the huge man's face. Stefan was so surprised by Boguslaw's obvious show of affection for Hanna that he stood gaping. Never once, in all the fifteen years he had known Boguslaw, had the giant ever shown the slightest hint of emotion. That he would do so here, in front of all the men, obviously indicated that he cared a great deal for Hanna.

Stefan felt a sweep of jealousy and irritation at their embrace. "Let's go inside," he ordered sharply. *"Now!"*

Boguslaw instantly released Hanna, and she saw his scarred face redden. Astonished at the tone of Stefan's voice, Hanna turned to face him. She flinched at the fierce scowl on his face. *What have I done this time?* she thought. She stood staring at him in dismay until he impatiently motioned for her to enter the tent.

Disappointment clogging her throat, Hanna hastily brushed past Boguslaw and disappeared into the tent. Mikhail shot his brother a long look and then followed her. Still frowning, Stefan grabbed the tent flap to follow, but paused when he felt a hand on his arm.

"You care for the girl, do you not?" Boguslaw asked, his eyes meeting Stefan's evenly.

"It is no business of yours," Stefan said curtly, shaking off Boguslaw's hand.

Boguslaw folded his thick arms across his chest, not offended by Stefan's sharp tone. The two men had been friends for years and neither doubted each other's friendship or loyalty.

"Perhaps," Boguslaw said mildly.

"What the hell is that supposed to mean?" Stefan asked, glaring ferociously at the giant.

"Perhaps it is my business. I care for Hanna too."

Stefan's face showed surprise at his friend's confession. "You shouldn't," he commanded tersely.

Boguslaw raised an eyebrow. "I shouldn't?"

Stefan frowned fiercely. "She is my responsibility."

"Ah, I see."

Stefan growled in irritation. "Damn it, Boguslaw, this is none of your concern."

"Anything that affects my commanding officer and my friend is my concern. You know that."

Stefan's scowl deepened, but he did not answer. Boguslaw lightly put his hand on Stefan's shoulder. "I know what you are feeling. Tell me, will she stay at the camp?"

Stefan ran his fingers through his hair tiredly. "Frankly, I don't know what I am going to do with her."

Boguslaw looked up at the glittering stars in the sky. "If she does stay, I suggest that she be removed from your immediate presence."

Stefan raised an eyebrow. "Are you giving the orders around here?"

"In this case, perhaps. You need no distractions, and she could be a dangerous one."

"Don't lecture me, Boguslaw."

"I speak the plain truth. You would be wise to put her out of your sight and mind, friend."

"That will not be necessary," Stefan said flatly.

Boguslaw exhaled deeply. "I suggest you reconsider. You owe it to the men to give your full concentration to the task at hand."

"This camp is my first concern."

"Is it really?"

Stefan was quiet for a moment before exhaling his breath in one frustrated hiss. "Hell, Boguslaw, she needs me."

"She deserves more than you can offer."

Stefan winced at the hard truth of Boguslaw's words. The giant was right. Hanna deserved a man who could protect her and put her safety above all else. As the commander of the camp, responsible for the safety of every man under him, it was impossible for him to put her life above the others. He glared at his friend, but no argument came to mind.

Boguslaw leaned close, his eyes gleaming in the moonlight. "Hanna is a rare woman, Stefan. Beautiful, brave, and loyal. The man who wins her heart will be lucky indeed."

"She's a damn sight too strong-willed and stubborn, if you ask me," Stefan muttered under his breath.

Boguslaw laughed softly. "Ah, the same traits that remind me of a colonel I know."

Stefan looked at his friend and grinned wryly. "Very touching."

Boguslaw smiled in response. "I only ask you to think about what is best for everyone, including Hanna. You know I'll respect whatever decision you make."

Stefan sighed deeply. "I know you will. In return, I will consider your advice, old friend."

Boguslaw nodded slightly and then moved away into the darkness. Shaking his head, Stefan lifted the tent flap and ducked under it.

Alexander, Marek, and Mikhail were seated around a small wooden table, showing Hanna something on a map. She said something softly and then looked up at Alexander, smiling shyly. The balding man beamed happily, and then coughed nervously when he saw Stefan staring darkly at him.

Still scowling, Stefan pulled his stool toward the table. Did all of his men have to be so damn accommodating of her? he thought moodily.

"Report," Stefan snapped.

Alexander came to his feet quickly. "We've been busy, sir. So far we have determined the location of the Swedish military headquarters in Warsaw, several of their ammunition depots, and two supply buildings."

"Any word from the king?"

Alexander nodded. "He has gone to Silesia, where he awaits word from you. He has two complete divisions outside of Krakow and another on the Lithuanian border. We will try to coordinate our efforts."

"Who is commanding those divisions?" Stefan asked.

"Grand Hetman Robert Pawinksi in Lithuania, and Colonels Adam Piotrowski and Jerzy Smolenski in Krakow," Marek answered.

Stefan nodded in satisfaction. "They are good men. What are our orders from the king?"

Mikhail leaned forward on the table. "Small, concentrated attacks on Swedish outposts in and around Warsaw. We are to steal, sabotage, and destroy, focusing on ammunition depots and supplies. Above all, we are to grow in numbers and strength, accepting all men from both the gentry and peasantry willing to fight."

Stefan rubbed his chin thoughtfully. "I see. And I am to lead these bands of armed gentry and rebel peasants who will harass the Swedes into leaving Warsaw?"

"It has been a successful tactic before," Marek answered quickly. "The Swedes will soon weary of their conquest."

"And what of Charles Gustav?"

"He is in residence at Warsaw Castle," Alexander answered. "I hear he plans to lead a division south toward Częstochowa."

Hanna became sleepy as the talk droned on about military divisions and tactical strategy. She hadn't realized how tired she was both physically and emotionally. Shaking her head, she rested her chin on her hand and tried hard to look interested. But despite her best efforts, her eyelids grew too heavy to keep open.

The talk continued for a while longer before Stefan glanced at her and saw she had fallen asleep sitting up. Sighing, he stood.

"Enough discussion tonight. We'll continue in the morning."

Nodding, the men filed out one by one except for Mikhail, who hung back to speak privately with his brother.

"What happened at the Czarnowski estate?" Mikhail asked as soon as they were alone. "We heard no word of the death of Jozef Czarnowski."

Stefan shook his head, his expression grim. "I didn't kill him. I bargained for Hanna's life."

"Bargained?" Mikhail asked, not able to hide the surprise in his voice.

"Czarnowski held a knife to her throat, threatening to kill her unless I let him go."

Mikhail swore succinctly under his breath. "Had he harmed her?"

"He hit her as I came in through the window. I know nothing other than that."

Mikhail had noticed the red welt across Hanna's cheek. "Blasted coward."

Stefan managed a tired smile. "Hanna didn't take it passively. She cut him badly across the face. He was dripping blood by the time I arrived."

Mikhail whistled softly under his breath. "Good for her. I'm only sorry she missed his heart."

"I'm not," Stefan said, his voice hardening. "I'll not relinquish that task to anyone."

Mikhail nodded silently and then looked over at Hanna. "What are we going to do with her now?"

Stefan shook his head. "I don't know."

"Certainly she can't stay here. It is a military camp, for God's sake, Stefan. This is no place for a woman."

Stefan frowned. "I realize that. But she has no home, no one to turn to for safety."

"Surely she has someone in England?"

"An uncle who beat her."

A look of concern crossed Mikhail's face. "It is most unfortunate. But surely even that is safer than letting her stay here."

Stefan shrugged. "Perhaps."

Mikhail let his arms fall to his side. "Lord, Stefan, I don't want to send her into harm's way. I've become rather fond of her." He felt the blood rush to his face, and he quickly lowered his head.

Stefan looked at Mikhail in surprise. *Had even his brother succumbed to her charm?*

"Rest assured, I have no intention of sending Hanna into harm's way," Stefan said wryly.

Mikhail straightened. "Of course not. But what about tonight? Shall I have someone set up a tent for her?"

Stefan cast a brief glance at Hanna. "It would be proper, but she is so exhausted and I do not have the heart to wake her. Besides, I'll have to make additional arrangements to see that she is properly guarded. A lone woman in a camp of men is not safe without protection. But the hour is far too late for us to make such arrangements now. For tonight, she'll stay here, under my direct supervision. She'll be safe with me."

Mikhail raised an eyebrow in surprise. "I see."

Stefan heard the note of interest in his brother's voice. "You can stop speculating, Mikhail. I want only to keep an eye on her."

"Because you care for her?"

"I never said that," Stefan retorted sharply, regretting his tone the moment the words left his mouth. He sighed, softening his voice. "I'm too tired to think, Mikhail. Right now all I want is a decent night's sleep."

"As you wish," Mikhail said, staring at his brother for a long moment before leaving the tent.

Stefan turned to look at Hanna. She was sound asleep, her head resting in her hands, her chest rising and falling with every breath. Her face was smooth in sleep, unburdened with the heavy worries of life. She looked as peaceful as a child, although he was very much aware that she was no child. She was a lovely, vibrant woman to whom he found himself extremely attracted.

He let his eyes feast on her quiet beauty. She had been through a great deal in the past several days, and yet she had never once offered a word of complaint. In fact, she had shown courage, strength, and good judgment in the face of danger. He felt a sudden rush of pride. Hell, he couldn't have asked for more from one of his men.

Carefully, he swept her into his arms and lay her on the pile of animal skins, gently removing her shoes. Once she was settled, he put out the lamp, coughing slightly as he directly inhaled a bit of the thick smoke. He unfastened his belt, letting it drop to the floor before stripping off his tunic. Quietly, he eased himself into a sitting position on the skins and pulled off his boots one by one. Out of deference to Hanna, he kept his breeches on as he stretched out beside her, pulling a blanket over them.

Tonight, she would sleep beside him. He had no wish to wake her by ordering one of his men to bring in extra skins. Come morning, however, he would have to make some decision about her. But for tonight, at least, they would share each other's warmth.

He had barely relaxed when Hanna cuddled closer to him, making small, sleepy noises. Rolling to his side, he gently pushed a strand of hair from her forehead. He liked to feel the soft, silky strands between his fingers. Slowly, he ran the pad of his thumb lightly across her cheeks, smiling when she gave a contented sigh and snuggled closer.

Damn, he thought, frustration coursing through his veins. *She is worming her way into my heart and there is nothing I can do about it. I am completely and utterly helpless when it comes to her.*

He put his arm across her waist. He liked sleeping next to her, and that surprised him. He had never slept the night through with any woman; he had preferred to be done with the bedding and leave. It had always been easier that way. Yet Hanna felt so right in his arms. His chest tightened with emotion. *God forbid, I'm falling in love with her.*

As much as he wanted her, he knew he could not allow it. He had sworn an oath to protect and fight for the honor of Poland. And now Poland was fighting for her very existence.

I do not have the luxury of caring for someone. It is the wrong time, the wrong circumstances for both of us.

Honor demanded that he give her up now, before he became even more attached to her. But as he stroked the smooth skin on the back of her neck, he didn't know how he would do it. She would look at him one time with her blue-green eyes and he would be unable to hold himself at a distance.

He winced at the weakness she had created in him. *What have you done to me, Hanna Quinn? How will I be able to send you away?*

He held her tightly, wishing that things could be different between them. But he could not change history or the course of their lives, no matter how much he wished it.

He lay there unable to sleep until the faint rays of the morning light crept beneath the tent. Slipping from underneath the warm animal skins, Stefan stretched, letting the cool air refresh him. He dressed quietly, buckling his sword around his waist. Lifting the tent flap for a quick look outside, he saw that dawn colored the sky with a breathtaking display of red and gold streaks. Turning back to Hanna, he knelt down beside her and brushed a light kiss across her lips.

"The Lord giveth and the Lord taketh away," he whispered softly before rising and leaving the tent.

Chapter Nineteen

Hanna awoke with a start, unsure of her surroundings. Sitting up, she saw she was alone in the tent, warmly cocooned under a pile of thick furs. Frowning, she tried to remember how she had come to be in this bed. The last thing she remembered was sitting at the table, listening to the men talk about military strategy. She pressed her hands to her cheeks in embarrassment. Good heavens, she must have fallen asleep in front of everyone.

Looking around, she wondered where Stefan had slept. She saw no other bed. Had she slept beside him again?

Pushing her hair off her shoulders, she rose and looked ruefully at her gown. Two nights in a row she had slept in her clothes, and she knew she looked a sight. She smoothed down her skirts before sitting on the edge of the furs and pulling on her shoes. It was a cool morning and the air was crisply refreshing.

Cautiously, she lifted the tent flap and squinted at the bright sunlight. Boguslaw stood guard at the tent, and he smiled when she came into view.

"*Dzień dobry,*" he said, bowing slightly to her. "Good morning."

"*Dzień dobry,* Boguslaw," she answered happily, a smile lighting her face.

"It is good to see you, milady. Did you sleep well?"

Hanna looked away from him quickly as she wondered again where Stefan had slept. "Very well, thank you, Boguslaw." Before she could say anything else, her stomach growled loudly.

"Hungry?" Boguslaw asked, a twinkle in his eye.

Hanna nodded ruefully. "Aye, I'm famished. But I would like to clean up a bit first."

Boguslaw nodded and graciously led her to a nearby stream. "I'll provide you with a bit of privacy, milady, yet I'll not be too far away. If you require my assistance, just shout."

Hanna nodded gratefully as he left. Quickly, she stripped off her gown and the shift beneath it, gasping as she slipped into the cold water. She splashed herself thoroughly, unable to stand the dirt and grime on her body for another moment. She debated whether she should wash her hair but decided against it; the wind was particularly cool.

Shivering but clean, Hanna emerged from the water shaking the droplets from her body. Grabbing her shift, she pulled it on, and she had just reached for her gown when she heard a branch crack behind her. Whirling, she saw Stefan emerge from behind the trees.

"Stefan, my God, you gave me a fright," she cried. Then, abruptly realizing her state of undress, she hastily clutched her gown to her breasts. "I've not yet dressed."

Stefan let his eyes linger on her bare legs. "I am well aware of that," he said wryly. Holding out his arms, Hanna saw several gowns and a cloak.

Hanna looked at him and then at the clothes in amazement. "Where did you get them?" she asked, her eyes wide.

"This morning I led a successful raid against a Swedish supply wagon en route to Warsaw Castle. We uncovered no weapons, but we did discover a cache of women's clothing and jewelry, as well as several bottles of fine wine. It seems Charles Gustav planned on charming a woman to his bed. I suppose he'll have to rely on other means now."

Hanna lowered her eyes as she imagined what those other means might be. "Thank you," she said, raising her eyes to meet his.

Stefan grinned and held out his hands. "Please take your garments, milady."

Hanna smiled and reached out to take the clothes in her arms. Nodding politely to her, Stefan turned on his heel and left.

Hanna fingered the elegant material thoughtfully, watching him disappear into the trees. Taking stock of her new clothes, she quickly donned a yellow gown with red threads, squirming to fasten the hooks and buttons by herself. The bodice was cut much lower than she was used to and the hem was a bit too long, but otherwise it was a near perfect fit. Still shivering from the cool air, she slipped into the cloak and pushed her hair from her shoulders. She would braid it later.

Once dressed, she hurried back to the tent. Boguslaw no longer stood guard; in his place was the young soldier who had knocked her off the horse.

"Good morning, milady," he said, standing stiff at attention. Hanna smiled at him, and the young man returned her smile shyly.

Hanna entered the tent and found Stefan sitting at the table, deep in discussion with Mikhail. Both men rose when she entered, Mikhail's mouth falling open in astonishment.

"By God, you are lovely," he breathed.

Stefan frowned at his brother's words, yet he let his own eyes sweep over her. She did, indeed, look beautiful. Her hair was unbound and spilled over her shoulders in a cascading river of glory. The bodice of her gown was low and gave him a tantalizing view of the top of her creamy white breasts when her cloak fell open. He swallowed and then nudged his brother rudely. Mikhail abruptly closed his gaping mouth.

"Some food has been prepared for you," Stefan said, pointing at the table. "Please, sit down."

Hanna obeyed, perching on the edge of the stool. Quietly, she took a small piece of bread in her mouth and chewed it.

Forcing himself to dismiss her from his thoughts, Stefan turned from her, and the two men resumed their conversation. Hanna listened to their discussion with half an ear. They were planning another raid on a Swedish supply building. She took a drink from a goblet on the table and then grimaced as she tasted warm ale. Still, it helped wash down the bread, so she didn't complain. She nibbled on more bread and was just about to sample a piece of dried meat when Mikhail came to his feet abruptly.

"I'll discuss the strategy with Marek and let you know what he thinks," Mikhail said, heading for the exit. Turning, he bowed his head slightly at Hanna, a smile touching his lips.

Hanna smiled at Mikhail as he left. Then, turning back to the table, she saw Stefan was staring at her with a frown on his face. Neither spoke, and the silence stretched into a long, uncomfortable pause.

"I'd like to have a word with you," Stefan finally said.

His voice was so serious, Hanna's heart skipped a beat. The expression on his face did not bode well.

"I'm listening," she said, clasping her hands tightly in her lap. She suddenly wished she hadn't eaten anything, her stomach felt so full of butterflies.

"I'm sending you back to England," Stefan said, his voice flat and unemotional.

Hanna looked at him in stunned disbelief. "You're doing what?" she finally managed to say.

"You will return to England on the next available ship. If I don't get you out of Poland soon, the English Channel will freeze and you will be forced to stay here until next spring."

Hanna came to her feet slowly. "I'm not going back to England."

"Aye, but you are," Stefan answered calmly. "Your life is in danger here."

Hanna shook her head, putting her hands firmly on her hips. "I said I'll not return to England, Stefan. I've nothing there."

"And you've nothing here," he answered quickly, hating himself for the pain that flashed across her face and the way his own hands clenched in protest at his sides.

Hanna fought to keep her lower lip from trembling at his bluntness. "That may be true, but I'll not go back to Uncle Mason, no matter what you say. Poland is my home now."

"We are at war, for God's sake. It is not safe for you here."

"Nonetheless, I intend to stay in Poland."

Stefan sighed, running his fingers through his thick hair. "This is a military camp. We are fighting a war and many of us will die trying to oust the Swedes from Poland. It is no place for a woman."

"I'm not afraid."

Stefan rose, frowning at her from across the table. "Regardless of what you feel, I fear for your safety, Hanna. I know you have no desire to return to England, but I have no other recourse. What would you have me do?"

Hanna placed both her hands on the table, leaning toward him. "You haven't given me a chance to prove myself useful here," she said quietly.

"Useful?"

Hanna nodded, noting the surprised look on Stefan's face. "Aye. I can handle a sword as well as many of the men out there. I can ride a horse and am willing to be trained with a bow and arrow."

Stefan looked at her, astonished. "Train?" he bellowed when he managed to find his voice.

"You said you needed all the able-bodied people you could find to help you resist the Swedes."

"I said able-bodied men." The tent shook with the force of his voice.

Hanna stamped her foot in frustration. "What should it matter if I can match a man at swords?"

"It matters to me." Scowling, he took a deep breath to calm himself. Lord, she had made him lose control again. He tried to arrange a more reasonable expression on his face.

"Besides, you could be hurt," he added gruffly.

"Every person in this camp takes that chance," Hanna insisted.

Stefan growled softly. She was the most infuriating woman he had ever met. The worst part was that her argument had merit. He badly needed anyone who could hold a sword, and she was a damn sight better than many men he presently had under his command. He hit the palm of his hand hard against the table in frustration.

"Nay," he said emphatically.

Hanna drew herself up straight. "I'm not going back to England, Stefan. All my life people have been telling me what to do. But not anymore. I'm taking a stand now. I'll not return to England and that is final. You may punish me in whatever way you see fit, but I'll not go."

Stefan met her eyes and was surprised to see a strange emotion in them. A mixture of pain and determination, he thought. Her breasts were heaving furiously and her hands were clenched tightly at her side. She really meant what she said.

Stefan felt his resolve weakening. Lord, she put up one hell of a fight. And God help him, he knew he didn't have the heart to hand her another defeat. She had already lost too many battles in her life.

Stefan sighed and sat down heavily on the stool. "Do you realize what you ask of me? Hanna, please don't ask me to override my better judgment."

She walked over to him and put a hand on his shoulder. "I understand the risk. I wish only to help in whatever way you'll allow. If it is women's work you want of me, I'll do it. Please, just don't send me away."

Tears filled her eyes, and Stefan could see she was fighting to hold them back. He felt his determination wane. *Had he no strength when it came to her?*

"What am I going to do with you, Hanna?"

A tear fell on his hand, and he took her arm. He heard her sniffle, and in one movement he pulled her into his lap, gently pushing her head onto his shoulder.

"For God's sake, don't cry," he whispered, stroking the silky softness of her unbound hair. "I can't bear to see you sad." He lifted her head from his shoulder and gently cupped her face between his hands. "Stop crying, Hanna. I'll not send you away. Do you hear me?"

Hanna closed her eyes in relief, tears trickling from beneath her eyelids. He would allow her to stay. He would not force her back into an unbearable life with her uncle. More tears slid down her cheeks, and she took a shaky breath to try to calm herself.

Stefan felt a tightness settle in his chest as he leaned over and gently kissed the tears away from her cheeks, tasting the salty wetness with his tongue. "Shh, *moja aniotek,* you have my word."

Hanna's eyes opened slowly. *"Aniotek?"* she whispered, choking on a lump in her throat.

Stefan smiled. "Little angel."

Hanna smiled back through her tears, and for a long moment they stared at each other in silence. A spark of fierce desire and tenderness kindled deep within the pit of Stefan's stomach as he let his fingers trail up the length of her arm until he reached the soft skin of her neck. Gently, he caressed her skin before lifting his hand to cup her cheek.

Hanna saw his eyes darken as he touched her, and she closed her eyes, marveling at the way his hands could make her feel.

"I want to kiss you, Hanna," Stefan suddenly said, his voice ragged. "You'd best remove yourself from my lap, for I've not the strength to push you away."

Hanna's fingers tightened on his shoulders as her heart began to race so furiously that she struggled to breathe.

Her eyes fluttered open, and Stefan saw desire pooling in those dreamy depths. His breath caught in his throat. "Sweet Mother of God," Stefan whispered, his hands gripping her fiercely, not knowing whether to pull her closer or to hold her away from him. "Remove yourself now, Hanna."

"B-but I want to kiss you too," she whispered back, her eyes searching his face.

A small groan escaped his lips. Faintly, he tried to remind himself of his duty even as he slid his hands beneath her neck, tilting her head back. "You shouldn't tempt me so, Hanna. I can't stop thinking about you," he murmured, his mouth lightly brushing across her lips.

Hanna shivered in pleasure and then closed her eyes, allowing the thrilling sensations to sweep over her. Her thoughts were spinning crazily; his touch made her ache for something she did not fully understand. A small moan came from deep within her as Stefan's large, sword-callused hands lightly skimmed over her body. He made her feel so warm, so desired. Lord, the heat was nearly unbearable.

"Stefan," she whispered. "You make me feel so . . . hot."

What little control Stefan had left snapped as he heard her words. He pressed her tighter against him, raining hot kisses along the length of her neck. "Lord, Hanna, I swear you will be the end of me."

She barely had time to take a breath before Stefan's mouth fiercely took hers, hot, hungry, and searching. Her lips parted willingly to his sweet onslaught. His mouth slanted over hers again and again until Hanna could hardly think coherently. Her fingers entwined in his hair and she pulled him tighter to her, reveling in the way her body responded to his fevered touch.

"So sweet," Stefan whispered, kissing a hot trail from her lips to her earlobes. "God help me, but you are sweet."

Hanna shivered in delight as his mouth moved languorously down her neck to her chest. He placed slow, nibbling kisses at the top of her bodice until she arched against him, her breasts straining to be free from the material. She was melting in the arms of this handsome soldier.

"Sir?"

Hanna and Stefan both jerked their heads guiltily toward the sound. Seeing Staszek standing in the entrance to the tent, Hanna scrambled to her feet, attempting to adjust her bodice, her face burning. Stefan leaned back in his chair, an amused smile on his face.

"Nice timing, Staszek."

Flushing, Staszek looked slowly from Hanna to the commander. "I can come back, sir, if it would be more convenient."

"That will not be necessary," Hanna said firmly. "I was just leaving." She gathered her skirts and rushed past the scout, her cheeks still flaming.

With a low grunt, Stefan waved Staszek to a stool. The scout sat, pulling the stool closer to the table.

"I have the information you requested, sir," he said quietly. "The English ship, the *Albatross,* leaves for England one week from Tuesday. I think it possible to secure safe passage for the girl."

Stefan sucked in his breath and held it before exhaling deeply. "She will not be returning to England," he said flatly.

"She'll not?" Staszek asked, raising an eyebrow.

Stefan shook his head. "Nay, she will not."

Staszek nodded deferentially. "As you wish, sir."

Stefan rubbed his nape and looked at his scout. "My wishes have little to do with it. She has no desire to return and I have not the heart to force her."

"Then she will stay with us?"

Stefan nodded. "For now. She has nowhere else to go. But I'll need to find her something to do. She insists on performing some kind of task in order to earn her keep."

"Perhaps she can assist Henryk with the cooking."

Stefan stroked his chin thoughtfully. "Perhaps. Talk with him and see if he is willing."

Staszek nodded and began to stand, but Stefan waved him back to the stool. "I also want you to arrange a private tent for her, complete with guard. Is that understood?"

"Aye, sir. I don't think there will be any problem, but I will personally keep an eye on her, just in case."

Stefan nodded with satisfaction as Staszek left, his fingers massaging his temples wearily. In order to preserve what was left of Hanna's reputation, she'd have to be removed from his tent at once. He knew if he didn't do it immediately, he'd never do it. She was becoming too dear, too important to him.

"Curse it," he muttered, a frown crossing his face. "It's better this way."

One day she would thank him for it. Or at least he hoped she would.

Chapter Twenty

Hanna moved into her own tent that same day without a word. Her heart tore in two, grateful that Stefan had let her stay at the camp, strangely saddened by the truth of their situation.

Duty above all. Particularly above you, Hanna Quinn.

Still, Hanna was determined to prove she could be useful. Staszek immediately introduced her to Henryk, the camp cook and doctor. Hanna liked him at once. She thought he had the face of an apostle, with wise eyes, a long, thin nose, and a flowing white beard. His rheumy blue eyes had a twinkle, and they smiled at Hanna every time he looked at her.

As the days turned into weeks, Henryk slowly warmed to Hanna, seeing that she was determined to work hard and learn from him. He taught her how to find herbs in the forest that were good for cooking, and she quickly learned how to season the food with them. She watched him prepare traps to catch rabbits and small game. Eventually, he allowed her to build and set traps of her own.

Hanna was an apt pupil, eager to learn all she could

from the old man. As the weeks flew past, Henryk taught her the medicinal use of many herbs and plants. He also instructed her on how to set bones and treat burns and small cuts. She was pleased that the men began to trust her enough to treat them. The men had finally accepted her ministrations, except for Stefan. He kept a careful distance, only nodding briefly if they crossed paths. Hanna tried to maintain her composure and not show outwardly the hurt she felt at his coolness.

In her spare time, Hanna often met with Boguslaw. She asked endless questions about the camp's raids, strategy, and progress, until Boguslaw teasingly began to call her lieutenant. Still, she never ceased her questioning, her curiosity always overcoming her shyness.

One late autumn afternoon, Hanna was sitting with Boguslaw beneath a tree, sorting her herbs into different baskets. Boguslaw was cleaning his sword with a dry cloth, trying to remove any moisture that might cause the steel to rust.

"Boguslaw," Hanna suddenly asked, shaking the dirt from her fingers, "don't you ever worry about Stefan? He has been away from the camp for four days now."

He lifted an eyebrow but continued to clean his sword, his eyes never leaving the cloth. "Nay."

"Never?" she asked, surprised.

"Never," Boguslaw answered.

Hanna frowned. "How can you say that? Are you not his friend?"

Boguslaw set his sword on his lap with a sigh. "We are soldiers, milady. If you had been in as many battles and campaigns as I have with the colonel, you would know what a fine soldier he is."

Hanna fell silent for a moment. "Perhaps you're right. I shouldn't worry. What good would it do anyway? He pays me no heed." She flushed as soon as the words were out of her mouth, mortified that she had spoken such thoughts aloud. "Please forgive me," she said haltingly, pressing her hands to her cheeks. "Of course, he has much more important things on his mind."

The giant was quiet for so long, Hanna wondered if he had even heard her momentary outburst. Good God, he must think her a spoiled child. Embarrassed by her outburst, Hanna started to gather her things when she felt Boguslaw's hand on her arm. Startled, she looked up at him.

"He cares a great deal for you, milady. I've known of Stefan's concern for you from the beginning. He has been my friend for a long time."

Hanna's blue-green eyes reflected her vulnerability. "I'm sorry I even mentioned it," she said softly. "It is only that sometimes I lay awake at night and wonder what he is thinking. And each time he leaves the camp I wonder if I'll ever see him again."

"His thoughts are on battle. But I daresay they are also quite often on you, milady."

"On me?" Hanna said, her voice reflecting genuine astonishment.

Boguslaw did not offer an explanation, resuming his cleaning. A long silence stretched between them, both of them lost in thought.

"Boguslaw, are you afraid of dying?" Hanna suddenly asked, causing the giant to look up in surprise.

"Nay, not really. But I don't welcome it either."

"I think it is far worse to see the people you care about die. Wouldn't you agree?"

Boguslaw picked up the sword again and resumed his careful cleaning. "Aye, I would."

There was again a long silence between them before Hanna stood. Quietly, she gathered her baskets, hanging them over her arms.

"Milady?" Boguslaw said softly, looking up at her.

"Aye?"

"Don't worry about the colonel . . . he'll be back. Stefan Tarnowski is an excellent soldier; the best I have ever had the honor of serving with. He's not one to be careless."

"You are right. It is just that I can't help but worry a little . . . here." She patted her chest gently with her hand.

Boguslaw nodded. "War is a terrible waste, Hanna, a waste of precious human life. Stefan Tarnowski knows that better than any of us. He would not take unnecessary chances."

Hanna smiled. "You are a good friend, Boguslaw. One of the best friends I have ever had. Thank you for your kindness." She turned and walked away from him.

Boguslaw was a bit uncomfortable at her words, but whistled an off-beat melody as he resumed his cleaning.

The next day, Stefan returned to the camp dirty and exhausted, but unharmed. Hanna met Boguslaw's eyes across the camp before he nodded at her slightly.

But Hanna became increasingly concerned as autumn slowly drifted into the biting cold days of winter. Snow blanketed the forest, making it almost impossible to ride, and the raids became more difficult and dangerous. Yet the rebels did not cease their activities. The men knew that new supplies would be just as hard for the Swedes to obtain, and each raid yielded more needed items for the camp.

Hanna was kept as busy as ever. It was hard to find the leaves and herbs she needed for medicines, and many of the men fell ill. She treated as many of them as possible, collapsing in exhaustion at the end of each day.

Stefan continued to watch her from a distance. He often spoke with Henryk, getting reports on her progress. He was pleased to learn that she had taken to her duties with the old man quite well. She had shown herself to be quite capable and useful.

More than useful, Stefan corrected himself. Her presence was good for the camp. Hanna insisted on freshening the tents with herbs and spices, until Stefan actually looked forward to returning to the command tent. The men adored her and behaved better around the camp; her laughter was contagious and uplifting. More than that, she performed tedious tasks such as mending, visiting the men who were sick, and cheering up those who missed their families. She was a tremendous help, and Stefan knew the winter would have loomed endlessly if not for her cheerful smile and helpful hand.

Yet at night she tormented him in his thoughts and dreams. More than once, he had almost called her into his tent just to talk to her, to be near her. Yet he could not allow himself a moment in her presence without risking pulling her into his arms. He kept himself at a careful distance, always watchful yet never too close.

Hanna easily fell into camp routine as the days turned into weeks and the fiercely cold winds of winter blew through the camp. One freezing morning, Hanna had just left the tent of a young man who was burning with fever. He had been tossing and turning since the previous nightfall and she was worried. As her feet crunched in the snow, she made a mental note to ask Henryk to visit him for a diagnosis. She had just walked past the command tent when she thought she heard her name being called. Quickly, she turned around and saw Stefan motioning to her.

Surprised, she hastened her step toward him, and he quickly ushered her into his tent. The tent was warm, and Hanna marveled again at the clever invention of the charcoal fire. Until she had come to Poland, she had never seen it before. A metal container surrounded several lumps of charcoal that glowed red, trapping the heat in the tent quite thoroughly. It was especially welcome, given the frigid Polish winter.

Shaking the snow from her gloved hands, Hanna threw back the hood of her cloak and gasped. The most fierce-looking man she had ever seen sat at the table, grinning at her. His black bushy eyebrows met in the middle of his forehead and a long mustache swirled about his cheeks. He was dressed in a black and gold tunic, and a short, curved saber lay on the table. Her eyes still wide in wonder, she looked questioningly at Stefan.

Stefan was amused at the surprise in her eyes. "Hanna, this is Hamid-Bey, commander of the Tartar forces in the service of His Majesty King Yan Casimir."

Hanna looked at him, taking a step back. "T-tartar

forces?" she said, her voice squeaking.

Hamid-Bey came to his feet and moved around the table, sweeping her hand into his. "May Allah strike me down if I speak falsely, but you, milady, are the most beautiful woman I have ever seen." He pressed a lingering kiss on Hanna's hand. Half fascinated, half frightened, Hanna could only stare at him.

Stefan rolled his eyes, clearing his throat purposefully. Hanna lowered her eyes, her cheeks growing pink from the attention. As she looked down, she noticed the Tartar's other hand. It was swollen and an angry red.

"My God," Hanna breathed, taking his hand gently into her own. "What happened to you?"

"Hamid-Bey received a bad cut a few days ago," Stefan said quietly. "I insisted that he allow you to take a look at it."

Her fear forgotten, Hanna carefully probed the wound. She felt Hamid-Bey tense at her touch. "Infection has set in," she said quietly. His skin was hot. "I'm going to have to reopen the wound and clean it out. Then I'll wrap the hand in a warm herb poultice. It is going to hurt something fierce, so I suggest a bit of whiskey or ale to ease the pain."

Neither man moved to act on her suggestion. She looked up with irritation at Stefan. "I said it would hurt," she said again, stressing each word as if speaking to a child. Stefan met her eyes calmly and still said nothing.

Hamid-Bey laughed and led Hanna to the table, where they both sat. "I suggest, madam, that you do not worry about my threshold of pain. Just do what you must."

Hanna met Stefan's eyes, and he nodded slightly at her. Shrugging, she reached into her pack and pulled out a small knife and a package of dried herbs. She instructed Stefan to boil some water while she unrolled a few of her linen strips. Carefully, she wiped the knife with a piece of the cloth until she was satisfied it was clean. Slowly, she returned to the table. Grasping Hamid-Bey's wrist firmly, she drew the knife across the wound. Foul-smelling pus spilled out.

Hanna felt the Tartar stiffen, but he did not draw his hand away. She looked up at him in concern, but he smiled at her. Bending over his hand, she worked tirelessly until all the pus had been removed. Then, kneeling near the charcoal fire, she dipped a piece of cloth into the hot water and waited a moment for it to cool. Gently, she cleaned his wound. Afterwards, she applied a warm herb poultice to his hand and tied it tightly with a clean, dry piece of cloth.

"The hands of an angel," Hamid-Bey said when she was finished, flexing his hand within the bandage. He smiled widely at Hanna, and she flushed at the admiration in his gleaming eyes.

Stefan frowned, swallowing his irritation at the Tartar's apparent attraction to Hanna. He was in no position to instruct the Tartar on how to behave with her, but he damn well might start if Hamid-Bey didn't stop looking at her like that. A sharp tapping on the outer pole holding up the canopy of the tent thankfully interrupted his thoughts.

"Enter," Stefan called out.

Staszek moved into the tent, the wind blowing in a fair amount of snow with him. Amused, Stefan looked at his scout; Staszek had been careful to announce his presence ever since he had stumbled across Stefan and Hanna locked in an embrace.

"A messenger just arrived with this, sir," Staszek said breathlessly, removing a parchment from his belt.

Stefan took it and unrolled it on the table. Moving the lamp closer, he bent over it, reading carefully. After several minutes of silence Stefan sat down hard on the stool, running his fingers through his thick hair.

"What is it, sir?" Staszek asked, concern lighting his eyes.

"Assemble the officers," Stefan ordered. When Staszek hesitated Stefan waved his hand impatiently. *"Now,"* he said sharply.

Staszek nodded crisply and left the tent. As Hamid-Bey rose to leave, Stefan motioned to him. "Sit down, Commander," he said tiredly. "I would like you to hear this as well."

Hanna seemed to be all but forgotten as she slowly gathered her things, taking care to clean each of her instruments before putting them away. She purposely stalled, curious to know what message was in the parchment and why Stefan looked so worried. As no one had yet ordered her to leave, she busied herself with her medical supplies.

Stefan's officers were present in his tent within five minutes with the exception of Alexander, who had left earlier on a raid of a small Swedish outpost on the outskirts of the city. As soon as everyone was seated, Stefan stood.

"I have bad news to report," Stefan said quietly. "Colonels Piotrowski and Smolenski have been captured."

Marek's mouth fell open. "Captured? Both of them?"

Stefan nodded. "Apparently, there was a concentrated effort on the part of the Swedes to secure the area surrounding Krakow. The strikes against the two camps took place simultaneously."

There were murmurings of surprise among the men. *"Jezus Maria,"* Mikhail whispered under his breath.

"More than two hundred men were captured or killed," Stefan continued. "The remaining men have regrouped under the command of Captain Gorlewski."

"Gorlewski?" Hamid-Bey asked, quirking an eyebrow.

Stefan looked quickly at the Tartar. "You know him?"

Hamid-Bey stroked his mustache thoughtfully. "Somewhat. Inexperienced, but completely loyal to the Polish state. He could prove to be a formidable presence if he gets some help."

Stefan cocked an eyebrow. "Help from your reinforcements, Commander?"

"Reinforcements?" Mikhail said, looking at his brother in puzzlement.

Stefan nodded, spreading his hands on the table. "Six Tartar regiments are presently on the outskirts of the city of Zamość, at the disposal of Polish forces."

Marek whistled softly. "Six regiments?"

Hamid Bey nodded. "They could be in Krakow in one day, on my orders. And a thousand more Tartar dragoons are coming to the aid of Yan Casimir. We are no friends of the Swedish empire."

A stunned silence filled the tent, and Hanna could practically hear the men thinking. A sudden crash outside broke the silence, and Alexander appeared in the entrance, covered in snow, his nose red from the cold.

"It is colder than the arse of a Swedish woman," he said, stamping his feet. Looking around, he saw Hanna sitting on the floor, her bag near her. His face flushed. "Begging your pardon, milady," he said.

Stefan impatiently waved him to the table. "Sit down, Alex. There is a lot you have to get caught up on."

Alexander shrugged out of his coat, tossing it into a corner. "Sir, if you'll permit me, I'd like to give you a brief report of this morning's activities. I think you'll find what I have to say quite interesting."

Stefan nodded, and Alexander sat heavily on a stool across from his commander.

"Quite by accident we came upon a very heavily guarded Swedish convoy coming from the south. I had never seen anything like it; there must have been nearly a hundred soldiers, but no wagons. Of course, our curiosity was peaked. What cargo could be so precious that it would be carried without a wagon, yet guarded by a hundred soldiers?" He paused for a moment, rubbing his balding head with his hand.

"I sent my spies to find out. We waited nearly four hours in the freezing cold until they returned. But they came back with some extraordinary information. That precious cargo was none other than two of our colonels from Krakow, Piotrowski and Smolenski. It appears they have been captured by the Swedes and are headed for interrogation in military headquarters near Warsaw Castle."

A moment of shocked silence was interrupted by the soft laughter of the Tartar. "By Allah, the Poles have the luck of the devil."

Alexander looked puzzled at Hamid-Bey's words and Stefan motioned to the parchment with a wave of his hand. "We just received word of their capture, Alex. No doubt our Tartar comrade believes their proximity now allows us the opportunity to plan a rescue."

Mikhail leaned forward on the table, nodding eagerly. "God's wounds, Stefan, we could rescue them. It would be a worthy victory to steal back two of our colonels from right under their noses."

Stefan frowned, turning slightly toward Alexander. "Are you sure they are being held in the Swedish military headquarters?"

Alexander nodded. "At least for now. It is the best-guarded building in Warsaw, after all. More than likely, high-ranking Swedish officers are most interested in hearing what the colonels have to say."

Marek interrupted, scowling. "Strategically, a rescue would be damned dangerous."

"There are guards posted around the building and on every floor," Staszek added. "The headquarters are virtually impenetrable."

"Nothing is impenetrable," Mikhail argued hotly. "Besides, we need those men. It would be worth the risk."

Stefan listened to his men argue, lightly drumming his fingers on the table. Finally, when all eyes turned toward him, his face was grim and thoughtful.

"As tempting as it may be to try a rescue attempt, we have another more pressing issue to contend with." He pointed to the rolled-up parchment on the table. "The king has ordered us to destroy as many Swedish cannons as possible. According to his intelligence, the Swedes are preparing for a massive attack against Częstochowa."

Stefan searched the faces of his men as a deathly silence filled the room. Częstochowa was the spiritual center of Poland and home to her most sacred icon, the Black Madonna. Legend had it that Saint Luke had painted the portrait of the Madonna and her child on a piece of the table of the Last Supper. A Swedish victory in Częstochowa would be a death knell to the country.

Stefan let his words sink in before continuing. "But without the cannons, the Swedes are vulnerable, especially now, given the good news brought to us by Hamid-Bey."

Alexander looked puzzled. "What news?"

The Tartar leaned forward, his black eyes glittering from the flickering light of the lamp. "More than a thousand Tartar dragoons are now at the disposal of King Casimir."

"My God," Alexander exclaimed, looking at Stefan for confirmation.

Stefan nodded slowly. "It makes our mission to destroy the Swedish cannons even more imperative."

A heavy quiet fell over the group until Marek broke the silence. "The cannons are in the Swedes' most well-protected ammunition depot, deep inside the city, not far from Warsaw Castle. A frontal attack by a large number of men is not possible; we'd never get past the troops on the outskirts of the city. I would recommend a smaller, more concentrated approach by a few men. However, this, too, will be exceptionally difficult, as depot sentries are scattered every few meters around the building. The odds that one of our men could slip through each of the sentries, enter the building, complete the sabotage, and come out again are virtually nonexistent. Even worse, if we failed on our first attempt, the Swedes would know our plan and would tighten security."

Mikhail frowned thoughtfully. "The depot is located in old man Krupa's stable, if I remember correctly. Don't thick groves of trees line the path to the stable?"

Marek nodded. "Aye. But don't be mistaken; the trees won't offer us cover. The grounds around the depot are completely secure and well-patrolled."

Mikhail shook his head impatiently. "That is not what I had in mind. What if we approached the depot through the trees? There is a trapdoor on top of the stable. One of us could lower himself down from the roof."

"Or simply set fire to a long fuse and let the fire start the explosion," Alexander added.

Marek shook his head. "Those trees are not for climbing. Most of the branches wouldn't support a man. In fact, they wouldn't support a person who weighed more than seven stone."

Alexander guffawed. "Seven stone? Why, that is hardly the weight of a child."

"I weigh seven stone."

The men turned in astonishment as Hanna rose slowly, her hair falling loosely over her shoulders. "I could climb the trees and lower myself down through the trap door on the roof of the stable. The branches would hold my weight."

Stefan had completely forgotten that Hanna was still in the tent. "Nay," he thundered when he could find his voice. "Absolutely not."

The other men looked similarly shocked at Hanna's proposal. Everyone, that is, except Hamid-Bey. His face remained calm, a spark of interest flashing in his dark eyes.

"But you need me," Hanna insisted. "I could do the very thing you require."

Stefan rose from the table and went to stand beside her. "Hanna," he said, his voice exceptionally soft, "I think it would be best if you would leave now."

"Then you will not consider my offer of help?"

Stefan's arm was firm but gentle on her shoulder. "I will not." He steered her to the entrance, lifting the tent flap.

"See that the lady is escorted back to her tent," Stefan ordered the soldier on guard outside. The young man nodded crisply.

His expression dark and unreadable, Stefan returned to the tent, sitting down on his stool with a thud. None of the men spoke for a long time.

"May I be so bold as to ask why you rejected the lady's proposal?" Hamid-Bey asked after several minutes.

Stefan looked at the Tartar in surprise. "Need you ask? She is a woman."

Hamid-Bey laughed. "Rest assured that I noticed, Commander. Yet she appears quite capable of carrying out such a responsibility."

"I will not put her in danger." His voice was cold and final.

Alexander sighed. "As loath as I am to admit it, Stefan, she would be a good choice for the mission. Even if she is discovered, I have never known the Swedes to execute a woman."

"More than likely they would do worse," Stefan said, growling.

Mikhail stood. "I agree with Stefan. It is too dangerous."

"Aye, enough said on this matter," Stefan answered quietly as he met the eyes of each of his men. "And now, gentlemen, I suggest we put our minds to thinking of another way into that depot."

Chapter Twenty-one

Hanna hurried back to her tent as quickly as possible. She did not say a word to the young guard who escorted her or to the sentry who stood in position outside her tent. She simply ducked inside as the two men briefly exchanged words.

Hastily, she threw back her hood and bent over her charcoal clumps. She blew twice, in quick succession, on the charcoal, causing it to glow red. Quickly, she removed her gloves and held her hands over the warmth. When her hands were adequately heated she shrugged off her cloak and laid it near the heat to dry. Sitting down, she put her chin on her knees, staring emptily at the glowing coals. She felt frustrated and alone.

She had not expected Stefan to be so adamantly opposed to her offer of assistance. God in heaven, the man could be so stubborn. Why couldn't he see that her offer was the best hope they had of taking out the cannons? Angrily, she picked up a stick and began poking at the coals.

After a few minutes she heard Henryk's voice outside her tent, and she scrambled to her feet, lifting the flap.

"Henryk, what are you doing out there? Please come in."

The old man shuffled in, shaking the snow off his shoulders. Hanna helped him out of his cloak and then motioned for him to sit by the fire.

"I came to see how you fared with your patient this afternoon."

Hanna had completely forgotten about the young man. "Oh, Blessed Virgin, I meant to ask you to visit him. I was able to bring his fever down somewhat, but he was tossing and turning so much, I could barely examine him. I wanted you to take a look at him."

Henryk nodded. "I visited two more like him this morning. Cold and damp weather is very difficult on the body. It makes one susceptible to the fever and much more." He rubbed his long silver beard between his hands. "I'll visit the young man when I leave you. I'll just take a moment to warm these old bones of mine."

Hanna drew her knees to her chest and clasped her arms around her legs. "Sometimes I wonder how we will survive the winter, let alone the war."

He raised an eyebrow at the frustration he heard in her voice. "Is there something wrong, child?"

"I don't know, Henryk. I feel so . . . useless." She looked down at her hands. "Sometimes I wish I had been born a man," she blurted out.

The old man looked at her, so astonished at her words that he could not speak for several moments. "My God, child, whatever made you wish that?" he asked as soon as he could find his voice.

"I am quite good with a sword," she said defensively, "and I have other skills that could be useful to the camp. But I am forbidden to use them because I am a woman. It's not fair."

"Tsk, Hanna," Henryk gently chided her. "The skills you have developed and the work you do in this camp are very important. Why do you think Stefan constantly asks about you?"

"He asks about me?" Hanna asked with shocked incredulity.

A Touch of Fire

Henryk nodded firmly, his eyes searching her face. "He comes around nearly every evening he is in camp, inquiring after you. I believe he is quite fond of you, Hanna."

Hanna's eyes momentarily lit up as she looked into his milky blue ones, but her joy quickly faded. "I wish it was true, Henryk, but I'm afraid you are mistaken. He hardly acknowledges my presence in the camp and treats me as if I have the plague."

Henryk laughed. "Perhaps there are other reasons he avoids you. A woman can do strange things to a man's mind. But it does not mean he cares not for you."

Hanna lowered her eyes, sorry for her outburst. "My apologies for complaining. I just felt that as a man, I could take on more responsibility and better earn my keep here."

Henryk touched her cheek. "What you do here is important, my dear. You will learn that being a woman does not make your responsibilities any less relevant. In fact, Poland has had many such women who served their homeland as well, or even better, than her men."

Hanna lifted her head and looked at him. "Truly?"

Henryk smiled at the hopeful tone in her voice. "Truly. Have you ever heard the tale of Queen Wanda?"

Hanna shook her head slowly. "Nay. Who was she?"

At her wide, expectant expression, Henryk cleared his voice and began to speak. "Long ago, when the Polish capitol was in the city of Krakow, a much-beloved king named Krak ruled the country. When he died the throne was sought by both of his sons. Although by right the throne went to the oldest son, the younger was fiercely jealous and also desired to rule the land. The need for power gnawed at him until one night he stalked his brother and killed him with one fell of a sword. But God did not allow the crime to go unpunished and the act was quickly discovered. The younger brother fled into the forest, never to be heard of again.

"As Poland was still without a leader, the councilors met at Wawel Castle in Krakow. It was their responsibility to make sure that a proper king was found, and they argued fiercely among themselves until one of the younger councilors spoke up.

"'We mustn't forget that King Krak also has a young daughter,' he told the group.

"'A woman to rule us?' another councilor said, horrified. But the idea was intriguing, and the councilors began to seriously consider her competency.

"'She is wise,' one man said.

"'She is brave and good,' said another.

"'Most important,' shouted someone else, 'she is fair and just.'

"With these words, the councilors began to talk among themselves until the eldest called for a vote. And in spite of some who had doubts, Queen Wanda, daughter of Krak, was elected to the throne by the councilors.

"Wanda was beautiful and wise. The people loved her with all their hearts, and peace and prosperity reigned for many years over the region.

"However, the Germans, who were neighbors to the west, grew in military strength and began to attack Polish hamlets and cities more and more often. The people urged Queen Wanda to take a stand against the Germans. A call to arms went out throughout the country, and Wanda brought together her knights in armor. The knights were pleased by the queen's firm stand against the Germans but were surprised when Wanda decided to personally lead them into battle.

"'Queen Wanda is truly strong and brave,' were the words whispered around the kingdom.

"Queen Wanda left one hundred men to defend Wawel Castle and led the rest of the men into the countryside to face the Germans. 'Our ancestors have fought bravely and shed their blood for this land, and we will also defend it and emerge victorious,' Wanda shouted as she led them into battle.

"The battle was fierce, but Wanda was a clever leader and the Poles defeated the Germans. It was a glorious sight to see Queen Wanda and her knights ride back to Krakow victorious. There was much celebration and talk of the strength and courage of their wise ruler.

"But the German commander, Rytygier, was furious at his defeat by a woman and searched for another way to bring down the Polish queen. 'I will have those rich Polish lands if it is the last thing I do,' he muttered for days. Finally, he came up with a clever trap for Wanda.

" 'Send an emissary to Krakow to ask for the hand of Queen Wanda in marriage,' he ordered gleefully, rubbing his hands together.

"Wanda, of course, was shocked at the proposal, but she found herself in a difficult predicament. Her refusal of the German would insult his honor, leaving him only one recourse: war. This meant plunging her country into a long and bloody war with the Germans. But to accept meant uniting her lands with the hated Germans.

"Wanda thought for many days until she finally came up with only one possible course of action. 'Rytygier will not leave me or my people alone as long as I am queen,' she cried. 'He will stop at nothing to gain the Polish lands. But if I rule no longer, Rytygier has no reason for war. I must do what is necessary to preserve the kingdom.'

"With these words, Queen Wanda went down to the edge of the Vistula River, where she threw herself into the water. Two fishermen found her body the following day. The people mourned their queen for weeks, but they realized that she had made the ultimate sacrifice for them and the country. Her example was an inspiration to all Poles."

The old man stopped and took a deep breath. Hanna was looking at him, her eyes wide and luminous.

"Is it a true story, Henryk?"

"Aye, it is a true story, child."

"Wanda . . . she actually ruled Poland?"

"That she did, Hanna."

"And she gave her life for the country?"

Henryk nodded. "So you see, fate has a role for all of us, regardless of whether we are men or women. Remember that, child." The old man rose. "Now I am off to visit that young man to see if I can't bring down his fever."

Hanna stood and impulsively gave Henryk a hug. "Thank you, Henryk. For everything."

He smiled and patted Hanna on the shoulder before leaving. Turning back to the coals, Hanna sat for a long time, the tale of Queen Wanda running through her head. Eventually, she got up and looked for her bag. When she could not find it she pursed her lips, remembering she had left it in Stefan's tent when he had so unceremoniously escorted her out. Frowning, she reached for her cloak. She would have to retrieve it now or run the risk of waking him in the morning when she would need her things for her early rounds.

Lifting the flap of the tent, she told her guard, who was huddled over a small fire, that she would be back shortly. Pulling the hood of her cloak tighter over her head, she began to walk to Stefan's tent. When she reached it she asked the young soldier on guard to retrieve her bag. He called out to Stefan, and as soon as admission was granted, disappeared behind the tent flap. Moments later he returned—without her bag.

"Where is my bag?" Hanna asked, surprised.

"The Colonel wishes to speak with you. Please enter, milady." He held open the flap for her.

Hanna hesitated, not wishing to face the men again. But she set her lips in firm determination and, taking a deep breath, entered the tent.

Much to her surprise, Stefan was alone. He was bent over the table, elbow-deep in a pile of maps. He looked up as she entered, and Hanna suddenly felt as nervous as a child.

"I'm sorry to bother you," she said quickly. "I only came for my bag." She began to reach for it when Stefan commanded her to sit. His voice was cool and hard. Not a good sign, she thought, her heart sinking to her toes. Turning slowly, she pushed back the hood of her cloak and perched on the edge of the stool.

Trying to calm her racing heart, she studied his face. She had been right. He was angry; she could tell from the muscles that tightened in his jaw. His eyes were dark and his fingers drummed steadily on the table as he stared at her so fiercely, she wished she could melt into the floor.

Why does he glare at me? Why doesn't he speak? Her hands began to tremble and she held them tightly in her lap, taking a deep breath to steady herself.

God in heaven, he is angry with me for suggesting I help on the mission. I've become exactly what he feared, a nuisance and a distraction. He will tell me he has no other recourse than to send me away to some village for safekeeping. Oh, dear God, nay.

Her eyes began to fill with tears and she swallowed hard, fighting to prevent them from falling. As odd as it was, the camp had been the only home she had known since she had left England. She did not want to leave. More than that, she didn't want to leave Stefan. She couldn't imagine her life without him.

Stefan's fingers abruptly stopped their drumming and lay still on the table. After several long moments he rose, leaning forward on the table.

"Come here, Hanna." His voice was soft but firm.

Hanna stood slowly, her shoulders beginning to tremble. She took one shaky step toward him and then stopped. Good God, she always seemed to forget how big he was. The tent seemed much smaller whenever he stood. His sleeves were rolled up to his elbows, revealing his muscular forearms, and she was reminded again how utterly masculine he was. And at this moment, utterly unapproachable, as well. She swallowed hard.

Stefan waited for her to move toward him. When she did not he sighed and took two long strides around the table until they were face to face. He loomed above her, clearly aware that his stance was intimidating. He damned well hoped she would be frightened into listening to him for once.

Hanna kept her eyes fastened on the tips of his boots, dreading the words he would say. Her hands shook so badly that she clasped them tightly in front of her.

Stefan lifted her chin in his hand. "Look at me," he ordered her quietly.

Slowly, Hanna raised her eyes to meet his. They were cool and stormy gray. His jaw tightened as she looked at him.

"Tell me one thing, Hanna. Why in God's name did you volunteer to put yourself in such danger? Do you wish to drive me to madness?"

It took a moment before his words registered. "M-madness? You think I volunteered simply to drive you to madness?"

"Is that not so?"

Hanna's mouth dropped open and then she closed it firmly. "Nay, it is not so. I truly meant that I could climb the trees and lower the fuse into the depot. Do you doubt that I could do it?"

Stefan marveled at how quickly she went from being frightened to furious as he watched her eyes flash angrily. One prick of her stubborn pride and she became a tigress. He decided that he preferred her angry rather than frightened. His lesson could still be taught. His hands behind his back, he thought for a long moment and then cocked an eyebrow at her.

"The mission is dangerous. Extremely dangerous. I'd think twice before I sent my most experienced man to complete such a task. But even to consider sending a woman . . ." He shrugged, letting his sentence trail off.

Hanna was outraged. "Is that what worries you? May I remind you that Poland was once ruled by a woman? Queen Wanda personally led her soldiers into battle."

Stefan's mouth opened as if to say something and then shut. This was not going as he had planned. "Queen Wanda?" he managed to ask in a strangled voice.

Hanna moved closer to glare at him more effectively. "Aye, Wanda, daughter of King Krak."

She wasn't making any sense, and Stefan suddenly felt annoyed. Damn it, he was trying to instruct her and she was distracting him with some old legend about a Polish queen. If he wasn't so irritated, he might have laughed.

"Doubtless you have been privy to Henryk's legends," he said dryly.

She looked at him suspiciously. "He said it is a true story."

"It most certainly is, I assure you. Polish women have always been considered quite capable."

"*Ah ha,*" Hanna said triumphantly. "I am half Polish. So you see, I could easily carry out such a mission."

At that ridiculous statement, Stefan threw back his head and roared with laughter. Sweet Lord, Hanna Quinn was the most outrageous, outspoken and utterly unpredictable woman he had ever met.

Hanna stared at him for a long time. "I fail to see what is so amusing," she finally said.

Stefan quit laughing and took a deep breath. "Lord, Hanna, I don't know whether to hug you or put you over my knee."

"Why not simply allow me to try and get into the depot?"

At her words his smile vanished, replaced instantly by a dark frown. He walked over to the table and stood there for a long moment. Hanna suddenly began to regret her words. He looked downright furious.

Stefan slammed his fist down on the table. Hanna jumped back as maps flew everywhere. "Damn it, woman, have you not understood a word I said?" he thundered.

Hanna took a deep breath and tossed her hair over her shoulder, refusing to be intimidated. "Stefan, you must listen to me. I am the only person in this camp who weighs seven stone or less. I could do it, I know I could. The risk would be minimal."

"*Minimal?*" he roared so loudly it caused Hanna to move back. "You think your life is minimal?"

She looked at him squarely. "Any commander would risk the life of one to save the lives of thousands."

He jerked her toward him so hard, she landed against his chest with a breathless thud. His grip on her shoulders tightened and her heart pounded painfully.

"I will not risk your life, Hanna."

"But . . ." she started, and then stopped as the fierce scowl on his face deepened.

"Is that understood?" he repeated, his eyes dark with fury and something else Hanna could not read.

"Aye," she whispered, wondering if her voice wavered because she was frightened or because she stood so close to him.

He loosened his grip slightly. "There is something you have to learn about me, Hanna. I do not make decisions lightly. I have pledged to protect you and I mean to keep my word."

"Stefan . . ." she protested, but he reached out and placed a finger firmly over her lips.

"There will be no further discussion of the depot. Is that clear?"

Her eyes searched his face, but his expression was firm and unrelenting. When she nodded at last he lifted his finger and turned away from her.

"Then that will be all," he said sharply.

He was dismissing her! Hanna stared at his back for a long moment. She was simply unable to believe he was treating her so rudely. Tears of anger and frustration formed in her eyes. Everything was so wrong between them. And it was mostly her fault. A tear ran down her cheek and she angrily brushed it away. Well, not entirely her fault. If he wasn't so horribly stubborn, he'd see that she was more than capable of carrying out such a task. Sniffling, she marched to where her bag was and thrust it under her arm. She was just reaching for the flap when she felt his hand on her shoulder.

"Wait; you forgot this," Stefan said, giving her a roll of clean linen bandages. He inhaled sharply when he saw the brightness of her eyes.

Hanna snatched the bandages from him and turned to leave, but he pulled her around to face him. She resisted him, but he drew her closer anyway.

He sighed deeply. "Good God, Hanna, you will surely force me into madness. One moment ago you were furious with me. Why do you cry now?"

She looked away from him, but he gently nudged her chin up until she looked directly into his eyes. "Why are you crying?" he softly repeated again.

"I am not crying," she insisted fiercely even as a tear slipped from her eye. She struggled against his hold, but he held her tightly.

His voice softened. "Hanna, you had to be taught a lesson. I am the commanding officer of this camp. You cannot continue to countermand my every order."

"I do not countermand your every order," she argued fiercely.

Stefan nearly smiled. This woman was a contradiction in terms. He pulled her close despite her struggles, resting his chin on her head. "Why is it that no matter what I do, I always bring tears to those lovely eyes of yours? Am I such an ogre?"

Hanna bit her lower lip. "Aye, an ogre, and the most stubborn, arrogant, and insufferable man I have ever known."

A husky rumble came from his chest. He was stubborn? Why, she was by far the most willful and undisciplined woman he had ever come across. Then why in hell did he find her so irresistible?

He already knew the answer. He admired her strength, determination, and loyalty. She had been through nothing but hardship all of her life, yet never once had she allowed herself to be defeated by it. Aye, perhaps she was stubborn, but he suspected it was motivated by pride.

Hanna began to feel warm in his arms. "For God's sake, Stefan, enough of this lesson," she said after several moments had passed and he had not said a word. "Let me go." She pushed her arms against his chest and saw his eyes darken as he looked down at her, his arm circling around her waist.

"Nay."

"Nay?"

"Nay, I'll not let you go, Hanna," he replied quietly, gazing into her magnificent blue-green eyes. "Not yet."

Taken aback by his words, she waited for an explanation, but he offered none. He simply stared at her for an agonizingly long moment before his mouth settled on hers with surprising tenderness.

Hanna trembled at the hot pressure of his mouth and the wave of heat that swept over her. She told herself to push him away, to prevent him from tearing out her heart as he had done by carefully avoiding her for the past several weeks. But her body would not respond to her commands. Instead, she instinctively curled her arms around his shoulders, letting her fingers stroke the soft skin of his nape.

Gently, Stefan coaxed her mouth open and tasted the sweetness of her tongue. He was acutely aware of every movement she made, the way her tongue played with his, the light brush of her fingers on his neck, the tickle of her hair against his cheek. Emotions so thick overwhelmed him and he couldn't breathe. God help him, at that moment he wanted nothing more than to hold her in his arms forever, uncovering all the mysterious secrets of this beautiful red-haired nymph who fired his blood.

Yet even as his tongue stroked the soft cavern of her mouth, he knew he could not have her. She deserved more than he could give and he cared too much about her to take what he could not offer in return. *Damn, why had he started something he could not finish?*

Regretfully, he broke the kiss and put some distance between them. Her eyes were closed and her lips, beautifully moist and swollen from their kiss, were still lifted to him. God, she was beautiful. He felt a painful burst of longing course through him. He nearly gathered her back into his arms, but he forced himself to remain motionless, knowing that it was for her sake that he stop it now.

Slowly, Hanna opened her eyes. When she saw that Stefan had moved away from her she looked at him questioningly.

Taking a deep breath, Stefan closed his eyes, forcing the words from his mouth. "I apologize for my unwarranted behavior. You had better leave."

Hanna looked at him, stunned. "Leave?" she finally managed to whisper.

Stefan ground his teeth together. "Aye, leave, Hanna." They were the hardest words he had ever had to say.

Hanna flushed, his words wounding her to the quick. Then, with a small cry, she whirled from him and fumbled for the tent flap.

"Nay, damn it, wait," Stefan said, blocking her exit.

"Release me," Hanna demanded, trying to get past him. "For God's sake, Stefan, let me leave with dignity."

"I want to explain..." Stefan started, but Hanna retreated, the blush deepening into a blazing scarlet color.

"Just leave me alone. I have already humiliated myself enough for one day, thank you."

"Hanna..." Stefan started, but at that moment she wrenched herself free of his arms and ran out into the night.

Cursing, Stefan lifted the tent flap, bellowing her name. When she did not reappear, the young guard standing duty at his tent politely asked if he should fetch the young lady.

Stefan sighed loudly and then shook his head. "Nay. Just ensure that she returns to her tent safely." The young man saluted sharply and ran off after her.

Stefan went back inside and immediately headed for a wooden crate that stood in the corner of the tent. He leaned over and lifted the cover, pulling out a bottle of whiskey. He never drank while in command, but tonight was an exception. He leaned back in his chair and took a large swig, grimacing as the burning liquid seared his throat.

He should never have kissed her. Lord, it had all been going perfectly until he had seen her tears. And then his resolve had vanished. He had absolutely no strength when it came to her. She simply had to turn her lovely eyes on him and he melted. Hell, he was worse than an untried schoolboy. He took another swig and closed his eyes in order to see her face.

Damn the war.

Damn his duty.

He was a fool. He had fallen in love with a woman he could not allow himself to have.

Chapter Twenty-two

Hanna had just finished her morning rounds and stood for a moment, sharing the warmth of the fire with the guard outside her tent. She never felt right about having someone stand outside in the freezing cold just to guard her tent, and had on several occasions protested to Stefan. But he had refused to listen to her, insisting that the guard remain.

As usual, she thought wearily. He never listened to what she had to say. Leaning over the fire, she rubbed her hands together and looked up at the soldier who stood across from her. He was staring, but he hastily dropped his eyes when she looked at him.

"Tadeusz," she asked quietly, noticing his cheeks redden. "Is there something wrong?"

The man shook his head. "Nay, milady. I just thought that you looked unusually tired this morning."

She *was* tired. She hadn't slept a wink after her encounter with Stefan. To think how she had once again thrown herself at him; it was downright shameless. And in the end he had thrust her away, as always. Good God, she had been foolish to hope for anything with such a man. Why couldn't she seem to get that through her head?

"I'm fine, but thank you for your concern." The fire warmed her hands and face and she stood for a moment, allowing the heat to penetrate her cloak.

"Have you seen Colonel Tarnowski this morning?" she suddenly asked, her voice catching on his name. *Could she not even say his name without emotion?*

"Aye, milady, he left the camp early with several of his men."

"I see. Do you know if Boguslaw Dobrowolski was among them?"

Tadeusz shrugged. "I don't know, but I could find out, if you would like, milady."

Hanna nodded. "Aye, I think I would like that very much indeed. If he is around, would you be so kind as to tell him that I would like to see him?"

Tadeusz nodded, and Hanna ducked into her tent. Blowing on the coals, she waited for the tent to warm up before discarding her cloak. She sat down beside the coals thoughtfully, wrapping her arms around her legs, resting her chin on her knees. She had a plan and she wanted to talk to someone about it. Someone who would listen to her.

She sat there for a long time, mulling over her ideas until she heard someone call her name. Scrambling to her feet, she lifted the flap and saw Boguslaw standing there.

"Thank God you are here," she said, grabbing her cloak and thrusting her arms into it. She pulled the hood over her head as she grabbed Boguslaw's elbow. They walked slowly, their footsteps crunching in the brittle snow. They walked in silence until Hanna stopped and looked up at him.

"May I ask you something?" she asked.

"Of course, milady."

"Do you know what Stefan plans to do about the Swedish cannons?"

The giant raised an eyebrow. "Why should you trouble yourself about that, milady?"

"Please, it is important for me to know."

Boguslaw tapped his foot on the snow, not answering for a long time. Hanna met his gaze pleadingly until he looked away.

"I know you offered to enter the depot through the trees, milady. It was a brave thing to say."

"I meant what I said, Boguslaw. It is the best course of action."

The giant shrugged, brushing the snow off the back of his uncovered hands. "Perhaps. But it is not the one the colonel has chosen."

Hanna put a hand lightly on his arm. "Please, Boguslaw, tell me his plan. I need to know for my own peace of mind."

The giant pursed his lips together. When she pleaded with him like that he had little strength to refuse. He thought for a moment and decided no harm could come from telling her. Stefan and his men had already left; it was too late for her to do anything.

"There will be a small frontal attack on the depot, drawing attention away from the back, where several of the men will attempt to enter and light the fuses."

"A frontal attack?" Hanna exclaimed. "For God's sake, the depot is in the middle of the city, surrounded by armed sentries. As soon as the first alarm is sounded, the place will be flooded with Swedish soldiers."

Boguslaw looked mildly surprised. "You question the colonel's strategy?"

Hanna nodded vigorously. "I most certainly do. Can't you see? A frontal attack will kill nearly all of those who go on this mission."

Boguslaw shrugged. "It is war, milady."

"It is madness." Hanna was so upset by the thought of it, she was shaking. "All those men needlessly killed," she whispered.

"I would not say needlessly, milady," Boguslaw answered, crossing his arms. "We must destroy the cannons. Their deaths would not be in vain."

"B-but is there no other recourse? Must we destroy

the cannons? Are not thousands of Tartar soldiers on our side?"

Boguslaw shook his head. "Against the huge cannons of the Swedes, even the Tartars will be of little use. The cannons must be destroyed."

She thought for a moment before suddenly looking up at Boguslaw. "My God," she whispered as another thought came to her. "Who will lead this frontal attack?"

Boguslaw met her gaze and then looked away.

"Stefan," she whispered, her voice catching in her throat. "Stefan will lead the attack."

"Milady," Boguslaw said gently, putting his arm on her shoulder. "I think we should end this discussion. You are clearly upset."

"Of course I am upset. Good God, Boguslaw, is that where Stefan went this morning? Is he planning the attack on the depot?"

"It is too late for your concern, milady," he said quietly.

"Too late? They plan to do it today?"

Boguslaw shook his head. "They will make their attempt two nights from now. But you must have faith that everything will turn out all right."

"Two nights from now?" she asked, appalled.

Boguslaw tried to soothe her. "Please, milady, I beg you not to worry."

Hanna's mind reeled. She clutched her hands tightly in front of her and then whirled to face Boguslaw. "Why didn't you go with them?" she asked, her voice rising near hysteria.

The giant looked away, but not before Hanna saw something in his eyes. "The colonel thought I could be of better use here."

"Nay," she whispered. "He left you behind to protect me, didn't he?"

Boguslaw remained silent and Hanna yanked his arm. "Answer me, Boguslaw." She was crying now, the tears coursing down her face. "My God, he left you behind because he doesn't think he will make it back."

With a small cry, she turned away from him and began running. The giant strode after her, grabbing her arm just before she entered the tent.

"It is the way it must be, milady. You must trust the colonel's judgment. All of us trust him with our lives. His plan is the best one under the circumstances."

"It is not," Hanna insisted, brushing angry tears from her face. "I was his best chance to get into the depot and you know it."

Boguslaw shook his head sadly. "You do not understand the man behind the commander. You were wrong to think he would ever risk your life."

Hanna stamped her foot. "And he was wrong to think I would sit back and watch him throw his life away."

With those words, Hanna disappeared into her tent. Boguslaw stood looking after her, clearly unhappy at the despair in her voice, and even more unsettled by the strange spark of determination in her eyes.

He would have to keep a close eye on her. He was already regretting their discussion and his frank answers, but he had hoped it would prepare her for what might happen. He had never expected such a fierce reaction from her.

Boguslaw sighed deeply, rubbing the knuckles of his large, callused hands. He had never understood women. But one thing was certain: he would never again underestimate Hanna Quinn. At that moment, he decided this fiery, redheaded woman was probably more dangerous than all of the Swedes' largest cannons put together.

Chapter Twenty-three

Hanna made her way down the hill with sure but careful steps. Her heart was beating so loudly, she was sure any Swedish soldier in a five-kilometer radius could hear it. Pale moonlight slid through the clouds, occasionally lighting her way across the snow and through the trees. She walked carefully, to make as little noise as possible.

She was dressed in black from head to foot. She had quickly sewn herself a warm tunic and comfortable breeches that would allow her to climb easily. Her hair was braided and hidden beneath a black cap. A small dagger, her only weapon, hung from her belt. A pack containing all the equipment she would need was strapped to her back.

Earlier in the day, she had questioned her guard at great length about the city, the location of Warsaw Castle, and about old man Krupa's barn. The young soldier clearly thought she was a bit daft but saw no harm in humoring her. When she had all the information she thought necessary, she went about secretly gathering the equipment she would need to carry out her plan.

Hanna stopped for a moment, watching the small cloud that appeared. It was a freezing night, but Hanna hoped the weather would work to her advantage. If she was lucky, perhaps there would not be as many sentries as usual on duty.

She looked up at the moon as it peeked through the clouds and judged it was at least an hour past midnight. She had informed her guard that she would be attending an ill soldier for a couple of hours and had immediately slipped out of sight. She had waited patiently until the soldier guarding the horses went into the trees to relieve himself; then she led a horse away, mounting it quickly. She was careful to avoid the areas where she knew sentries were posted, saying a small prayer that none had recently been assigned to the path she had chosen. Luck was with her, and she moved through the forest quietly until she reached the outskirts of the city. She dismounted when she reached a small ridge and tied her horse to a tree. In the golden glow of the moonlight she could see the silhouette of the city of Warsaw. She was less than one kilometer from the city.

"Well, let's get on with it, Hanna Quinn," she whispered to herself. Exhaling a deep breath, she started down the ridge; suddenly, she felt a heavy hand on her shoulder. A scream froze in her throat and she whirled around, her hand reaching for her dagger.

"Just where do you think you are going?" she heard a familiar voice ask, and she saw Boguslaw standing behind her, frowning fiercely.

She waited until her heart began to beat normally before she opened her mouth to speak. "Good God, Boguslaw, you nearly scared me to death. What are you doing here?"

Boguslaw rested a hand on his hip. "You didn't really think you would get away with this, did you, milady? Come; we will return to the camp immediately."

Hanna shook her head, planting her feet firmly on the ground. "Nay. I will not return."

Boguslaw sighed. "I will force you, if I must."

Hanna frowned, realizing the giant meant what he said. "Boguslaw, I beg you not to stop me. You know this is the safest course of action. For God's sake, all those men will die needlessly. If I am caught or hurt, it is but a small loss. But if Stefan is killed, Poland will lose a most important military leader. I ask you not to think of me, but think of what Stefan's death could do to Poland's struggle to survive."

Boguslaw was silent for a long moment, and Hanna realized with astonishment that he was actually weighing her words. She held her breath, praying with all her might that he would heed her.

After several moments he spoke. "You may be right, milady, but I have never disobeyed an order from the colonel. It goes against everything I believe in."

"If you do not let me try, you will most likely never see him again. Good God in heaven, I beseech you, Boguslaw. Let me try."

Hanna could see the pain of indecision on his face, and she realized the situation was far worse than she had suspected. Good Lord, if Boguslaw was actually considering disobeying a direct order, their situation must be near hopeless. She had been right to assume the loss of Stefan's leadership would be a terrible blow to the resistance struggle.

"I swore to protect you, milady. If anything happened to you . . ."

"If anything happened to Stefan, I would not want to live," Hanna answered quietly. "And knowing that perhaps I could have prevented needless deaths but didn't, I wouldn't be able to live with myself."

Boguslaw inhaled deeply. Precious minutes slipped away, and Hanna thought them the longest moments of her life. Finally, after what seemed like hours, the giant turned toward her.

"All right, milady, I will allow you to try. But on one condition."

Hanna closed her eyes in relief and then opened them again quickly. "Condition?"

"I shall accompany you."

"Accompany me?" Hanna began to protest, but Boguslaw stood firm in front of her, his hands on his hips. "I'll wait for you at the base of the tree."

She thought for a moment, and then she nodded. In all actuality, she had little choice, and besides, the thought of the giant waiting for her return did have its appeal.

"Agreed," she said slowly.

He reached for her pack. "Then show me what you have in here."

Hanna slipped it off her shoulders and he opened it. Boguslaw counted at least ten scaling ropes, a flint and scraper, and a small bundle wrapped in linen strips with a fuse hanging from it.

"Gunpowder inside?" he asked, poking the bundle. Hanna nodded.

Boguslaw grunted in admiration. She had done her homework and had taken only what she needed. He closed the pack and fastened it securely to her back.

"You have what you need. Let's go before I change my mind."

They climbed down the ridge and through more forest before they entered the city. Hanna could hear the voices of Swedish patrols on their rounds.

Boguslaw abruptly stopped to listen, motioning her to be silent. Hanna drew up beside him, suddenly very glad for his reassuring presence. They stood motionless until he was satisfied their way was clear. He began to move again, making his way cautiously and quietly. Hanna kept close on his heels, forcing herself to take deep breaths of the cold air to calm her racing heart. He took her in a direction she never would have gone, but pressing his mouth close to her ear, he explained that his way was a safer approach to the stable.

They soon came to a dirt road lined with rows of evenly spaced trees. Abruptly, Boguslaw stopped behind a tree and peered into the darkness. Hanna froze as she heard the low murmur of the sentries' voices. She knew the depot was at the end of the rows of trees.

Suddenly, the sound of footsteps crunching in the snow split the night. Swiftly, Boguslaw swept Hanna behind a tree, flattening her between his body and the bark. His entire body tensed, and she felt him place his hand on the hilt of his sword. Hanna held her breath. The footsteps drew closer, and a sentry passed within a few meters. Hanna thought she might faint from sheer terror, but the guard's pace did not slow. As the sound of his footsteps faded, Hanna exhaled in relief. Boguslaw turned her to face him.

"It is time," he whispered. "Are you sure you want to go through with this?"

"Aye," she whispered. "I'm sure." She hoped he couldn't hear the tremor in her voice.

"Then I'll wait here for you. I'll not leave without you, no matter what happens."

Hanna shook her head furiously. "Don't be silly. If I don't come back, you must go."

The giant shook his head. "If you do not return, neither do I. I'll make my final stand here, waiting for you, milady. I'll not go back empty-handed. I would rather be dead."

His voice was flat and final, and Hanna swallowed hard. She knew what Boguslaw was thinking. If they came out of this alive, Stefan would never trust either of them again. Her eyes filled with tears, but she held them back. *A small price to pay for his life, Hanna Quinn.*

"All right, Boguslaw. Rest assured I'll be back."

He nodded solemnly and then glanced up at the tree, judging the distance he would have to lift her. Holding out his hand, he motioned for her to put her foot in it. She did so, and he lifted her to the first branch. Grabbing it, she nimbly pulled herself up. She looked down at Boguslaw once more, but he had already vanished.

Taking a deep breath, Hanna reached for the next branch, saying a brief prayer as she cautiously tested its strength. For once in her life she was glad for her small size. She moved quietly through the branches until she found a thick, extended branch that stretched almost parallel to the adjoining tree. Reaching into her pack, she pulled out the first of the many scaling ropes she carried and threw it at the tree. There was a heavy thud as the metal hook landed against the tree and Hanna paused, listening for any sounds of alarm. When there were none she pulled hard on the hook until it caught on a branch. Hanna yanked on it, but it held firm. She coiled and tied the remainder of the rope around the thick branch until it stretched tightly between the trees.

Carefully, she climbed out to the edge of the branch and looked down. She neither heard nor saw anything unusual. It would be now or never, she decided. Whispering another prayer that the branches would hold her weight, she grasped the rope between her hands and let her legs swing into emptiness.

She hung there, suspended between the two trees, long enough to take deep breaths. Then hand over hand, she pulled herself across the rope and into the next tree. Once safely on the other side, she paused to force herself to calm down. Her hands were trembling so badly, she was afraid she would fall. She sternly ordered herself to be calm and quiet. She wasn't so much in danger of being seen as she was of being heard. It was dark in the shadow of the trees and she was up high enough so that the thick branches would shield her rope, and probably most of her body as well, from prying eyes below. But if she fumbled or misstepped, that would alert the guards. Every move had to be perfect; this was no place for a frightened girl.

As soon as her anxiety lessened, she resumed her climb. She found another suitable branch and, pulling the next scaling rope from her pack, she repeated her previous actions until the rope was stretched taut between the two trees. She pulled herself hand over hand to the next tree, where she continued the same movements. A part of her felt as if she was in a dream, while the cold edge of fear and discipline kept her mind razor sharp.

Soon the voices of the sentries beneath her became much louder. She took painstaking care to make as little noise as possible. Her movements began to become instinctive and routine. She crossed tree after tree, finally realizing that she had arrived at the tree next to the old barn. Once safely in the haven of the branches, Hanna allowed herself a few moments to rest. The next several minutes would be crucial and she wanted to be fully alert.

After a few minutes she continued her climb. This time she had to move upward until she was even with the roof. This was the most dangerous part, as the branches were thinner and weaker the higher she climbed. She moved with agonizing slowness, carefully testing each branch before pulling herself up. Finally, she saw the edge of the roof and sighed in relief. As she gingerly pulled herself to the next branch, she heard a loud cracking noise. Quickly, she grabbed an adjoining branch and froze as she heard a sentry shout.

"Vem där?"

The sound of a Swedish voice struck terror in her. Hanna held her breath, not daring to move. It seemed like ages, but she finally heard the sentry mutter something and move away. She waited a while longer, just for good measure, and then resumed her climb. When she was parallel to the roof she realized that the tree was farther away from the barn than she had expected. Silently, she judged her options. She could either try to leap from the branch to the roof or climb higher, hoping to find a sturdy branch and lower herself down with the rope.

"Mary, Mother of God," she whispered, and then she closed her eyes. Either option would leave her completely exposed for a few moments. Forcing herself to open her eyes, she thought for a moment and then decided to climb higher, looking for a way to lower herself down onto the roof. It would leave her exposed for a longer time, but it would be quieter.

She climbed up, searching until she found a sturdy branch she thought would hold her weight. Taking out a scaling rope, she tied it tightly around the branch and then waited for the right moment to move.

Finally, she heard the sentries laughing loudly, and she slid down the rope till her feet touched the rooftop.

Quickly, she fell to her stomach, her heartbeat roaring in her ears. Lying still on the cold roof, she listened for a shout of alarm, but none came. She came to her knees cautiously. Time was of the essence now.

Hanna crept along the roof, carefully feeling for the trapdoor. She could not find it after her first quick sweep, and she feared her search had been too hasty. She felt like weeping with frustration, but she forced herself to start again, this time much slower. She nearly shouted with joy when her fingers finally encircled an iron ring. Grasping it firmly, she tugged with all her might. The trapdoor didn't budge. She looked at the door in astonishment.

Oh God, I've come all this way and can't get the trapdoor open. She felt like laughing hysterically at the irony of it.

Slowly, her eyes narrowed in determination. She could be just as stubborn as that trapdoor and she wasn't leaving until it opened. She pulled her dagger free from her belt. Slowly, she moved the dagger around the outline of the trapdoor, loosening the dirt and grime. This time when she pulled on the iron ring she was rewarded with a slight movement. Her enthusiasm renewed, she slowly began scraping again until the trapdoor finally opened.

The overpowering acrid smell of gunpowder hit her. Good God in heaven, there would be a huge explosion when this building went up. Quickly, she reached into her pack and pulled out the thick bundle with the long fuse. She lowered it carefully down into the darkness until she felt it hit bottom. Putting the string between her teeth, she reached into her pocket for the flint and an iron scraper.

Now came the most dangerous part of her mission. She waited until she heard the murmur of the sentries' voices and swiftly struck the flint. Immediately, the sentries fell quiet. Holding her breath, Hanna waited. When they began talking again she struck again. Still no spark.

This time, she heard the sentries' anxious voices and feared she had been discovered. She struck the flint again and again, no longer worrying about the sound. Finally, a small spark appeared. Nursing it carefully, she took the fuse from her mouth and held it to the fire. The flames licked greedily at the rope and began its slow descent into the darkness below. Hanna waited a precious moment more to make sure the flame hadn't gone out before she scrambled for the rope. The shouting beneath her was loud and she could hear the alarm being sounded.

Praying that the branch would hold, she grabbed the rope and pulled herself up quickly, fear giving her strength and speed. Once safely on the branch, she climbed down, branches tearing at her face. When she reached her first rope bridge, she hastily swung herself across, scrambling in an attempt to find the next rope. It continued this way for at least three trees, until she heard someone beneath her shaking the tree.

"Han är här," someone was screaming. Hanna held her breath. *Merciful God, she had been discovered!*

The tree shook madly as the man beneath seemed determined to dislodge her from it. Hanna closed her eyes and clung to the tree for dear life. When she thought she would not be able to hold on for another moment the shaking stopped and she heard a gurgling noise. Not daring to waste another moment, Hanna hastily reached for the next rope as she heard a hoarse voice below her.

"Hanna?"

Her heart leaped to her throat. "Stefan?" she whispered back.

"Get down here, now."

Hanna obeyed, partly out of fear and partly out of an overwhelming relief that Stefan was so close. She began her descent recklessly, practically sliding down the branches. At one point her tunic snagged on a branch. She yanked on it so hard, it tore halfway down her side. She was nearly at the bottom when she felt a strong hand grab her by the britches and lift her from the tree.

She landed hard in Stefan's arms. He hugged her tightly and then pressed a fierce kiss on her lips. But before she could even open her mouth to say something, he quickly set her on her feet. Hanna gasped in horror as she stumbled over a Swedish soldier with a jagged wound in his throat. She had no time to dwell on it, for Stefan grabbed her arm so painfully, she nearly yelped.

"We had better get out of this alive, Hanna Quinn, because when we do I am going to kill you myself," he warned grimly.

Hanna opened her mouth, but no words came out. Desperately, she filled her lungs with air. "The depot is about to go," she said finally.

Stefan's eyes narrowed and he gripped her hand, dragging her behind him. They ran, not caring who saw them or how much noise they made. Hanna could hear the shouting and the running feet of those in hot pursuit, but Stefan had a firm hold on her hand, relentlessly pulling her along until her lungs screamed for air yet again.

Hanna tried to stop, but he would not let her. "B-Boguslaw . . ." she managed to cry out.

"He is safe," Stefan called out over his shoulder.

They were still running when the terrifying roar of an explosion knocked them to the ground. Hanna hit the earth hard and immediately felt a strange tingling sensation in her leg.

"Stefan," she screamed, but her cry was muffled by shouts of pain and rage.

Stefan heard her scream and quickly rolled on top of her, covering her body as shards of iron and stone flew through the air. There was a moment of silence, and Hanna wiggled in an attempt to get up and flee.

"Stay down," she heard Stefan order firmly. She immediately realized why he had ordered her to do so as another set of secondary explosions filled the air with more flying shrapnel. As the fireworks exploded around them, Hanna suddenly felt light-headed.

"Stefan," she whispered, "I feel so odd . . ." Before she could finish her sentence a yawning emptiness came rushing up to greet her.

Stefan rolled to his feet, his heart leaping to his throat when he saw Hanna lying limply on the ground, her eyes closed. In one swift movement he swept her into his arms.

"Hold on, love," he whispered to her as he headed for the spot where his men were waiting.

Boguslaw breathed a sigh of relief when he saw Stefan come into view, but his relief faded at the grim look on Stefan's face and the iciness in his eyes. Stefan handed Hanna up to him without a word and then mounted his own horse in one quick motion.

"Give her back to me," he ordered the giant, wheeling his horse around. Stefan cradled Hanna carefully in his arms, resting her cheek against his chest.

Spurring their horses on, they made for camp while some of his men stayed behind to confuse any pursuers who might follow. As soon as they arrived, the word quickly spread of Hanna's success. Many of the men cheered and shouted as Stefan rode past, but he ignored them, instead ordering Mikhail to fetch Henryk to his tent.

When they arrived at the command tent Stefan lowered Hanna to Boguslaw. Quickly, the giant took her into the tent and lay her gently on the furs. Stefan knelt beside her, taking stock of her injury. A thick piece of shrapnel had lodged itself in her leg.

"Jezus Maria," Boguslaw whispered as Stefan's face grew dark with concern. Stefan looked at him, and for a moment, their eyes locked. Stefan said nothing, but Boguslaw clearly understood the look of pain in his commander's eyes. Stefan had been betrayed by two people he cared for deeply. A deep slash of pain and regret shot through Boguslaw's heart. Swallowing hard, he lowered his eyes to look at Hanna.

"I accept full responsibility for tonight's events," Boguslaw said quietly.

Stefan did not answer for a long time, unmoved by Boguslaw's surprisingly shaky voice, and simply brushed back a lock of hair that had fallen across Hanna's forehead. When he finally looked up at the giant he said curtly, "Leave us."

As Boguslaw studied Stefan's stony face, he realized that it was the face of a stranger. He rose slowly and without another word left the tent.

When the giant was gone Stefan removed his dagger from his belt and carefully cut the cloth away from her wounds. Hanna began to moan and come around.

"Where the hell is Henryk?" Stefan asked sharply, his voice hoarse with worry.

As if he had heard his name, Henryk entered the tent and knelt down beside Stefan. Mikhail and Alexander rushed in after him.

Henryk took in Hanna's condition at a glance. The wound was deep, but the piece of iron lodged in her leg had stopped the bleeding. As soon as he pulled it out, he would have to clean the wound and then sew it up. Hanna would feel intense pain, and Henryk did not relish his role as the one who forced it upon her. Yet the task had to be done, and soon.

Henryk stood and ordered everyone out of the tent with the exception of Stefan. He doubted if an entire regiment of Cossacks could pull the man from her side.

"Bring her around completely and give her some vodka," Henryk ordered Stefan as he reached into his bag.

Stefan retrieved the vodka and sat behind Hanna, cradling her head in his lap. Gently, he patted her cheek until her eyes fluttered open.

"Stefan . . . wh-what happened?" Hanna asked, dazed.

"Shh," Stefan said softly, raising the bottle to her lips. "Take a drink of this."

Hanna swallowed a mouthful, coughing as the liquid burned her throat. As she moved slightly, she felt a horrible pain in her leg. With a small cry, she raised her head to look, but Stefan pressed down on her shoulder, preventing her from seeing the wound.

"Everything is all right. Just take another drink, Hanna."

As Hanna bit her lower lip, her blue-green eyes glazed with fear and pain, Stefan felt his insides tightening. Good God, he wished with all his heart that he could bear the agony for her. Gritting his teeth, he lifted the bottle, and Hanna obediently took another sip.

Henryk had assembled the instruments he needed and now bent over Hanna. "I'll need to pull a piece of iron from your leg, child. You'll first feel the pressure of my weight on your hip, for I must hold your leg still. Then I will pull out the iron. There will be some pain."

Hanna's lower lip trembled, but she met Henryk's gaze steadily. "I'll try not to move, Henryk."

Stefan's hold on her shoulders tightened. Judging from the size of the shrapnel, there would be more than just some pain.

The old man raised his eyes to meet Stefan's. Grimly, Stefan nodded and bent over Hanna.

"Hold on to me, Hanna," he whispered. "I'll be right here."

Hanna held out her hand and Stefan gripped it hard. She inhaled a sharp breath as Henryk leaned against her, pressing hard against her hip. With both hands, the old man reached out and took the iron between his fingers, pulling hard on it. An intense pain swept through Hanna's body, and her mouth opened in a silent scream. Stefan murmured soothing words to her, his face gray with concern.

"I've got it," Henryk announced, dropping the piece of iron next to the coals. Quickly, he pressed a pile of clean linens against the wound to stem the bleeding.

"I've got to close the wound before she loses any more blood."

Stefan nodded, his lips pressed tightly together as Henryk reached for his needle and held it over the coals until it glowed red.

Hanna weakly lifted her head and watched in fascinated horror as Henryk came toward her with the heated, glowing needle.

"Don't look," Stefan whispered, turning Hanna's head aside just as Henryk pressed the needle to her tender skin.

Hanna's body jerked suddenly at the searing pain, her breath expelled in one anguished rush. "Stefan," she managed to cry before her head fell to the side and she slipped into merciful unconsciousness.

Chapter Twenty-four

Hanna floated in a haze of pain and nightmare. A constant burning thirst ached in the back of her throat and she was so hot, so bloody hot. She tried to kick the covers off her but felt a sharp pain jackknife through her body. Her mouth opened in a silent scream and then she faded into blackness.

Dimly, Hanna was often aware of strong hands lifting her head and making her drink something to ease her aching throat. Sometimes she felt hands prodding her painful leg, but she did not have the strength to move away or even open her mouth in protest. Faces swam in and out of her sight. She heard someone ask her a question, but the voice came from so great a distance, she could not understand the words. Yet she clearly remembered hearing someone whispering soothing words and warm fingers entwined with hers, giving her strength.

Finally one morning, Hanna opened her eyes and struggled to a sitting position. She pressed her hand to her brow as her vision blurred, causing all the images to whirl about her. *Where was she and what was she doing here?*

She closed her eyes and then opened them again, forcing the objects around her into focus. She was alone in the command tent.

Her memory came rushing back. *The cannons. Good God, had she done it?* She held her hands against her temples, forcing herself to remember what had happened. She had been running when an explosion had knocked her to the ground. Stefan had been there as well. Then she felt the pain in her leg.

Her leg. Quickly, she lifted the skins and saw that the full length of her right thigh was bandaged. Gingerly, she tried to move it and found that it only invoked a little pain, nothing like the burning agony she had felt before. She closed her eyes in relief and then opened them again abruptly, snatching the skins away from her body.

She was completely naked! And she was in Stefan's bed again.

She could hear her heartbeat—loud and fast—as she remembered the look of fury on Stefan's face when he had pulled her from the tree. *How had he found her? Where was Boguslaw? What in God's name had happened?*

Anxiously, Hanna struggled to her feet, favoring her injured leg. Hastily, she was looking for something to wear when she heard a noise at the front of the tent. Before she could move, Stefan threw open the flap, his shadow falling across the opening.

His eyes widened as he saw her standing stark naked in the middle of his tent. Hanna took an unsteady step back, clutching her hands to her breasts in an attempt at modesty.

"S-Stefan," she whispered, as she felt her cheeks blaze. She took in several things at once: the huge dark circles beneath his eyes, the lines on his cheeks that indicated deep-seated exhaustion, and the look of relief that flooded his face when he saw that she was all right.

Stefan let his eyes sweep boldly across Hanna's body. Her hair tumbled across her shoulders and fell down her back like a shining red river. Her young breasts were taut, and the rosy pink of her nipples peeked through her fingers, which had not completely covered them. His breath caught as he let his gaze fall to the soft curls of red hair between her thighs. Lord Almighty, she was beautiful despite the heavy bandage that encumbered her right leg.

Slowly, he raised his eyes to meet hers, and Hanna felt her heart sink as a cold shutter seemed to fall in place over his stormy gray orbs. A lump settled in her throat.

This time I have gone too far. I have pushed his patience beyond reason. And I have broken the fragile bond of trust that had been building between us.

She felt like shouting, *I did it for you, Stefan. Because I couldn't bear the thought of anything happening to you. No matter what the punishment, if you are alive, it was worth it.*

But she said nothing, simply twisting her hands together tightly in front of her, waiting for the explosion of his wrath.

It didn't come. Stefan stood motionless for several moments until he abruptly turned from her. Leaning over, he picked up a gown and stockings, tossing them at her.

"Put them on," he said.

Hearing the coolness in his voice, Hanna grabbed the gown off the ground and quickly pulled it over her head. She fumbled with the hooks, her hands shaking nervously. Stefan strode over and helped her fasten the rest of the hooks. Hanna felt a shiver run through her from his warm fingers against her skin.

Plucking her stockings from the floor, Stefan led her to a stool, motioning for her to sit. She perched there obediently, although the bandage made it difficult to sit. Kneeling, Stefan carefully lifted the edge of her gown before sliding the stocking over her toes. Slowly, he drew the delicate material up the length of her thigh, where he fastened it securely with a garter. Hanna felt her cheeks flush, both in embarrassment and wonder, that he was so skilled at such a thing. She thought about jerking away from him as he reached for her injured leg, but the dark look on his face boded no argument. Her helplessness brought tears of humiliation to her eyes, but she sat completely still as he eased her into the second stocking. Afterward, he helped her into her boots, not uttering a single word the entire time.

When he was finished he stood abruptly. "Wait here," he instructed. He stepped out of the tent and spoke rapidly to the soldier on guard.

Hanna obeyed him, folding her hands in her lap. A finger of ice wrapped around her heart. Stefan's voice was so cold and distant that it frightened her more than whatever punishment he had in mind for her.

She had no idea how much time had passed before he returned. Her mind had explored every possible means of his wrath until she was exhausted. When he came back into the tent she raised her eyes slowly.

He had her cloak in his hands and he gestured for her to stand. When she did he wrapped it around her shoulders and abruptly lifted her into his arms. He was careful not to jar her leg, and Hanna marveled at how a man so large could be so gentle. She looked up at him questioningly, but his face was expressionless. Her stomach began to churn uneasily.

Stefan carried her out into the bright, cool morning. Hanna shielded her eyes from the sun with the back of her hand. When her eyes finally adjusted to the light she saw all the men were oddly quiet. No one looked at her, except for the Tartar officer, Hamid-Bey. He gazed at her with amused interest, his hand slowly stroking the long hairs of his mustache. Hanna began to feel increasingly nervous.

"What is happening?" she whispered.

Stefan did not answer, but abruptly handed her over to Mikhail. Panic seized her and worriedly she looked up at Mikhail for an explanation. Stefan's brother stared straight ahead, not acknowledging her despite the fact that his grip on her was so tight she could barely move.

Frightened, Hanna glanced back at Stefan, unable to take her eyes from his face. He stood calmly in front of his men, one hand on his hip. His face was unreadable, but his jaw was clenched, giving his features a hard edge.

Hanna felt her heart skip in fright. She had never seen his anger so icy and controlled.

"Boguslaw Dobrowolski, come forward," Stefan called out, his voice ringing clearly among the trees.

Hanna drew in her breath sharply as the giant stepped forward. The huge man stood before Stefan, his head raised. A deathly silence fell over the men, and Hanna felt fear sweep through her.

"Boguslaw Dobrowolski, soldier of Poland and servant of King Yan Casimir, the charges against you are as follows: disobeying a direct order from your commanding officer, jeopardizing a sensitive mission, and betraying the trust of your fellow soldiers. What have you to say for yourself?"

Boguslaw met Stefan's eyes evenly. "All that you have said is true, sir."

Hanna began to struggle in Mikhail's arms. "Nay," she cried out. "I forced him to help me. For God's sake, he didn't want to do it."

Stefan did not so much as glance her way; his gaze was locked with Boguslaw's. "Do you know what the sentence is for such an offense?" Stefan asked, his voice quiet yet steady.

Boguslaw nodded. "Aye, sir, the sentence is death."

There was a murmur among the men, and Hanna jerked in Mikhail's arms. "Oh God, Stefan, please listen to me. What he says is not true. It was all my fault. Please, let me go." She pounded her fists against Mikhail's chest, but he would not release her.

"Silence her," Stefan barked harshly, and Mikhail clamped his hand down over her mouth.

Stefan clasped his hands behind his back, slowly walking back and forth in front of his men. "I will not tolerate disobedience. Not when our lives and the country depend on my judgment. I want that to be clear to every man here."

There were some murmurs of agreement. Hanna suddenly realized that Stefan's public punishment of Boguslaw, a close friend, displayed to everyone that each man under his command was to be treated equally and fairly. She bit her lower lip so hard, she drew blood.

There was silence, and then Stefan and Boguslaw locked eyes for another long moment. Finally, Boguslaw crossed himself and murmured something softly. Hanna shook her head mutely, her heart thudding with dread and fear.

God in heaven, it was sheer madness. If Stefan wasn't so stubborn, he would see that they had done it for him. Because the country needed him and because . . . because, oh God, she loved him. A sob escaped her lips, and Mikhail lifted his hand from her mouth.

"Nay, please stop," Hanna cried out, the tears choking her voice.

No one seemed to hear her. Boguslaw slowly knelt on one knee, his eyes never leaving Stefan's face. Stefan carefully drew his sword from its sheath, raising it above his head. Stefan paused for a split second before he brought his sword down, slashing through the front of Boguslaw's tunic.

Hanna let out a small cry and buried her head in Mikhail's chest, sobbing uncontrollably. After a moment she felt Mikhail gently lift her chin. She raised her tear-streaked face and gulped in astonishment. The material from Boguslaw's tunic had fallen away from his skin, leaving him bare-chested but miraculously unmarked. Hanna felt her heart leap in joy and confusion. *Stefan had not killed him.*

Boguslaw appeared to be surprised as well. The giant looked up at his commander, clearly bewildered by his actions.

"Rise, son of Poland," Stefan said softly. "I will spare your life. You have served fifteen years honorably in the service of our country. I choose not to impose the sentence of death upon you, yet you will be punished for your disobedience." Stefan jerked his head at one of his men. "Bind him to the tree."

Boguslaw stood and held himself erect as the rest of his tunic was stripped from his back. He was led to a nearby tree and his arms were lashed around the trunk. A young lieutenant stepped forward with a corded whip.

"Twenty lashes for his offense," Stefan instructed the lieutenant.

"Nay," Hanna shouted, and Stefan turned his head slowly to look at her. "The punishment should be mine as well." She lifted her chin proudly, a trail of tears still visible on her cheeks. Stefan nodded imperceptibly.

"And give him fifteen more for the girl's offense," he said calmly.

Hanna's mouth fell open, her eyes wide with horror. "Nay, Stefan, it is barbaric." For a moment, she thought she saw regret in his eyes, but when he spoke, his voice indicated no such emotion.

"You will watch this man suffer for your disobedience, Hanna. Perhaps the next time you consider disobeying one of my orders, you will remember the consequences."

With a small cry, Hanna turned her head, squeezing her eyes shut. Stefan walked over to her, reaching out to catch her chin firmly in his hand. He waited until she opened her eyes.

"For each lash that you turn away from or close your eyes to he will receive two more. This is your punishment too. Is that understood?"

Hanna pressed her lips tightly together, her eyes filling with tears. "You are a beast. I h-hate you," she whispered fiercely as the tears slipped from her eyes and down her face.

Their eyes met and held—hers full of pain, his dark with an emotion she could not read.

Turning, Stefan nodded curtly to the lieutenant. The man lifted his hand, the whip snaking through the air. It landed on Boguslaw's back with a cracking thud. The giant did not utter a sound. Hanna watched silently, her lips pressed tightly together.

Stefan was as impassive as stone. He stood stiffly watching as the lieutenant lifted his arm again and again. With each crack of the whip, Stefan felt a bone-deep weariness fill him. He knew full well what Boguslaw's and Hanna's motives had been. But a commander could not allow any man to defy his orders. Punishment had to be meted out, and it had to be made clear that disobedience within his ranks would be severely punished. Even if it meant that he would have to whip a man he had known and called his friend for fifteen years.

Damn them for putting me in such a position. He felt heavy and burdened, beyond simply tired. The weight of his thoughts bore down on him.

Thirty-two, thirty-three, thirty-four, thirty-five.

At last the whip was silent, but no one moved. Finally, Stefan stepped forward, ordering one of his men to cut Boguslaw from the ropes. Once free of his bonds, the giant took one step from the tree and stumbled. Stefan gestured, and two men rushed forward to help Boguslaw steady himself.

"Take him back to his tent and see that his wounds are attended to," Stefan commanded sharply. Turning from the men, he strode back toward the command tent. As he passed his brother, he nodded once. Mikhail abruptly turned, carrying Hanna to her own tent.

Hanna remained silent as Mikhail lay her carefully on the bed and leaned over to revive the embers in her coal bed. When the coals finally began to glow red Mikhail looked over his shoulder at Hanna and saw that she had turned her head and was staring at the side of the tent.

Sighing, Mikhail came to his feet and stood over her still form for a long moment, seeing the tears streaming down her face. "He did what he had to do, Hanna. His duty requires him to make decisions . . . difficult decisions. Though we might not always understand his motives, his judgment is always sound and fair. In return, he demands complete obedience from his men. To disobey him is a direct challenge of his abilities and judgment. Despite your success at the depot, to let yours and Boguslaw's challenge pass unmentioned . . . would have been unwise."

"His actions were cruel and unfair," she said so softly, he barely heard her.

"I don't expect you to understand. War is a difficult and complex matter. In spite of the fact that what you did was wrong, I understand your motive. And I thank you for it. But I warn you, don't ever cross my brother again. Next time, he will be unable to act so generously."

With those words, Mikhail left the tent. Hanna waited until long after his footsteps faded before struggling to her feet, wincing afresh from the pain in her leg. Angrily brushing the tears from her cheeks, she grabbed her bag and went out into the cool morning. She ignored her guard's questions and strode directly for Boguslaw's tent. She tapped lightly on the tent pole, but when no one answered, she lifted the flap and entered. Boguslaw was lying on the bed, stomach down, his back covered with linen strips. With a small cry, Hanna sat beside him.

Carefully lifting the linen strips, she saw that Henryk had cleaned the wounds and placed salve on them. Her eyes filled with tears at the injustice of it.

"Oh, God, Boguslaw," she whispered. "I'm so sorry."

He lifted his head to look at her. "Nay, milady, have no regrets. We did what we thought was right. The cannons have been destroyed and our commander is still alive."

She was silent for a long moment. "How did Stefan find us?" she finally asked softly.

Boguslaw sighed. "His men were doing a last survey of the grounds for their attack when they came across me. Marek nearly slit my throat before he figured out who I was. Stefan was summoned and I was sent back to the rendezvous point. The colonel wished to wait for you himself."

Hanna smiled wryly. "Aye, he was there, all right." Her eyes lingered on Boguslaw's bandaged back. "I only pray to God we did the right thing. But what price did we pay? You almost lost your life."

"My life was forfeit the moment I agreed to help you, milady," Boguslaw said softly.

"Wh-what?"

Boguslaw closed his eyes for a long moment before opening them again. "In time of war there is often no time for a commander to explain a decision. If he had to outline the reasons behind each of his actions, there would be confusion and chaos. He must be able to count on his men to obey his orders without question or hesitation. Every soldier knows that and takes an oath of obedience." He paused for a minute before resuming. "When I agreed to help you I directly disobeyed my commanding officer. The price of such disobedience is death. I knew that."

"It's m-madness," Hanna said, overcome with horror.

Boguslaw shook his head firmly. "It is a matter of honor, milady."

Hanna felt ill at the thought that Boguslaw had willingly agreed to forfeit his life in order to help her. She took a deep breath to keep her stomach from heaving. "Yet your life was spared," she managed to say.

She saw pain appear in Boguslaw's eyes.

"Aye, the colonel spared my miserable existence. Still, his mercy has cost me my honor. For a soldier such punishment is far worse than death."

Hanna's eyes widened. "Th-that is why Stefan spared you?"

Boguslaw inhaled deeply and shook his head. "Nay. The colonel showed compassion in the face of my treachery. It is what pains me the most."

A sob escaped her lips as she touched his cheek. "I had no idea. Oh, Lord, please forgive me for all the anguish I have caused you, Boguslaw. I wish you had never had the misfortune of meeting me."

Boguslaw reached up, his hand encircling her cool one tightly. "You are gravely mistaken, milady. You are a remarkable woman . . . brave, kind, and fiercely loyal. I consider it an honor to be counted among those who had a chance to know you."

Hanna squeezed his hand as a tear fell from her eye. Boguslaw reached up and brushed it away. "Had I been different . . . a man of rank and wealth . . . I would have risked everything for the love of a woman like you, milady. As it is, I have but my life to offer you. I would not have done it any differently."

Another tear slipped from her eye and rolled down her cheek. "I d-don't know what to say," Hanna whispered, her eyes wet.

"There is nothing to say, milady. I know your heart lies elsewhere. It is the will of God, and I have known it for a long time." He lifted her hand to his lips and pressed a soft kiss against her skin. "I ask only one thing of you: Find it in your heart to understand and forgive. Do not judge Stefan Tarnowski so harshly."

They stared at each other for a long moment before Boguslaw dropped her hand. With a small groan, he laid his head back on the bed. Hanna sat watching him, carefully adjusting the skins until she heard the steady rhythm of his breathing. When she was sure he slept, she slowly came to her feet.

Suddenly the enormity of all that had happened swept over her. She took a shaky step and then paused to regain her bearings.

Good Lord, it sounded so easy. Understand and forgive. That was all there was to it. She closed her eyes, remembering how Stefan looked as he ordered the lashings for Boguslaw. His face was cold and emotionless. Her hands clenched at her sides.

Taking a deep breath, she opened her eyes and left the tent. Somehow, she doubted that she and Stefan would ever be able to find a way to bridge the gap that now yawned endlessly between them.

Chapter Twenty-five

Stefan rubbed his eyes wearily. He and his officers had been seated around the command table for hours. The smoke from the lamp filled the tent with a haze, making it seem full of fog.

Stefan kneaded the muscles in his stiff neck and exhaled deeply. He had called a meeting as soon as he had been informed of the planned execution of the two Polish colonels, Piotrowski and Smolenski. He knew that the public hanging of the men was an attempt by the Swedes to draw him out, force him to tip his hand. In spite of this, Stefan did not intend to leave the challenge unanswered.

He looked around the table at his men. Alexander was involved in a fierce discussion with Marek, his bushy mustache twitching rapidly, his face the color of a ripe beet.

"It is a trap if ever I've seen one," Alexander said heatedly, banging his hand against the tabletop. "They know damn well that we will try to rescue the men."

Marek spread his hands across the table. "Of course it

is a trap. But that doesn't mean that we can't spring it and still rescue the men."

Alexander leaned forward. "I say it isn't worth the risk."

Mikhail jumped in. "I disagree. Freeing the colonels would be an enormous victory for us, not only strategically, but it would certainly lower the morale of the Swedish troops. It could have far-reaching consequences."

Staszek nodded. "I agree with Mikhail. We can't just let them die without even trying to save them."

The men began arguing loudly until Stefan stood slowly, clapping his hands. Everyone looked up at him in surprise. "Cease your arguing. I have heard enough." He waited a moment until he was sure he had their full attention and then slowly paced the length of the tent, his large hands clasped behind his back.

"There is no question that the Swedes hope to flush us out with the public execution of the colonels. They expect us to try to save the men in the hopes of killing or capturing any one of us. Since the successful attack on the depot they certainly are more than anxious to discover the location of our camp. We must be extraordinarily careful, but I think we can strike against them and be successful. Therefore, I have decided that there will be a rescue attempt, but one with a rather unorthodox strategy."

Marek raised his head sharply, immediately interested. "Unorthodox?"

"Aye, unorthodox." He paused for a moment, deep in thought. "Marek, where do you think the best place to attempt the rescue would be?"

Marek thought for a moment before answering. "On the road between the headquarters and the main square, where the execution will take place. They will be the most vulnerable to attack then."

Stefan stroked his chin thoughtfully. "Agreed. And I think that is exactly the conclusion the Swedes hope we will come to. Nay, we shall not fall into their trap."

Mikhail looked up at his brother. "Then where shall we strike, Stefan?"

"We will make our move as the men are being led to the platform for their execution."

There was a concerted gasp in the room. "Amid the crowd?" Marek said in astonishment.

Stefan nodded. "Aye. We shall be disguised as common folk attending the hanging. We will strike as soon as the men are taken from the wagon. There will be a few moments when the men and their guards will be surrounded by the crowd. We will strike then, using the cover of the crowd to make our escape."

Marek leaned forward. "But how will we get through the gates of the city? Surely the soldiers will seal the gates and search the crowd for us."

"We will carry disguises for the colonels as well. A heavy cloak with a hood will be enough. It will conceal their identities for a short time, long enough for us to escape. But we will not leave the city via the gates. We will cross the Vistula River to safety."

Alexander gaped. "Cross the river? In the middle of the day?"

"Aye. The Swedes will not expect us to make our escape across the river. Their security will be weakest there. A small detail of our men will take care of the sentries shortly before our arrival. We shall then make our escape in many different rafts. When the Swedes finally discover our escape route, we will offer them only a few small, scattered targets. Hopefully, by that time we will be far enough out of range that they will be unable to hit us. They will not have time to drag a cannon, even a small one, to the river. We will surely be gone by then."

Marek whistled under his breath. "My God, Stefan, it is a brazen plan. Imagine crossing the Vistula in broad daylight. But it might just work. Aye, strategically, I can find little fault with it. Except..." He paused for a long moment and then spoke the thought that was on everyone's mind. "Except that it puts you at risk, Stefan. It would not serve us if you were somehow captured by the Swedes."

Stefan frowned, kneading his nape. "Aye, that is true.

But I'll not put my men at risk and then watch from a distance. Not under any circumstances."

An uncomfortable silence filled the tent before Mikhail stood up and faced his brother. "We need you, Stefan. Alive. Marek is right. You are much too valuable to be put at risk."

Stefan's frown deepened. The thought of someone other than himself implementing the plan was unfathomable. Yet the cold, rational part of his brain told him that putting himself unnecessarily in danger was foolish and would undermine everything they were trying to do.

"Damn, this is an intolerable situation," Stefan cursed softly, clenching his fists tightly at his sides. He couldn't agree to such a thing; he wouldn't. He began pacing furiously before finally stopping abruptly in his tracks.

"I understand that your concern for my welfare is well founded," he said curtly. "But I'll be damned if I will stay behind." He paused a moment to deliberately unclench his hands. "I'll lead the detail to the river's edge. That should keep me busy but still within reach, should anyone require my assistance."

The men gave a sigh of relief in unison, and Alexander rubbed his balding head nervously. "Lord Almighty, Stefan, it tightens the balls just to think about waltzing into the middle of an execution and dancing out across the river with our colonels. It is damn tricky, but I have to say it is bold."

"Aye, it is bold," Mikhail said enthusiastically, "and it has a good chance of success. I could lead a group of men across the river the night before and conceal the rafts on the other side."

Stefan nodded slowly and then looked at Staszek. "I want you personally to scout the area to determine the best places to cross the river. Keep in mind the need for some thick underbrush to conceal the rafts."

Staszek nodded as Stefan sat back down at the table. The conversation quickly turned to the details of the operation.

They talked for some time longer before Stefan stood

A Touch of Fire

and dismissed them. Wearily, the men left the tent, filing out one by one. When the last man was gone Stefan went outside to have a breath of the crisp, cold night air. It was a clear night; the moon hung in the sky like a round, golden orb, throwing flitting shadows across the pale snow. He walked away from the tent and the guard who stood there, in search of a few moments of solitude.

A gentle wind blew across his face, lifting his long hair from his shoulders. The sounds of the night were comforting and peaceful. Yet it was when he was alone that his thoughts most often wandered to Hanna. He had not seen her since his public punishment of Boguslaw. She was careful to avoid him, and he found himself thankful for it. He had no desire to see the look of disapproval and repulsion in her eyes, clearly horrified by his harsh actions against his friend.

For Christ's sake, how did everything get so tangled? Duty, friendship, loyalty, and honor had been blurred until nothing was clear anymore. In war, survival became all important . . . and survival depended on good and solid leadership. That responsibility had fallen squarely on his shoulders.

But it had been a mistake to let Hanna remain at the camp. His foolishness over her had nearly cost him his command . . . and her life. *Try living with that, Colonel.*

Stefan smiled bitterly as he thought of all the times Hanna had defied him, challenged his authority and knowingly disobeyed him. Aye, she infuriated him, all right. It was enough to drive a man into certain madness.

Yet, surprisingly, he could not seem to dwell on his anger. Instead, unbidden images of her sweet smile and the way she blushed so innocently leapt to mind. He exhaled deeply. How could he possibly forget the way he felt when her soft curves pressed against him and strands of her silky hair trailed between his fingers?

Stop, he ordered himself sternly. *You have let your better judgment be overruled in every decision you have made about her. Put her out of your heart and mind, soldier.*

Stefan started as he felt a hand on his shoulder. Instinctively, he turned, reaching for his dagger. Hamid-Bey stepped slowly out of the shadows.

"Forgive me," he said softly. "I have startled you."

Stefan dropped his hand from his dagger. "I'd advise you not to approach me so quietly, Commander. I nearly put my dagger through your throat."

Hamid-Bey smiled. "Rest assured that I will remember that advice next time."

Stefan nodded slightly. "What brings you here? I thought you would have left camp by now."

"I shall soon depart. There is, however, a matter I would first like to take up with you."

Stefan felt vaguely disturbed. Years of training had conditioned him to sense what went on in the minds of the men who served him. At this moment, he had an uneasy feeling that he would not like what the Tartar was about to say. Yet as he looked at Hamid-Bey, he let none of these emotions show on his face.

"I am listening."

Hamid-Bey slowly fingered the curl of his mustache. "I wish to ask a favor of you."

"I see," Stefan said slowly, his face indicating none of the surprise he felt. "How may I be of service to you?"

"I wish to ask for the girl."

Stefan was stunned into silence. "Girl?" Stefan finally said, hearing his voice choke slightly.

"Yes, the girl called Hanna. I wish to own her."

Stefan hesitated. Here was a problem he had not foreseen. As no man had an obvious claim to Hanna, the Tartar clearly saw no reason not to ask for her. In all aspects, to Hamid-Bey, it was a perfectly legitimate request.

Stefan was disconcerted. This had suddenly become a delicate matter. He could not afford to anger the Tartar, yet the thought of turning Hanna over to Hamid-Bey made him tense uncomfortably.

Stefan struggled against the feeling, forcing himself to harden his heart. Why shouldn't he consider it? Giving

Hanna to the Tartar would relieve him of all responsibility for her. He knew she would do quite well as the woman of a Tartar commander. The riches and booty Hamid-Bey would lay at her feet would surely be beyond her wildest imagination. She would be well taken care of, protected, and treated like a queen.

Aye, he should certainly entertain the idea. From his point of view there would be benefits, as well. There would be no more of Hanna's fiery temper, her constant interference and disobedience. Things would be quiet again and he could resume his duty without the continual disruption she caused to his concentration. He told himself that several times until he almost believed it. *Almost.*

Stefan crossed his arms and looked at the Tartar thoughtfully. "Why her?" he asked slowly. "Surely you could have any woman you desired."

The Tartar laughed, and Stefan saw a row of his gleaming white teeth in the moonlight.

"That I could, Commander. But this Hanna, she intrigues me like no other woman. She has hair the color of fire and a courage that would put a Tartar woman to shame. She will bear fine sons, good warriors, to the man who beds her."

Stefan felt fierce anger at the thought of anyone bedding Hanna. Except perhaps himself.

"The girl is my responsibility," Stefan said carefully.

"I would release you from that responsibility once the girl became mine," Hamid-Bey answered smoothly.

Stefan was silent for a long moment. Arguments raged in his head until finally he realized that whatever absurd notions he was entertaining, he wouldn't turn Hanna over to the Tartar and he knew it.

Shrugging his shoulders, Stefan said, "I am sorry, Commander. It is simply not possible."

Hamid-Bey lifted an eyebrow. "You refuse my request?"

Stefan shook his head. "Nay, not exactly. I simply cannot fulfill it. You see, the girl is my reward for a revenge I extracted on my enemy. She is . . . well, symbolic of that victory."

Hamid-Bey's eyes held Stefan's gaze. "Perhaps I can tempt you with even greater rewards."

Stefan spread his hands. "Your offer is generous, but I wish nothing."

The Tartar laughed. "Come now, Commander. The girl has openly expressed her dislike for you. You and I both know that a warm and willing woman is quite preferable to a clawing, fighting one... or a cold one, for that matter."

"What the girl thinks of me is of no importance," Stefan said casually. "She belongs to me and I will do with her what I please, regardless of her feelings."

For a moment their eyes met again, like two sabers crossing and parlaying. Despite his mild tone, Stefan's eyes held a grim challenge. For a brief moment, something stirred in the dark, gleaming eyes of the Tartar. Then he bowed deeply.

"As you wish, Commander. I ask only that you consider my words. The next time we meet I will make my offer again. Perhaps you will have changed your mind by then."

Stefan nodded slightly as the Tartar melted into the darkness. Then, with a soft curse, Stefan turned sharply on his heel and returned to his tent.

Hanna was roused from a dreamless sleep by her guard. Anxiously, she sat up. "What is wrong?" she whispered, clutching the skins to her breast.

"I'm sorry to wake you, milady. It is the colonel. He wishes to see you at once in his tent."

Hanna fumbled with the furs sleepily. "Now? My God, it must be nearly midnight."

Her guard nodded. "Aye, it is, milady. I suppose you have been summoned for a most important matter. I'll escort you to his tent when you are ready." He turned and left the tent.

Hanna slipped from beneath the warmth of her furs, shivering in the cool air. Her leg was stiff, and she gently rubbed the area around the wound to get the blood circulating. Then, bending over the coals, she breathed some life into them before dressing hastily. Her hair was unbound and she considered braiding it. As she ran her fingers through her tresses, she shook her head. It would take too much time, and besides, she would only have to unravel it as soon as she returned to her tent. It wouldn't be worth the effort. Quickly, she grabbed her cloak and thrust her arms into it, tying the hood tight around her head.

She stepped out into the frigid night to where her guard was waiting for her. As they approached the command tent, Hanna could hear voices raised in loud discussion. The guard left her at the entrance and turned away quickly. Taking a deep breath, Hanna lifted the flap and entered.

Mikhail and Stefan were seated at the table and both jerked their heads up when she appeared. Stefan slowly came to his feet.

"Sit down," he ordered her shortly.

Hanna pushed back her hood, shaking out her hair before sitting. She could feel the tension in the room, and her heart started to flutter uncomfortably.

"I think we should discuss this further..." Mikhail started in a low voice, but Stefan interrupted him with a wave of his hand.

"There will be no more discussion, Mikhail. My mind is made up."

Hanna looked at the men in bewilderment. "Made up about what?" she asked, suddenly not sure she wanted to know the answer.

Mikhail looked at her, his brows furrowed in a frown. "The Tartar commander, Hamid-Bey, has asked for you."

"Is he ill?"

Mikhail exchanged a quick look with his brother and then sighed. "Nay, Hanna. He wishes to claim you."

"Claim me?" she said in astonishment.

Mikhail nodded. "He desires... well..." He struggled for a moment. "Curse it, there is no other way to say it. He wants you as his woman," he finished in a rush.

Hanna stood slowly. "His woman?" She suddenly had

an urge to laugh; the whole idea was so preposterous. Yet the way the two men were frowning at her, she suddenly felt a knot grow in her stomach.

"Nay," she whispered. When neither of the men answered her she moved to the table, putting her hands on the edge. "I will not be anyone's woman," she said firmly.

"Aye, but you will," Stefan said, speaking up for the first time.

His voice was frigid enough to send a chill through Hanna's body. She leaned forward on the table. "I see. So this is what you have decided. Is this more of my punishment? How fitting that you chose something worse than death for me."

Mikhail started to speak, but Stefan waved his hand to silence his brother. Stefan's eyes narrowed, but he let her insult pass.

"I see you are still harboring resentment for the punishment given to one of my men."

"You nearly whipped him to death," she said accusingly.

Stefan leaned forward, a thick lock of his hair falling across his eyebrow. "He deserved to die for his disobedience."

Hanna drew in her breath sharply. "He deserved nothing of the kind. He was only trying to help."

"He disobeyed a direct order. He put an entire mission in jeopardy."

"But he succeeded . . . we succeeded. Why can't that be enough?"

Stefan's jaw hardened. "You know the answer to that, Hanna."

She waved her hands in the air. "Of course, an order is an order. Well, haven't you ever disobeyed an order before? Even out of good conscience?" She glared at him, daring him to try and answer that.

Much to her astonishment, Stefan nodded. "Aye, in fact I have. On some occasions it even saved my life and the lives of others around me. Not all commanders make the right decisions, Hanna; I will be the first to admit that. Sometimes it comes to a point where a man must follow his conscience or be unable to live with himself. But for each time he does this, he must be ready to live with the consequences of his actions. There can only be one leader among men at war. To willingly choose to disobey could mean death for many who are counting on you to fulfill your assigned responsibilities."

Hanna swallowed hard and looked away. She had not been prepared for Stefan's quiet explanation, nor for the way her anger fled her when she heard it. She pressed her lips together, looking down at her hands, clasped tightly in front of her.

"Then what will you do with me?" she whispered.

Stefan sat down on the stool. "As I have told you before, I do not take my responsibilities lightly. It is my duty to see that you are well cared for."

Hanna lifted her head sharply. "I'll not become a . . . a concubine to that man," she said fiercely.

Stefan ran his fingers through his hair wearily. "Nay, you will not."

"B-but you said . . ." she started, and then let her words trail off.

"I said I do not take my responsibilities lightly. Hamid-Bey was turned away this time, but there would be no one to stop him, or anyone else for that matter, from taking you if something happens to either Mikhail or myself."

"I d-don't understand," she whispered.

Stefan sighed. "Aye, that statement is utterly true. You have no understanding of how precarious your situation really is, Hanna. You are a young and beautiful woman. Yet the truth of the matter is, you are alone, without family, or any kind of protection . . . except for my pledge to protect you."

Hanna lifted her head proudly. "I need no one. I can take care of myself."

Stefan laughed hoarsely. "Is that what you would tell Hamid-Bey as he draped you over his horse and rode off with you across the steppes?"

Hanna flushed but said nothing. There wasn't much she could say; Stefan was right and she knew it.

Stefan grimaced at the expression on her face and laid his hands flat on the table. "Hanna, by abducting you before you were properly wed, I have . . . well, let's say, *decreased* the chances of your making a suitable marriage. As the widow of Jozef Czarnowski, it would have been possible for certain arrangements to be made. You would have had the considerable wealth and name of the Czarnowski family to draw on. But as Hanna Quinn, you are a foreigner in our country, without title, status or coin to your name."

The truth of his words came closer to her heart than she cared to admit. "I need none of those things," she said adamantly.

Stefan felt the muscles in his neck knot with tension. Frustrated, he looked over at his brother, who sat quietly listening to the exchange. Mikhail's hands were laying loosely on the table, but as his eyes met Stefan's, they held a hint of challenge.

Stefan frowned. *This is not going to be easy. Nay, it will not be easy at all. God help me, but I'm going to have to fight both of them on this one.*

Stefan came to his feet, folding his arms firmly across his chest. "As I am responsible for the events that have left you in such dire straits, Hanna, it is my duty to see that you at least have some recourse in the event of Mikhail's or my untimely demise."

Hanna blinked, still not lifting her head. Oh, God, what more could he possibly say? Her pride was in tatters and now he was going to show compassion and generosity in the face of her humiliation. It would be more than she could stand. She held her breath, waiting for the ax to fall.

Stefan cleared his voice. "I have decided to give you the Tarnowski name." His words hung in the air for a long moment.

Hanna exhaled in a rush, as if someone had punched her in the stomach. "Wh-what?" she stammered, uncertain that she had heard him correctly.

Stefan leaned forward, his hands on the table. "Granted, right now it is a dangerous matter to be associated with the Tarnowski family, but you will find safe refuge wherever King Casimir and his court reside. The Tarnowski name will give you the protection and resources you need to have a relatively safe and comfortable life, even if it must be in exile. When Poland is ours again you can return proudly and honorably."

Hanna opened her mouth to say something, but nothing came out. Shocked, she pressed her hand to her chest to force herself to inhale.

At that moment, Mikhail suddenly leapt to his feet. "Stefan, I must insist that I be the one to marry Hanna. I am willing to fulfill my duty in this regard. Besides, I owe her my life."

Stefan could see the flush on his brother's cheeks and suddenly wondered if Mikhail thought himself in love with Hanna.

"Nay, Mikhail," he said brusquely. "She is my responsibility. Besides, I'll not have you marry her because of some misguided notion of duty." He reached out and put a hand gently on Mikhail's shoulder. "Come now, you know the responsibility is mine."

Mikhail's young face showed disappointment. Troubled, he began talking softly to Stefan, hoping to persuade his brother to change his mind. During the course of the conversation both of the men turned their backs to Hanna, as if she weren't there.

"M-marry?" she said finally, forcing the words from her lips.

The two men turned to her, surprised that she had spoken. Mutely, they nodded their heads and then dismissed her, resuming their discussion.

"Misguided notion of duty?" she shouted next at the top of her lungs.

Chapter Twenty-six

Hanna thought Stefan and his brother had gone completely and utterly mad. Marriage? Duty?

Hanna took a deep breath and squarely faced the men. "There will be no marriage and no more talk of duty and responsibility."

A smile curved across Stefan's handsome face. "Aye, but there will, Hanna." He sat back down on the stool, seemingly undisturbed by the fact that she was giving him her fiercest glare.

His casual attitude made her immediately uneasy. "I'm sure we can be reasonable about this," she said, moving closer to the table. "I have no wish to be a burden to anyone. I have tried to earn my keep here and have learned many useful skills. I'm certain there will be a position for me somewhere in a Polish household after the war is over. There is no need to rush to such a solution for a problem that doesn't exist."

Mikhail paced back and forth across the tent so furiously that Stefan grumbled in annoyance. "Sit down, Mikhail. You are making me dizzy." His brother plopped onto a stool with an unhappy sigh. Stefan turned his attention to

A Touch of Fire

Hanna. "You sit down as well," he ordered.

She remained standing. Stefan threw her a scowl so dark, she sat down immediately. No need to provoke his anger unnecessarily, she thought hastily.

Seeing that both of them were sitting dutifully, Stefan leaned forward on the table. "My decision has been made and I expect both of you to abide by it. Is that clear?" His eyes met Mikhail's evenly, and his younger brother looked away.

"Aye, it is clear, Stefan."

Stefan turned to Hanna, who sat quietly on her stool, rubbing her fingers anxiously. "Hanna?" Stefan said quietly.

Hanna raised her head and met Stefan's steel-gray eyes. "I am sorry, but I just can't agree to this. I'll not have anyone throw his life away, as you so bluntly put it, over a matter of duty. Nay, I will not do it. And that is my final answer."

Stefan nodded and was silent for a long moment. "I see," he finally said, drumming his fingers on the tabletop. "Well, you may both rest assured that your concerns have been heard and considered. Nevertheless, my mind has not been changed. The marriage will take place."

"Have you not heard what I said? I respectfully declined your offer," she stated, outraged.

Stefan raised an eyebrow. "Offer? I don't recall making any offer. I did, however, expressly give both of you an order."

"Order?" Hanna said, her voice raising dangerously near a shriek. "You are ordering me to marry you?"

Stefan shrugged. "I suppose you could put it that way."

Hanna leapt to her feet. "It is absolutely out of the question."

Stefan looked at her calmly. "I see. Then I suppose I have no other recourse than to present you to Hamid-Bey on his return to the camp. I only wonder what I might get in exchange for you. The Tartars can be quite lavish and generous, you know." He rubbed his chin thoughtfully, seemingly deep in thought.

"You wouldn't dare," she hissed.

"I wouldn't?" he said mildly.

Hanna stamped her foot. "This is blackmail. I will not succumb to it."

Stefan rose slowly, his patience at its end. "This is for your protection, Hanna. And if you weren't so damn proud, you would see why I am doing this."

Hanna clenched her hands at her sides. Lord, the man was impossible. He constantly pointed out her vulnerable situation. She didn't need his help and she certainly didn't need his protection. She would do fine on her own.

Her lower lip began to tremble. Why did she feel so wretched? Because he was right, damn him. She did need him. And despite her strenuous attempts to deny it, she did care for him.

She took a deep breath and faced Stefan resolutely. "I know why you are doing this. Because you feel sorry for me. Poor Hanna Quinn, a woman without a husband or a family to protect her. But it isn't necessary, I tell you."

Her entire face was flushed crimson, but Stefan could see her lower lip start to tremble. He shook his head slowly. "For God's sake, Hanna, I do not pity you. The marriage is a necessity, in name only. I will not force you to play the role of a loving wife."

Her hands were shaking and she hastily thrust them under her cloak. Stefan saw the gesture and admired her for it. Hell, she was frightened, but still too proud to show it.

Stefan toyed with the corner of a map, giving her a moment to compose herself. Pride was a dangerous thing, but it had often sustained a man in the worst of times. If it was her pride that had brought her this far and had protected her through all her troubles, then who was he to question it?

"You would do this for me . . . because you feel responsible for my safekeeping?" she whispered at last.

Stefan nodded. "Aye, because the moment I abducted you from the home of Jozef Czarnowski I sealed your fate, without even knowing it."

"You will not change your mind?"

Stefan shook his head firmly. "Nay, I will not. I will see my responsibility through to the end."

Hanna sat down on the stool. She sighed deeply and then looked down at her hands, deep in thought. After an extraordinarily long silence, she looked up.

"Then if the conditions are as you have stated, I will agree to the marriage."

Mikhail exhaled a deep sigh of relief and shot a glance at his brother. Stefan seemed outwardly unaffected by her answer, but his jaw relaxed considerably as she said the words.

Stefan slowly came to his feet. "Excellent. We shall ride to the church tonight."

"Tonight?" Both Hanna and Mikhail gasped the word in astonishment.

Stefan nodded slowly. "Aye, tonight."

"B-but . . ." Hanna started, and then she let her sentence trail off. She needed time to prepare herself for such an event. For God's sake, she was still in shock over the proposal.

"We need to ride at night under the cover of darkness," Stefan explained patiently. "And there is no reason to wait another day. It would serve no purpose. Now that it has been decided, we ride tonight and do the deed."

Mikhail opened his mouth to say something and then abruptly closed it. He quickly turned from his brother. "I'll see to the mounts," he mumbled, hastily leaving the tent.

Stefan reached for his belt and buckled it around his waist. "I suggest you dress warmly," he said calmly to Hanna as she stood, staring at him as if he had gone stark, raving mad.

She finally blinked and turned from him, walking out into the cool night. She felt dazed, as if someone had knocked her over the head with a blunt object. It was mad, this plan. But what was she to do?

Hanna returned to her tent and threw off her cloak. Hastily, she looked for her warmest dress, a dark blue wool one with a high collar. She changed into it, pulling the cloak across her shoulders. Her hair hung loosely about her shoulders, but she was too weary to braid it. Instead, she grabbed a ribbon and tied it at her nape.

Taking a deep breath, she lifted the tent flap and walked back to the command tent, where Stefan and Mikhail stood outside next to the horses, talking softly. Stefan looked up as she approached him. He had the audacity to smile at her, and she felt like hitting him for it.

"Come, Hanna. You'll ride with me," he said, lifting her onto the horse.

Her wounded leg bumped against the saddle and she winced in pain. Stefan looked up at her in alarm, but she smiled through clenched teeth. "I'm all right. It is just a little tender."

Mikhail quickly mounted while Stefan carefully climbed on behind Hanna. With a soft cluck, Stefan led the horses into the forest.

"There will be no talking," Stefan said, his mouth pressed against her ear. "Sounds carry far in the quiet of the night."

Hanna nodded, clutching her cloak tighter around her. The wind knifed through her cloak, causing her to shiver. She felt Stefan's hand circle her waist, pulling her back against his chest. Opening his own cloak, he wrapped her in it, giving her added warmth.

Hanna was touched by the gesture and felt her thoughts whirl with confusion. Stefan Tarnowski was the most contrary man she had ever met. That he could be so rigid and distant one moment, while being gentle and thoughtful in the next, was simply beyond her comprehension. No matter what he did, she could not understand him.

Or perhaps she did not want to understand him. *Because when you think about him for too long, you open yourself up to a world of hurt and pain, Hanna Quinn.* She thrust her hands deep inside her cloak, refusing to let her thoughts wander any farther.

They rode for more than an hour, following barely distinguishable paths. Hanna was about to ask for a short rest when Stefan suddenly raised his hand and slid off the horse. Mikhail rode up beside her, taking the reins into his hands.

Stefan was back in a few moments and reached up to help Hanna from the saddle. "It looks safe," he told his brother softly.

Stefan put Hanna gently on the ground, holding her steady until she was able to shake the stiffness from her legs. Mikhail dismounted and tethered the horses to a nearby tree.

"This way," Stefan said softly, as the three of them headed down a path. "Keep your cloaks pulled down over your heads and follow my lead." Both Hanna and Mikhail nodded.

They reached a clearing after a few moments. Hanna gasped as she saw the magnificent old church rising out of the shadows. A full moon hung in the sky over the church, bathing it in a delicate golden light. It was enormous in size, but its architecture dipped and curved delicately. Surrounded by huge trees that looked as if they had been there for centuries, the church was both a rustic and a regal sight.

Hanna exchanged an awed glance with Stefan, and he smiled at the look on her face. He, too, had always felt humbled in the presence of this beautiful church. Reaching out, he took her hand and led her toward the entrance.

When they reached the steps of the church Hanna paused to look up at the impressive structure. A tall spire on the top of the massive stone exterior seemed to reach up to the heavens, as if beckoning to a celestial visitor. Hanna felt a stirring in her soul at the elegant sight and, sighing softly, she allowed herself to be pulled into the church.

As they crossed the threshold, both Stefan and Mikhail removed their hoods. "Keep your head covered," Stefan ordered. "Someone will undoubtedly remember you as having been here." Hanna nodded, pulling her hood tighter around her head.

As they moved inside, Hanna gazed about the church. The interior was illuminated by hundreds of candles and shadows flickered eerily across the stone walls. An old peasant woman, her head covered by a tattered kerchief, knelt in a pew, praying silently. A lone priest was quietly lighting candles around the altar.

Stefan dipped his fingers into the holy water, bending to one knee as he crossed himself. Coming to his feet, he walked slowly toward the priest. Quickly repeating his actions, Mikhail and Hanna followed closely behind.

The priest raised his head, noticing them for the first time. Hanna saw that he was quite young and deathly afraid of them.

"We have no more supplies to offer you," the priest said shakily, his face drawn with worry. "Please, tell the marshal to cease tormenting us."

"Rest easy, Father," Stefan said softly. "I am not here for supplies, nor do I work for the Swedes. I have come only to see Father Witold."

The young priest relaxed slightly. He looked closely at Stefan, then at Mikhail. His eyes flickered over Hanna's face, which was partially covered by the hood. "I have not seen you here before."

Stefan smiled at the young man. "Nor I you. But I give you my word that I wish no harm to either you or Father Witold. I ask only that you tell him an old friend is here to see him."

"Father Witold is sleeping," the young priest said protectively.

"It is most important that we see him now. He will understand."

The priest fixed his eyes on Stefan, clearly trying to determine whether or not to believe his words. After several moments he seemed satisfied, for he turned on his heel and disappeared through a door behind the altar.

Some time passed before Father Witold appeared in the doorway. He was dressed in a heavy black robe that fell to his ankles. The silver cross that hung around his neck gleamed in the light of the candles. His eyes registered shock, and then relief, as he saw the Tarnowski brothers.

"Praise God," the priest murmured, moving forward to clasp Stefan's hand and pat Mikhail on the shoulder. "You both are alive and well. But what brings you here? Have you no idea how dangerous it is? The Swedes are looking for you, my son."

Stefan nodded. "I know, Father, but it is imperative that I speak to you." He motioned slightly with his head toward the old peasant woman, who was silently mouthing the words of a prayer while clutching a rosary in one hand. Father Witold nodded.

"Come; I have a place where we can speak privately." The priest glanced with interest at Hanna, whose face was still hidden in the shadow of her cloak, but did not question her. Instead, he immediately led them to a small adjoining room. The furnishings were sparse, but a sturdy table and four wooden chairs stood in the middle of the room and a fire blazed cheerfully in the fireplace.

The priest motioned for them to sit and then walked over to the fireplace, turning the logs slowly with a fire iron. "You may speak freely. What has brought you here to see me?"

Stefan stood and held out a chair for the silver-haired priest. "Please sit, Father."

Father Witold carefully propped the fire iron next to the fireplace and took the offered chair.

Stefan remained standing. "I need to ask a favor of you," he finally said slowly.

The priest dipped his head. "It must have been terribly important to have brought you here. What is it, Stefan?"

Stefan knelt down at the priest's feet, taking his wrinkled hand into his own. "I want you to perform a marriage ceremony for me, Father. Tonight."

Father Witold's mouth dropped open in utter astonishment. "What?"

"I must marry in order to protect a woman I wronged, an innocent victim caught in the middle of my revenge on Jozef Czarnowski."

The priest closed his gaping mouth and put his hand on top of Stefan's head. "Are you sure this is what you want to do, my son?"

"I am certain of it."

Father Witold looked over at Mikhail, who nodded in confirmation. The priest's eyes fell to the hooded shape who sat quietly, head bowed.

"Then if it is so important, I shall wed you tonight. But I must first insist on hearing your confessions. The two of you will enter into this union with clean hearts."

Stefan came to his feet, nodding his agreement. He walked over to Hanna, taking her gently by the elbow. She stood, and Stefan led her to stand in front of the priest.

"First, I would like you to meet my bride, Father," Stefan said quietly.

Hanna untied her cloak, gently pushing back the hood from her face. As the cloth slid from her head, the ribbon fluttered from her hair, causing her flaming tresses to tumble freely about her shoulders.

Father Witold stood slowly. "Come into the light, child," he urged softly.

Hanna stepped forward and the priest drew in his breath sharply as he looked at her. "My God," he whispered hoarsely, taking a faltering step back. "Is that you, Alexandra?"

Chapter Twenty-seven

There was a moment of stunned silence before Hanna took an involuntary step back. "Alexandra?" she whispered, her heart lodging uncomfortably in her throat. "Th-that was my mother's name."

There was a long silence. Finally, the priest ran his hand across his brow and sighed deeply. "Forgive me, child. I am an old and foolish man. You simply reminded me of someone I knew a long time ago. The Alexandra I knew disappeared years ago, never to be heard of again."

"B-but perhaps you are not wrong, Father. My mother was Polish. She left Poland many years ago, and I never knew anything about her life here. She died when I was very young. Please, do you know anything about her?" Her request came out in a breathless rush. She could barely speak over the pounding of her heart.

The priest thought for a moment before a stricken look suddenly crossed his face. "My God, child," he whispered. "How was it that you became involved in Stefan's revenge against Jozef Czarnowski?"

Hanna clasped her hands in front of her, lowering her

head slightly. "Stefan Tarnowski abducted me on my wedding day. I was to be Jozef Czarnowski's bride. But I had no wish to marry him. I was forced into the betrothal."

Father Witold gasped, clutching his heart, and then groped for a chair. Alarmed, Stefan reached out and took the priest by the arm, easing him into the chair. Hanna twisted her hands together, thinking her words must have shocked the priest. She knelt and grasped Father Witold's cold hands between her own, anxious to reassure him.

"Although Stefan's intentions were wrong, Father, you must believe that he saved me from an evil man. Stefan never harmed me and has only treated me with kindness. M-most of the time," she added softly under her breath.

Stefan stepped forward firmly. "Just who was this Alexandra, Father?" he asked, his voice suddenly grim.

The priest did not answer and Hanna squeezed his hands. "Please, I beg you, Father. Tell me what you know about her . . . about my mother."

Father Witold reached out and took her chin gently in his hands, turning her face closer to the firelight. "The resemblance is remarkable. And I hear a slight accent in your voice. Where are you from, child?"

"England," Hanna answered him.

"Ah, England," the priest murmured. "Yes, I can see how that would have been possible."

"What would have been possible?" Stefan asked, his uneasiness rising. *What in God's name was going on here?*

Father Witold closed his eyes for a moment and then opened them again. "Your name. What is your name, child?"

"Hanna."

"Your full Christian name," he repeated slowly. "What is it?"

Hanna's brows furrowed slightly in a puzzled frown. She looked at Stefan, who nodded slightly. "Hanna Christina Quinn," she answered quietly.

The priest drew in his breath sharply, pressing his fingers to his temples. "My God," he said hoarsely. "It is true. You are her daughter."

Hanna's eyes widened. "Please, Father, what can you tell me about my mother?"

The priest did not answer for what seemed like an eternity. The silence stretched on until Hanna thought she would scream. She closed her eyes, praying for strength and patience. Finally, Father Witold took a deep breath and placed his hands on the table.

"Your mother, Hanna, was a young and beautiful woman, the daughter of a very powerful family. She had a kind and gentle heart and was loved by all who knew her. She was courted by many Polish noblemen but fell under the dark charm of a young and ruthless man by the name of Jozef Czarnowski. They were engaged to be married, but a scant two weeks before the wedding your mother changed her mind about Jozef. It seems she had come across him beating a young peasant boy. It turned out the lad had fallen ill and was unable to manage his work. The boy died from his beating two days later. Your mother was horrified. She had seen a cruel streak in the man she was to marry and it frightened her."

Hanna clasped her hands over her mouth in horror. "M-my mother was to wed Jozef Czarnowski?" she asked after a few moments of shocked silence.

The priest nodded sadly, his eyes reflecting a heartfelt sympathy. Hanna thought she might be ill, and she forced herself to swallow the bile that rose in her throat. The horrible pieces of her life were slowly falling into place, all of them seeming to revolve around Jozef Czarnowski. Shakily, she forced herself to her feet, looking up at Stefan's stony face in dazed disbelief and dread.

An anger so fierce it boiled through his veins caused Stefan to clench his fists at his sides to keep his fury from exploding. *That sick, twisted bastard. No wonder he was so obsessed with Hanna.* He closed his eyes for a moment, commanding himself to become calm.

"Your mother was to marry him," Father Witold continued. "But she disappeared a few days after her discovery. At first, the rumor was she had returned home."

"H-home?" Hanna whispered, her voice scarcely audible. Her thoughts were whirling madly. She felt dizzy and weak, and she wondered if she might swoon.

Father Witold took a deep breath. "You were wrong about your mother's heritage, Hanna. Your mother was not Polish by birth. Poland was her adopted homeland. She was sent to the Polish court for diplomatic reasons. But she fell in love with the country and adored it with all her heart. She was Polish by choice and would have lived here all her life, had circumstances allowed her."

Hanna nodded mutely, remembering the soft tales of brave heroes and beautiful princesses. *And she had taught her daughter to speak Polish.*

"Th-then where was my mother's home?" Hanna asked softly, the room beginning to spin slightly.

The priest paused a moment, his eyes meeting Hanna's evenly. "Are you sure you must know, child?"

Stefan stepped forward, gripping Hanna's arm tightly. Whatever the priest was about to say, he knew instinctively he would not like it.

Hanna nodded, her hands trembling. "Please, Father, I beg of you. Tell me everything."

Father Witold sighed deeply. "Alexandra Christina Gustavus was the younger sister of Charles Gustav the Tenth. She was born into the royal family of the kingdom of Sweden. Of course, she disappeared long before her brother ascended to the throne. But now I'm afraid that makes you, my dear child, the niece of the self-appointed King of Poland."

Stefan felt as if someone had dropped him headfirst into a vat of freezing cold water. *It was impossible. Hanna a member of the Swedish royal family? Why, it was so absurd he should be laughing. Except, for some reason, he didn't feel like laughing at all.*

Hanna pressed her hand against her brow and then slumped in a dead faint. Stefan caught her in his arms. He lifted her, holding her tightly against his chest, and then forced himself to take a deep breath to clear his mind. Still holding Hanna, he turned to face the priest, many unanswered questions on the tip of his tongue.

But Father Witold had already turned away, staring deeply into the fire, his thoughts on a time long ago. A chair scraped across the floor and Mikhail came to his feet, his eyes wide with shock. He stared at Stefan, his hands shaking uncontrollably.

"M-my God, Stefan. Can it be true about Hanna?"

Stefan carefully set Hanna down in one of the chairs and then looked up grimly at his brother. "I don't know, Mikhail. But I do vaguely remember hearing something about this story. But I never saw this Alexandra."

"B-but it doesn't make sense. If Alexandra did not want to marry Jozef Czarnowski, why didn't she simply refuse to marry him or just return to Sweden?"

Stefan rubbed the back of his neck where his muscles felt like corded knots. "Remember, Mikhail, Alexandra would have also been the cousin of Polish King Wladyslaw IV, also a member of the Swedish royal family. Perhaps she feared angering her cousin and thought he might force her to go through with the marriage anyway, against her will. Don't forget, the Czarnowski family has been a powerful force for many years in Poland."

"Then if she could not refuse, she had no other recourse than to disappear," Mikhail said slowly. "Yet it is inconceivable. Princesses do not simply disappear."

Father Witold lifted his head. "King Wladyslaw spent years looking for her. He was furious when she disappeared. But Alexandra had money and a circle of friends who protected her well. She vanished, never to be found."

"Except by Jozef Czarnowski," Stefan said quietly.

Mikhail threw up his hands in frustration. "I simply cannot believe it. Perhaps it is just a coincidence."

Father Witold shook his head. "It is no coincidence. She is Alexandra's child. I am certain of it."

Stefan banged his hand against the table. "Christ, it does make sense. Jozef Czarnowski must never have stopped looking for her. When he finally found Alexandra she was probably already married and had a child . . . a little girl, much to Jozef's sick delight. Then he just bided his time until the child was old enough to be married off."

"Good God, Stefan, you aren't suggesting that her parents would have allowed it?" Mikhail exclaimed.

Stefan sat down heavily in the chair, resting his forehead on the palms of his hand. "Fortunately for Jozef, both of Hanna's parents were dead by the time she was eleven. She was raised by a greedy uncle who beat her and kept her unmarried until she was sixteen. Hanna told me Jozef had come for her when she was twelve, but her uncle forbade it, preferring instead to use the extra years to spend her fortune until she turned sixteen and gained control of it."

Father Witold put his head in his hands. "My God, I had no idea that Jozef Czarnowski was going to marry this poor child. I heard only that he had chosen an Englishwoman for his bride."

Stefan sighed deeply. "No one could have anticipated such a twisted act, Father. But simply put, the implications of this discovery are staggering."

Mikhail leaned forward on the table. "That is certainly an understatement. Sweet Mary, Stefan, do you realize what we have here? Hanna is a member of the Swedish royal family. She is a hostage worth a thousand Polish generals."

Stefan lifted his head, but his eyes did not register any surprise. Fleetingly, Mikhail understood that his brother must have already realized her worth.

"She is also the cousin of our own King Yan Casimir. Had you thought of that as well, Mikhail?"

Mikhail swore softly under his breath. "No wonder Jozef Czarnowski wishes to wed Hanna. She is his access to both the Swedish and Polish courts. He must have been rubbing his hands together with glee when the Swedes decided to invade Poland."

Stefan nodded wryly. "Undoubtedly, Jozef has political ambitions of his own."

Mikhail snorted. "Then Czarnowski is a fool. Charles Gustav already has a son."

"Do not speak so hastily, brother. That son is only two years old. Jozef's marriage to Hanna could give him a claim to either throne."

Mikhail closed his eyes, letting Stefan's words sink in. "*Jezus Maria.* God save us from that traitorous bastard."

Father Witold looked up, and Stefan could see the deep lines etched on his face. The war had not been easy on any of them, least of all the priests who sought to preserve the Catholic tradition of Poland beneath the heavy hand of their Protestant conquerors.

"What are we to do about the girl?" Father Witold asked softly, looking over at Hanna, who still lay unconscious in the chair. "She has suffered much."

Stefan stood, clasping his hands behind his back. He paced for several minutes across the room. Neither Mikhail nor Father Witold spoke, both letting Stefan collect his thoughts. Finally, Stefan halted. His face was etched with concern and worry.

"How, in good faith, can I possibly go through with this marriage now, Father? My primary concern was to give Hanna the protection of the Tarnowski name, as I thought she was penniless and alone in this country. But now I discover that she is royalty. For God's sake, I am a mere soldier, and now, a man outlawed in his own country. I cannot make such an offer to a woman of her status."

Father Witold stood. "You are wrong, my son. The Tarnowski family has shown courage and honor in the face of mortal danger. King Casimir would certainly not see the marriage as improper."

Stefan frowned. "It isn't so simple, Father. I'm afraid she doesn't really wish for the marriage and I have not properly asked for her hand." He ran his fingers through his hair wearily. "Besides, there are other matters to be considered. Hanna lives at my camp in a tent. It cannot continue. For God's sake, she is a princess."

The priest walked over to Stefan and put a gentle hand on his arm. "Royalty or not, Stefan, she is still a young woman who needs your protection. If she were to fall into the hands of the Swedes now, she would be returned to Jozef Czarnowski, and his twisted plans would be fulfilled."

Mikhail took a deep breath and sighed. "He is right, Stefan."

Stefan looked over at Hanna. Her hair had spilled across her cheek and the expression on her face was smooth, unburdened from the harsh realities of their situation. As much as he wanted to deny it, Father Witold spoke the truth. He could not afford to let her fall into the hands of Jozef Czarnowski. What had once been a matter of personal honor had now become an issue of political concern. Whether she liked it or not, Hanna would have to become his wife. The stakes had just increased tenfold.

Stefan gazed at her. Lord, she had already been through so much. All her life, people had done nothing but use her for their own gain. Now, in the same way, he would force her into a union she did not want.

It is for your protection, Hanna. I wish you could understand. Lord, why do I always have to hurt you in order to help you?

"All right. Let's bring her around and get this over with," Stefan said resignedly.

Father Witold bent over Hanna and tapped her gently on the cheeks until her eyelashes fluttered and she began to awaken. She opened her eyes, and for a moment they were blank until they fell upon Stefan. Quickly, she struggled to a sitting position.

"Is it true?" she said, pressing her hand to her brow. "Is everything you said about my mother true?"

Father Witold nodded. "Yes, and it makes your situation more perilous, child. If you were to wed Jozef Czarnowski, his position within the Swedish court would be ensured. And even if we are able to win back our country, Jozef could not be punished despite his treasonous behavior because you are still cousin to Yan Casimir."

Hanna pushed a stray curl from her forehead, her eyes resting on Stefan. He stood stiffly in front of the fireplace, staring into the flames. His profile was serious and she knew that he was as shaken by the news as she was.

"Then what am I to do?" she whispered.

Father Witold took her hand. "You must marry Stefan, my child. It is the only way to keep you safe from Jozef Czarnowski."

Hanna swallowed hard. Stefan was clearly upset at the turn of events. Good God, why shouldn't he be? He was being forced to marry the niece of his most bitter enemy. How ironic that the Swedes' most feared Polish colonel would now take under his protection the niece of their king. And neither of them had a choice. Fate could be most cruel.

She wished Stefan would say something, *anything,* but he refused to look at her, keeping his gaze focused on the fire. Hanna twisted her hands in her lap for a long moment and then stood, smoothing down her dress.

"Then I am ready," she said quietly.

Stefan lifted his head slightly and their eyes met. Hanna saw pain and regret in his gray eyes, and she bit down on her lower lip to keep from crying. *Oh God, I never wanted this to happen. Now I will burden him for life with my presence and he will only end up hating me. Yet he is still too honorable to relinquish his responsibilities.*

Hanna took a deep breath as Father Witold led her toward Stefan. There would be no confession, he told them. The hour was fast approaching dawn and they would be at risk traveling in the daylight. The priest quickly stood them side by side in front of the fireplace. Mikhail stood to Stefan's left.

In soft tones, Father Witold began to recite the sacrament of marriage. After some time, they kneeled on a cloth Father Witold had provided, still listening to the low hum of the priest's voice.

They stood again, shortly after that. Soon the ceremony became a blur to Hanna. She could not stop thinking about what Father Witold had revealed about her mother. Her thoughts whirled dizzily until she could barely stand. At one point she felt Stefan's hand beneath her elbow with reassuring steadiness. Father Witold's voice droned on until she no longer heard the words.

Suddenly, she felt Stefan nudge her. Startled, Hanna looked up and realized Father Witold had asked her a question. She glanced at Stefan and saw he was staring long and hard at her.

Father Witold smiled. "Hanna Christina Quinn," he repeated again. "Do you take this man for your husband?"

She looked again at Stefan and saw his eyebrow raised in expectation of her answer. His eyes were calm, and Hanna realized he was resigned to his fate. Still she hesitated, unable to say the words. Father Witold cleared his voice once and then twice.

"Aye, I do," Hanna finally whispered.

Mikhail gave an audible sigh of relief as Father Witold asked the same question of Stefan. He did not hesitate with his answer, and Hanna got the distinct impression that he was in a hurry to get the entire ordeal over with as soon as possible.

Father Witold finished with the rest of the ceremony and then gave the blessing. A silence fell over the group.

Hanna was suddenly paralyzed with fright. *Good God in heaven, she had done it. She had actually married Stefan Tarnowski.* Her shoulders began to shake uncontrollably.

Stefan turned toward her and put his hands on her shoulders and squeezed them reassuringly. Then he bent over and kissed her. It was gentle and surprisingly tender.

"Come," Stefan said, reaching for her cloak and draping it over her shoulders. "We must leave at once."

Hanna fastened her cloak while the men exchanged words in a low voice. Finally, Stefan pressed something into Father Witold's hand as the priest led them out of the room and through the church.

"God be with you, children," the priest whispered, giving each of them a kiss on the cheek. As he stood in front of Hanna, he took her hand gently in his.

"Tell me one thing, Hanna. Was your mother happy? I was quite fond of her."

Tears filled Hanna's eyes. "My father loved her very much. When she died it was as if a dark shadow fell over our house. My father was never the same after that. But when she was alive our lives were full of love, warmth, and happiness. Aye, Father, I believe my mother was happy. We loved her dearly." Her voice broke with emotion.

Father Witold patted her hand softly. "Fear not, child; that happiness will be yours too. Just remember that with love everything is possible."

Her eyes fell upon Stefan, who was talking softly with Mikhail. "Love?" she whispered shakily.

The priest nodded. "Yes, love, Hanna. It is the most sacred of emotions. Now, go with God, my child."

Hanna kissed his cheek softly before turning and leaving the church. The three of them made their way quickly across the clearing to where they had left the horses. The dark shadows of night were already making way for the softer light of morning. They rode quickly, anxious to be out of sight by the time the sun rose in the sky. They reached the camp just as the yellow rays of the sun burst over the forest.

They were challenged three times by sentries before they were allowed admittance to the camp. Stefan dismounted as they reached the command tent and reached up to help Hanna. She was so exhausted, she nearly fell into his arms. He held her until she was steady on her feet.

"Go back to your tent and get some sleep," Stefan ordered her gently. "There will be more time to talk about our situation later."

Hanna nodded, too tired to argue. Once inside her tent, she stripped and pulled a heavy sleeping gown over her head before sliding beneath the heavy furs. Although her mind was whirling with a thousand thoughts, she fell asleep almost instantly.

Chapter Twenty-eight

Hanna awoke to the sound of voices outside her tent. She sat up abruptly, the memory of the past night rushing back to greet her. Closing her eyes, she pressed her fingertips to her temples. *My God, what have I done?*

Shaking her head, Hanna slipped from under the skins and pulled a wine-colored gown over her head. Lifting the flap, she saw the sun was high and realized that it was already midday. She let the flap fall into place before grabbing her cloak and reaching for her bag. So many thoughts crowded her head, vying for her attention, but she pushed them all aside. There would be time later, when she was alone, to contemplate all that had happened to her. But now there were sick men who needed her attention. They deserved to be taken care of as soon as possible. Taking a deep breath, she stepped out into the bright sunshine, stifling a groan from the pain in her wounded leg.

Her guard gave her a cheerful greeting as she headed for Henryk's tent. The old man was not there when she arrived, so she headed off to see her first patient of the day. The young soldier had a deep cough and liquid in his lungs. Hanna prepared a cup of steaming hot tea made of bitter herbs and then piled extra furs on him to keep his chest warm. There was little else she could do but talk with him softly, reassuring him that he would soon be well.

The day dragged on slowly and it was nightfall before Hanna finished the last of her rounds. She shared some bread, cheese, and hot wine with her guard before wearily entering her tent to relax. She had just started to take off her cloak when she heard the guard speaking to someone. Curious, she lifted the flap and saw Mikhail standing there.

"Good evening, Hanna," he said softly. "I have just left my brother's tent. He wishes to speak with you."

Hanna felt her heart flutter unexpectedly in her chest. She had hoped to have a little time to think matters over before she had to talk with Stefan. But her late start had cost her this luxury. Now she would have to face him unprepared.

Frowning, she took Mikhail's offered elbow and walked with him to the tent. He did not enter but simply left her at the entrance and walked away. Bracing herself, Hanna lifted the flap and moved inside.

She was astonished by the sight that greeted her. A huge wooden tub with thick steam rising from it stood in the middle of the tent. She moved closer to it and then jumped as she heard Stefan speak.

"You may consider it a wedding present," he said, grinning.

Hanna turned to face him. "A bath?"

Her face lit up with such happiness that Stefan laughed. "Aye, a bath, Hanna."

"B-but are you . . ." she stammered and then stopped, unsure how to give voice to her fears.

Stefan rose, sparing her further embarrassment. "I will leave you alone. But when you are finished I will talk with you."

Hanna nodded as he turned and left the tent. Then,

with a wide smile, she stripped off her garments and gingerly put one leg over the side of the tub. She tested the temperature with her toe and then sighed. The water was deliciously warm. She sank into it, certain that she had never felt anything so wonderful in all her life. After a while she sat up and saw that Stefan had thoughtfully left a rough cake of soap and a small vial of rosewater beside the tub.

Hanna picked up the soap, running it slowly across her skin. Then she slid her head under the water, thoroughly wetting and then soaping her hair. Reaching down the side of the tub, she picked up the vial of rosewater, wondering where Stefan had managed to find such a treasure.

She muffled a delighted giggle. Frankly, she didn't want to know, nor did she care. All she wanted to think about for this moment was the wonderful way she felt. She slipped her head beneath the water again and then rinsed her hair clean with some of the scented rosewater.

Hanna closed her eyes, letting the velvety soft water soothe away her aches. She stayed that way until the water cooled. With great regret, she finally stood and stepped out of the tub, reaching for the thick cloth nearby. She rubbed her skin vigorously until it glowed pink. Then she wrapped herself in the cloth, running her fingers through her waist-long tresses, hoping to smooth out the tangles. She was sitting near the coals when she heard Stefan request permission to enter.

Before she could answer he entered, bringing with him a momentary blast of cold air. Hanna shivered, clutching the cloth around her body.

"I did not grant you permission to enter," she cried. "I'm not dressed."

Stefan simply stared at her. She was utterly beautiful. Her skin was freshly scrubbed and damp tendrils of hair clung to her bare shoulders. Stefan felt his breath catch in his throat. Lord help him, this beautiful woman was his wife. *In name only,* he reminded himself regretfully.

Frowning, he took off his cloak and tossed it in the corner of the tent. "I am fully aware of the fact that you are not dressed. However, you are my wife, Hanna. Such modesty is not necessary."

"Necessary?" she choked. "You said it would be a marriage in name only."

He sat down on a stool and began pulling off his boots. "Indeed I did. But you might as well get used to having me in close proximity because you will be staying here, in my tent, from now on."

Hanna's eyes widened. "What?" she demanded, horrified.

Stefan pulled his tunic over his head, baring his chest. "Appearances must be kept, my dear. A wife usually lives with her husband."

"W-why, it is indecent. What will the others say?"

He laughed. "I have made an announcement concerning our marriage. It will be understood, even expected, that we live together."

"Did you also make an announcement about my . . . heritage?"

Stefan shook his head. "That will be our secret, Hanna. It would only put you unnecessarily at risk. Understood?"

She nodded and rose slowly, still clutching the towel. "B-but if I am to stay here, where will I sleep?"

Stefan swept his arm wide. "Wherever you want. I'll have an extra pile of furs brought in, if you so desire it."

"Thank you," Hanna said with obvious relief. Stefan noted wryly that it was not the best compliment he had ever received from a woman. Frowning, he reached for the front of his breeches.

"What are you doing *now?*" Hanna nearly shouted.

Stefan paused, trying for patience. "I am going to take a bath. It is a luxury that does not often come my way."

"But the water is already cold," she stammered, suddenly ashamed that she had taken so long.

Stefan shrugged. "It doesn't matter. It will be enough." He unfastened the top of his pants and Hanna hastily looked away, feeling the heat rushing to her cheeks.

Stefan nearly laughed as he saw her so carefully averting her eyes from his physique. Despite her fiery temperament, she was unsure of herself when it came to him. Somehow, that greatly pleased him, as if there was still a part of her that he could reach, somewhere behind the formidable wall of her stubborn pride.

He stepped into the water and sighed as the dirt fell away from him. He ducked his head beneath the water, rubbing the soap thoroughly through his locks. The water was cool, but it felt good, damn good. Finally, he stood, stretching the full length of his body like a satisfied cat.

Hanna was still sitting in front of the coals, her eyes carefully lowered. Lord, the man did not have a shred of modesty or decency. Why, he stood stark naked in front of her without a second thought. She told herself firmly that she would not look up, no matter what he said to provoke her. She fixed her eyes firmly on her hands, which lay clasped in her lap.

Stefan shook the water from his hair and then glanced over at Hanna. She sat staring at the ground, but he could see the telltale pink on her cheeks. He smiled to himself, finding her shyness enchanting. Smiling, he got out of the tub and walked across the tent looking for a dry cloth. He finally found one and quickly dried himself. Then he carelessly wrapped the cloth around his waist and leaned over to pull something out of a small wooden crate.

"I would say that this evening deserves a bit of a celebration, wouldn't you agree?" he asked, holding up a flask of wine.

Hanna raised her head in surprise, forgetting her vow not to look at him. "Celebration? Have you gone completely mad? We were forced into this mockery of a marriage."

Stefan frowned in exasperation. "We have few choices in this lifetime, Hanna. Whether by choice or not, we are married. We will have to learn to live with it."

She looked away quickly, but Stefan saw the pain and despair that crossed her face. Scowling, he walked to the table and set the flask of wine on it. Sitting down on the stool, he lifted the flask to his mouth and took a long drink. When several moments had passed and he had not said anything Hanna finally looked up.

"What are you doing?" she whispered as he took another drink.

"I am celebrating alone," he answered curtly.

"Oh," she said in a small voice, looking back down at her hands. As much as she wanted to deny it, he was right. Whatever the reason for their marriage, they had been bound together by vows that she had taken willingly. Some kind of truce would have to be established.

Ignoring the nervous flutter in her stomach, Hanna stood, walked over to Stefan, and slowly held out her hand. "All right. I wish to have a drink."

Stefan looked at her with a raised eyebrow and then handed her the flask. She tipped it slightly toward him.

"To us."

"To us," Stefan agreed as she lifted the bottle to her lips and tilted it back. She took a long drink and then put the flask down hard on the table, coughing. Stefan patted her on the back until she was breathing properly.

"Care for another sip?" Stefan asked, amused, holding up the flask. Hanna hastily shook her head. Stefan smiled before taking another drink himself. When he was finished he set the flask on the table and rose.

"All right, Hanna. It is time to discuss some important issues regarding our rather unusual situation." He motioned her toward a stool. "Please sit down."

Hanna sat gingerly, feeling terribly self-conscious, wrapped only in the cloth. She found it a bit absurd that they were about to have their first serious discussion as man and wife while she was half clad and he himself was barely covered. *You are a married woman,* she reminded herself, but she felt little comfort from the words.

"May I get dressed first?" she asked, quickly looking down at her folded hands.

"You may," Stefan answered slowly. "But I will not leave the tent."

She looked at him incredulously. "You would watch me?"

He shrugged. "Perhaps. But I will not step outside in the freezing cold every time my wife wishes to change her gown."

"You . . . you have no shame. Even husbands and wives maintain some kind of decency."

Stefan's mouth curved into a smile. "I suppose you have a lot to learn about me, Hanna."

She clamped her lips together tightly. "All right, then, say what you must. I will dress when I may be afforded some privacy."

"As you wish," Stefan drawled.

There was a warm glint in his eyes as his gaze raked across her bare legs and shoulders. Hanna felt her heartbeat quicken at the look of stormy desire in his eyes, but then quickly looked away.

Stefan smiled briefly as he ran his fingers through his damp hair. After a moment, his face became serious. "All right, Hanna, this is how I evaluate our situation. We are married and marriage is a complex matter. It can be successful only if the appropriate strategy is applied. As long as the correct steps are taken in a series of carefully calculated moves, the marriage will proceed on a proper and suitable course. Therefore, I have taken it upon myself to form such a strategy."

Hanna thought he had gone completely daft. "Strategy?" she said in a choked voice.

He nodded, pleased that she was following his train of thought. "Precisely. Marriage requires discipline and strict regulations. I think we should be able to chart the course of our marriage within these guidelines."

Hanna thought about saying something, but then decided against it. Stefan made it sound as if they would march along through life, stopping only to conquer their problems before moving forward again . . . until they met their next enemy. It was so silly, a smile touched her lips. Looking up, she watched him pace the tent, continuing to speak about his battle plan for their marriage.

Her eyes strayed to his body. He was magnificent. His flesh was golden and the muscles in his thighs knotted as he walked, his strides smooth and powerful. There were still a few droplets of water on his shoulders and one of them trickled down his chest until it slid beneath the cloth at his waist. She felt curiously breathless just looking at him.

"Hanna?"

She looked up guiltily. "Aye?"

"Have you heard a word I said?"

She nodded vigorously. "Of course I have."

"Then I assume you agree with what I said."

"Wh-what you said?"

He stared at her blushing face before throwing his hands up in resignation. "I said that a great many things happened to us yesterday. I am still trying to sort everything out. But one thing I know for certain. You do not belong here, especially given your . . . status."

Hanna's eyes widened. "Status?"

"Your rank. You are royalty, Hanna. You do not belong in a camp of rebels. I have decided to send you to Silesia, to King Casimir. You will be welcome there, and safe. I will come for you when the war is over."

She moved toward him. "Leave the camp? You wish me to go?" Her voice wavered slightly.

Stefan laughed, but the sound was a hoarse rasp. "What I want is of no consequence. You will go."

Hanna folded her arms stubbornly across her chest. "It's not fair. You need me here, and the men need someone who can treat them. Henryk already has more work than he can handle."

Stefan strode across the tent until he stood directly in front of her. Hanna looked up, meeting his frowning silver eyes.

"You wish to disobey me again, *wife?*"

The way he stressed the last word made her look up in surprise. "Nay, I don't wish to disobey you," she said slowly. "I simply wanted to point out that . . ."

He interrupted her impatiently. "I am your husband. From this moment on, I expect you to obey everything I ask of you."

"What?"

Stefan smiled. "Must I remind you that you took a holy vow to obey me? You are my wife, Hanna, and by the sacred vows we exchanged in front of Father Witold, you agreed to obey your husband."

She looked absolutely shocked, and Stefan was pleased with her reaction. Theirs was a test of wills and he fully intended to win it.

Pressing her lips together, Hanna met his eyes evenly. "Did you not also vow to love and cherish me?"

"Aye, I did," he answered slowly.

"Then you should respect my wishes, as well. I do not want to leave."

Stefan threw back his head and roared with laughter. "You expect me to love and cherish a wife who won't obey me?"

Hanna frowned, trying to think of an appropriate answer. "I am simply asking that you not treat me, or this marriage, like one of your soldiers."

He was dumbfounded by her words. "Soldiers?" he spluttered, his voice rising considerably. If there was one thing she was not, it was a soldier. He didn't think Hanna had ever taken a single order from anyone. She was reckless, undisciplined, and headstrong. Aye, all the things that drove him to distraction . . . and the primary reasons why he couldn't stop thinking about her.

Damn.

"Hanna—" he started warningly.

"I know you are as unhappy about this marriage as I am," Hanna interrupted. "But I won't allow you to order me about, even if I am married to you."

Stefan didn't think the entire Polish army could order her to do anything she didn't want to do. He opened his mouth to say something and then changed his mind. Instead he took a deep breath.

"I am your husband, Hanna. I will do what I think is best for you. You will go to Silesia and there will be no further discussion. If you refuse to comply, then I can only assume that you are willing to break a holy vow between man and wife. Somehow, I cannot believe that of you."

Hanna swallowed hard and looked away. "I see. Is this part of the reason you married me? So you could bend me to your will?"

Stefan sighed. "I have promised to protect you, Hanna. That is all I wish to do."

She was silent for a long moment before speaking. "I will not break a holy vow. If you wish me to go to Silesia, then I shall go."

Stefan closed his eyes in relief, even as a small part of him protested. It had been a blackmail of sorts, but he didn't give a damn as long as it worked. Her safety was his priority now.

"When must I leave?" she asked quietly.

"Soon," he answered. "Very soon."

Stefan opened his eyes and looked down at her. Her hair had begun to dry and fiery tendrils curled about her face. Her cheeks were slightly flushed from their argument, but her blue-green eyes showed no defeat. Stefan felt something stir deep within him. She still refused to let go of her pride, despite everything she had been through.

He took a strand of her hair between his fingers. Damn, she was soft and warm. Her sweet, feminine scent drifted to his nostrils and he took a deep breath. *Lord, he wanted her.*

He sighed inwardly. This arrangement was not working out as he had planned. He had promised Hanna it would be a marriage in name only and he fully meant to live up to that promise. But she felt so right in his arms that he wished for just a moment more to hold her and forget about everything that stood between them.

Hanna suddenly took an unexpected step backward. Stefan's fingers were tangled in the cloth around her body and as she moved the entire fabric slid away, fluttering slowly to the ground.

Stefan inhaled a ragged breath as his eyes swept across her body. The creamy whiteness of her skin dramatically contrasted with the strands of red hair that fell in cascading waves about her shoulders. Her breasts thrust out proudly, the pink nipples erect. He turned his head and looked away, fighting for control.

With a small cry, Hanna bent over and scooped up the cloth from the floor. When Stefan looked back at her she was readjusting the cloth around her body, her face flushed crimson. He stared at her in amazement and then reached out to take her by the arm. He wasn't sure what he wanted to do, other than offer her some solace. He had wounded her pride badly this night and he knew it.

"I'm sorry, Hanna," he murmured softly, drawing her into his arms. "I am sorry for everything that has happened."

She struggled against his embrace. "Nay. I can't bear your pity."

He cupped her chin, lifting her face to his. "I do not offer it."

She turned her head away from him. "L-leave me alone. I d-don't know who I am anymore," she whispered.

Stefan rubbed his fingers gently against her cheek. "Whatever Father Witold revealed about your past, it does not change the person you are, Hanna."

She closed her eyes. "And who am I?"

"A very brave and beautiful woman. A woman to whom I find myself very attracted, despite her constant defiance of me."

She smiled through her tears, and Stefan leaned over and kissed her. It was a natural and easy gesture; he had not planned for it to happen. As he pulled away, he looked deeply into her blue-green eyes. He marveled again at the shifting color of her eyes, like the rippling waves of the sea. *Would he ever be able to reach within those depths and strip away the walls she had built around herself?*

After a moment, Stefan was startled to realize that she had not pulled away. He let his hand drop from her chin but could not tear his gaze from her eyes. He drew in his breath sharply.

"Before God, Hanna, you had better move away from

me or I will relinquish my promise to keep this a marriage in name only."

Hanna felt her heart skip a beat. Stefan's touch made her feel so warm and wanted. And vulnerable. *Oh Lord, so very vulnerable.* She opened her mouth to say something, but her voice was locked in her throat. Slowly, she lifted her hand, cupping the side of his warm cheek tenderly.

Looking into her eyes, he saw her need, her desire. "Lord, I need you, Hanna," he whispered as he leaned toward her, giving her plenty of time to move from his embrace. But she did not pull away; instead, he felt her hands grip his shoulders, as if to pull him closer. Bending over, he settled his mouth over hers, claiming it as his own.

Hanna moaned at the heat of his passion. His tongue moved quickly between her parted lips and probed hotly and expertly in the soft recesses of her mouth. Her legs grew weak and she put her arms around his neck to steady herself.

Roughly, Stefan pulled her tight against him, his mouth searching, seeking. Lord, he wanted a response and he got it. Hanna clung to him as if she were drowning and he was her only anchor. God, she was so warm and soft, he wanted to take her right then and there.

Hanna could not think over the pounding of her heart. His hands were everywhere, stroking, touching, setting off waves of pleasure that swept through her body. As his grip tightened around her, a sob of soft pleasure came from the back of her throat.

Stefan heard her whimper and it nearly drove him wild. He had never met a woman with such passion and sensuality. She fired his desire and imagination like no other woman. He tangled his fingers in her damp hair, kissing her until her lips were swollen with passion.

Suddenly, Hanna pushed him away with a small cry. "Nay," she whispered with wide eyes, her lips trembling. "This is wrong. You do the strangest things to me, Stefan. I cannot think."

Stefan pulled her against his chest. "We are man and wife, Hanna," he said, forcing himself to take a deep breath to calm himself. "What we do is not wrong." Still, he knew he had moved too fast. Lord, he hadn't even planned on kissing her. But when he had looked into her beautiful eyes she had tempted him beyond his endurance. Again.

Looking down at his wife, he saw her eyes were filled with confusion. Yet there was something else there that he had never seen before: trust.

He cupped her face gently between his hands. "Do you wish me to stop?" he asked quietly. Her face was flushed, her eyes hazy with passion. He knew it wasn't fair; she was making her decision under duress.

Frowning, he let go of her face and stepped back. "I will stop if you command it, Hanna." His voice was as rough as the storm that had begun to howl outside.

"You are not ashamed of the way I respond to you . . . so willingly," she whispered so softly he could scarcely hear her.

Stefan was thoroughly puzzled. "Ashamed?" he said hoarsely. "My God, you think I am displeased with your response to me?"

She looked away quickly, her cheeks flushing, and Stefan had the answer to his question. He reached out, taking her by the arms, shaking her gently until she looked up at him. "Lord, Hanna, you excite me like no other woman ever has. I have always wanted you, from the first ridiculous moment I saw you, half clad and fighting off two of my men. And doing quite an admirable job of it, I might add."

A tight emotion settled in his chest. Everything he said was true. He had wanted her from that moment on. All the denials and torture he had put himself through had been useless. What was happening between them now had been inevitable from the moment his eyes had met her flashing blue-green ones.

"B-but I am the niece of your most hated enemy. Does it not matter to you?"

Stefan cupped the side of her cheek with his hand. "I'll not lie to you; it does change things between us. But not the way I feel for you. There is a lot of pain and misunderstanding that we need to put behind us. And that will take time. God willing, we will have that time someday." He lightly traced her cheekbone with his fingers. "You are the most exciting woman I have ever known. I want you, Hanna. I've wanted you for a very long time."

It wasn't a declaration of love or an affirmation of the sanctity of their marriage, but it was a start. And for now it was all Hanna had in the whole world. She wanted to embrace it and hold it close, if only for this moment in time.

Hanna felt her heart flutter from his warm gaze and the gentle stroking of his fingertips. A fire sparked in her stomach and began inching its way slowly through her body.

"Y-yet you always push me away."

Stefan laughed, his voice rasping. "Good God, Hanna, you have no idea how many times I nearly ravished you. One touch of your hand, one look in your eyes . . . well, it can drive a man to do things he never anticipated. I pushed you away for your own protection . . . before I had my way with you, whether you were willing or not."

A long silence fell between them. Stefan still cupped her cheek, and after a moment, Hanna turned her face toward his hand.

"I'm so tired of fighting," she whispered. "So tired of trying to be strong, trusting no one but myself. As much as I try to deny it, I have always trusted you, Stefan."

"I'll never hurt you, Hanna." He leaned over and gave her a kiss so tender and gentle it brought tears to her eyes. "Don't stop trusting me, wife."

With those words, Hanna slipped her arms around his neck and pressed her cheek against his. She was silent for a moment.

"Tonight we're not going to stop, are we, Stefan?"

He kissed the top of her head. "Nay, we are not, Hanna."

He slid his hands down the length of her body, coming to rest on her hips. Hanna could feel the heat from his hands, and a shiver of pleasure washed across her stomach.

"You are so soft," Stefan murmured, breathing deeply of her scent, marveling at the way it clung to him. How many times had he dreamed of her, the soft fragrance of her scent calling irresistibly to him? He moved his hands slowly up her back, caressing every inch. He wanted to take his time, to ease her anxieties. But the feel of her nearly caused his tight control to unravel. She was achingly beautiful, yet fragile in a way that touched his heart. Gently, he stroked the smooth skin of her arms and shoulders.

Hanna's breath caught in her throat. Her body responded so easily to his touch, leaving her yearning for more. She rubbed her cheek against the side of his neck before timidly pressing a soft kiss beneath his earlobe.

Stefan inhaled sharply, a shudder moving through his body. He pulled on her cloth, letting it slide to the ground in a small puddle. Slowly, he brushed the hair from her shoulder, revealing the soft white skin of her neck. He kissed the hollow of her throat and she moaned in pleasure. Deliberately moving down her neck, he tasted every inch of that ivory column until she trembled in his arms.

Hanna shamelessly pulled Stefan toward her, winding her fingers in his hair. She let her eyes close and her head fall back, losing herself to the exquisite sensations flooding her body.

Stefan marveled at her beauty, the way her hair spilled about her shoulders in a cloud of red fire, the way her long eyelashes lay upon her ivory skin, and the full, sensual pout of her lips. She was utterly magnificent and thoroughly honest in her passion. He forced himself to master the impatience building in his loins. Slowly, he leaned over, his lips lightly brushing against hers, teasing and coaxing. He sensed a need in her that matched his own and he wanted to bring it to a roaring fire. God, how he wanted her.

Hanna pressed against him, her breasts straining against his chest. Her hands ran lightly over the iron-hard muscles in his shoulders and down his arms before she slipped her hands across his broad chest, touching and exploring.

Stefan uttered a small groan as his mouth descended on hers, hungry and needing. Her mouth parted willingly, welcoming his tongue and his heat, matching his kiss with a wild abandon that threatened to reel Stefan out of control. He drank of her sweet nectar again and again until he finally pulled himself away, shaking.

"Sweet Mary," he said in wonder. "I have never felt this way for a woman, Hanna. You enchant me with your eyes, your body, your soul. I desire all of you."

"And I you," she said shyly, her face flushing.

Leaning over, he gave her a tender kiss. Emotions he could not express adequately in words he tried to express to her with his lips and tongue. He pressed her tighter against him, seeking to claim her body and heart.

Hanna had never known such a feeling of love and warmth. Stefan's kisses were so gentle and loving, they brought tears to her eyes.

Pulling away for a moment, Stefan swept Hanna into his arms, carrying her to the furs. As he lay her down gently, he felt the blood roaring in his ears and wondered if the echo he heard faintly was the pounding of his own heart. He stood over her, and she looked up at him, desire clouding her eyes.

"Hanna Tarnowska, will you take all of me this night?" he whispered, his voice ragged. "My heart as well as my body?"

He stood motionless, waiting for her reply. Hanna knew he would leave her at the slightest hint of doubt in her eyes. She searched her heart but felt no uncertainty or doubt, only a deep longing to join with this man in body as well as mind. She held out her hand.

"Come to me, husband," Hanna said softly.

Stefan stripped the cloth from his waist and cast it aside before stretching out beside her. He half expected her to shy away from him; some women were more than intimidated by his size, and he had no experience with virgins. But she watched him with open curiosity, awe, and desire. Timidly, she reached out and traced the line of the scar that started above his ribs and ran down to where the thick dark hair curled below his stomach.

Stefan groaned, grabbing her fingers and pressing them to his lips. "God, Hanna, your touch burns my very soul."

He pulled her toward him and Hanna moaned as her breasts met his hot skin and the crisp hairs of his chest. Slowly, he lay her on the skins, kissing a hot trail to her breasts. Hanna shivered in delight as his thumbs relentlessly circled her tender nipples. Every touch of his fingers ignited a fire within her and she squirmed against him, a deep, primitive longing within her. She moaned as he took her rosy tips in his mouth, his tongue soft and relentlessly circling until Hanna thought she would die from sheer pleasure. Shifting, she arched against him, her hands clutching the skins beneath her. His mouth continued its sweet torture until she cried out his name, begging for release.

Stefan lifted his head, taking a ragged breath, marveling at how good she felt and how much he desired her. She was utterly exquisite. His breath caught as she brushed against his stiff arousal, and his hands tightened around her in response.

Hanna clutched his shoulders, not understanding the wild emotions he stirred in her. She wanted him to touch her everywhere at once, but he was infinitely patient and slow. She moaned, pressing her body against his.

Stefan pulled away for a moment to admire her. "Beautiful," he murmured, struck by the alabaster smoothness of her skin. His finger lightly traced the wound on her leg, and he saw with satisfaction that it was healing properly.

Instinctively, Hanna moved to cover herself, but Stefan captured her hand and held it tightly.

"You are exquisite," he whispered. "I want to cherish this moment. Let me look upon all of you, Hanna."

She lay still and Stefan drank in the sight of her. Her cheeks were flushed, her body as smooth as ivory. His fingers touched the fluttering pulse at her neck and he slowly traced a line between her breasts down to her thighs. His fingers brushed the soft curls and Hanna held her breath, partly in fear and partly in longing.

Hanna trembled, and Stefan frowned slightly, looking at her face. He took her small hands between his, holding them against his heart.

"You are afraid?"

Hanna nodded shyly. "I d-do not know how to please a man. Perhaps I will disappoint you."

Stefan laughed hoarsely. "Disappoint me? Hanna, rest assured you will not disappoint me." He brushed a kiss across her forehead and then held her mouth in a long, searing kiss. His fingers kept stroking the soft hair between her thighs until she felt an aching building up inside her.

She had almost forgotten her fear when Stefan slipped his fingers into her tender folds with agonizing gentleness. He nearly lost control when he felt her wetness. "Lord, Hanna. You are ready for me."

"Wh-what?" she cried, but he captured her question with his mouth. He kept up his slow movements until he felt her relax, her hips moving slightly with each thrust of his hand. She moaned with pleasure and his desire increased as he realized how much she was enjoying it.

Ablaze with heat and desire, Hanna melted from his searing kiss and the slow penetration of his fingers in primal rhythm until she could no longer bear it.

"Stefan, cease your torture or I shall surely die," she whispered.

"The best is yet to come, my darling," he whispered thickly. She was ready for him, yet he held back, wanting the moment to last as long as possible.

Slowly, he lowered himself on top of her, his hands seeking hers. When he found them he laced their fingers until they were joined, limb to limb. He pressed a kiss on her forehead and the bridge of her nose.

Hanna opened her eyes and Stefan saw they were cloudy with passion. He inhaled a shaky breath, forcing himself to calm the slamming beat of his heart.

"It will hurt a bit at first, Hanna, but I promise you it will quickly fade." She stared at him. "Put your arms around my neck," he said softly. "And don't be afraid. Everything will be all right."

He gave her a long, searing kiss. She slid her arms around his neck. "I am not afraid," she whispered, but he could feel her body tremble beneath his.

He settled himself between her thighs and moved forward, pausing as he felt the shield of her virginity blocking his entrance. He hesitated for a moment and then plunged forward. Hanna cried out in surprise and pain. Stefan immediately stopped his movement, giving her a moment to adjust to his invasion.

"Hush, love. The pain will soon be over."

His breath was hot against her cheek and she could feel the fierce undercurrent coursing through him.

Stefan clenched his teeth, every muscle in his body aching to move.

Hanna felt the throbbing pain gradually give way to a warm, tingling ache. Slowly, he began to move, and instinctively, Hanna raised her hips to meet him. He answered with a low growl as his thrusts became deeper and more demanding.

"God, you are so tight," he groaned as he kissed her.

Hanna felt her body and mind in a turmoil. A blinding white heat had spread from her stomach and now coiled tightly within her, threatening to explode. She grasped his shoulders, suddenly terrified.

"Stefan," she gasped.

"Shh, Hanna. It will be all right. Trust me."

She did trust him, with all her heart. With those words, she fell back on the skins, surrendering to his body and his need. He never stopped stroking and touching her, urging her to join him on a magical journey. The heat within her built until she was sure she would explode.

Stefan thrust again and Hanna realized he had not given her all of him. Clutching his shoulders, she twisted against him, pulling his body closer.

"Nay, Hanna. It is too much, too soon."

A Touch of Fire

But she did not listen and pulled at him until he was fully embedded within her.

Stefan threw back his head, his breath escaping in a tight hiss. "My God, so hot . . . so sweet."

Hanna writhed beneath him, lost in the burning sensations branding her body. A magical passion surged between them, carrying her toward a mysterious end. When the shattering climax finally came upon her she cried out his name, her fingers gripping his shoulders tightly.

Stefan found his release a moment later with a fierce thrust; then he clasped her to his chest so tightly, she could not breathe. Gradually, his grip loosened and he collapsed against her, breathing heavily.

Hanna could feel his rapid heartbeat against her chest, and she lightly stroked the skin on his back. She had never felt so utterly vulnerable and yet so completely loved at the same time. Impulsively, she gave him a hug.

Stefan rolled to his back and pulled the warm skins over them. Hanna rested her head on his chest and he wrapped his arm possessively around her. As they lay there, husband and wife, a deep feeling of contentment and fulfillment settled over him. It was something he had never felt before, even in the glorious aftermath of victory, and it took him by surprise. Hanna had touched a hidden part within him and it was both rewarding and unsettling. He pressed a kiss on the top of her head, squeezing her tightly.

"You mean so much to me, Hanna," he whispered, stroking her hair.

"And you to me," she whispered back. "I have never felt so . . . wonderful." She flushed slightly, remembering how eagerly she had given herself to him.

Stefan put his hand under her chin, lifting her head from his chest. "I often wonder what strange twist of fate brought us together."

Hanna shook her head. "I don't know, but I thank God for it. All my life I have felt alone. Until I met you, Stefan Tarnowski. With you I feel complete, whole and safe."

He kissed her softly on the lips. "You will never be alone, Hanna. I promise you that."

She laid her head back on his chest and they rested in silence, enjoying the warm glow from their lovemaking. It was such a splendid, contented comfort that neither of them wished to move for fear of breaking the magic of the moment.

Within minutes, they had both fallen asleep in each other's arms.

Sometime in the middle of the night, Hanna awoke from a most sensual dream. Warm hands were softly stroking her skin, urging her into a fever. She reached out to touch the burning hands, but she felt nothing but an ache of desire deep within her. She moaned once and then opened her eyes.

It was not a dream. Stefan was nuzzling her neck and grazing her earlobes with his tongue and teeth. She felt the warmth of his body as he stroked the soft curls between her thighs, causing a slow warmth to spread outward from her stomach.

Her sleepiness vanished. Timidly, she reached up to touch his cheek. His eyes were closed, but when he felt her light touch on his face, he opened them.

"I want to make you mine, Hanna, at least once more." His breathing was ragged.

She did not understand his words and had no time to dwell on it for he lowered himself on top of her, slowly entering her. She gasped in pleasure, and Stefan captured the sound with his mouth, giving her a deep and searing kiss. When he finally lifted his lips from hers Hanna closed her eyes, sliding her fingers into the crisp hairs on his chest and arching her back to deepen his thrusts.

Soon Hanna felt again the pressure building within her and she cried out with blissful agony. "Stefan, please," she begged.

He stopped for one moment to look deep into her eyes. "My wife," he whispered, tracing a line along her cheekbone and stopping on her lips.

A tear rolled down her cheek. "I love you," Hanna whispered. "By God, I love you, Stefan Tarnowski."

He smiled and then held her close, surrendering to his need. He thrust again and again until he heard her cry out and shudder with release. Unable to hold back any longer, he thrust once more, allowing his seed to pour into her. He exhaled deeply and then collapsed, rolling to his side and bringing her with him. He was still embedded within her, and he decided he would be satisfied to stay this way for the rest of his life.

Hanna raised her head from his chest and looked at him. He touched her lips with his fingers, silencing the questions he saw forming there.

"Sleep, Hanna. There will be plenty of time for talk later."

She nodded reluctantly and tucked her head beneath his chin. He heard the deep, steady sound of her breathing minutes later.

Stefan held her tightly until he, too, succumbed to the deep folds of slumber.

Chapter Twenty-nine

When Hanna awoke she was alone. She came to her feet naked, shivering in the cool air. She felt the heat rise in her face as she took a step and felt a tender soreness between her legs.

Looking for her dress, she came across all of her things in a corner of the tent. Someone had thoughtfully packed her belongings and moved them into the tent while she slept. Bending over, she pulled a chemise and her pale blue gown from the pile and dressed quickly. She pulled a comb through her tangled hair and then parted it into three separate pieces, braiding it tightly. She shrugged into her cloak, pulling the hood around her head. Then she picked up her bag, moving outside to start her rounds.

The young soldier she had met upon her arrival stood guard, and he smiled widely at her. "Good morning, Milady Tarnowska."

Hanna could not help but smile back. It was the first time someone had used her married name. "Good morning to you too."

As she made her way through the camp, she noticed

it was oddly empty. Only a handful of soldiers could be seen. She stopped at Henryk's tent, but it was empty. Frowning, she called out to a passing soldier.

"Do you know where everyone is?" she asked him, pushing her hood back from her forehead.

The soldier stopped, stomping his feet and rubbing his hands together for warmth. "I'm not sure. Several of the men, including the commander, rode out at dawn. They made an awful ruckus."

Hanna flushed, realizing she must have slept soundly through the whole thing. Stefan had made her thoroughly, yet pleasantly, exhausted.

"I see. Did that also include Henryk?" she asked.

The soldier shrugged. "Perhaps. Someone else was looking for him this morning."

Hanna's heart immediately leapt with fear. There was only one reason Henryk would go along on a mission. It meant there was a good possibility that injuries, even casualties, could occur.

The soldier saw the concern on her face. "Don't worry, milady. The men will be back soon." Dipping his head politely, he continued on his way.

Hanna moved along as well, her head whirling with conflicting emotions. *Why hadn't Stefan said he was leaving in the morning?* Her face deepened into a frown. Perhaps he had tried to tell her, when he had made love to her a second time last night. *"I want to make you mine, Hanna, at least once more."*

"Once more before what?" she mused under her breath.

Hanna suddenly stopped dead in her tracks, her heart freezing in her chest. *The captured Polish colonels.* Good God, Stefan was probably trying to rescue them from the prison in the Swedish military headquarters. That might explain his secrecy and his decision not to tell her about it. Quickly, she rushed to Mikhail's tent and then to Boguslaw's. They were both empty.

Hanna stopped to catch her breath, pressing her hand to her brow. She had to stop tormenting herself or she would be sick with worry. Taking a deep breath, she tried to calm herself. Worrying would not help. She could at least go on her rounds to keep her mind off the thought of Stefan being in danger.

She made her rounds slowly. The hours dragged by, and nightfall came and went. At dusk she returned to the command tent, straining her ears for any sound of the men. Only silence met her waiting ears. Anxiously, she paced the tent until she finally collapsed on the skins and fell into an exhausted sleep.

Some time later, she awoke still in her clothes. She rose from the bed and lifted the flap. Dawn already blazed across the sky. The guard on duty shook his head at her question. Sighing, she went back inside to prepare herself for another day.

The morning and afternoon passed with agonizing slowness. Hanna completed her rounds in a daze, scarcely able to concentrate on her tasks. When the sun sank beneath the hills and the men still had not returned, Hanna thought she would surely go mad with the waiting. She had a horrible feeling that something had gone wrong and she felt utterly helpless. She sat in front of the coals, her eyes filling with tears. *Dear Lord, did I fall in love with a man only to have him torn from me? Please God, I cannot bear the thought of losing someone else who is dear to me.*

She must have dozed off for she came awake suddenly as she heard the sound of horses' hooves. Anxiously, she leapt to her feet and rushed out of the tent. The sky was pink with the first light of dawn and she could see the men riding toward her.

Her breath caught in her throat. She gripped her hands together so tightly, the knuckles turned white. Finally, Mikhail came into view. Her breath caught in her throat when she saw he was carrying someone on his saddle. With a small cry, she flew across the snow, heedless of the distance between them.

As she reached him in a breathless rush, she saw with a mixed feeling of relief and concern that it was Alexander. He had taken a bad cut across his neck and shoulder. It had been bandaged, but the movement of the horse had jarred the wound open. Blood soaked through the linen strips.

"My God," she said, gently grasping his wrist and feeling for a pulse. She found one, but it was weak and erratic.

"Move him inside," she told Mikhail. He nodded and carried Alexander into the tent. Turning, she bumped squarely into Marek. He held out a bloody and twisted hand.

"Dear God," she whispered. "What happened?"

Marek grinned. "We had a skirmish with a few Swedes. But we got what we came for."

"W-where is Stefan?" she asked, her voice a whisper.

Marek frowned, looking around. "He isn't here? Why, he should be here by now."

"He isn't coming," a deep voice said from behind her. Whirling around, Hanna saw Boguslaw standing behind her, his face grim. "You must be brave, milady."

Hanna's heart stopped beating. "N-nay," she said, taking a step back.

Boguslaw nodded sadly. "I'm sorry, milady. He tried to rescue two of the men who had fallen behind. He was taken prisoner. The Swedes . . . they will not spare him."

She covered her mouth in horror as the tears streamed down her face. Her mouth opened as if to say something before she slid to the ground, sobbing. Boguslaw lifted her gently, carrying her to the command tent. Once inside, he set her down carefully on her feet.

"Are you going to be all right, milady?" he asked her gently.

Hanna pressed her hand to her eyes and took a deep breath. Looking around the tent, she saw wounded men who needed her help. Her pain would have to wait. Resolutely, she brushed the tears aside and bent over Alexander. He opened his eyes, and Hanna saw they were glazed with pain.

"It was a damn fine plan," he gasped. "If only those two young fools had not fallen behind. Stefan should not have gone back for them."

Hanna's eyes filled with tears. "Shh," she whispered, lifting his head gently to unwind the bandage from his neck. He groaned in pain and she carefully put his head back down on the bed. Then she went to her bag and brought some clean linen strips, laying them out beside her.

"You are going to be all right, Alex," she whispered softly, and he smiled weakly at her.

She cleaned the wound and pressed a poultice to the area, wrapping a bandage tightly around it. She cleaned Marek's bloody hand next, and Henryk, who had just arrived in the tent, set the bone.

She moved to treat a tall, thin gentleman whom she had never seen before. He had a receding hairline and a thick brown mustache. His face was one big bruise, his left eye swollen shut and his lips cracked and bleeding. A shorter, stockier man sat next to him. His arm was in a makeshift sling and his ankle was twisted at a most uncomfortable-looking angle.

She knelt down beside the tall one. He looked at her and smiled as she placed a cool hand on his forehead.

"You must be the foreign woman, Hanna Quinn, I presume," he said quietly.

Hanna looked at him in surprise. "Aye. How did you know?"

"You are already a legend among the men. Quite a job you did on the ammunition depot. You certainly have my thanks."

She flushed. "I'm afraid you have me at a disadvantage, sir. I do not know your name."

"Colonel Jerzy Smolenski, at your service."

Hanna gasped. "You are one of the colonels Stefan freed."

Jerzy nodded. "Aye, and this is Adam Piotrowski."

The stocky man nudged his companion in the side. "She is Lady Tarnowska now. That giant of a fellow over there told me she is the colonel's wife."

Jerzy dipped his head. "Pardon me, milady. The colonel has certainly done Poland a service by taking such a beautiful and courageous wife."

Pain crossed Hanna's face, and Jerzy noticed and touched her hand. "I know what you are thinking. But don't fret, milady. He may still be alive."

Hanna took a deep breath and smiled at the colonel. "Thank you," she said softly.

She treated their cuts and bruises while Henryk set Adam's ankle. There were a few more minor wounds to be taken care of, and Hanna treated them carefully. Finally, she stood wearily, looking about her.

Henryk and another soldier had taken Alexander to his tent. Mikhail sat at the table silently, his head in his hands. Marek sat next to him, nursing a flask of vodka, and the two colonels still sat on the floor where Hanna had treated them. At that moment, Staszek entered the tent and walked over to Boguslaw, and the two began to talk softly. Suddenly, the knowledge of all that had happened swept over Hanna, making her legs feel weak. She staggered toward a stool and Marek stood hastily, reaching out to help her with his good hand.

She put her head in her hands for a moment before looking up at Mikhail. He raised his head and Hanna saw a look of agonized pain in his eyes. She closed her own eyes, knowing they were only a mirror to his pain.

"By God, Hanna," he whispered. "It was not supposed to work out this way."

Marek shook his head in disbelief. "I had no idea Stefan wasn't with us. I just now made the rounds and we are all accounted for, except for Stefan and two of Staszek's scouts. We didn't lose a single man, and only Alexander suffered a serious wound. It was a brilliantly executed plan."

Staszek stepped forward, and Hanna opened her eyes and saw that his face was red with shame. "It is my fault. My men were too inexperienced. They froze in the face of danger. Stefan saw they had fallen behind and went to help them. H-he was too late. I saw him and the others being taken prisoner. It was exactly what we feared might happen. My God, and it is all my fault."

Mikhail shook his head. "It is not your fault, Staszek," he said gently. "Fear has a strange way of affecting men. No one knows what any of us will do in such a situation. The most important thing is that we achieved our objectives. We rescued two important leaders to our movement, inflicted a terrible blow on Swedish morale, and provided a rallying point for many in the country. It was exactly what Stefan had hoped to achieve. We c-can carry on w-without him." His voice choked as he said the words, and he quickly lowered his head.

Hanna listened to the exchange in silence. Finally, she spoke. "Are we not going to try and save them?"

Marek answered with a deep sigh. "It is doubtful that they are even still alive. The Swedes are surely furious at the escape of our two colonels and will certainly sentence Stefan and the others to death. That is, unless they can be provoked into keeping them prisoners. Then they may keep them alive to . . ." Marek didn't finish the sentence as Boguslaw suddenly shook his head warningly.

"Keep them alive for what purpose?" Hanna asked, demanding an answer.

Mikhail let his hand fall heavily to the table. His eyes were hopeless as he looked at her. "To torture them, Hanna."

"Torture?" Her voice was filled with dread.

Jerzy Smolenski struggled to his feet. "I think that is not a topic to be discussed with a lady."

Mikhail sighed. "She is his wife. She has a right to know."

Hanna stood slowly, swallowing her fear. "B-but you think there is a chance that Stefan might still be alive?"

Marek shrugged. "Perhaps. But not for long."

Hanna looked around at the men before she took a determined breath. "Well, I don't know if anyone else plans to do anything, but I do."

Mikhail looked up at her dumbfounded. "You do?"

"Aye. I have decided to trade myself in exchange for Stefan's life."

"Trade? What are you talking about?" Marek demanded.

Mikhail stood, understanding evident on his face. "I cannot allow you to trade yourself for Stefan, Hanna. No matter who else you happen to be, you are still my brother's wife."

Boguslaw stepped forward, frowning. "I don't know what is going on here, but I don't like it. The last time she got that look in her eyes, all chaos descended."

Hanna put her hands on her hips and faced the men squarely. "You have not been told this, but you should know now. I am the niece of Charles Gustav."

Jerzy Smolenski gasped once. The silence that followed was deafening. Boguslaw's mouth dropped open and Marek stared at her at her as if she had said she was the queen of England. Staszek took a step forward and then stopped. All of them looked to Mikhail for confirmation.

Mikhail came to his feet. "It is true, although we discovered this only a few days ago."

Marek whistled under his breath. "*Jezus Maria.* Why didn't anyone tell us?"

Hanna flushed. "Stefan wished to protect me, but that is not important now. What matters is that we have a way to save his life, if he is still alive."

Adam Piotrowski suddenly burst out laughing, and everyone in the tent turned to him in surprise. He wiped tears of mirth from his ruddy cheeks and took a deep breath.

"Your courage is astonishing, milady, as is your information. God help us if we only had a hundred soldiers like you on our side. But niece of Charles Gustav or not, the young man over there is right. There is no need to risk your life. We may be a bunch of tired old men, but no one has ever accused a Pole of cowardice. I have no intention of letting Colonel Tarnowski or the other two men rot away in that prison."

Hanna looked at his injuries and then back at his face doubtfully. Adam saw the expression on her face and smiled. "I will be the brains behind the operation, milady. I'll leave the fancy footwork to these gentlemen here."

A ripple of laughter went through the men, easing the tension in the tent.

Hanna smiled back at him in spite of herself. It was such a relief that *someone* was doing *something* to help Stefan that she nearly burst into tears.

"Come, big fellow, help me to the table," Adam said, pointing at Boguslaw.

The giant reached down and helped the colonel to his feet. The stocky man hopped to the table on his one good leg and sat down heavily on the stool. The rest of the men joined him around the table, their faces becoming serious.

The dark mood that had fallen over the men seemed to change miraculously to one of hope as they heatedly discussed their options. Hanna listened, pacing across the tent, adding her comments every now and then. No one seemed to mind her presence, and on a few occasions the men even welcomed her advice. Hours dragged on as they mapped out the details of their strategy. When a plan had finally been formed and the details worked out all involved seemed satisfied.

Except that they still lacked the aid of one more man.

Mikhail pulled Marek aside. "We'll have to move the camp as soon as Hanna and I return. We are vulnerable now that they have three of our men. Under certain circumstances, one of the younger ones might be tempted to reveal the location of the camp."

Marek nodded with understanding. "I'll have things ready to go by your return." He was silent for a moment before he asked the question that had been burning on the tip of his tongue.

"Mikhail, do you honestly think you'll be able to secure his help?"

Mikhail's face was grim. "Hanna and I will do our best. God help us, he is our last hope."

Chapter Thirty

Swedish Field Marshal Ingmar Ahlstrom occupied the center seat at a long, polished mahogany table, flanked by several officers, some of whom were wearing Polish uniforms. Sizing up the situation at once, he watched the large man who stood in the center of the room. The man was clearly an officer, and showed no outward sense of nervousness or despair despite his situation. The other two men with him were young, quite young, and trembling like leaves in an autumn wind, and Ahlstrom knew they certainly would be no problem to deal with.

His eyes flicked slowly back to the leader. The big one looked formidable. His strength and calmness seemed to give the younger ones courage. He stood slightly in front of them, as if to protect them. Ahlstrom stored this away as interesting information.

He snapped his fingers, motioning for the guards to bring the tall prisoner closer. "What is your name?" he asked curtly.

The prisoner said nothing, but Ahlstrom thought he glimpsed something in the man's dark eyes. Startled, he realized it was amusement. Frowning, he shuffled some papers in front of him before looking up at the prisoner again.

"I fear you do not understand the gravity of your situation. You are part of the rebel band who interfered with the execution of two known traitors to His Majesty King Gustav. Do not deny it."

"I do not deny anything," the prisoner answered calmly.

There was an uneasy murmur among the men. The tall soldier did not show the slightest bit of fear despite the fact that he faced certain death. Instead, he actually looked bored with all that was going on around him.

"Why did you do it?" Ahlstrom asked.

The prisoner shrugged. "Because we could. Your security is weak; your defenses are pathetic. You will not last long in this country, Marshal. You are not welcome here."

Ahlstrom's eyes narrowed as the officers looked at each other, stunned. He knew his men were shocked that someone would speak so rudely to him, the king's highest officer. Why, it was near blasphemy.

Ahlstrom clenched his fists. "You have interfered with the king's justice. You will die."

"Ah, I see. A matter of justice. Why don't you tell me, Marshal, just what justice is that? A justice that executes men pledged to protect their country from foreign invaders?" When Ahlstrom did not answer the prisoner laughed, the booming sound filling the chamber. "Your sense of justice, I'm afraid, is that of a backwards ass."

There were gasps about the room as Ahlstrom pounded his fist on the table for quiet. Suddenly, one of the Polish officers leapt to his feet.

"My God, I recognize him now. It is Colonel Stefan Tarnowski. I served with him in the Ukraine."

A hushed murmur went through the group as Ahlstrom slowly came to his feet and leaned across the table. "Ah, Colonel Tarnowski," he said. "I should have known. Your impertinence is unacceptable and unbecoming. But you have earned the right to taste a little of the king's justice."

Stefan leaned forward to meet the marshal halfway across the table. A guard rushed forward, but Ahlstrom waved him back.

"I await your demonstration, Marshal," Stefan said softly. "Perhaps it will be more impressive than your tactics at Pila."

There was something so cold in the Pole's eyes that Ahlstrom felt himself shiver. Annoyed at his reaction, he ground his teeth together. "You will die slowly, you bastard," Ahlstrom hissed. "At my hands personally."

Stefan shrugged. "There are hundreds and thousands more like me, Marshal, willing to give their lives for Poland. Are you planning to kill all of them as slowly?"

Ahlstrom gripped the edge of the table, his knuckles white. "Your resistance against us is futile."

Stefan shook his head. "You are wrong, Marshal. You may take pleasure in my death, but it will not hinder the rebellion. We will not stop until every single one of your soldiers is gone from our soil." He turned to take in the Polish officers in one contemptuous glance. "That goes for traitors, as well."

The conviction in Stefan's voice and the sudden gleam of triumph in his eyes chilled Ahlstrom to the bone. "Get him out of my sight," he ordered. "Take him to the dungeon and string him up. I'll soon be visiting the prisoners."

Stefan bowed slightly at the waist, his shackled hands held in front of him. "Until we meet again, Marshal."

Stefan's laugh echoed throughout the room as he was led away.

The old priest stood quietly at the gate, staring up at the oppressive gray sky. He was clad in a robe so long, it swept the ground. He absently pushed his hood back, exposing his gray head to the cool air. As he murmured softly to himself, his gnarled fingers clutched a heavy silver cross that hung around his neck.

"Father, cover your head or you will catch a chill," the young priest who stood beside him chided softly. "Dusk is already upon us."

The old priest shook his head. "We will not have long to wait, my son."

A few moments later, a Swedish guard opened the gate, admitting the priests. Two more soldiers came forward to escort them to their destination. When they reached the building a sentry standing out front snapped to attention, allowing them to enter. The younger priest kept his head lowered as they were led along an echoing corridor and then down a winding staircase. The air was damp and cool as they descended below the ground. Although it was dark, their way was lit by several torches placed along the stairway.

They eventually came to a barred doorway where one guard stood at attention. He pulled over the escorts and whispered loudly.

"You'll have to wait. The field marshal is in there with the prisoners. He said he didn't want to be disturbed."

One of the escorts snorted. "What good will it do to have the priest here, if all he has to do is pray over a couple of dead bodies?"

"Who cares?" laughed the other one. "I don't see why we have to allow priests in here at all."

They began talking in low tones, completely ignoring the priests. The young priest saw this as a blessing and took the opportunity to move closer to the doorway. He could hear the low murmur of voices and pressed his face closer to the barred window. He was not prepared for what he saw.

Colonel Stefan Tarnowski was chained to the wall, completely naked, while two men amused themselves, pricking him with heated swords. He had already been beaten; his body was covered with bruises and one eye was nearly swollen shut. Although the men drew blood with their swords, Stefan did not cry out. His good eye was open and alert, and he gazed steadily at the men who

A Touch of Fire

tortured him. Angered by his refusal to break, they cursed in harsh disappointment.

Finally, one of the men stepped forward with a jagged knife and pointed it at Stefan's face. The priest saw the man had the markings of an officer and realized it must be the Swedish field marshal.

"Beg for mercy," the marshal ordered Stefan, a cold sneer in his voice, "and I will spare you further pain."

Stefan's eye fixed coldly on the marshal. "I beg from no man."

With a snarl the marshal took a step toward Stefan, raising the knife. The young priest cried out in alarm. The guards had not been paying attention to him and, muttering, they dragged him away from the door. Moments later, the door opened and the field marshal stood in the entrance, a look of annoyance on his face.

"What is this?" he demanded. "I said I was not to be disturbed."

One of the guards swallowed nervously. "I am sorry, sir. The priests have come to give the prisoners their last rites. The young one here must have seen or heard something through the door. It frightened him, I guess."

The field marshal frowned at the young priest, who had bowed his head and now looked studiously at the floor. Sighing, the marshal turned toward the older priest.

"Hello, Father Witold. Bringing help this time?"

The old priest nodded. "I am an old and frail man. And I have been at this prison too often of late."

The marshal's eyes narrowed. "I don't know why you insist on giving these prisoners their last rites. They are nothing but traitors."

"Every man is precious in God's eyes," the priest murmured.

The field marshal bowed slightly and stepped aside. "All right. Allow them in." He motioned to the other guards. "Let the prisoner down for the time being."

The two guards unlocked the chains and Stefan fell heavily to the floor. One of the guards kicked him on his way out, laughing. The two younger prisoners were huddled in a corner, shivering. Both of them had been beaten as well, although it was clear they had been spared the torture inflicted on their commander.

Father Witold ducked through the low entrance, followed closely by the young priest. The guards shut the door behind them with a clank. The young priest walked slowly to Stefan's side as Father Witold went to administer to the other two prisoners.

"Are you all right?" he asked quietly, rolling Stefan over to his side.

Stefan opened his good eye and grasped the priest's hand with surprising strength. "Greetings, Father."

The young priest slowly pushed back his hood. "Hello, Stefan."

Stefan blinked once and then twice. "Mikhail?" he whispered hoarsely.

Mikhail nodded, looking hastily over his shoulder. "Aye, Stefan, we have come to rescue you. Are you all right?"

Stefan nodded. "They haven't had much time with me yet. No bones broken as far as I can tell."

Mikhail reached under his robe and pulled out a dagger. "Father Witold is arming the other men. We shall trick the guards into the cell and take their uniforms. You will exchange places with Father Witold; his robe will hide your bruises. We will then leave the grounds as we came in . . . right through the front door."

Stefan raised an eyebrow. "Father Witold is a part of this?"

"He succumbed to a touching request from a certain red-haired woman," Mikhail said, smiling tightly.

Stefan frowned with understanding before lifting himself to a standing position, leaning heavily on Mikhail's shoulder. He took a moment to shake the stiffness from his limbs, his anger ready to explode at what had been done to him and his men. Then he took the dagger from Mikhail and motioned the other men to move behind the door. The young soldiers scrambled to obey, gripping their daggers in their hands.

Mikhail nodded at the priest, and Father Witold suddenly cried out for help. The door swung open and the first guard rushed in. Stefan stepped from behind the door, wrapping his muscular arm around the guard's neck, thrusting upward with his dagger. The other guard, who had followed close behind, was tripped by one of the younger soldiers as he came into the room. He hit his head against the stone floor and lay still. Mikhail ran out into the corridor, tackling and then silencing the last guard, who was trying to escape. Grunting, he dragged the man into the cell.

Father Witold immediately shut the door as Stefan reached down to pull the uniform off the guard. Murmuring a soft prayer, Father Witold quickly made the sign of the cross over each of the fallen men.

"Make haste," Mikhail ordered the two young soldiers. "We do not have much time." They nodded and began hastily stripping the guards of their uniforms.

Father Witold shed his robe and handed it and the silver cross to Stefan. "You are more easily recognizable with those bruises on your face. I have a cap that will partially cover my face. It will be enough. You need the hood."

Stefan frowned but took the robe, throwing it hastily over his large form. "You will have to come with us, Father. It will not be safe for you to return to the church."

The priest nodded. "I am aware of that. I will go with you."

Stefan looked for a long moment at Father Witold. "We will not forget what you have done," he said softly, reaching out to clasp the priest's hand in his own. "For us and for Poland." Father Witold nodded slowly, a tired smile crossing his face.

Mikhail leaned down and pulled the guards out of sight. Their uniforms were rather ill-fitting on the soldiers and Father Witold looked almost comical in his, but Stefan thought they would pass anything but a close inspection. He pulled the hood of Father Witold's robe over his head.

"We have only to get to the entrance of the building," Mikhail explained. "A diversion will be created as soon as we are outside that should allow us to escape."

Stefan nodded, and they moved out into the corridor. Mikhail led them to the spiraling staircase and the men quickly climbed it. They paused for a moment before moving calmly out into the hallway. They all knew their greatest chance for detection would come during their walk down the long corridor.

Stefan heard Father Witold murmur a prayer under his breath as they started down the hallway. The soldiers walked stiffly, acting as the escorts of the priests. One Swedish soldier passed them but said nothing. Mikhail sighed faintly in relief. Everything was going as planned.

They were almost at the entrance of the building when disaster struck. An armed soldier stepped out from an adjoining room and bumped squarely into one of the young soldiers. Still weak, the boy fell to the ground, his cap sliding from his head.

The soldier looked at the boy, understanding dawning on his face. He opened his mouth to shout when Stefan slid his dagger from beneath the robe and thrust it into the guard's throat. The soldier gurgled and then slid to the ground. In a flash, Stefan reached down and grabbed the boy who had fallen, pushing him toward the entrance.

"Get them out of here," he hissed at Mikhail as someone shouted an alarm. Turning, Stefan covered their backs until they were safely to the entrance.

Out of the corner of his eye, Stefan saw two more soldiers rushing down the hallway. Turning, he sprinted the final meters toward the doorway. He threw a glance over his shoulder as he reached the entrance and saw the entire corridor had filled with men.

From outside he heard a bloodcurdling shout, and all hell broke loose as someone grabbed his arm and hauled him out into the night air.

Chapter Thirty-one

Hanna paced anxiously at the rendezvous point. She hated the waiting, but was thankful the men had allowed her to come at least part of the way. Henryk had strenuously insisted that he was not up to the excitement of another mission and needed to remain with the injured colonels. Secretly, Hanna was certain that the old man had decided to stay behind because he knew how very much she wanted to go. Although the men had furiously debated the wisdom of allowing her to ride with them, in the end Mikhail had reluctantly permitted it because they needed her medical skills. But she was allowed to ride only as far as the rendezvous point.

There were not many men on the mission. Marek and the two colonels were supervising the relocation of the camp and needed all the men Mikhail could spare. After some discussion Mikhail took sixteen men and Hanna, agreeing to meet up with the others at the new site as soon as the rescue mission had been completed.

Now, restless, Hanna was unable to sit still. Leaning down, she checked her bag for the hundredth time, making sure everything was in place. She wanted to be ready to help anyone who needed attention. Her heart twisted with worry. *What was taking them so long?*

She was interrupted from her thoughts by Tadeusz. He was one of the five men who waited with her at the rendezvous. He held out some bread and cheese, but she shook her head regretfully.

"Thank you, Tadeusz, but I couldn't possibly eat a thing. My stomach is in knots. I'm afraid I'll go mad with the waiting."

"You should eat, milady," he prodded gently. "It will help you keep up your strength."

Hanna felt her stomach turn over at the thought of putting anything in it. "Nay. I can't. But I thank you for your concern." She patted him gratefully on the shoulder.

Tadeusz shrugged and moved away. He had barely gone two steps when he heard a noise. With a small cry, he whipped around just in time to see an arrow come whistling through the air. It lodged in his shoulder, throwing him to the ground.

"Get down," he shouted at Hanna as he saw an enemy soldier raise his bow for a second time. Hanna let out a frightened cry and immediately fell to the ground. Hastily, she began crawling toward Tadeusz, the sharp stones tearing holes in her gown. Her heart was pounding so hard, she was having difficulty breathing. As more screams of rage and pain filled the forest, the terrified Hanna realized that they were under attack.

She had almost reached Tadeusz when she felt a heavy hand on her shoulder. She screamed and kicked, but to no avail. Someone dragged her roughly to a standing position.

Twisting around, Hanna saw she was held by a Swedish soldier. Faintly, she realized that a patrol must have stumbled upon them. The Swede grinned evilly at her, and she answered his smile by thrusting her knee directly into his groin. Howling in pain, the soldier released her and she hit the ground, her breath knocked out of her in a whoosh.

Gasping, she scrambled to her feet as the soldier staggered toward her, raising his fist.

He hit her once across the face and Hanna felt an exploding pain before she collapsed.

Fire. Everywhere Stefan looked there was red, raging fire. Thick black smoke plumed above the Warsaw skyline, darkening the angry evening sky. Sounds of screams and hoarse shouts filled the air. Yet even as Stefan's eyes swiftly registered the chaos, he twisted his body around, ready to do battle with whomever had grabbed him.

His eyes barely had time to register surprise when Boguslaw thrust him out of the way of a saber that nearly sliced into his shoulder. With a grunt, the giant swung his sword, finding its destination in the soft underbelly of his Swedish attacker. The man screamed in pain as Boguslaw shouted at Stefan to head for the forest. Turning, Stefan sprinted for the trees, the giant following closely on his heels.

"Nay, they are too close. Follow me," Boguslaw puffed, swerving to the left behind a small building.

As they ran, they could hear the shouts of Swedish officers trying to establish some kind of order among their men while also trying to put out the fires. Although chaos had broken out, none of the soldiers knew whom to fight. The attackers had come, set fires, and melted into the darkness.

Boguslaw and Stefan slowed down, making their way carefully. After several minutes had passed Stefan realized they were headed for the river.

"A boat?" he whispered quietly to the giant, and Boguslaw nodded.

They increased their haste until they came to the riverbank. Boguslaw pulled a small boat from a clump of bushes and dragged it to the water.

"Fresh horses await us on the other side," Boguslaw said softly. "We will be safe once we reach them."

Pausing, Stefan put a hand on the other man's shoulder. "You have done a fine job tonight, my friend."

Boguslaw felt his heart tighten. To hear words of praise from his commander so soon after his dishonor was surprising. Shame swept over him. He did not deserve such forgiveness.

Stefan sensed the large man's discomfort and said, "Let's not allow this cursed war to come between us, Boguslaw. You did what you had to, as did I. Let's put it behind us and start anew. We are too old for such foolishness, my friend."

Stefan held out his hand, and Boguslaw looked at him for a long moment before taking it. The two men stood for a moment hand in hand, letting the wounds of war slowly begin to heal. Finally, Stefan moved away and Boguslaw reached down for two long oars. The sound of horses' hooves suddenly split the night.

Motioning with his hand, Stefan drew his dagger, waving the other man into the bushes and hiding himself behind a tree. Moments later, they heard heavy footsteps coming in their direction. Stefan's hand tightened on the dagger as he listened intently. He could tell by the sound of the footfalls that only one man approached them.

Stefan waited until the man had walked a few paces past his position before stepping out from the tree and grabbing the man around the neck from behind. His hand clamped around the man's mouth and he raised his dagger to strike.

Something stopped Stefan from completing his thrust. Perhaps it was the way his captive trembled or the smallness of the man's form. Without really knowing why, Stefan roughly turned the man to face him.

It was a Swedish soldier, all right, but nothing more than a boy. His eyes were wide with shock and fear, and they quickly filled with tears despite his attempt to give Stefan a defiant look.

Stefan raised his dagger again and then lowered it. War or no war, he would not kill children. Boguslaw moved out of the darkness to stand by Stefan's side silently. He said nothing, but looked questioningly at Stefan.

"Let's tie him up and gag him," Stefan said quietly. "Someone is bound to come across him sooner or later."

Boguslaw offered no comment but simply nodded. In one swift movement he removed the boy's cloak and tore the shirt off the young man, ripping it into long strips. Carefully, he bound and gagged the boy, sitting him up against a tree. Stefan reached down and wrapped the cloak warmly around the boy so he would not freeze. The youth watched silently, his eyes filled with a mixture of confusion and relief. As they turned to walk away, Stefan saw a tear slide down his young face.

A strange regret swept through Stefan. War made animals out of people; the instinct to survive overtook all shreds of civilized behavior. If war could justify a man killing a child, then that man was no better than an animal.

The image of the young boy's face burned its way into Stefan's memory. It was a sight of war he would never forget.

Cold and stiffness crept into Hanna's bones as she lay tightly bound, draped uncomfortably across a horse. The bounce of each step jarred her so hard, her teeth rattled. She was slightly nauseous and her face felt as if it were on fire. Weakly, she lifted her head but was rudely shoved back down on the horse.

"Ligg ner!" her captor said curtly in Swedish.

Despair and fear swept through Hanna as she fought to keep from crying out. *What had happened to the other men? Had Stefan been rescued?* Her thoughts whirled with a hundred questions, but her body was exhausted from the beating and the ride. Each step of the horse's hooves knocked her face against the saddle, causing such agonizing pain that she thought she would be ill.

Eventually, her captors stopped for rest, and a bright light was thrust into her face as she sat beneath a tree. Squinting, she looked up and saw faces crowded above her, staring down. She could hear someone speaking rapidly in Swedish from far off. After some time, their curiosity appeared to be satisfied, for her bonds were loosened and she was permitted to drink some water.

She was bound anew as soon as they decided to ride on. A Swedish soldier grunted as he picked her up, throwing her over his horse. Nausea filled her stomach again as her tender, bruised face knocked against the saddle. Her eyes filled with tears and she swallowed hard to keep from retching.

Her Swedish captor mounted shortly afterward. Digging his heels into the side of the horse, he galloped off into the darkness toward a destination that Hanna was certain she did not wish to know.

Chapter Thirty-two

As scattered snowflakes swirled in the wind, softly carpeting the frozen ground, Stefan and Boguslaw moved silently through the forest, purposely choosing the narrowest paths through the thickest part of the forest. Ever cautious, they had decided to approach the rendezvous point by stealth.

Stefan strained to see through the darkness, trying to ignore the biting wind. The cold gusts easily penetrated his thin robe and he blew on his hands to bring some warmth to his numb fingers.

More than an hour later, Boguslaw told Stefan in a low voice that they had nearly reached the rendezvous. Quietly, the men slid off their horses, tethering them to a tree. They went the rest of the way on foot. Both men stopped abruptly in their tracks when they heard the low murmur of voices. Silently, Boguslaw drew his sword and Stefan gripped his dagger in his nearly frozen hand. They moved forward slowly, Stefan circling to the right to approach from behind the voices.

The murmuring was louder now. Stefan could see the telltale signs of a fire; smoke rose and swirled into the air. He wondered who was guarding the rendezvous; he and Boguslaw had approached with relative ease.

Frowning, Stefan gave a small whistle, and the voices stopped immediately. Moments later, a similar whistle sounded in response. Stepping out of the shadows, Stefan moved toward the voices. He knew Boguslaw would wait to see that all was well before revealing himself. Mikhail quickly came into view.

"Thank God it is you," Mikhail said, clasping his brother's hand. "I was beginning to worry." He looked down in surprise at Stefan's hand. "You are as cold as ice. Bring him a cloak immediately," he ordered one of the soldiers.

A moment later, Boguslaw emerged from the forest.

"Who the hell is guarding this place?" Stefan asked angrily as someone handed him a cloak. "Where are the sentries?"

"Here," a young soldier said, coming forward sheepishly. "I was heading for your position, sir, when I heard the whistle."

Stefan still fumed as Mikhail drew him close to the fire. In the flickering light, he saw Father Witold and the young soldiers who had been interned with him. They looked exhausted, but they abruptly came to attention when they saw him. There were a handful more of his men sitting around the fire, clearly the men who had taken part in the rescue mission.

Turning back to Mikhail, Stefan saw his brother's face was drawn and grim. "Are all the men accounted for?" he asked shortly.

"One team was attacked. We lost five men and..." Mikhail let his sentence trail off.

"And what?" Stefan asked sharply, his heart suddenly slamming in his chest.

"Hanna was taken captive," Mikhail finished in a small voice. "I'm sorry, Stefan."

A hollow ache thundered through Stefan's stomach. *Hanna taken captive?* He clenched his hands at his sides, struggling for control. When he finally spoke his voice was as icy as the wind. "Would you be so kind as to explain to me, Mikhail, what in Christ's name Hanna was doing here?"

Mikhail hung his head. "Henryk said he was too weary to travel. He feared he would not make the grueling journey. I thought we needed Hanna along in case someone was too badly injured from the mission to ride. All necessary precautions were taken, I swear. We checked the area thoroughly; I thought it was safe. B-but a Swedish patrol must have stumbled upon them. I am sorry, Stefan. I was wrong."

A long, weary silence followed.

"Did you move the camp?" he finally asked.

Mikhail nodded. "Aye. Marek is overseeing the move."

"The colonels?"

"Safe and well. They will be heading back to Krakow soon. I dispatched a messenger to Silesia to inform the king of the new developments. I daresay he'll be pleased with your accomplishments."

Stefan did not bother answering. He had lost five men tonight, all in an attempt to save him. Although another blow had been struck to the conquering Swedes, Stefan derived no satisfaction from the way things had turned out.

"Take the injured men and Father Witold and ride back to the camp. The other men and I will remain behind to discover the whereabouts of my wife. But first, show me on the map the new location of our camp."

The men huddled around the light of the fire until Stefan was satisfied that he had memorized the location. As dawn broke across the sky with breathtaking splendor, the two brothers parted ways.

Hanna awoke groggily and struggled into a sitting position. She was no longer bound, but red welts marked where her hands had been tied. Carefully, she reached up to touch the side of her face and winced. It throbbed as if a stampede of horses had trampled across it. Feeling it gingerly, she determined that nothing was broken.

Her physical state determined, she quickly examined her surroundings. She appeared to be in some kind of library. A long desk with a chair sat in one corner, and tall shelves filled with books lined the walls. There were two chairs in front of the hearth and a fire was blazing, the logs crackling as the sparks danced on and off them.

Slowly, Hanna lifted herself off the divan and moved across the room to the door. She pulled on the latch, but it held firm. She was a prisoner. Pummeling her fists against the door, she shouted, but no one answered.

She leaned against the door before she crossed the room to the window. Carefully, she lifted the heavy drapes and looked outside. A sickening realization filled her. She was in Jozef Czarnowski's castle.

How had they known?

Hanna swallowed the bile that rose to her throat. Dizzily, she sank into a nearby chair, urging herself to be calm. Whatever the reason, she was here. She had to think, to figure out some way of escape.

After several minutes, she stood determinedly and walked to the desk. Perhaps she could find a weapon or something that she could use to help her get away. She opened the top drawer and sifted through some scrolls and parchments. Nothing of any interest here, she thought. Quickly, she shut it and pulled open the next drawer and saw a fat ledger covered by thick pieces of parchment paper. Frowning, she yanked open the bottom drawer. It was deeper than the others and it contained a pair of leather gloves, a bundle of wax, and several uncut wicks. She was just about to shut it when something wedged in the back of the drawer caught her eye. Reaching down, her fingers circled something soft. She pulled on it until the object came free. Holding it up, she inspected it closely.

Her heart skipped a beat. Forgotten memories suddenly welled within her, stimulating thoughts she had not had for years. And along with the memories came the terror. She sagged against the desk as horror wrenched through her, still clutching the object to her breast. "My God," she suddenly whispered, before sliding down the side of the desk, her legs no longer able to support her. "Oh, my God, nay."

Chapter Thirty-three

Jozef Czarnowski flung open the door to the library. His eyes narrowed as they fell upon Hanna sitting on the floor, clutching something protectively to her chest. Crossing the floor in three angry strides, he pulled her roughly to her feet, yanking the object from her hands.

"Look at me, woman," he snarled at her.

Hanna lifted her tear-streaked face to his angry one. The scar she had given him ran down the right side of his face, across his cheekbone, stopping at the top of his lip. Although the skin had healed, it was clear he would be permanently disfigured. Hanna blinked; the scar only enhanced the evil look on his face as he sneered at her.

"You don't like what you see?" Jozef said, cruelly gripping her arm and forcing her back a few steps. "Get used to it, my dear. You will be seeing a lot of it."

"Y-you bastard," Hanna whispered through her tears. "That is my doll."

Jozef frowned, his grip tightening around her arm. "I'm afraid I don't know what you are talking about."

Hanna pointed at the doll he held in his hand. "That

belongs to me. I haven't seen that doll since the night my mother was murdered. You killed her, didn't you?"

"Don't be absurd. You are obviously distraught and do not know what you are saying."

"I know that my mother was Alexandra Christina Gustuvas. Once betrothed to you, Jozef Czarnowski."

"Wench," he hissed, enraged. "Who have you been talking to?"

She tried to yank her arm from his grip. "Did you really think I wouldn't find out? Your scheming is finished, Jozef. I will not go along with it."

He grabbed her roughly by the shoulders. "Don't make the mistake of trying to cross me, Hanna. I will not be denied a second time. Your mother defied me and ruined all of my plans, just as you are trying to do. Well, this time it won't work."

Tears rolled down Hanna's face. "She tried to protect her child from you. I would have done the same. Oh God, and look what it has come to."

Jozef leaned close to her. "It came out exactly as I wished. You are your mother in every way. You even have her eyes." He gripped her chin in his hand, turning her face toward the light. "I will still have my Alexandra through you."

His grip tightened painfully. "Stop it, Jozef," Hanna whispered fearfully.

He held her chin a moment more before finally dropping his hand. "Your protests are useless, Hanna. Tonight we are to be presented to the king as man and wife."

"Th-that is impossible."

"You will do what I say."

"You can't do this, Jozef. I am the king's niece. I will expose your plans."

Jozef released her chin and cupped her face between his hands. "You are too late, Hanna. We will already be married by the time you see your uncle. A priest is on the premises; he will do my bidding, whether you are willing or not. I took all precautions this time. You'll not slip through my fingers again."

With a cruel laugh, he thrust her away and she stumbled backwards, landing hard on the floor.

She looked up at him slowly. "Nay, Jozef, you are wrong. I am already m—" The words froze on Hanna's lips as Jozef stood above her with a raised fist.

"Cease your words, Hanna, or I will be forced to harm you."

The gleam in his eyes indicated that it would be a pleasurable experience for him. Hanna shuddered in horror and turned her head away.

"Now, I urge you to be ready, my little rose," he said softly. "I'll have someone come to escort you to your room so you can be made presentable for me." He tossed the doll into her lap carelessly. "Remember, sweet, if you don't obey me, you will end up just like your mother . . . God rest her soul."

He laughed and turned on his heel, slamming the door behind him. His malevolent laughter rang in her ears until Hanna desperately covered them to block out the sound.

She was living a nightmare.

Hanna paced across the room, anxiously pulling on the gold and ivory threads of her wedding dress. It had been meticulously repaired and cleaned. She felt like tearing it off her body again, as she had with her sword, but instead she clenched her hands tightly at her sides.

She had tried to explain to the maids that marrying Jozef was impossible; she was already married. But they had simply looked at her as if she were daft and had continued bustling around her. She had tried to make them listen again while they had bathed her and washed her hair. Gradually, Hanna had realized no one was going to listen to her. They were clearly terrified of Jozef Czarnowski, and not a single one of them would dare cross him. Sick with frustration, Hanna had sat on the bed, folding her arms stubbornly across her chest. If no one would listen, then she would not cooperate.

The maids had begged and pleaded with Hanna to get into her gown, but she had adamantly refused. She had glared so fiercely at the women that no one had known what to do. Only after a grinning vassal of Jozef's had appeared in the doorway, offering to help her into her gown, had Hanna allowed the maids to dress her. She had known the man would make good on his threat. Still, she had to be restrained while the maids had combed, arranged and twisted her hair in a number of styles until the right one had been found. Finally, with sighs of relief, the women had quickly left the room, happy to be free of their difficult charge.

Hanna continued her pacing until she heard a soft knock on the door. After a moment of indecision, she opened it and was quietly informed by a manservant that her presence was required in the library. He led her down the stairs, opening the library door for her. When she hesitated he indicated firmly that she was to enter.

Breathing deeply, Hanna walked into the room. Jozef stood in front of the hearth, clad in a burgundy *kontusz* with a striking silver sash, black breeches, and knee-high boots. He was talking softly with a priest. Both men looked up at her.

Hanna moved forward, her mouth opening in surprise. Standing next to Jozef was the young priest she had seen at the church the night she had married Stefan Tarnowski. Running across the room, she threw herself at his feet.

"Do you remember me, Father?" she cried. "I came to the church the other night with two men looking for Father Witold. I married one of those men that night. Please, do not allow this mockery to continue."

The priest inched back, clutching his cross in his hand. His expression was one of horror and astonishment. Shocked, he raised his eyes to Jozef.

But Jozef had eyes only for Hanna. Abruptly, he reached down and yanked her to her feet, tearing the sleeve of her gown in his haste. "You lying wench," he shouted. "You did nothing of the sort."

He twisted her arm so painfully, Hanna yelped in fear. "I did, Jozef. You are too late. I am a married woman. Your plans are finished."

Jozef slapped her hard across the face, and the priest gasped in surprise. "Enough lies, Hanna. You will marry me without another word."

The priest came forward. "I must protest the treatment of this young lady . . ." he began, but he stopped as Jozef stared icily at him.

"How I behave with the lady is none of your concern. I order you to marry us at once."

The priest looked at Hanna and Jozef, aghast. The woman was crying, and a red welt had risen on her bruised cheek. The priest shook his head doubtfully.

"I am sorry, sir, but I think the girl speaks the truth. There were visitors at the church recently, looking for Father Witold. One of them was a woman, but I did not see her face clearly. It could have been her."

Jozef reached out and grabbed the priest by the collar, dragging him toward the fire. The priest clutched Jozef's shoulders, a small cry escaping his lips. Jozef's hands fastened around the priest's neck and he pressed into the soft flesh slowly but steadily.

"It was not her," Jozef hissed. "This woman belongs to me and me only. Let there be no doubt on this matter. Do you understand me?" The priest nodded rapidly, his eyes bulging with fear. Jozef abruptly released him, thrusting him away. The priest fell to his knees, gulping for air.

"Excellent," Jozef said, smoothing down his hair and shirt. "I am pleased that we understand each other so well. Now, let us proceed with the ceremony." He threw an arm around Hanna, dragging her close to him.

The priest staggered to his feet, rubbing his neck gingerly. His face was red with exertion and fear.

Hanna raised her head defiantly despite her tears. "I will say it again, Father. I am already a married woman and have lain with my husband. Perhaps I even carry his child."

Jozef grabbed her by the shoulders, thrusting her against the wall. She hit her head hard against the stone, her ears ringing from the blow.

"I said cease your prattle!" he shouted at her.

The priest recoiled in horror. "N-nay. I cannot do this. In good conscience, I cannot."

There was a moment of stunned silence. Suddenly, Jozef turned, swinging his fist directly into the priest's face. Surprise crossed the young man's face before he crumpled to the ground. Cursing, Jozef reached for the fire iron as Hanna threw herself at his arm, screaming.

"Jozef, stop it." The weight of her body caused him to stagger sideways a few steps, and the fire iron clattered to the ground. "He is a priest. For God's sake, stop it." Tears of horror streamed down Hanna's face. Never in her life had she seen anyone strike a priest. And in a country where priests were so highly revered, it was unthinkable.

Jozef turned to look at her, and Hanna felt her heart freeze in fear. His eyes were glazed with madness; the scar on his face twisted his mouth into a sneer. She dropped her grasp on him and slowly moved away from him.

"You bitch! You think you can ruin my plans again. Well, it won't work." He reached out, grabbing her by the shoulders. "You will be my wife no matter what it takes."

He snatched a handful of her hair and dragged her to the door, flinging it open. Hanna screamed, trying to pull herself free, but his hold on her was iron tight. Over her screams, Jozef called for one of his vassals. The man appeared moments later.

"Gather eight men and prepare the horses. We will ride to the church to find ourselves another priest."

The vassal looked slowly at Jozef, and then at Hanna, who still struggled to free herself from Jozef's grasp. "B-but, sir," he stammered, "darkness is falling and a storm will be upon us at any moment."

Jozef turned to face his vassal. "You dare to question my order?"

The man straightened abruptly, seeing the rage in Jozef's eyes. "Nay, sir, I shall do your bidding at once." Turning quickly on his heel, he rushed off to fulfill his master's request.

After he had gone, Jozef turned to Hanna, winding his fingers deeper into her hair. "Now, my dear," he whispered, "we are going to have a little talk about what we will and will not say to the next priest. You will obey or else you, and the priest, will be sorry. Very sorry, indeed, my little rose."

His face curved into a smile and Hanna shuddered as he pulled her back into the room, shutting the door firmly behind them.

Chapter Thirty-four

The blizzard struck with little warning. Stefan cursed his luck as he and his men stealthily approached the Czarnowski castle. They were on foot now, having tied their horses to trees several meters back. The snow hindered their progress and the biting wind was cold enough to steal their breath. Stefan signaled a stop while Staszek and two of his men crept forward to the castle wall. The three quickly disappeared into the blinding snow while Stefan and his other men sought the shelter of the trees to await their return.

Staszek and his men were gone less than an hour. The young scout gave his report while vigorously stomping his boot-clad feet.

"There are not many sentries on guard, sir. The weather has moved all but a handful inside. However, I did see an interesting sight. Horses are being saddled. It appears as if someone is planning to ride in this foul weather."

Stefan was genuinely surprised. "Horses? How many?"

"I counted eight, sir, but I can't be sure."

A Touch of Fire 355

Stefan stroked his chin thoughtfully with a gloved hand. What the hell was so important that Jozef Czarnowski would risk eight of his men in such weather? Stefan had six of his own men with him; eight of Jozef's men would be relatively easy to handle in spite of the weather. If he could manage an ambush, it could prove to be useful in many ways. Prisoners could tell him just what Jozef Czarnowski was up to; if necessary, he and his men could pose as the men, forced to return to the castle because of the bad weather. At the very least, it would get them inside the castle gates.

"Ready the horses," he told Staszek, "and bring the men around. We'll follow Czarnowski's men until we can determine in what direction they are heading. Then half the men will ride ahead and prepare for an ambush while the other half will bring up the rear, preventing an escape."

Staszek nodded, and Stefan's orders were quickly passed around. Within minutes, Staszek returned with the horses and the men mounted, positioning themselves behind the trees to watch.

Stefan and his men didn't have to wait long. The gates to the Czarnowski castle soon opened and a group of heavily cloaked riders exited. Silently, Stefan counted ten. The first two riders carried torches, which were useful for traveling in the dark but rendered the group clearly visible and vulnerable. Stefan frowned again, wondering what was so important that these men had been forced to ride in a blizzard. He had no time to dwell on the thought for the horsemen quickly headed for the trail that led to Warsaw. Stefan motioned sharply with his hand, and Staszek reined in beside him.

"Take your men on the parallel path and intercept them about two kilometers from here," Stefan said in a low voice. "Be certain to cut off their trail. We'll be right behind you."

Staszek nodded sharply and rode off. With a wave of his hand, he and several of the men disappeared in a cloud of white. Stefan signaled the remaining men and they spurred their horses forward in pursuit of the Czarnowski party.

They followed behind at a discreet distance, careful to stay well out of sight. The air was cold and sharp and the swirling snow caused a chilling dampness to settle deep in their bones. Still the men followed doggedly, finally coming to an abrupt stop as the path suddenly curved.

Stefan could hear shouts and he urged his men forward. As they approached, the clash of swords and shouts became louder. Staszek had engaged the riders. Stefan charged into the middle of the fight, his sword already drawn. Without hesitation, he unleashed his sword on one of Jozef's men, who slashed at him with a bloodcurdling yell. The man was flung out of his saddle. A second horseman charged Stefan, but he, too, was thrown as his mount stumbled over the fallen body.

Stefan saw that Boguslaw had dismounted to engage another of Jozef's men on foot. Pulling on his reins, Stefan's powerful horse bolted toward a soldier who was rapidly approaching the giant's unprotected back. Stefan rose in the stirrups, his sword raised above his head. Too late, the soldier saw Stefan and fell where he stood, the commander's sword easily finding its mark.

"I want some of them alive," Stefan shouted, wheeling his horse around. His eyes swept coldly across the scene before he noticed a circle of three men forming a ring around two of the riders. Frowning, Stefan yanked on his reins, bringing around his steed. Staszek had just approached the group, engaging one of the mounted soldiers. The two clashed swords, and Staszek forced the man's horse back a step. The frightened horse crashed into a nearby stallion. The horse whinnied and flung its head up with fear. Its cloaked rider nearly tumbled off the horse. At that moment, a fierce gust of wind ripped through the clearing, blowing the hood off the rider. Long tresses tumbled free, whipping madly in the wind. Stefan's breath caught in his throat.

"Hanna," he cried.

He thought she might have heard him; her head jerked up for a moment. Suddenly, her horse reared its forelegs again, lashing out with fear. She screamed as she fought to stay in the saddle, her thick curls streaming out behind her.

Stefan charged toward her and saw one of Jozef's men grab for her bridle. He saw her feebly try to slap his hand away, but the man grabbed her arm firmly, dragging her from the rearing horse onto his. Then, digging his heels into the side of his horse, the man galloped off into the forest, the other men protecting him from behind.

Stefan knew at once who was on that horse, and his eyes narrowed. Urging his steed forward, he determinedly removed the last soldiers who stood in his way. Then, slapping his steed on the rump, he plowed into the forest, hot in pursuit of the fleeing man. The storm whipped the branches around him, but Stefan did not notice. His concentration was on one man and one man only.

It was easy to follow their path. Two riders on one horse made for heavy marks in the snow. Hanna was probably fighting him as well, Stefan thought grimly, which would slow his pace considerably.

It did not take him long to overtake them. He guided his horse alongside Jozef's as they reached a small clearing. Clamping a heavy hand on his shoulder, Stefan pulled him from the horse with one strong yank. Jozef shouted, pulling Hanna off the stallion with him. Both of them tumbled headfirst into the snow.

Stefan tugged hard on the reins, bringing his steed to an abrupt stop. In one fluid motion he dismounted and drew his sword. Jozef came to his feet, reaching for his own sword as Hanna rolled a safe distance away from him. Jozef started toward her but froze at the sound of Stefan's voice.

"I'd advise you to stay away from my wife, Czarnowski."

Jozef stopped dead in his tracks. "Your wife?" His surprise quickly gave way to seething hate. "You filthy dog. So you think you can take what is rightfully mine?"

Stefan stood amid the whirling snow, one hand on his hip. "She was never yours to take."

Hanna staggered upright, moving closer to Stefan. She could barely see; her hair whipped madly about her, the wind bringing tears to her eyes. But for a moment her eyes met Stefan's through the storm, and she saw such concern and love in them that she felt like crying.

"Are you all right, Hanna?" he called out.

His face was calm but set in cold, dangerous lines. She nodded, gathering her wits and courage. Stefan motioned with his head that she was to move behind him.

"Stefan, I could help . . ." she started before he interrupted her with one harsh word.

"Now!"

She stumbled toward him, slipping in the snow until she was safely behind him. Heaving, she leaned against a tree at the clearing's edge, using it to help brace her trembling legs.

The two men circled, grimly facing each other. Slowly, Stefan raised his sword. Jozef moved cautiously to meet him. Hanna started as the swords abruptly crashed against each other, striking a dazzling fan of sparks.

Despite his cowardice, Jozef was well trained and met each of Stefan's thrusts with blocks of his own. Given the fierce storm that raged around them, Stefan knew it would be a fairly even fight. Although Stefan was clearly the better swordsman, he knew that a man backed into a corner was a dangerous one. Stefan continued to press his attack, carefully waiting for the right moment to strike.

Jozef began panting heavily as the exertion of fighting off Stefan's blows seemed to tire him. His eyes scanned the forest behind Stefan wildly, as if he expected his men to ride through and save him at any moment. Stefan kept up a balanced attack, his eyes never leaving Jozef's face.

"Bastard," Jozef hissed as Stefan nearly knocked the sword from his hand.

The storm lashed at them, blinding them with snow. Stefan nearly slipped a dozen times and knew that he would have to watch his footing. The smallest error could be fatal now.

"You should have sided with us." Jozef strained between his teeth, holding off Stefan's onslaught. "We need the Swedes. My marriage to Hanna will secure Poland's future."

"Need I remind you that she is my wife, Czarnowski? And she'll stay that way."

Jozef shook his head. "Not for long, Tarnowski. She'll soon be a widow." He laughed evilly as their swords clashed.

"I'm afraid you'll not be so lucky, Czarnowski. Not this time." Stefan advanced, neatly slashing a deep gash in Jozef's sword arm. Jozef howled in pain as steel met flesh, blood dripping from his shoulder.

"You whoreson. You've not the vision that I have. I will be king someday, and I'll have your head displayed for all to see."

Stefan's sword clanged hard against Jozef's. "You will be dead, Czarnowski. Now. By my hand."

"Even you would not dare to kill me in cold blood on my own property," Jozef said, his voice howling with the wind. "You have no just cause to do so. Hanna was my intended bride, not yours. I brought her from England with the clear intention of making her my wife. King Gustavus will certainly support my claim on Hanna and will surely assist me with gaining an annulment of your marriage. Even Yan Casimir would not be so foolish as to stand in the way of my marriage to Hanna, given the fact that she was my bethrothed from the beginning. So you see, Tarnowski, you've already lost her. Surrender your sword now and perhaps I'll allow you to die with dignity."

Stefan laughed as his sword made a hissing arc through the air. "I'm afraid you flatter yourself if you think to gain the approval of King Casimir. Your treachery is well known and greatly despised by him. Be well advised, Czarnowski, that when we regain our country your name will bear the shame of treason for many generations to come."

Jozef circled carefully to his right, forcing Stefan to retreat. "I'm afraid it is your name that will be stained, not mine. Once wed to Hanna, I shall vie for the crown and it is I who shall name the traitors. Rest assured, dear gentleman, your name shall be first on that list."

The swords clashed together with such ferocity that it forced both men back a step. Stefan took a moment to catch a deep breath. "Your grandiose plans were doomed from the beginning, Jozef, first with Alexandra and now with Hanna. How does it feel to know that both women preferred other men to you? Not much of a statement to be made about someone who believes himself strong enough to be king."

Jozef lunged at Stefan, and Stefan saw the madness in Jozef's eyes.

"You don't understand anything. Hanna is my destiny."

Another fierce exchange followed. Stefan took a serious cut to his forearm and could feel the warm blood running down his hand, making the sword slippery. Gripping the curved handle as best he could, Stefan pressed forward, forcing Jozef to retreat slightly.

"You have no destiny, Czarnowski," he said, panting slightly. "Your destiny ended the day you dared to touch my sister."

Jozef's eerie laughter whirled amid the snow. "Your sister was nothing but a passing fancy to me . . . a silly child. It meant nothing."

Stefan felt a fierce anger coil deep in the pit of his stomach, but he forced himself to contain it. He knew well that rage was a swordsman's worst enemy. Three jagged scars across his torso were a constant reminder of that lesson.

"Come now, Tarnowski," Jozef taunted. "Have you nothing to say to that? She was quite a tasty piece, but a bit too weepy, if you must know."

He laughed again, a sick smile widening across his face.

Gritting his teeth, Stefan advanced, his attack coming hard and steady. While countering his blows, Jozef glanced at Stefan's face and was momentarily chilled by the icy fury in his eyes. Frightened, he took a fatal step back, slipping on the snow.

It was the opening Stefan had been waiting for. Swiftly, he charged forward, raising his sword.

"For Danuta's honor," Stefan shouted grimly as he thrust the steel blade of his sword cleanly into Jozef's chest. "And for Hanna's," he added softly.

A look of surprise crossed Jozef's face as his sword slowly slid from his hand, disappearing into the snow. Dazed, he looked at Hanna. He held out his hand to her as he staggered in her direction. He took only two steps before slumping to his knees and falling face first into the snow. A crimson stain slowly seeped into the blurry whiteness around him.

Hanna stood watching in horror before she ran toward Stefan. He caught her in an embrace so fierce she could not breathe. Tears slid down her face, freezing into brittle ice and blowing away in the howling wind.

"He killed my mother," she said, her voice filled with grief and pain. "Oh, God, Stefan, he took my mother from me and he almost took you, as well."

Stefan held her tightly. For a long moment they stood in each other's arms, saying nothing, while the blinding storm raged around them. Then, slowly, Stefan tilted her head back and looked deeply into her stricken eyes before cupping her face in his hands.

"He'll never hurt anyone again. It's all over."

Hanna closed her eyes before catching his hand in hers. "I'm sorry for everything, Stefan. I wanted only to be a good wife to you. I insisted on going along on the mission. It wasn't Mikhail's fault and . . ."

Stefan silenced her by placing a finger firmly on her lips. "Hush, Hanna. I know full well how undisciplined, willful, and reckless you are." He shook his head in disbelief. "I can't believe I'm about to say this, but God help me, I wouldn't want you any other way. I am madly and completely in love with you, Hanna Tarnowska. Exactly the way you are." He stared into eyes that were filled with a wonder and disbelief. Her red tresses whirled around her as she shook her head. "Oh, I love you, too, Stefan. And I swear I shall never, ever, disobey you again."

Stefan flung back his head and laughed as he had not laughed in years. He didn't believe her for a minute, yet, strangely, he didn't care in the slightest. He only cared that she was finally safe and that he could at last look forward to a lifetime of challenges with her.

He gave her a hard, possessively tender kiss. "No promises that you do not intend to keep. Come on, wife. Let's go home," he whispered huskily.

He hugged her tightly before sweeping her into his arms and carrying her to where his men were waiting.

Epilogue

With his friends and family, Stefan Tarnowski stood in the churchyard as a plain wooden coffin was lowered gently into an open grave. Father Witold bowed his silvery head over it, murmuring a prayer and making the sign of the cross. As Stefan watched him, he knew that Father Witold had been right after all. Now that it was all over, Stefan felt not avenged but justified.

The war between Sweden and Poland had continued for two more terrible years. But Stefan had been correct in his prediction that the ordinary people of this fiercely Catholic nation were not willing to succumb to their Protestant oppressors. Appalled by the imposition of Swedish traditions on their beloved Church, the resistance against Sweden became a moral struggle of good versus evil. People from every village, hamlet, city and town in the nation had risen up against the invaders.

Dismayed by the fierce resistance to their occupation, the Swedes fought back savagely. Soon, however, it became evident that the Scandinavian soldiers no longer had a taste for conquering and pillaging these proud people. Morale among the Swedish troops plummeted as bands of Polish rebels continued to chip away at their spirits and supplies. Even more damaging was the shocking news that the king's long-lost niece had married the legendary Colonel Stefan Tarnowski and was actively participating in the struggle against the Swedish soldiers.

As promised, Tartar troops led by Hamid-Bey thundered across the southern part of Poland, dealing a death blow to the Swedish conquest of Poland. Colonels Smolenski and Piotrowski soon recaptured the ancient city of Krakow, flying the Polish flag once again from the high steeple of Mariacki Church. The Swedes gradually retreated to Warsaw. Step by step, inch by inch, Polish soil was won back by her people.

By the autumn of 1657, Warsaw had been liberated and Stefan led the Polish troops and King Yan Casimir back into the city. The people celebrated for seven days and seven nights, the same amount of time that Stefan had held off the invaders at the battle of Pila.

At last, a merciful peace fell over the land. The horrid years of occupation had finally ended. Yet for Stefan there was still one more task to be done before things were finally set right in his household.

Father Witold had personally brought Danuta's case to the Warsaw Council of Bishops. After much discussion, it had been determined that Danuta Tarnowska had died spiritually the day she had been raped by Jozef Czarnowski. As she had not been in control of her mental faculties after that brutal event, the Council had ruled that she couldn't have committed suicide willingly or knowingly. Therefore, the Council conceded, it would be permissible for Danuta to be buried on holy ground.

Now, Stefan stood quietly at one side of his sister's grave, looking at the faces of his family and friends, who had stood by him through the worst of times. Mikhail, Boguslaw, Staszek, Alexander, Marek, and the others; these were the people he would always be able to count on. He knew firsthand the price they all had paid. He also understood that beneath the pain and suffering that each had endured, they were men strong in their faith in God and their love of country.

Someone began softly singing an old Polish song:

> *An eagle soars from high above,*
> *Over the rich and fertile plains of Poland,*
> *A mother, she joyfully calls to her children,*
> *Welcoming them home with open arms.*

Stefan wondered how such a simple song could make him feel so strong and happy. He turned to his wife, who stood beside him, her face calm and peaceful. She held their one-year-old son, Julian, in her arms, and the graceful swell of her stomach indicated that another child was on the way. Stefan's heart filled with such pride and contentment that it nearly burst.

He put his arm around her, drawing her close. Hanna smiled and looked up at him. "What is it, Stefan?" she asked softly.

Stefan paused for a moment before answering. "Sometimes it takes a tragedy before one realizes how precious life really is. Had Danuta not died, I might never have met you. And if I had not been so set on revenge—" he broke off.

Hanna took his hand, pressing it to her cheek. "Hush, Stefan. Our destinies were written long before we ever met each other. Somehow I am sure that Danuta and my mother are smiling down on us this very moment."

He smiled at the thought of it and their eyes met and held, blue-green and gray, filled with love, tenderness, and happiness.

The soft notes of the song trailed away on a breeze. One by one, the people left the grave site, hugging each other and wishing the Tarnowski family well.

Hanna, Stefan, and their son stood near the church on top of the hill long after everyone else had left, looking over their beloved city, the enchanting sound of the poignant song still echoing in their hearts.

They were home . . . at last.

Author's Note

As Polish history may be foreign to many readers, I wanted to add a few historical footnotes.

In the summer of 1655, Swedish King Charles Gustav deliberately broke the Treaty of Sztumska Wies and mounted a major offensive against the Kingdom of Poland on both an eastern front (through the Duchy of Lithuania) and a western front (through Pomerania). There was no major battle at Pila, although the Swedes did sweep through the city. In truth, the formidable Swedish army initially marched in and across Poland with little or no resistance.

However, the Swedes' particularly brutal treatment of the Polish people, their land and their Church, caused many among the population, especially the peasants, to rise up against the Scandinavian invaders. The turning point in the war came when the Swedes attacked the revered Catholic monastery in the city of Częstochowa. Home to the nation's most sacred icon, the Black Madonna, the Polish monks rallied in the fortress, preventing the advancing Swedish army from entering the monastery.

Revitalized by the monks' success, the entire country rose up in protest, beating back the invaders step by step. Especially effective were the small bands of rebels who consistently stole from, attacked, and harassed the Swedish soldiers, drastically lowering their morale. Eventually, the Polish army was reorganized under the brilliant command of a general named Stefan Czarniecki. He led the Polish army on a series of successful campaigns that contributed greatly to the ousting of the Swedes from Poland.

Some other notes of interest:

◆ It is true that some noblemen of the Polish parliament, called the *Sejm,* did, indeed, conspire to welcome the Swedish king in exchange for promises of preserving their rank, wealth, and status.

◆ The icon of the Black Madonna can still be seen today at the monastery in Częstochowa. The legend that the icon was painted on a piece of the table from the Last Supper by Saint Luke was told to me by a tour guide when I visited the monastery.

◆ The legend of Queen Wanda is also true. I first heard the story when I was a student at Warsaw University. I found it a delightful testament to the strength and ability of women in Europe during medieval times.

For the clarification of many historical, linguistic, and cultural matters, I must acknowledge the valuable assistance of my husband, Robert Czechowski, a Pole by birth, and his brother, Waldemar Walczynski. As complicated as it seemed at times, their unflagging enthusiasm always made me smile, reminding me how justifiably proud they are of their culture and heritage. I would also like to thank my mother-in-law, Maria Czechowska, for welcoming me, in such a warm Polish fashion, into the family. Also, hats off to Jolanta Karbarz, my Polish roommate of one year while I was a student at Warsaw University. Her patient explanations of the Polish language, culture, and history will always stay with me, as will her friendship.

Finally, thanks Mom, Winifred Braden, and Marty Sholten for reading the manuscript, Elizabeth Davidson for helping me with the Swedish, and Dad for keeping me straight on all the military terms. I can't tell you how useful it is to have a real colonel in the family!

Any atrocities found within the story, however, are unquestionably mine alone.